"Eva Marie Everson is a talented storyteller with a passion for relationship stories that will touch your heart."

—**Tracie Peterson**, bestselling and award-winning
author of the Land of the Lone Star series
and *House of Secrets*

Past Praise for Eva Marie Everson

"Everson's work is neatly done and her fans will find value in her presentation of life's lack of tidiness, which reads both realistically and convincingly."

—*Publishers Weekly*

"Everson's evocative writing puts the reader in the midst of the gorgeous seaside setting."

—*RT Book Reviews*

"Written in an easy-to-read style, including chapters that convey scenarios from the past, *Chasing Sunsets* moves quickly and captures any romantic's attention. Everson knows how to create a well-crafted tale."

—**Alice Wisler**, author of *A Wedding Invitation*

"Eva Marie Everson charms her readers with characters you'd love to have as friends. Then she places them in a setting where you'd love to be."

—*Novel Reviews*

"Eva Marie Everson's latest story shows her versatility as a writer as she pens a contemporary fiction undertones."

D0828034

Books by Eva Marie Everson

Things Left Unspoken
This Fine Life

CEDAR KEY SERIES

Chasing Sunsets
Waiting for Sunrise
Slow Moon Rising

Books by Eva Marie Everson
and Linda Evans Shepherd

The Potluck Club
The Potluck Club—Trouble's Brewing
The Potluck Club—Takes the Cake
The Secret's in the Sauce
A Taste of Fame
Bake Until Golden
The Potluck Club Cookbook

a cedar key novel • book 3

SLOW MOON RISING

EVA MARIE EVERSON

Revell
a division of Baker Publishing Group
Grand Rapids, Michigan

© 2013 by Eva Marie Everson

Published by Revell
a division of Baker Publishing Group
P.O. Box 6287, Grand Rapids, MI 49516-6287
www.revellbooks.com

Printed in the United States of America

Library of Congress Cataloging-in-Publication Data
Everson, Eva Marie.
    Slow moon rising : a Cedar Key novel / Eva Marie Everson.
        pages cm
    ISBN 978-0-8007-3438-1 (pbk.)
    1. Family secrets—Fiction. 2. Islands—Florida—Fiction. 3. Christian fiction.
4. Domestic fiction. I. Title.
PS3605.V47S58 2013
813'.6—dc23   2012050044

This book is a work of fiction. Names, characters, places, and incidents are the product of the author's imagination or are used fictitiously.

The internet addresses, email addresses, and phone numbers in this book are accurate at the time of publication. They are provided as a resource. Baker Publishing Group does not endorse them or vouch for their content or permanence.

13   14   15   16   17   18   19   7   6   5   4   3   2   1

Dedicated to

Shellie Arnold
Loyd Boldman
Craig Duddles
Jessica R. Everson
Mark Hancock
Larry J. Leech, II
Edwina Perkins
Linda D. Schoonover
Dan Walsh

and to

Word Weavers International, Inc., Orlando Chapter

1

Anise
July 2000

Some memories come with distinction. Exactness. Moments I recall with precision as to what I was wearing. Where I was standing. The music playing on the radio.

What I was thinking.

The day I met Ross Claybourne is no exception.

I had put in a full day at the Calla Lily, my floral shop. Up until two years ago, when my mother died, the shop had been known as Kelly's Floral Shop, appropriately named for the woman who'd opened it, Gertrude Kelly.

"Gertie" she'd been called by family and friends.

Not by my brother and me, of course. We called her "Mom."

And Dad . . . well, in the beginning he'd also called her Gertie. But soon after my tenth birthday, he called her "plaintiff." After that, simply "your mother." For the life of me, I don't believe I heard him call her by her name ever again.

But that's another story. A sad one. And I tend to stay away from sad stories.

I was making floral arrangements for the Stockford wedding reception, ten to be exact. I'd filled the plastic glasses with wax crystals, covered the wide opening with a circular piece of cardboard, and then hot-glued a mat of duckweed to which I affixed golden-yellow preserved gardenias and freeze-dried orange rose petals.

I placed them in a carrying container, along with yards of white and peach netting, which would be used to form a cloud at their bases. I reached for the on/off knob of the radio; Faith Hill's song "Breathe" wafted from its small speakers. The song expresses passion. Something I'd never really known. Oh, I'd thought I had—once—but then . . .

The phone rang.

I switched off the radio before turning toward the old wooden countertop where the phone rested, the black rotary my mother had installed in the midseventies and I'd not been able to part with.

"The Calla Lily," I said. "This is Anise."

"Oh good, Anise. I caught you. I was afraid you'd already headed out to the church." My caller was Lisa MacNeil, co-owner of Harbour Inn, one of the oldest bed and breakfast inns in New England. She was also my best friend.

I sighed appropriately, knowing Lisa would understand. I had forever decorated for everyone else's weddings. Never my own. Weddings exhausted me more than funerals. At least I *knew* I would get one of those. Some day. "I more or less have everything in the car. One last box to carry out to the van. Cheryl is already there so . . ."

"Are you planning to stay once you get everything set up?" Panic rose in Lisa's voice.

"Goodness no. You know me and weddings." I allowed a giggle to escape my throat—forced but effective.

"Oh good. Because . . . I need you. Can you bring a fresh arrangement for the front hall after you're done?"

"What happened to the one I brought yesterday?"

Now it was Lisa's turn to sigh. "An unsupervised child just *had* to inspect it."

This time my laughter was real. "I think I have something here that will suffice. I'll be there around . . . five?" I reached for a pad and pencil to make myself a note.

"Perfect. Dinner afterward with Derrick and me? At the inn, on us?"

I paused. Saturday evenings were nearly always spent with my brother Jon and his wife—and my assistant—Cheryl and their family. My *not* being there would hardly be a tragedy. And, since I'd sometimes rather spend an evening with Lisa and Derrick, I decided to take her up on it. "Sounds good," I said. "I could use some Lisa and Derrick time."

"See you when you get here."

I delivered the remainder of the flowers and other arrangements to the Chapel of Saint Mark and found Cheryl already busy at work. I watched her with amazement. What she'd managed to accomplish in the short time she'd been there was nothing short of miraculous. White linen cloths and runners the color of burnt sunset had been laid over the tables. The chairs had been swathed in white and tied off with ribbon matching the runners. Peach-colored napkins had been fanned at each place setting, the silver and the crystal arranged. The reception hall looked ready for the one hundred guests who would celebrate in just a few hours, though I knew we had a few touches left to arrange, including the bride and groom's table.

As soon as Cheryl spotted me, she met me at the first table I'd come to, which had been set up as a place for staging our boxes and containers. "Before I forget," I said, "I have to go out to the inn this afternoon to replace the front hall arrangement. Lisa has asked me to stay for dinner. I hope that's not an inconvenience."

Cheryl—a tall, willowy redhead—pretended to pout, but I knew her better than to take it to heart. "Well, I can't say I blame you. Although little Aleya will be devastated."

"Tell her I'll see her tomorrow and I'll bring her a lollypop."

Cheryl brightened. "Well, with news like that, I can guarantee you she'll get over the devastation."

We reached into the box with the floral table arrangements simultaneously, our chatter complete and work about to begin. "Go ahead and start the bride and groom's table," I said. "I'll get to work on these centerpieces."

"Will do," Cheryl said.

She walked away, leaving me alone with my work, and my gratitude that I had somewhere else to be.

A few hours later, my Land Rover rambled toward the seashore and the inn. My windows were down; a cross breeze of thick air ruffled my recently ordered linen cropped pants and a long-sleeved linen tunic. Though the summer sun warmed our eastern Maine town during the day, I tended to get cold in the evenings when the wind blew in from the surrounding hillsides, skipping across Seaside Pointe's shoreline. Because the inn was only a stone's throw from both, I slid a long, narrow scarf that I kept in the car's front passenger seat around my neck as soon as I pulled into the personnel parking area behind the grand inn.

The back of Harbour Inn rose regally before me. With the evening still early, faint light poured from nearly every one of the twenty windows stretched across the second and third floors. The first-floor windows were dark, save those of the inn's restaurant at the right-hand corner.

I slipped out of my car, closing the door quietly behind me. Such peace as was felt in the gentle rustling of the shrubs, the lapping of water, and the salty-sweet air should not, in my opinion, be disturbed. I opened the back door, pulled the container holding the front hall arrangement—a summer collection of apricots and greens—toward me, and closed the door with a click. With the vase held tight against my body, I mounted the seventeen steps leading to the wide porch. A quick glance upward showed that the porch lights—though few—had already been turned on in anticipation of night's fall.

Lisa purposefully kept the lighting muted. Too much, she said, deterred from the romantic feel of sitting in the rockers in the evening, listening to the quiet sounds of the sea, the music from the restaurant.

With it not being quite sunset, the flap-flap of the American flag—proudly displayed at the left side of the house—greeted me. I watched it as I climbed, proud of all it meant, paying no attention to where I was going. I'd gone up these steps a thousand times or more. I knew each one. Just how high to step. Just when I had reached the landing.

But this evening's ascent was complicated by one of the inn's guests coming down. Rather quickly. Looking out toward the harbor rather than to where he was going. We crashed into each other without warning; the vase slipped from my grip, falling to the step at my feet, then tumbling down those behind me.

As though in slow motion, I turned and watched as it shattered. The small amount of water I'd placed in the bottom splashed against the white boards while colors of green and apricot sprayed the brick landing. Too late, I reached for it. As dizziness washed over me, a strong arm wrapped around my waist while a hand gripped an upper arm.

"Are you all right?"

"Oh no!"

Our words were spoken together; mine but a whisper, his a deep baritone. I looked from the disaster below to celestial blue eyes etched by laugh lines. "I . . ." I righted myself, gripping the clean-white board railing to my right. My assailant's hands fell away. Just as easily, they returned to slip under my left elbow, to guide me the remaining two steps to the landing.

"I am *so* sorry," the man said, though rumblings of laughter echoed within the words.

I shook my head as I studied him. An older man. Well-built. His white hair neatly trimmed and receding. Clear skin. Handsome to a fault and with an easy smile, nearly irresistible. Nearly. "You don't sound sorry."

Peals of laughter escaped him. He pressed a hand against his chest as he said, "No, really. Really. I am." He looked toward the busted vase and dying flowers. "That could have been a real accident."

I planted my hands firmly on my waist; the linen tunic billowed like a puffy cloud. "That *was* an accident. What could have possibly made it more real?"

The man took a breath before extending his hand. In frustration, I stepped backward, nearly losing my balance again. Instead of shaking the man's hand, I reached for it in desperation, lest I topple and lie among the tossed flowers. I felt a jerk, my body slammed against his—rock solid and smelling of expensive aftershave—my arms locked around his neck as he took several steps backward.

Just then, Lisa barreled out a back door. "What in the world."

Now it was my turn to laugh . . . so hard, I had to find one of the rockers to sit, the man not far behind me. Together we rocked and hooted—I still have no idea why—while Lisa stood at the top step, looking to the ground, shaking her head. When we finally sobered and I had wiped the tears from my cheeks, Lisa turned to us and said, "I take it you've met."

When the man stood, I noticed his attire. Pressed slacks. Blue dress shirt, unbuttoned at the neck and cuffs, which were rolled to the elbows. Casual confidence exuded from every pore of his being, even as he, again, extended his hand. "Ross Claybourne," he said. "Nice to bump into you. Twice."

I laughed again, this time more subdued. I slipped my hand into his. It was warm. Soft for a man's. "Anise Kelly."

Lisa joined us, pointing toward the railing and the scene below. "I take it that was the floral arrangement for the front hall."

I leaned back, crossing my legs. "I'm afraid so."

Ross Claybourne shook his head. "My fault entirely. If you'll let Lisa here know about the cost to replace it, I'll be more than happy to pay."

"Don't be silly," I said. "I wasn't watching where I was going either." I stood. "Lisa, I'll run back to the shop, get another arrangement, and be back within forty-five minutes."

Lisa waved her hands toward us, as if to say "Pshaw." The overhead light shimmered within her dark blonde curls—cut short and framing her face—as they bounced in the fair breeze. "No, no. Just come in and we'll have dinner. I'll send Derrick down to salvage the flowers while I find a vase somewhere." She looked to the man standing nearby. "Dr. Claybourne, were you planning to go out for dinner or will you join us in the restaurant tonight?"

His gaze slid to the harbor, then to the hills, before resting on the two of us. "I hadn't really decided yet. I just thought to get some fresh air first." He nodded at me. "Nice to meet you, Mrs. Kelly."

I swallowed. "Miss."

A blush rose from the collar of his shirt to his cheeks. "I apologize. Miss Kelly." He nodded at Lisa. "Enjoy your dinner, ladies," he said, then skipped down the stairs, stopping halfway. By now Lisa and I had stepped to the railing and peered down. His attention returned to us. "I'm more than happy to pick up the damage. The least I can do."

"Don't you dare, Dr. Claybourne," Lisa said. "We have staff for that, and you're here for a much-needed break, remember?"

Even from where I stood, I could see the whisper of a cloud

as it filled his eyes. Not entirely obscuring their blue brilliance, but enough to tell me the man's heart had been wounded.

Derrick and Lisa filled me in on Dr. Claybourne's story over steamed garden vegetables and halibut, broiled and seasoned to perfection by Derrick—a master chef. We dined in their private quarters of the inn: a sitting room, kitchen with eating area, bedroom and bath beautifully decorated in seaside blues and greens, yellows and reds.

"He's a widower," Lisa said.

I stabbed a piece of cauliflower with a silver fork. "Recent?"

Derrick, a handsome, fortysomething man with a remarkable full head of sandy blond hair, stuck the pad of his thumb to his lips to gather some of the seasoning of the fish. "Last year. He came here to get away for a while. To heal, if a man can heal after losing his wife of thirty-five years." He pointed an index finger first at me, then at Lisa. "Don't you two go cooking up anything for him, you hear me?"

Lisa gave him her best "get over yourself" look. "First, Mr. MacNeil, your words would have a much better chance of warning us if there were not such a delightful twinkle in your eye."

Derrick rolled his green eyes in protest.

"Second," Lisa continued, "just how is it that you know so much about Dr. Claybourne?"

Derrick took a long sip of his iced tea. "I have no idea what you mean," he said after a deep swallow.

"You most assuredly do. You know exactly how long the man was married."

Derrick's hands shot up as though he were being held at gunpoint. "Can I help it if he told me?"

Lisa's eyes—a matching shade of green to her husband's—narrowed. "What else did he tell you? Spill, Derrick Mac-Neil, or you may find yourself sleeping on that sofa in there tonight."

I could only smile at their banter, fully aware of where it was all heading. My sweet friend had always wanted for me what she and Derrick possessed, a loving marriage. Completion in each other. Their love was second only to their devotion to God, in spite of the years of prayer for a baby that never came.

I was not far behind them, however. Only my prayers had been for someone to love me. The way Derrick loved Lisa. The way my brother Jon loved Cheryl. The way our father had loved . . . *her.*

Derrick chuckled. "His wife's name was Joan, they have four daughters—all but one grown—and Joan is deceased."

I blinked. "From?"

He shook his head. "Didn't say."

Lisa's shoulders dropped. "How sad. For him and for the girls. One still left at home, did you say?"

Derrick nodded. "Yes. But I didn't get her name. Her social. Her blood type or her favorite musical group. Nothing on the other girls, either. Sorry, ladies." He grinned as he picked up knife and fork and cut his thick slice of tomato into bite-size portions. "Oh," he added. "One he did mention. She's a doctor, like him."

"What kind of doctor?" I asked.

Lisa stood, made her way over to the L-shaped kitchenette. "He's a pediatrician. I'm going to put on some hot water for tea. Anise?"

"Do you have any of the herbal raspberry like you had the last time I was here?"

Lisa stared at me as if I had three heads. "Of course."

I smiled. "Then, yes."

"Is Dr. Claybourne's daughter a pediatrician as well?" Lisa removed the stainless steel teakettle from a back burner and set about filling it with water.

"I guess so," Derrick said from beside me. "He said they were in practice together."

I shrugged. "Well then, that would make sense," I said, as though I knew what I was talking about. I wiped my mouth with the rose-colored linen napkin that had rested in my lap, laid it beside my plate, and stood. "Let me get the tea set ready."

"You know where it is," Lisa said.

Indeed I did. I also knew how special it was to her. The creamy white bone china from England with a spray of yellow daffodils and green ivy had been a gift from her mother-in-law on her wedding day, passed down two generations. I also knew how it must pain her that she had no one to pass such a treasure along to.

"Are you going to service in the morning?" Lisa asked after I'd arranged the tea set on a carrying tray.

"It's a Sunday, isn't it?" I asked with a smile.

She leaned in and whispered, "Good, because Dr. Claybourne asked to go with us."

"I heard that," Derrick said.

Oh, dear . . .

2

Lisa could not have been more obvious the following morning at church. She reminded me of Yenta the matchmaker in *Fiddler on the Roof.*

"Don't sit with your family this morning," she said through a smile as we walked in the double doorway of the sanctuary. "Sit with us. Balance us out." She cut her eyes toward Dr. Claybourne.

I blushed; I'm sure I did. But I made my apologies to my brother and his family, then sat with Lisa, Derrick, and Dr. Claybourne.

Matchmaker, matchmaker . . .

Even as we sang hymns of worship, my mind danced with a tune from the film. *He's handsome, he's young! All right, he's sixty-two.*

When the service was over, the congregation spilled out onto the sidewalk that stretched along one side of Main Street. Lisa immediately requested I join them for lunch at a nearby café and that Dr. Claybourne do the same. If I hadn't blushed before, I know I did then. I could feel the heat rising from my chest, spreading up my throat and across my fair cheeks.

With absolute charm, Dr. Claybourne said, "I appreciate the offer, Lisa. But I think I'm going to walk a little." He looked down the sidewalk, toward our small town. "The weather here is so nice." He glanced at me. "We have rather humid summers in Orlando."

I nodded once.

"Perhaps then," Lisa said, "Anise can give you a tour."

Derrick audibly sighed. "Lisa . . ." Then to Dr. Claybourne. "I'm sorry, Dr. Claybourne. I'm afraid my wife . . ."

But Ross Claybourne threw back his head and laughed, just enough to put us all at ease.

"I'm sure my brother and his family—" I started to say, just as Dr. Claybourne said, "Well, if she doesn't mind—"

"But if you need to be with your family . . ." he continued.

"Don't be silly," Lisa answered for me. "She's always hanging out over there. She's due a break."

"Lisa." I feigned shock. But to Dr. Claybourne, I said, "It *is* a nice day for walking. Let me tell my brother and sister-in-law I won't be joining them today."

Dr. Claybourne waited while I told Cheryl of my plans. "Who is this man?" she wanted to know, her sea-blue eyes narrowing toward him as she slipped sunglasses over her ears and up to the bridge of her nose.

"He's staying out at the inn. I met him last night and . . . it's a very long story, Cheryl. I'll fill you in tomorrow, I promise."

Just then my brother Jon joined us. Younger by six years but nearly identical in looks to me. Both tall. Slender. Dark blond hair, fair skin, and gray eyes. There was never any doubt we were Chris Kelly's children. The only question was whether or not he regarded himself as our father.

"What's going on here?" Jon asked. Four-year-old Aleya and eight-year-old Adam were right behind him. They wrapped themselves around my legs and waist.

I placed a hand on their heads before pulling lollypops from my shoulder purse and handing one to each. "Just like I promised." I looked to my brother. "I'm going to lunch with a new friend." I turned, looked over my shoulder at where Dr. Claybourne stood with Lisa and Derrick.

Jon grimaced. "The old guy?"

"Jon," Cheryl said. "I'm sure he's a nice man."

"A nice man, a good catch. True?" I said.

Cheryl smirked. We shared a love of classic movies. "True."

I placed my hand on Jon's arm. "I'll be fine, brother."

"I can run a background check if you'd like."

"Stop being a police officer and just be my brother."

He gave me a long look, then leaned over and kissed my cheek. "I *was* being a brother. If I were being a police officer, I'd arrest him . . . for something."

I laughed lightly, said good-bye, and returned to the three waiting for me under the shade of a bushy maple.

"Well," Lisa said. "We're going to leave you two to your walk." She linked her arm with her husband's.

"Dr. Claybourne," Derrick said, extending his hand for a shake, "for what we are putting you through, I am sincerely sorry."

Dr. Claybourne shook his hand and laughed just as easily as he had earlier. After Lisa and Derrick walked away, I turned to my "date" and said, "The village green is just down this way. We can walk the sidewalk toward town, then cut over to the harbor if you'd like."

"Sounds nice," he said.

Dr. Claybourne took his proper place, walking on the outside of the sidewalk. Our pace was slow. We said nothing. I was grateful I'd worn flats and a soft, all-cotton madras skirt that fell just below my knees. Once we came to the harbor, the cotton and rayon cap-sleeved top I'd chosen would also serve me well against the afternoon sun.

I felt odd. Out of place. I didn't know this man, really. Didn't know him at all. And yet I felt . . . something. Familiarity? As though we'd known each other all our lives, I thought, but had run out of things to say. But then, he said, "So you work in a floral shop?"

I clasped my hands in front of me. "I own it, actually."

"Own it? How nice."

"It was my mother's . . . until she died two years ago."

"I'm sorry."

"I'd always worked *with* her, and because my brother . . ." I looked at the man walking beside me. "You saw him at the church. Jon, my brother, is a police officer and . . ." I chuckled. "Well, he wouldn't be caught dead with his hands in potting soil or arranging flowers."

"Too much of a man's man?"

"Something like that."

I pointed to our left where a sidewalk met the one we were on; it wove through the village green. "This is a pleasant walkway," I said.

"I'll follow your lead."

As we stepped into the heavily shaded areas of the footpath—lined with lush green grass, clusters of shrubs and flowers, park benches, and the occasional kerosene oil replica street lamp—the temperature seemed to cool considerably. I crossed my arms, wishing I'd brought a light sweater.

"This place . . . the whole town . . . it's so relaxing."

I smiled. "We call them villages."

"Villages. Well, it reminds me of a place near my home. Winter Park."

"You're from Orlando."

He glanced over at me but only for a moment. I could tell his eyes were drinking in the experience of the green, even looking beyond to the rows of storefronts up ahead where Main Street bustled. "Lisa tell you?"

"No. You did. Earlier. You said your summers were humid there."

"So I did." He chuckled. "Yes. Actually I live in a community called Windermere." His gaze shifted from the setting around us to his feet. "So then, what *has* Lisa told you about me since our impromptu meeting of last night?"

I took in a deep breath. "Only that your wife died last year. I'm sorry for your loss."

"My Joan. Yes."

"And Derrick mentioned that you were married a long time."

"Right at thirty-five years." His eyes remained focused on his shoes, or so it seemed.

"How simply horrible for you." I spoke sincerely but didn't want to linger on death and dying. I'd had my own to deal with. Even after two years, it was difficult to discuss the loss of my mother. I couldn't imagine being married to someone for so long, sharing so much, and then having to let go. If the man wanted to relax, this was no way to begin. "I understand, as well, that you have daughters?"

We neared a white-latticed gazebo with a drinking fountain out front. I pointed to it and he looked up. I was in need of a drink and thought perhaps Ross would enjoy sitting under the canopy. We veered to the left, stepped across the thick carpet of grass. I took a drink from the cement and stainless fountain; Ross did the same.

"Would you like to sit for a while? Since no one else is here?" An odd coincidence, but a pleasant surprise.

"That would be nice."

We sat on the far side of the gazebo so as to watch the strollers, the runners, the bikers. To our left, two twenty-something-year-old men tossed a Frisbee. They threw hard, leaping high with the catch. Beyond a track of trees—the red maples, the elms, the weeping willows, and the oaks—our village boasted a variety of colors along the storefronts, each one painted to reflect the personality of the owner and the variety of life here in Seaside Pointe. Quiet. Hardworking. Unobtrusive. Yet, with vistas, as far as I was concerned, one could find nowhere else in the world.

"To answer your earlier question," Ross said from where he sat to the left of me. "I have four daughters. Yes." He leaned his elbows against the low railing behind us, bowing his chest. I couldn't help but notice that, for a man of his age, he appeared—at least underneath his shirt—to be well built. Muscular. Not like a bodybuilder. Just . . . maintained.

I crossed my legs, slipped my hands underneath my thighs. "Tell me about them."

"Kimberly is the oldest. Then there's Jayme-Leigh. She's a doctor, like me."

"I understand you are a pediatrician. Is she as well?"

23

Ross chuckled again. "Yes. Yes, she is. One day she'll take over the practice, I'm sure. She's a fine doctor. Just getting started, of course, but she's good with the little ones."

"Does she have any of her own?"

Ross shook his head. "No. She and her husband, Isaac . . . I think they are choosing to remain childless." He looked me directly in the eyes. "Not that they've discussed it with me, but . . . you know . . . it's a feeling ol' Pop gets in his gut. Joan, she thought the same thing. I asked her once if Jayme-Leigh ever discussed it with her." He smiled. "She said, 'No, hon. You know how our second born is. She's hardly one to share.'"

I took in a breath and sighed so deeply my shoulders dropped. "If I had married, I cannot imagine *not* having children."

Ross shifted, bringing his right knee to rest between us on the bench. Now, only his right forearm remained on the railing. I watched him, watched his face soften as though he were deeply interested in me. In my life. The blue in his eyes intensified. "You've never been married?"

I shook my head. "No."

He blinked. "I have to say, Anise, that I'm truly surprised to hear that. If you don't mind my saying so."

So was everyone in my family, not that I would say so to this man who was still a stranger to me. My family, my friends. Everyone and no one. Everyone was shocked and no one could understand it. Least of all me. "Thank you. I'm sure you mean that as a compliment."

"I mean it as an insult to the men of this . . . *village*. What are they, blind? You're a beautiful young woman. Surely suitors have stood in line from your front door, across your porch, and down the steps to the sidewalk."

I laughed out loud at the sheer poetry of his words. His eyes smiled, but his face remained somber.

"So answer a question for me, then, Miss Kelly."

"What's that?"

"How is it that you have remained single so long?"

3

It was a question without an answer. Not one I could give, anyway. Not easily, without a lot of words. Words I'd not bothered to say out loud except to Lisa.

"I thought . . ." I swallowed hard, shook my head. A breeze blowing from the direction of the bay entered the green, whipped around the gazebo, and slapped a long lock of hair across my cheek. It came to rest over my nose.

As though he'd been doing so all his life, Ross reached over, plucked the strand with his fingers, and tucked it behind my ear. "Go on," he said. "You can talk to me."

It must have been the physician's heart that spoke, I reasoned. He was accustomed to hearing the issues of others, those crises that drove mothers and fathers into his office with their little ones. Some real, some the imaginings of overly fearful parents. I pictured him patiently listening, nodding, making notes in the child's chart. Smiling knowingly, assuring the frantic parents their child would be all right.

I took a deep breath, willing myself to say what I'd only admitted once before. "I thought I'd met 'Mr. Right' a few years ago. But . . ." I shrugged.

EVA MARIE EVERSON

"The young man was a fool to let you slip away," Ross said, straightening himself to again face forward, elbows resting on the railing. He tilted his chin upward. Breathed in the salt air from the bay. Air that lay heavy but lifted the spirits anyway.

"Not so young, I'm afraid." I laughed lightly and slipped my hands from under my thighs to clasp them in my lap. "Don't take this the wrong way or misunderstand what I'm saying here, but I've only dated older men."

Ross looked at me sharply. "Is there a reason for that?"

I gave a quick pout. "Lisa says I have a father complex."

Ross's eyes widened. "Ah." Then, "I'm sure you dated plenty of boys your own age when you were in high school."

"High school . . . that was a couple of hundred years ago."

"More for me than for you."

"When did you graduate high school, Ross?" I felt myself pink. "If I may call you 'Ross.'"

"I'd like that very much." He sighed with dramatic flare. "Oh, let me see . . . Columbus sailed the ocean blue, Jamestown colony . . . and then I graduated from high school in 1957." He winked at me. "And I bet you weren't even a glint in your daddy's eye back then."

"I was born in 1962. So maybe a twinkle but not quite a glint."

"You are a mere child, not that much older than my Kimberly-Boo."

I laughed again; it came easily with him. "A mere child of thirty-eight."

"Ah . . . and I'm an old man of sixty."

"I would have guessed fifty."

27

It was his turn to find delight in the words. "Oh, you're good, Miss Kelly. Very good."

"Anise."

He looked me fully in the eyes. A strange level of understanding shot between the blue in his and the gray in mine. It reached into my soul and stirred my heart. "Anise."

The sun danced through the latticework of the gazebo, and the wind played with my hair again, interrupting the moment. "Would you like to walk through the square?" I asked. "I don't know about you, but I'm a little hungry and the Rexall"—I pointed—"which you can see from here, has a wonderful fountain grill if you like greasy hamburgers made to order. Loaded, of course."

"I love greasy hamburgers made to order, loaded, of course." His salt-and-pepper brows drew together playfully. "And I don't believe I've heard the name Rexall in years."

I stood; he did the same. "Some things around Seaside Pointe never change. The Rexall is one of them," I said, stepping to the lawn. "Been here since the early fifties." I cut my eyes playfully at him. "The 1950s, when you were nearing adulthood."

We returned to the sidewalk. Ross crooked his arm and extended his elbow toward me in invitation to slip my hand into its protective embrace. I complied and, for the sweetest of moments, felt as though I'd been doing so my whole life.

Seaside Pointe natives called Holmes Drugstore "the Rexall" because that was its name in the beginning. The old sign—somewhat rusty and fading, but welcoming nonetheless—still hung above the glass door of the redbrick storefront. Over the years, the tiles on the floor had been replaced,

28

the paint on the walls and ceiling refreshed, and the items on the shelves modified to match the era. But nothing about the corner café had been altered. Updated, yes, but not altered. The booth seats were retro puffy glitter-vinyl, the tabletops Formica. Chrome napkin holders kept neatly folded but too-thin paper napkins at the far end of each booth, along with what would now be considered vintage salt and pepper shakers, glass sugar dispensers, and squirt-top ketchup bottles. The countertop bar matched the tables; a long row of swivel stools matching the booths' seats ran along its length. And, across the years, from the other side, meat sizzled on the griddle, ice cream was dipped high into sundae bowls and topped with whipped cream and cherries, and cola shot into tall Coca-Cola glasses from a bright red fountain.

This Rexall had been a favorite of mine since childhood when my father would bring me here after my dental appointments for a cherry cola. Provided, of course, I didn't cry or give the hygienist a difficult time. After Dad left our family, Mom would bring Jon and me for lunch after church. Provided we'd not misbehaved. When I was a teenager, these booths had been the setting of many after-school meetings with friends. This was where we'd planned school functions, dances, and the prom, which I did not attend.

I'd been madly "in love" with our history teacher at the time, not that he was even remotely aware of my fantasies. No *boy* from the senior class would begin to suffice as an escort. My cousin Trace, older by one year, had offered to take me, but I'd opted for spending the evening sitting on one of the piers along the bay, feet dipped in the water as I swished them back and forth and listened to the rippling, the call of the gulls, the boats and fishermen. There I daydreamed about the day I would graduate from high school, just a few weeks away. That very day I would boldly approach Mr. Pearson and tell him of the passion burning within me. I imagined he would gaze down at me for a moment, stunned by my declaration of love, take me in his arms, kiss me most ardently, and say, "My darling Anise."

"There's a booth open over there," Ross Claybourne now said.

"Perfect." I felt heat rush to my cheeks, as though the good doctor had read my thoughts.

"Are you all right?"

I nodded, unable to speak.

"Sure?"

"Yes."

I said hello to a few of the people I knew, not lingering or making introductions, though I knew anyone who saw me was bound to wonder. Instead, I moved Ross along until we sat in the wide booth he'd pointed out. Our server was right behind us; we placed our orders for cheeseburgers (mine a veggie burger), fries, and cola, and returned our attention to getting to know each other. "You were lost in thought," Ross said, "when we walked through the door."

"I know. I was remembering being here. As a young child, a teenager. Now. Funny how just walking through a door can bring back such a flood of memories."

"Do you come here often?"

Our drinks were served before I could answer. Ross and I set about removing the bendy-top straws and wadding up the tubular paper that remained. "I come about once a week,"

I told him before taking a sip of my drink. "My shop is just around the corner. I typically bring my lunch to work, but about once a week I treat myself to being here." I took another sip before adding, "Tell me more about your daughters."

Ross had taken a drink as well, swallowed, and answered, "Kim and Jayme-Leigh . . . after Jayme-Leigh, there's Heather. She's married to Andre, who is a pharmacist. They have three kids, two are twins. Then Ami. She's the baby."

"How old are your girls?"

Ross smiled in the beaming sort of way fathers do. Good fathers. Not mine. At least, not to Jon or me. "Kim is thirty."

"You called her . . . something . . . a few minutes ago."

Another bright smile. "Kimberly-Boo. It's a name I gave her when she was just a toddler. She loved peekaboo and . . . well, you know how parents can be when their children are young."

Yes, I thought, but not really. "Is she married? You said Heather is, but what about Kim? Does she have kids?"

"Yes, she's married to a great guy. Good husband. Great father. Charlie. They have two boys. Chase is four this year and Cody is only a year. He, ah, was born about nine months before Joan . . . passed."

I allowed the moment to settle before asking, "And Jayme-Leigh, you said, is married but no kids."

"That's right. Isaac's a doctor as well, but he's in research with a pharmaceutical company. They're both bright people, they enjoy their time together when they're not working. Jayme-Leigh is a good doctor. It's a real pleasure for me to watch her do her job."

"You look very satisfied when you speak of her."

"I am. Her mother and I wanted . . . we wanted her to have

31

children, of course. Our children were sometimes the driving force in our marriage, if I'm to be honest."

"Why not be honest? After all, I told you about my 'father complex.'"

We shared a laugh as our burgers and fries were served in plastic baskets covered by emblem-plastered sheets of paper. The scent of grease and meat and potatoes drifted upward. Both Ross and I inhaled deeply before saying, "Smells good!"

We laughed again. Ross offered a brief prayer of thanks to God, adding that he hoped whatever damage was being done to our arteries by the food on this table would not be of any lasting harm.

"That was cute," I said. "That last part."

"God and I are on good terms," he said. "Even if I was a little mad at him seven months ago."

"Is that how long it's been?"

He took a bite of his burger, nodding.

A natural part of me sank. Seven months. As if we were telepathic, I sent a warning to Lisa: *Too soon, Lees* . . . I decided to broach the subject. "Do you want to talk about it? About Joan?"

Ross swallowed, took a sip of his cola, and popped a fry into his mouth. Chewing around it, he said, "No, do you?"

"No."

"You're not eating," he said. "And by the way, a *veggie* burger?"

"I don't eat red meat," I said. I picked up a fry and bit into the warm saltiness of it. "Tell me about . . . Heather?"

"Ah, Heather . . . now, she's the little mother of the group."

"In what way?" I took a bite of my burger, felt the juiciness of the "meat," cheese, sliced tomato, and shredded lettuce burst into my mouth. Heaven on earth, even if it wasn't a *real* burger.

Ross placed his back into the basket, pulled a napkin from the holder, handed it to me, then pulled another for himself. He wiped his mouth, wadded the paper in his hand. "For starters, she's an actual mother and takes the role very seriously. 'Too seriously,' Joan would say. Joan worried that when Heather's children are ready to leave the nest, she won't be able to handle it.

"Beyond that, she's the one who flits in and out of everybody else's life. Cooking and bringing home-cooked meals to Jayme-Leigh and Isaac because she worries they don't eat right. She became a mother before Kim, so, of course, she's always checking to make sure her big sister knows what she's doing in the maternal department. She even watches Cody while Kim works, and Chase is in day care or pre-K or whatever they call it these days."

"How amazing of her. She and Lisa would get along great."

Ross picked up a fry, pointed it at me, and said, "I'd already thought that. Only . . . Lisa and Derrick have no children, do they?"

I shook my head, saying nothing more. It really wasn't my place to share their heartache with a man who was, in reality, still very much a stranger. "Your youngest, Ami? She's how old?"

"Seventeen. Eighteen in a half a year. She'd insist I add that last part especially considering she acts with more maturity than many adults I know."

"Really?"

Ross smiled. Or winced; the movement of his lips was difficult to decipher. "She certainly doesn't have the youngest child syndrome, and once Joan got sick, she seemed to take on more responsibility. More . . ." His voice trailed until it disappeared entirely.

"And she's still at home, of course."

Ross nodded as he gathered the thick burger between his hands. "Not often enough. Not these days." He took a bite, chewed, swallowed. "She's passionate about ballet. I've got her enrolled in a high school that specializes in art programs, so when she's not studying—which is never enough in my opinion—she's en pointe, if you get my meaning."

"I took a little ballet. Years of it, actually, though I can't say I showed any real talent. Your Ami must be very gifted."

"I have to admit, she is. I'm very proud of her."

"Being so young . . . it must have been difficult losing her mother. I was thirty-six when Mom died, and it nearly killed me."

Pain creased Ross's brow and shot into his eyes. "Ami . . ." He sighed.

I dabbed at the corners of my mouth with the pathetic napkin. "What is it?" I asked, my voice so soft, I wasn't sure he heard.

His eyes met mine. "With Ami . . . there's something . . . I haven't even shared with the family. Not yet."

"Something . . . serious?" My heart felt heavy for this young woman I knew only by the love and hurt in her father's eyes.

Ross looked away from me, from the booth, beyond the tables filled with diners and the fountain and the high countertop. He looked past the storefront window to the sidewalk where people were passing in Sunday afternoon clusters.

To a place where life appeared idyllic but seldom was.

4

Ross shook his head, unwilling to go on. "It's okay." He forced a smile, looked at me and then down at his half-eaten burger. "You were right about these burgers. This has been a tasty meal." His grin grew genuine. "And the company, delightful."

I wondered if I blushed; it felt as though I should have. "Thank you. I feel the same way."

"I say we finish our meal, walk down to the bay—if you have nothing else planned for the afternoon—and enjoy an ice cream cone after we've walked off a few of these calories." He appeared surprised by his own suggestion. "Is there a place for ice cream near the bay?"

"I can think of little else I'd like to do. I know the perfect spot."

We finished our meal with little conversation, now both eager to get to the bay. Ross paid for our meals and left a nice tip for our server before escorting me toward the door, his hand resting along the small of my back. I nearly shivered under his touch, which was odd for me. We strolled under the awnings of the storefronts. I pointed to various buildings, giving him the name of the establishment, its history, and telling him the story each held for me.

When the Calla Lily was viewable from across the street, I pointed to it with pride. He commented on the window dressing, the green and white striped awning, the painted bench sitting beneath the wide single-paned window. I told him that the stained-glass calla lily embedded in the front door was what led me to call the store by its new name and that, before my ownership, it had been called Kelly's Floral Shop.

"What made you change the name?" he asked.

I couldn't answer at first. Then, "It was what she wanted." My voice barely reached above a whisper. "She wanted me to make it my own." I shrugged. Forced a smile. "So I did."

I told him more about Mom, about what a delight she was to all who knew her, strong in character, gentle in spirit. I told him that my parents had divorced when I was ten and Jon was four, and how this one little shop, added to Dad's child support, kept us fed, sheltered, and happy.

"Is your father still alive?"

I nodded. "He is."

"Live here?"

I shook my head. "No. He lives in upstate New York."

"Did he remarry?"

I nodded again. "Yes, he did. I have three half siblings. A brother and two sisters."

"Are you close? To your siblings, I mean?"

"No."

The bay was in plain view; bright sunshine glittered along the tiny peaks of blue-gray water. The smell of the sea had already reached us, the salt, the sun, the marine life. Boats with brightly colored sails glided between the shoreline and the green of the barrier islands. Wildflowers grew multihued and resplendent where the Ladies of Seaside Pointe had scattered seed. They gave a colorful offering against the sea-washed, sun-bleached buildings where boats docked, or were rented, where lobster and clams could be purchased fresh and eaten outside on one of the metal picnic tables. Along the line where fences and railings kept folks from walking straight into the water, a tiny shack opened its sliding windows to locals and tourists, offering hand-dipped ice cream in a variety of delicious flavors.

I pointed to it, grateful for the diversion. "There's the Ice Cream Shack."

Ross smiled. "The name is fitting. What's your favorite flavor of ice cream?"

"Here's a hint: I'm a fairly simple girl."

"Then I guess vanilla."

"I said simple, not plain."

Ross roared with laughter, then took my hand in his to guide me across the wide street separating us from the bay. I prayed he'd not let it go when we reached our destination, and he didn't.

"Strawberry," I said as we ambled down a wide ramp heavy with pedestrian traffic.

"What?"

"Strawberry ice cream. That's my favorite flavor."

His hand squeezed mine. "My next guess was chocolate."

"What about you?" We walked past the Cook's Nook, a rambling, oddly shaped shack that served a variety of fresh seafood. Take it home or eat it there. The advertising sign—shaped like a ship's helm—creaked in the breeze off the water. Beneath it, a variety of red and black containers were stacked haphazardly along the outer walls. Some so high they'd nearly toppled over.

"Mine? Well . . . I should make you guess, I think."

We stopped walking. Still holding hands, I turned to look at him and stared deeply into his eyes, trying to read his mind. Beneath us, the boardwalk creaked under the weight of those walking past. Overhead, the gulls cawed. In the water, the waves lapped against the shore, sails billowed and flapped, and boaters called to each other. But I kept my focus intent. "Moose Tracks," I finally said.

He blinked. "How'd you do that?"

"What?" I smiled broadly. "I was right?"

"Yes. Yes, as a matter of fact, you are." We resumed our walk. "That's amazing; it's like you've known me for years."

I was beginning to feel the same way.

"Do you think this little ice cream shack of yours has Moose Tracks ice cream?"

"Of course," I said. "You're in Maine, remember?"

As the day slipped away and we made our way back toward the green, Ross told me about his vacation home, a place he and Joan had purchased in the early years of their marriage. "When we were down at the bay, I couldn't help but think about it."

"Where is it?"

"A little place called Cedar Key, Florida." He winked at me. "You'd like it. You'd fit right in there, I'd say."

"Why's that?"

He pointed to the gazebo, again empty. A gift from God, twice in one day. "Care to sit again?" he asked me.

38

I was thrilled to. The most disappointing thing about the afternoon was that it was swiftly coming to an end. "That would be nice."

"Cedar Key is an island off the west coast of Florida. It's . . . it's like time forgot to call it and say, 'March on.' And you can't get there on your way to anywhere else. It's like it's . . . the end of the world. It's a place where I can sit at the edge of the water and forget everything I left behind in Orlando. I can get up early in the morning and watch the sunrise. I can walk to the west side of the island, which is really just across the street from the house, in the evenings and watch the sunset. And everything in between is pure relaxation."

"Sounds lovely."

"It is. It's rustic and simple and . . ." He shook his head as though trying to find the right word. "Glorious." He nudged me with his shoulder. "You should come down sometime. Visit."

I wanted to smile but forced myself to remain calm. "I'll have to look into taking a vacation down there. I've never been to Florida."

"Never been to . . . are you serious?"

"Nope. Like I said earlier, Mom's job kept us fed and sheltered and happy, but we never got to go on vacations. Not even to the number one vacation destination in the world." I spoke as though I were a voice-over in a commercial. "Mom used to say we lived in a vacation village, be happy with that. So Jon and I made our own adventures every summer. It was the best we could ask for. Plus she did manage to pay for my dance and Jon's tennis."

"You're close, you and your brother."

"Very."

"What about summers with your dad?"

"Once or twice we went. Maybe three times. But, we were both so uncomfortable with the others."

"Your stepmother and half siblings?"

I didn't answer; it was all too painful. Memories of sleeping on half-pumped air mattresses while the others slept on comfy beds . . . of having to ask every time I wanted to open the refrigerator for a drink of water while the rest pulled out bottles of cola without so much as a request. Wishing I could have just ten minutes alone with my father instead of watching him play "dad" with the three who got to spend every day of the year with him. Even when I'd asked, "Dad, can you and Jon and me go somewhere for lunch, just the three of us?" Dad admonished me, reminding me we were part of a larger family now.

We were, but we weren't.

"I'm grateful my girls are close," Ross now said from beside me.

"That is a blessing."

"Especially when Joan got sick. She needed them, they needed each other."

"How long was she sick?"

Ross stared off again. Swallowed. "Long, long time . . ." His voice trailed. "Too long." The words sounded as though they'd been forced past a knot in his throat.

I looked down, noticed his hands resting on the tops of his thighs. I laid my hand over one of his and squeezed. "I'm so sorry," I whispered.

He turned his hand over, and our palms fell flat against

each other. This time, the shudder nearly undid me. What was it about this man?

I smiled inside, thinking of Lisa then. She'd say, "There's that father complex again, Anise." But she knew me well. I did not fall in love—or anything remotely close to it—easily. I'd only allowed myself to be swept away—ridiculously away— by one man.

It had only been five years before. I'd met Garrett O'Dell when he'd stopped by the floral shop to purchase a plant for a funeral he'd come into town for. There had been instant chemistry between the older man and me, something I'd never really felt with anyone before. Not that I'd dated much over the years; Seaside Pointe was much too small a community for my interest in older men to be met without scandal.

Garrett worked for an office supply company, which kept him on the road a good deal of the time. As he once said, "About half the month I'm in my car." He lived in Portland, he said, in a small apartment perfect for a bachelor who's just not home enough to even hang a picture on a wall. He enjoyed his job but missed having things like a yard to mow and then relax in, a dog to love and be loved by. Those kinds of things. "Heck," he said, "I can't even have a goldfish."

I asked him, on one of our many dinner dates, how it was that a man as fabulously good-looking as he managed to remain unmarried for so many years. He shrugged like a schoolboy and said he'd just not met the right woman . . . until now.

Garrett was ten years my senior; I was thirty-three, he was forty-three. Our birth dates were only days apart. We often laughed about how easy it would be, in the years to come, to celebrate our special day. We'd take lavish vacations, Garrett told me. We'd go to Hawaii . . . to Europe . . . to Greece.

I mentioned that I'd always wanted to go on a Holy Land tour. He quickly remarked, "Consider it booked."

Our relationship lasted a little over a year. Twice a month he came into town, we'd dine, walk the bay on warm evenings, sit before a fireplace in the lobby of the Harbour Inn where he always stayed when the weather turned cold. He'd often surprise me with jewelry—bracelets, necklaces, brooches—and body lotions, one of my indulgences.

Then, one Thursday when Garrett was expected into town, he didn't show. By Friday morning, my mood had reached near-panic. I called Lisa, who reported she'd not heard anything from him either. We both agreed the whole situation was puzzling.

And frightening.

I had called Garrett's cell phone several times by then; it went to voice mail each time without so much as a ring. Later that afternoon, Lisa called with an idea.

"He puts his stays on his business credit card. I looked it up, and he works for the Cumberland Office Supply Company."

"Cumberland?" He'd always told me he worked for Portland Paper & Office Supply. "I thought he lived in Portland," I said, not wishing to reveal the rest.

"Well, maybe there's an office in Portland." She paused. "Besides, they're not so far apart that he couldn't live in Portland and work in Cumberland."

"So, what do you think I should do?"

"Call the office. See if something came up. Maybe he's even in his office. How many times has he left out of Seaside

Pointe early to make it back to the office before closing so he could file reports?"

"That's true." I chewed my lower lip. "Lisa, do you really think I should? I don't want him to think—"

"After a year, Anise? Seriously? I'd think you have every right. But . . . if you'd like, I can make the call. After all, he missed his reservation without cancellation. I can say I'm concerned, and that will make perfect sense."

It was a good plan and I told her so.

For the next half hour, I stayed busy in the back of the shop while Mom went over a few details up front. I forced myself not to imagine the worst. Like, he was in the hospital, deathly ill from food poisoning he'd gotten at some diner somewhere. Or, he'd been in a car accident. And he was in a coma, unable to tell anyone to call me.

Or worse, he'd decided we were not right for each other but didn't have whatever it took to come tell me . . . or even to call . . .

Over the quiet music of the radio humming through the shop, I heard Mom say, "What's Lisa doing here?"

My stomach dropped along with the cluster of baby's breath I held in my hand. Something was wrong. As though walking through seaweed, I made it to the front, watched the front door open, heard the chime of the bell. Lisa appeared with a halo of light behind her. She wore dark sunglasses, pulled them from her face, and said only one word. My name.

I fainted, sure by her expression that Garrett had been in a car accident . . . indeed, that he was dead.

5

"And was he?" Ross now asked from beside me in the gazebo, where I'd told him one of my darkest secrets.

"No," I said. "He wasn't. When Lisa and Mom revived me and I'd sipped on some hot lemon water, Lisa told me the truth. She'd called Garrett's office and relayed exactly what she'd said she would. They told her there had been an unexpected death . . . in his *wife's* family."

"His wife's?"

I looked at Ross, managed to bring my eyes to his. "I had *no* idea. None. There was no bachelor apartment. No life without a dog or a yard or even a goldfish."

"What was there?" Ross's hand tightened on mine as his other arm wrapped around my lower arm.

"Three kids, a mortgage on a house—a beautiful house, I know, because I made Lisa take me there just so I could see—and a golden retriever."

"You saw all this?"

Tears I didn't want to shed forced their way to my eyes and spilled down my cheeks. I used my free hand to swipe at them. "I'm sorry," I whispered.

I didn't see it coming, the compassion in Ross Claybourne. I didn't expect it, really. Yes, I knew he was a gentle man, but I had not thought the tenderness would be directed at me. One second I was wiping away tears, and in the next I was wrapped in his thick arms.

And I allowed it. Of course, I allowed it. It felt wonderful to be held by a man, something I'd not experienced since that doomed relationship years earlier. When we finally broke apart, I laughed nervously. "How silly of me," I said.

"How very Gene Tierney of you," he replied.

"I'm sorry?"

"In the movie *The Ghost and Mrs. Muir*, Gene Tierney plays—"

"Mrs. Muir," I said in unison with him. "I remember that movie."

"It's a classic. And, if you remember, Mrs. Muir falls in love with a man—another writer—who she believes loves her too."

"Only to find out he is married with children."

"It's a touching scene."

I looked out over the green. Afternoon was making way for evening. Visitors were few; most had gone home for the day. I sighed. "If I remember correctly," I said with a lilt, "Mrs. Muir died at the end."

Ross laughed. "Yes, but she was *old*."

We smiled at each other in silence. It seemed to me that Ross grew uneasy, as if something was on his mind but he couldn't quite bring himself to say it. Finally, he patted my knee and said, "I'd best get you back to the church so you can get home and I can return to the inn."

As was my Sunday habit, I'd left my cell phone in the cup holder of my car. A quick check showed I'd missed two calls from Jon and five from Lisa.

Mercy.

I drove home, the same house I'd lived in since birth. Shortly after they married, my mother and father purchased the quaint Cape Cod cottage situated on a quiet street just outside of town. Mom filled the yards with flower beds, herb and vegetable gardens. Dad worked little by little to add on to the house. A deck with French doors leading to the family room. An extra bath. A detached garage and, just before he left to start another family, a bonus room over the garage. When Jon and I were in our teens, we both used it to entertain our friends.

I parked in the garage, hurried across the stone walkway toward the deck, and then unlocked the French doors to step inside. I dropped my purse and me into the nearest chair, flipped open my cell phone, and called Jon. His main concern was that I had been kidnapped by this stranger and sold into slavery. I assured him I was fine, that he'd been on the police force about a day too long if he really suspected that, and that I would talk to him later. I then called Lisa, who was nearly breathless with worry.

"Why are you worried?" I asked. I stretched my long legs, pointed my toes, and kicked off the sensible shoes I was glad to have worn that day.

"Dr. Claybourne got here just a few minutes ago. He only gave me the briefest of smiles, then headed straight for his room."

"The cad," I teased.

"What happened?"

I had to admit, I was a little perplexed myself. "I think we had a fun day," I told her. "We walked through the green, we went to lunch at the Rexall, walked to the bay and got ice cream."

"What else? Anything else?"

I shook my head. "Lisa, you sound like we're in junior high."

She huffed. "I just want to know why he came back so . . . so somber."

"I don't have any idea. We walked a lot . . . maybe he's just tired."

I waited through a long pause before she said, "There's something you are not telling me. I can feel it."

Yes, there was. I could feel it too. Something had sparked between Ross and me that afternoon. I'd felt chemistry, though I didn't want to admit that just yet. Most of all to Lisa and after only seven months into his being a widower.

Still, I also felt as though I'd been dismissed at the end of our day. Like when we were kids and Dad came to see Jon and me for day visits. *Okay, here I am. There you are. Here's what we'll do. Now, I'll go home and pat myself on the back because I've done my duty as your father.*

How could I explain to Lisa that one minute he'd embraced me, the next we'd laughed over an old movie, and the next he'd patted my knee and sent me on my way?

"Seriously, Lisa. You're imagining things. It was a fun day. I'm tired, though, so I'm going to say good night and go take a long soak."

"Wait—"

"Good night, Lisa."

I ended the call and did exactly what I'd told Lisa I'd do. I took a bath.

Ross Claybourne walked through the doors of the Calla Lily at ten after ten the next morning. He looked remarkably handsome dressed in dark blue shorts, a polo shirt, and a pair of dark blue denim boat shoes. He smoothed his hair as he walked in the door while I fought the urge to smile from the sheer joy of seeing him.

I had only unlocked the front door a few minutes earlier and was standing behind the counter, looking over orders for the upcoming week. Cheryl had not made it in yet; Monday was her late day.

"Hi," I said. "Welcome to the Calla Lily." As if he were just any customer.

He looked around, admiring silk arrangements, bunches of long-stemmed summer flowers in large cut-glass vases, until his eyes came to rest on the section of stuffed bears and helium balloons. "Nice," he said, stepping closer to the old counter.

I noticed how much more tanned he was than the day before. "Your face," I said. "You got some sun yesterday."

Pink splashed across the brown. "I do that," he said. "Tan easily."

We stood awkwardly looking at each other for a moment. "Can I help you with . . . anything?" I asked.

"I need to send some flowers," he answered, shoulders broadening.

"Oh," I said, sliding an order pad toward me. "Well then, sir. Let me get your information. Name?" I asked as though I didn't know.

"Dr. Ross Claybourne." I heard the lilt in his voice. "C-l-a-y-b-o-u-r-n-e."

I looked up. "Oh."

"One of the many variances in spelling. I bet you were thinking more along the lines of how Liz spells it."

I had been. I liked her clothing line, so why not? "Maybe so," I answered. "Address?"

"Sixty-twelve Black Bear Court. Windermere, Florida. Do you need the zip?"

"Please."

He provided it.

"And what would you like to order?"

"Well . . . I really don't know. It's to say 'thank you.' What would you suggest?"

I looked past him to take in my own inventory. "Do you want live or silk?"

"Live."

"We have some lovely summer arrangements."

He turned. His eyes swept the front of the store. "I see that you do." He pointed to a bunch I'd arranged earlier and placed in one of the cut-glass vases with blue floral pebbles and water after I'd come in. "These are nice."

"Those are among my favorites," I said. And they really were.

He peered over his shoulder. "Oh. Well, then, by all means." He turned fully, reached for one of the cards in a counter display, and said, "Can I sign the card while you bring them to the counter? Get them ready to go?"

"Yes, of course," I said. I stepped from behind the counter, walked to the arrangement, clasped it firmly in my hands, and said, "Will you be going back to the inn any time soon? I have a new arrangement for Lisa. I should have brought it to the church yesterday . . ."

"I . . . um . . . I'm not sure. Depends."

I gave a light shrug. "Oh. Okay," I said, wondering how a man I'd felt so comfortable with just one day earlier now put me ill at ease.

I returned to the counter with the flowers, placed them between my new customer and myself, and said, "I'll just need an address to send them to and a method of payment."

Ross slipped the card into the tiny envelope, reached into his back pocket, and pulled out a thick leather wallet. "I'll pay with cash."

"This arrangement is $59.95 plus tax."

I watched as he slid the arrangement over to the right before pulling a one hundred dollar bill from his pocket. "This should cover it."

I blinked at the crisp bill. "Yes, I believe it should." I picked up my pen and said, "The address you'd like these sent to?"

"Eight-fifty-five Sunset."

My head jerked up. "Eight—"

Ross was now holding the front of the envelope toward me. In clear print it read: *To the most beautiful woman in Seaside Pointe.* "Ross . . ."

"I was rude at the end of our time together yesterday."

"No. You weren't. Really."

"Yes. Yes, I was. I just want you to know that . . . it felt . . . wrong somehow."

50

My chest hurt. For him, mostly. And for myself. Was the "wrong" having been with me for the afternoon? For holding me when I cried? For laughing at my jokes? "How?"

He didn't answer; he shook his head and said, "Can I take you to lunch?"

"Lunch? It's not even ten-thirty."

"Out for a cup of coffee then? Or . . ." The twinkle returned to the blue in his eyes. "An ice cream?"

I pondered for the briefest moment the work I had ahead. Cheryl would not arrive until noon. Still, I was the owner. If I couldn't walk out on this store of my accord, then who could? "I'd like that," I said. "But only if you promise to talk to me, to tell me the truth about . . . yesterday. Why you ended our day so abruptly. Because, honestly, Ross, I thought we were having fun. I mean, except for that little moment when I blubbered all over your shoulder."

He held his right hand up, extending three fingers toward God. "Scout's honor. I'll talk."

"All right then. Just let me lock up."

We took a long walk, past storefronts and along the bay. We decided against the ice cream, opting for cappuccinos at Mother's Café. Ross was so tickled by the name; he told me as we sipped the froth from our drinks that, in the true South, this coffee bar would have been named Mama's Café.

"All kidding aside," I said when enough time had passed for pleasantries, "what happened yesterday? And remember, you promised the truth."

Ross nodded, extended his "scout's oath" hand and fingers again. "I felt guilty."

"Guilty?"

We'd chosen to sit at one of the small round tables out-side. The day was only mildly warm for July. A sweet breeze coasted up from the water, enough to pick up wisps of my hair, forcing them to dance along my cheekbones. Ross admired the colorful avenue of storefronts. His eyes drank in the people passing by; one way on this sidewalk, another way along the opposite side of the street. I waited, know-ing that words like *guilty* don't come easily to a man like Dr. Ross Claybourne. He needed a moment to form his thoughts, in spite of having had an entire night and morn-ing to do so.

"I loved Joan. My wife."

"Of course."

"But there were . . . issues. The girls . . . they didn't know . . ." His voice trailed. I watched his eyes brim with tears. He must have felt them threatening to destroy some archaic myth of masculinity. His sunglasses were tucked into the front pocket of his shirt; he pulled them out and slipped them on. "Joan," he continued. "She drank. A lot. Started before we married, but back then I didn't see it as anything but social. She was a good woman. A godly woman." His jaw jerked toward me, and I imagined that, behind the dark shades, his eyes had just met mine. "Some people would argue that, I know. How can a woman who drinks too much be godly . . . but . . . she was."

"Some would argue that she couldn't drink at all and be godly."

"Do you feel that way?"

His words felt like a challenge, one I was up for. "No. I don't."

His face registered approval. "She was a good wife. Doting mother. She knew she had a problem. She went to rehab several times and even managed not to drink while pregnant. But . . . then she'd say she could handle *just* social drinking and, for some reason, I'd agree. But the next thing I knew, she was stumbling to bed every night and I was making excuses for her the next morning."

He paused, waiting for me to say something, I suppose. But I had nothing to say. I knew no one with such a problem. The closest I'd seen my parents come to drinking was communion wine.

He took a deep breath, allowed it to slip slowly from his nostrils. "I told the girls their mother had cancer. Joan and I agreed on that. Truth was, she had cirrhosis." The thumb and index finger of his right hand toyed with each other. "Even with such a diagnosis, she wouldn't stop drinking. Jayme-Leigh knew—being a doctor, she figured it out. She tried to talk to her mother about her drinking. After that, Joan didn't consume as much, but she didn't quit."

"Gracious."

"And then she died and I . . . I was both heartbroken and relieved. I didn't have to keep her secret . . . *our* secret . . . anymore."

I reached across the table, placed my left hand on his right. "Ross, I am so sorry."

He flipped his hand to hold mine. Took another deep breath. "And," he said within the exhale, "I told myself I could now concentrate on my practice. On my girls, who'd lost so much with the death of their mother. On my grandchildren." He looked away again. "Especially on Ami."

There it was again. Something about Ami. "Because she's the youngest?" I asked, hoping he'd reveal . . . anything.

"Mmm," he said, which was neither a yes nor a no.

"So where does the guilt come from, Ross? Because you've moved on?"

He chuckled, but not as though he was amused. "No." He took a few more breaths, these shallow. "I came here because I needed the time away. My daughter Heather said I haven't really mourned." He tilted his head in acquiescence. "And, she's right. Truth is, though, I cannot figure out what I'm mourning. Joan's passing? Joan's disease? Joan's drinking? What we lost? What we could have had?"

The questions settled around us. The foam atop my half-finished coffee had turned murky and nearly disappeared. I stared at the short mug for a moment, wondering if I should take a sip. Choosing against it. The coffee was probably tepid, anyway. Finally, I said, "You've thought this through, I think."

"Not really." Ross took a sip of his coffee, frowned at the cup, and returned it to its saucer on the linen-draped table.

"Yes, you have. To have this many questions, Ross, means you have begun the process."

He looked directly at me. "Process? Of what?"

"Getting your answers. You cannot answer questions you don't have." I smiled weakly. "I know. I've gone through these same questions . . . both when my father chose another family over ours and when Mom died."

Ross folded his arms over his abdomen.

"But that doesn't get you to the guilt you say you felt yesterday. Are you feeling guilty for even asking these questions?"

"No," he said, all too quickly.

"What then?"

His hand squeezed mine before traveling up my arm to clasp my elbow. He leaned over the table and spoke softly. Intimately. "For feeling something . . ."

"About?"

"About you."

6

Ross was leaving on Wednesday, two days away. Hardly enough time to start, experience, and finish a summer romance. He had called his daughter and practice partner, Jayme-Leigh, told her he was relaxing and enjoying his time and would she hold down the fort another week.

We had nine days.

We decided not to waste a single minute. I turned the shop over to Cheryl so as to spend my days with Ross. He planned every moment without a second of them held from me, although I sensed Lisa's hand in the details. We took biking tours, bird-watching tours, and an aircraft scenic tour in a Cessna 172. We spent hours in the Maine Indian Heritage Museum and Gift Shop and at the Cottage Street Arts Center, where we saw several independent films during the afternoons and live theater at night. We went kayaking and lobster fishing, and took two different tours for seal and whale watching.

Out of all our activities, the one we seemed to enjoy the most was the two-hour windjammer cruise. We took three: a morning tour, an afternoon tour, and—the most romantic— a sunset tour. It was on this tour that Dr. Ross Claybourne kissed me for the first time. Warm and sweet, like the night. Like the man.

On Sunday night—one week from our first afternoon together—I lay in my bed, sobbing. Earlier that day Jon had expressed such disapproval over my new relationship, I thought he would go after Ross with some made-up legal citation, although I couldn't imagine for what. Ross had taken it all in stride, but I was crushed. I had fallen in love with this man, deeply and passionately in love with this man. I couldn't bear the thought of his leaving, and I couldn't abide my brother's disapproval. He was, after all, my only family left. Truly.

I cried also because we had but three days left with each other. A week earlier they'd felt like a lifetime away, but now they hovered like death's blanket. I wondered if Ross felt the same; if our being together for that many days would only add to his angst rather than heal his grieving heart.

He never once brought up Joan and, for the most part, I didn't sense her ghost between us. How could I? There was no room for her displeasure; there was only space for love.

The following morning we were to meet for breakfast before a seal-watching tour, which we'd already done once and enjoyed immensely. My eyes were swollen from my tearful night; before dressing I applied damp green tea bags over them and lay flat on the bed, ankles crossed, and listened to the Celtic strings of harpist Áine Minogue playing on my CD player. Just as I pulled the nearly dry bags from my face, my cell phone rang. I had placed it next to me on the bed. I grabbed it as though it would get away.

The caller ID showed it was Ross.

"Good morning," I said, attempting to be cheerful.

"Good morning, my love."

I melted. "Hello."

"I need to cancel our breakfast," he said. "Can we meet at the harbor at the boat dock at nine-forty-five?"

Disappointment washed over me. "Uh . . . sure." Even an hour and forty-five minutes' loss in time was an hour and forty-five minutes too many.

"I'm sorry. I should have thought of this last night. I . . . I need to run by the Rexall and pick up a prescription I had my pharmacy call in on Saturday."

Disappointment gave way to concern. "Are you all right?"

"Oh yeah." He chuckled. "You forget you are dating an old man. Old men have to take medicine on a daily basis."

I pretended to pout. "You are *not* an old man, Ross Claybourne."

"You're just saying that because you love me." He paused. "You *do* love me, don't you?"

I closed my eyes, breathed in deeply through my nostrils. "Most desperately." I wanted to say more, to tell him that I couldn't bear his leaving on Wednesday. I wanted to beg him as I sat upon my bed to never leave me. To forget Florida and move to Maine. But that would have been selfish on my part. He had a practice to return to. Daughters. Grandchildren. Friends and colleagues. One day, I imagined, he'd tell them about this old maid he'd once made happy while in Maine, even if only for a few days.

"I love you too." He chuckled again. "Most desperately."

"You're poking fun."

"No, I'm not. I mean it. I'll see you soon. Good-bye, sweetheart."

An old fear swept through me. What if Ross, like Garrett, had no intention of being there this one time? What if he had an airline ticket already tucked into his pocket? His bags packed? What if, in some ego-driven desire, he wanted to picture me, standing there on the dock, wide-brimmed hat in my hand, waiting for him to come? But, like Garrett, he'd never show. What if everything he'd said had been a lie and there was already a special someone in Orlando who'd captured his heart after Joan died? What if this were nothing more than a summer romance?

I dressed in a pair of long linen shorts and a sleeveless matching top with a pair of thong sandals while dread cloaked my heart. I drove to the harbor in despair. But anguish fled as soon as my feet stepped onto the boardwalk and I saw him, waiting near the boat. For me.

He waved. I waved back. And when I reached him, he kissed me as though there was no one else in the world but the two of us. Never had been. Never could be.

During the three-hour tour along Maine's picturesque shoreline, we stopped in the blue-gray waters for lunch, served by the cook on the tall ship. We dined on lobster soup, homemade bread, and blackberry pie. Ross and I whispered thoughts and stole kisses between bites. When we'd had our fill of food and our plates and bowls had been taken away, we settled on one of the highly waxed wooden benches near the bow. I snuggled into Ross's arms, my back curved perfectly to meet the muscles of his broad chest. The sun was warm—hot nearly—but it felt good against my skin. I stretched my long legs, which had tanned over the week, and pointed my toes. Ross kissed the tip of my ear, sending goose bumps along my arms and legs. I showed him and he laughed.

An hour and a half later, we returned to the dock. Elation pulsed through my veins. The sea air, the wind and waves had always done that to me. But experiencing them with Ross was a tonic unlike anything I'd ever experienced. He'd seemed genuinely interested in the captain's dialogue about the marine life, the various ports and barrier islands, and the birds who call Maine their home. As he listened, he'd whisper into my ear about how this or that reminded him of Cedar Key. "CK," he often called her. Stepping back onto land with him, I wanted to see this Florida gulf shore paradise more than ever, and I wondered if I might be bold enough to broach the subject before he left for home.

Ross took my hand, said we were going now to get ice cream. I reminded him we'd just had blackberry pie.

"But we didn't have ice cream," he said.

"Ross Claybourne, I do believe Mr. Horner will be able to retire from his ice cream stand with what we've bought this week alone."

Ross smiled at me. "I like ice cream. I like eating ice cream with you. So sue me."

I patted my tummy. "I'm going to gain ten pounds before this week is over, if I haven't already. I need to call our family attorney. Maybe I can sue you for alienation of a waistline."

He squeezed my hand as we moved along the boardwalk, pulled me closer to him, and said, "Ready to get rid of me so you can diet?"

I stopped, forced my tears not to surface, and said, "Never. I'd gladly wear twenty extra pounds if it meant your being here."

His smile was faint but warm. Loving. "Bless you for that."

We moved on, toward the ice cream stand, where only a handful of people stood in line. I spied Mr. Horner behind the window, beaming as he watched us approach. I suspected the older man had enjoyed witnessing love bloom between Ross and me this week. Mason Horner had been a lifelong friend of my father and, when Dad left, had felt some sort of paternal obligation to Jon and me. He and his wife often expressed concern that I had never married, that I'd be alone—like Mom—until my dying day. They'd not wanted that for me, they said. So to see me with Ross had to have held some semblance of hope for them.

"Strawberry and Moose Tracks," Mr. Horner said before we had a chance to order.

Ross winked at me. "What would you like to do this evening?" he asked.

"Oh, I don't know . . . anything, really." I turned to watch Mr. Horner, but Ross turned my face toward him, his finger against my chin. "How about dinner at the inn?"

"Lisa would love that, wouldn't she?" I started to look again at Mr. Horner, wanting to see—as I'd always done—just how high he'd stack the scoops. I was the proverbial kid in an ice cream parlor.

"Look at me," Ross whispered.

Goose bumps returned; I shyly allowed my eyes to meet his.

"I love you," he said. "Do you know that?"

"I know that."

"What are we going to do come Thursday, Miss Kelly?"

I blinked, sorry he'd brought it up. "Maybe, if we close our eyes real tight, Thursday won't come."

"Strawberry and Moose Tracks," Mr. Horner said from behind the opened window. He stretched the waffle cones—piled high with three scoops each—across the white linoleum counter. I took them both while Ross paid.

"Thank you, Mason," Ross said. "Oh, and can I have a small cup of water, please?"

"Mason," I said as we walked toward the picnic benches with our delights. "To me, he'll always be Mr. Horner, but to you, he's Mason."

"That's what you get, young lady, when you take to dating old men."

"Old*er*, Ross Claybourne. Not old."

After sitting on a bench, he raised his cone to me in a mock toast. "To us."

I tipped my cone to meet his. "You got Moose Tracks on my strawberry," I said, after we'd pulled them apart.

"Consider it fertilizer."

We laughed and bit into our ice cream. For several minutes, said nothing. Just licking and biting and watching the sun dance over the water and listening to the gulls call overhead, the gentle murmur of locals and tourists. Wishing as hard as I could wish that these moments could be frozen in time, or dripped into bottles to be opened on lonelier, colder days.

I had managed to nibble and lick my way to the bottom scoop. I paused to watch a small flock of sandpipers in flight, hovering close to the shoreline just beyond the fencing. They sang *twee-wee-wee, twee-wee-wee*. I took another bite of ice cream, raking my teeth across something hard. Thinking it to be a frozen berry, I peered down, ready to pluck it and pop it into my mouth. Instead, the top of a scintillating diamond ring stared up at me.

Breathless, I looked from the cone to the man sitting beside me, smiling. Winking. He pulled the ring from the ice cream, swished it in the untouched cup of water, and held it toward me, thick fingers wrapped around its delicacy. Fire from the sun caught in its facets, sending a rainbow of color toward me. Blue eyes met mine as he began the words I could tell he'd rehearsed for hours. "There are those who will say I've lost my mind. How can I, after only a week of knowing you, ask you to be my wife? I've wondered the same thing, to be honest with you." He sighed. "Rarely is a man blessed with such a love as I had with Joan—even with all its flaws. To be blessed twice in a lifetime is nearly more than I could have ever imagined or even prayed for.

"Anise, you've brought me more life, more laughter, and more happiness in one week than I've felt in a very long time. Longer than most would ever realize or accept. I felt myself falling in love with you that first Sunday. I tried to talk myself out of it and I failed. I've failed miserably. Last night I decided to give up. Give in to this feeling. I drove to the jeweler this morning, bought this ring—I'll buy another one if you don't like it—and roped the delighted Mason Horner in on my plot."

I giggled. Looked over my shoulder at the man who clasped his hands together in happiness and then brought them close to his heart.

"So, Miss Kelly," Ross continued, bringing me back to the moment, "if you can love this old*er* man in the coming years with half the passion you have this past week, I will be the most fortunate of men. And, if you can forgive me for asking you to marry me with a proposal that includes the name of my late wife, I will be most blessed indeed."

He blinked.

"You're crying," he said, brushing my tears with the pad of his thumb. "I can only hope those are tears of joy."

I nodded.

"We'll be up against a lot, Anise. I know that. But I love you. And right now, that's all that matters. If you're willing, we'll tackle the rest together." He slipped the ring onto my waiting finger. "If you'll say yes."

"Yes."

Again his eyes met mine. We sealed the moment with kisses sweetened with the flavor of ice cream and salted by my tears. "You're right," I whispered as I kissed the side of his mouth. "We'll be up against a lot. Your girls won't know what hit them and my brother is probably going to call the FBI. But I'm up for the challenge, Ross Claybourne, because, silly as it sounds after only a week, I love you so much I could die. And, quite frankly, I'd rather survive the coming storms with you than not experience them and be without you."

And I did. Oh, how I did. But the truth is, with all that hope and promise, I had no idea what I would face when I returned with him to his home and his family in Florida. No idea at all.

7

Ami
December 2000

Anise came to live here as Dad's wife in August, and I *still* heard about it from Heather four months later. My *gosh*, my sister just didn't know when to give it up. Let it go. Move on. Couldn't she have found a million and one better things to waste her energy on? Like her kids? Her husband? Couldn't she just be happy for someone at least once in her life rather than trying to make everything about her? How she felt? What she wanted? Why didn't she just . . . *see*? Not to mention Dad's marriage to Anise was the tip of the iceberg. So not the real issue. Not that Heather would have known it. Not that anyone would. No one but me. And who could I have told? No one. For sure.

Four weeks before Christmas, on the one-year anniversary of Mom's death, Anise decorated our house so beautifully. No small feat considering how gigantic the place is. She used some of Mom's decorations and hung most of Mom's ornaments on the tree, telling Dad that it would make it more like "Joan did it than me." But did that even remotely make Heather happy? No. As soon as she walked into the entryway and saw everything, she crossed her arms, stalked from one room to the other like a drill sergeant, and then sternly said to Dad, "Can I see you a moment, please? In your office?"

Anise, Dad, and I had retreated into the kitchen by then. Heather made it only as far as the wide arched doorway leading into the family room. Like she couldn't stand to walk into the kitchen if Mom was not in it and Anise was.

Heather and Dad left, but not before Dad gave Anise a quick kiss on the cheek and she patted him on the shoulder, leaving me to wonder even more about their relationship. They had this way of communication through touching . . . something I didn't really remember between Dad and Mom. But maybe they had it and, a year later, I could no longer recall it.

I don't know.

Anise leaned against the small oak kitchen island and sighed after Dad left the room.

"I'm sorry, Anise," I said from the angular bar between the kitchen and the breakfast nook. I'd deposited my Sassi dance bag there not ten minutes before the front door opened and Hurricane Heather stormed in. I now glanced at my watch. I barely had time to get to the studio. Maybe I'd make it if I went five miles over the speed limit. Or ten.

Anise fought back tears, shook her head, took a deep breath, and said, "Have you got everything you need for today?" Which was just like her. She's about looking out for someone else. Maybe this had been the connection between her and me. The other being she had years of dance experience and she seemed genuinely interested in both my father *and* my training.

So, try hard as I may, I could not *not* like her.

I nodded. "I do."

"Did I hear you tell your dad you've got a dress rehearsal tonight for the winter showcase?"

"Yeah. I won't be home until pretty late."

"Can you define late?" She smiled at me in that way that says "I'm not trying to be your mother, I just don't want your father to worry."

"We're done at nine. I'll stay to help lock up and . . . I'd say by nine-thirty, nine-forty-five."

"Want me to save you some dinner?"

And there was another thing I liked about Anise. She cooked healthy and I was so into healthy. "That'd be super."

"No," she said. "That'd be *supper*."

We giggled, and I was thankful her spirits lifted before I'd left. I didn't think I could have concentrated like I needed to otherwise.

I threw my bag over my shoulder, gave a quick wave, and said, "Tell Dad . . . well . . . tell him I said bye." Within seconds, I was out the door leading to the garage.

Something else about Anise I admired was the way she handled the car situation. Just before Mom died, Dad and she bought me a new Ford Mustang. White exterior, red interior, fully loaded, convertible, brand new. Mom was so proud to see me drive away in it the first time, and Dad was equally as thrilled when I returned home an hour later. Their baby, they said, off in a Mustang. The whole thing had made them a little nervous, I guess.

By then, Mom had stopped driving and had given her car to a church charity league. She specifically asked that a single mother who needed transportation for getting to work be gifted with it. For a while there, I saw a young woman in Mom's car, driving around town, three kids in the backseat. I knew it was Mom's because she had this Jesus fish etched on the back window. Custom designed like the Mercedes itself. So I knew it was hers, and any time I saw this woman, I'd think of Mom—not that I didn't think of her all the time anyway.

When Anise moved to the house, she insisted I keep my car in the garage with Dad's. She had no problem whatsoever leaving hers in the driveway to suffer in Florida's torturous heat. "It's just a car," she said. "Not even special."

I made it to the dance studio—Straight to Broadway—in record time. I sped, but I didn't get caught, so it was okay. The winter showcase was coming up in two weeks, and there was much to be done. I had been asked to work with the three-year-olds this year. The same age I'd been when Mom first brought me to this very studio.

I went into the ladies' locker room and changed from my jeans and long-sleeved tee into a leotard, tights, and ballet shoes. I slipped on a pair of black shorts with "Straight to Broadway" embroidered on the right leg before darting out the door and to Studio A, where the little ones were already practicing.

An hour later, I left Studio A for Studio D, also known as "the big one." The one where my class met. It was a little after five o'clock, and I was running behind. But I stopped at my locker to check my cell phone anyway, to see if anyone had called or texted.

Only Heather. A voice message saying, "We need to talk. Call me."

I thought not.

I texted Anise instead: *Everything okay at home?* I put my phone back into my bag, shut the locker, and went into my studio where, already, most of my class had their feet up on the barres. I looked to Letya, my instructor, mouthed, "Sorry," and got in place, facing the barre. We had at least three hours of work ahead of us; our class was performing four numbers in the showcase.

I needed to stretch, which I'd not had time to do before working with the tots. I placed my feet in first position, bent my knees for a grand plié. My stomach growled loud enough to draw the attention of Avery, my best friend, who stretched beside me.

It was then I remembered: I hadn't eaten yet today.

———

I sat in a corner booth, my head bent over a copy of *Tess of the d'Urbervilles*, when I heard the bells chime at the front door. The hostess said, "Welcome to Denny's." Footsteps came toward me, but I didn't bother to look up.

"There you are."

I raised my eyes. My older sister Jayme-Leigh—born between Kimberly and Heather—stood near my table. Her long copper hair was tied back with a scrunchie at the base of her neck and pulled over one shoulder. She wore tight jeans, ankle boots, and an oversized sweater with a tank top underneath. A shoulder-strap purse dangled at her hip. She looked anything but pleased.

"What are you doing here?" I asked, feeling miffed but not knowing why I should.

She slid into the booth opposite me. "Do you have any idea what time it is?" A waitress approached the table. Jayme-Leigh gave her an exasperated look and said, "Cup of coffee. Decaf."

"Cream and sugar?"

"Black."

The waitress turned her attention to me. "Would you like a refill on your Coke?"

I grabbed the glass and tilted it toward me. "Ah . . . yes. Please." After the waitress walked away, I said, "What do you mean 'what time it is.' It shouldn't be *too* late."

"Try eleven-thirty, Ami." Jayme-Leigh used her best "I'm so aggravated" voice. "Dad is going stark mad. I've been driving *all* over looking."

I looked at my watch. "Oh my goodness." I started digging in the ballet bag resting on the booth seat next to me. "Dad and Anise. I need to call them." I found the phone and flipped it open, realizing then that, somehow, it had been turned off, probably after my earlier text to Anise.

"Don't worry. I called Dad from the parking lot. Told him your car was here. So what gives? You were supposed to come home after practice. At least that's what Anise said you told her."

"I thought . . . I meant to. I guess I was so hungry and"—I looked down at my book—"I've got to get this book read for school—it's pretty good, actually—and . . . I guess I just forgot to check the time."

Jayme-Leigh sighed in a way that reminded me of Dad. "You forgot." Her lips formed a thin line.

70

I didn't answer right away. I really couldn't. There was no excuse worth offering. Oh, I had my reasons, all right. For one, Heather and her tirade left me a little anxious about returning home. But . . . there was something else. Something that every quiet moment at home only made worse.

I hadn't talked to anyone about my life's complication, not even Avery. Hadn't told her what had happened right before Mom died. Because, honestly, what if Mom had been wrong about what she told me. She was nearly nuts at the end there, anyway.

Could I trust the words of a dying woman when little she said made any sense anyway?

"Jayme-Leigh, if I ask you something, can we keep it between us?"

"Depends, Ami. I'm not going to keep anything from Dad that I feel he needs to know about you. You're his daughter."

The waitress returned with the coffee and a brand-new glass of ice and Coke. She whisked away my old glass and the trash of my straw's wrapping, and said, "Anything else, just holler."

Jayme-Leigh sighed. I knew why; she hated words like *holler*. But she plastered on a smile and said, "We'll be sure to do that." It was about as fake as anything I'd ever seen her do, and I'd seen her do a lot of fake things. Not that she's a bad person. She's not. She's a great sister and an even better doctor. When Mom was sick, Jaymes treated her with the best daughter/doctor care any patient could have asked for. At least, she did when Heather allowed it. But Jayme-Leigh has this way about her that those who know her best can see and those who don't know her at all—which is most

71

people—can't. A sort of "I'm above all this" manner that is really just Jayme-Leigh keeping her distance. Sometimes even from family.

Jayme-Leigh stirred her coffee, took a sip, and said, "Why these kinds of places seem to have the best coffee but the stickiest floors is beyond me."

I laughed a little. Not a lot. I had too much other stuff on my mind to find a lot of humor in the moment.

"So, Ami . . . what? What do you want to tell me? Or ask me?" I figured it didn't matter if Jayme-Leigh said she'd keep this between sisters or not. What I was about to tell her would, no doubt, be a run-to-Dad piece of information. She'd probably tell me she wasn't going to say anything, but she'd tell Dad anyway. She'd say, "Don't tell Ami I'm telling you" and then Dad would promise and actually keep his word.

Maybe.

"Okay, so here's the deal, Jaymes. Remember at the end there? When Mom was pretty close to being gone?"

She wrapped her hands around the brown ceramic mug. The aroma of her coffee had reached my nostrils. I loved the smell of it, and the scent reminded me of Mom. Every morning, hearing the coffeepot gurgle and cough. The rich scent of coffee beans and hazelnut wafting through the house when Dad took a tray of breakfast sweets and caffeine from the kitchen to the master suite. Every morning, until drinking coffee meant spitting up blood.

"Of course I remember."

"Do people who are dying, like Mom . . . do they sometimes say things that are . . . I dunno . . ."

"Crazy?"

"Yeah."

"Of course. Mom's condition, the meds she was on, all of it could have led her to talk out of her head." She seemed to study me. "Did Mom say something that confused you?"

I shrugged. "Yeah, maybe."

"Do you want to talk about it?"

Did I? I wasn't sure. Even with Jayme-Leigh, who I was the closest to. She and I were so much alike. We looked alike. Same dark features. Nearly the same hair color. But more than that, our temperament is the same. Both quiet. Studious to what is important to us. Jayme-Leigh, medicine. Me, dance.

"Not really," I finally said. I took a long swig of my Coke. "I'm sure she was just . . ."—I shrugged—"affected by the medicine and the timing. She was throwing up pretty bad that night."

"What night?"

"Dad had to go to the hospital. He got called in. I don't remember why, but Mom was sleeping and he thought he'd only be gone for a short while."

"Hospice wasn't there?"

I shook my head. "No. Just Mom and me. We . . . we didn't know how close it all was, you know."

She didn't answer. She just drank her coffee and stared at the tabletop.

"Mom woke up, started vomiting blood again. Started talking wild stuff."

"What did you do?"

"What Dad had shown me."

She reached across the table, laid her hand on my arm. "Why didn't you call me, Ames?"

I shrugged. "I don't know."

We were quiet until I added, "Lately, Jaymes, I've been . . . having some bad dreams. Forgetting things. Feeling angry about nothing. Everything. Do you think it's because of Mom dying and all?"

And all . . . like what I saw. What I heard. Not just that night but all the years before. Living with an alcoholic means living with secrets. And secrets are things I couldn't talk about. Wouldn't talk about.

"Sounds like stress, Ami." She smiled at me—so gently— and took a sip of her coffee, keeping her hands wrapped around the mug. She rested her elbows on the table, the cup of coffee under her chin. "You've been through a lot. We all have, but especially you. You lost Mom when you needed her most and then . . . Dad bringing Anise home."

"Yeah," I said. "Maybe."

"Let me ask you this," she said. "Are you feeling guilty at all?"

"Guilty? What do I have to feel guilty about?"

"You like Anise, don't you."

It wasn't a question, and there was no reason to lie. This, after all, was not Heather I was speaking with. "I do. She's making Dad happy and she's nice." I met my sister's eyes with my own. "Heather is making me crazy, though. She was at the house before I left for dance."

"I know. Dad told me."

"What's her problem, anyway?"

Jayme-Leigh patted my arm before returning her hand to her coffee mug. "She loved Mom. I think she feels a sense of loyalty to her."

74

"I loved Mom," I said. Raw emotion took flight inside my stomach. "I'm just as loyal."

"It's different with Heather though, Ames. She's such a busybody." She smiled to soften the blow against our sister. "Always trying to make everyone's life perfect. This—none of this—fit in with her plans. Mom dying. Dad remarrying. You liking Anise. Any of us liking Anise, for that matter."

"Yeah. I suppose so."

Jayme-Leigh hunkered down toward the edge of the table. "Ami, are you experiencing any depression?"

I nodded. "Sometimes. But aren't teenage girls supposed to feel depressed?"

She didn't answer, just asked, "Worse around your period?"

"Mmmhmm." Sometimes, in the middle of my cycle, it washed over me. Overwhelming me. Like a wall of water I could not get away from, out from under.

"Periods regular?"

"Yeah. For me."

"Listen, I can prescribe a mild antidepressant if you'd like. Just something to take the edge off while you're going through the grieving process."

I buried my head in my hands. "I'll think about it," I mumbled. I looked up. "Oh, man. What am I going to tell Dad?"

She placed the coffee mug on the table, reached over, and patted my hand. "Don't worry about Dad. Let me talk to him. Daughter to father and doctor to doctor. Okay?"

"No, Jaymes. I don't want him to know that Mom said anything to me. Anything crazy."

"Why not? He's a doctor. He understands."

"But then he'll ask me what it was about, and I . . . I don't really want to go there."

My sister stared at me for longer than I was comfortable with. "Was it that bad?"

"Yeah," I said. "It was."

8

I had another dream that night, like the kind I'd been having since Mom died.

In the dream, I'm dancing in a large auditorium. I imagine I am performing with the Atlanta Ballet, which is my true dream. My *goal* would be a more accurate word.

I'd been in love with the idea of dancing with the Atlanta Ballet since I was eight. Mom and Dad had taken me to Atlanta; Dad for some pediatric association conference and to see a Braves game, Mom and me to shop and see the ballet. From the curtain's rising, when the lights reflected onto the oak slats of the floor and I saw the dancers glide onstage, I've worked toward dancing on that same stage with the company. In this dream, I am.

It is the Christmas season, so we are performing *The Nutcracker*, of course. And I am Clara. The scene is familiar to me; I should be able to perform it without any rehearsal whatsoever. I am dressed in a flowing white gown, the hemline brushing and billowing along my calves. My tights are white; my pointe ballet shoes are a satiny pale pink.

Onstage, Clara's beloved nutcracker has come fully to

life, and he is dancing, before the other live toys, toward her. Toward me. He stops, extends his hands, which is my cue. Until now, I have been—like the audience—transfixed by his graceful movements.

Mine are equally flawless. I come closer to him. I arabesque. I reach the nutcracker, slip my hands into his, tilt forward for an arabesque penchée. It is time for our much-anticipated pas de deux, the dance of two. Though I dance with him, I must remain focused on something out in the distance, visible only to me.

But instead, for a reason only understood in dreams, I look out into the crowd. I cannot see the faces of those who have come to enjoy the ballet; only the crowns of their heads are illuminated. Brilliantly capped, as though they are angels and I have been summoned by God himself to perform for a heavenly audience. Perhaps, even, for *him*, I decide. I cast my gaze upward to the rounded box seats draped in red velvet curtains held back by gold and silver entwined cords.

I have a curious thought. So strange for this time and place in the performance. The curtains, I decide, should not be red. They should be purple. The deepest, most royal of purples. I run forward, as though to look for God, to seek his crown, and to right this wrong. I throw my arms out, whip my head from side to side, but I do not see him.

The audience is laughing. A giggle at first, but then raucous laughter. I turn to where the other dancers should be—and my beloved nutcracker—wanting to know where we are now in the dance. But they are all laughing too.

I look back at the audience. Now I can see their faces. Eyes tightly shut, mouths wide open, cheeks blushing as they point and cackle. I must do something to change this. I decide I will impress them with my abilities. I will do something so spectacular they will stop in their merriment and, instead, stare in wonder. I place my feet in second position, bend my left knee, and thrust my right leg out for the fouetté en tournant. Each turn is executed en pointe and with precision. I whip around once, twice . . . five times. And the crowd, I can hear them now, they are no longer laughing. They are mesmerized.

Someone calls out, "Grand jeté!" which I know I can do. Beautifully, in fact. I've been told by Letya I perform the grand jeté as no one she has ever seen.

I attempt to leap upward and extend my legs, as though my body is elevated by wire from the rafters. But, for some unknown reason, I cannot stop the fouetté en tournant. Try hard as I may, I cannot. Eighteen, nineteen . . . like a windup ballerina on a little girl's music box. The faces of the crowd whip past me . . . again and again and again.

And the laughter resumes.

Then I hear Mom crying out, "If you want to stop turning, you must forgive him!"

I am somehow able to stop spinning. I scan the audience to find her. She is sitting front row. Center seat. She is dressed in a pale pink Kasper suit, the kind she always wore to meetings and to church.

"Mom!" I shout to her, running as far as I can without falling off the stage.

She opens her mouth to respond, but her words do not come. Instead, blood gushes from her O-shaped mouth. Her eyes roll back, her head lolls.

"Mom!" I shout again.

She straightens, as though she is now well enough to speak. Her words are direct, not haunting. Not strangled or confused. "Forgive him, Ami," she says, looking at me. "Forgive him as I have forgiven him."

I fall to my knees, press my face into the cupped palms of my hands. "Mom, don't tell me another word," I beg. "I don't want to know . . . I don't want to know!"

"Ami! Sweetheart! Ami!"

I bolted upright in my bed and into my father's arms. "No!"

Dad's arms came around, squeezing. His voice was, as always, strong and protective. "I've got you. I've got you."

I gasped as my eyes flew open. Anise stood at the doorway to my bedroom, looping the top button of a baby-blue Eileen West peignoir set. Her hair—thick and mussed—swirled around her shoulders. Even as I struggled to leave the world of sleep and enter my reality, I was struck by the thought it was understandable that my father fell in love with her. She was perfection.

"Is she all right?" Anise asked Dad. I thought it interesting that she asked him and not me.

Dad looked into my eyes. "Having a bad dream, sweetheart?"

I nodded. "Yeah, I guess so."

"Do you want to talk about it?" he asked.

Anise turned from the doorway. "I'll get you some water, Ami." From my bed I could see her padding down the staircase.

Dad rubbed my arms as though he thought I was cold. "You're okay now. Want to talk about it?"

I did but I didn't. I wanted to tell him about my dream. About Mom asking me to forgive him, just as she had done that awful night. I wanted to ask him about her accusations. But I could not because . . . because what if they were true?

"I'm okay." I smiled at him. "Silly dream brought on by too much practice, I think." But my heart hammered beneath one of my father's oversized tees I'd turned into pajamas. Like Mom sometimes did.

He brushed hair away from my face, kissed my forehead. "Well, your old dad is here now. If there's a dragon I need to slay, you just let me know. I'll go get my sword and send him to his death."

I giggled. "My knight in shining armor." With a dad who said things like this, surely Mom had been wrong.

I looked past his shoulder to where Anise climbed the stairs with a tall glass of water in her hand. She glided into the room, extended the drink, which I readily took and gulped down. I hadn't realized how dry my throat had become.

Anise ran a slender hand along the back of Dad's shoulders, allowed it to come to rest over the right forearm. Her other hand reached for the now-empty glass. The wedding rings Dad had picked for her shimmered in the room's faint light like broken glass in full sunlight. No wonder Heather was in a tailspin over Anise. Those rings alone must have cost Dad a fortune and—even though he can afford it, but knowing my sister—she must be counting all the money coming out of her inheritance and into Anise's life.

Heather being the one who thinks family is like a business and must be managed as such.

"How do you feel, Ami?" Anise asked as she took the glass.

I swallowed. "I'm okay." I looked at Dad. "I'll be fine now. I think I can sleep."

Dad kissed my forehead one more time, stood, and made a show of tucking me in like he'd done when I was a kid. "Daddy, you are so funny," I said, as though it were true.

"Only the best for my little girl," he said with a wink.

Anise had already made it to the doorway. "Good night, Ami. Give a shout if you need us."

I nodded. "Thank you," I said as she continued on into the hallway.

Dad followed behind her, stopping at the door to look over his shoulder at me. "Want me to leave the door open or close it?"

"Close it. I'm fine. Really." Beneath the taut covers, my feet had begun to wiggle but not enough so he'd notice.

The room grew dark by inches as my father faded from view. As soon as the door clicked shut, I allowed my feet to move with wild abandon. I listened for Dad's footsteps receding toward the master suite. As soon as their door closed, I slid up, pushing the cover off me. I turned the bedside lamp on—the cute retro one my sister Kimberly had bought for the big sixteen-year-old-bedroom-revamping Mom insisted on with each daughter—swung my legs out of bed, and darted across the room to the desk where my laptop was plugged in. I unhooked it, scampered across the floor, and got back into bed. I pushed the top up, booted up, and typed the dreaded words that had haunted me for weeks. Maybe months.

Stages of grief.

The first of the thousands of websites that appeared defined the five stages of grief. The second was listed as "Understanding the Seven Stages of Grief." I decided that understanding five would be difficult enough. I clicked on that link.

I read aloud, something I've always done when reading alone. "Grief is something we all go through at some point in our lives. We all, at one time or another, lose something or someone dear to us. A parent. A sibling. A child. A friend, a family pet, or even a job."

I tumbled out of bed again, lightly treading over the hardwood floorboards of my bedroom, and to the desk for a composition notebook and a pen. I returned, flipped the notebook open to a clean sheet, and wrote "What are the five stages of grief?" I returned my attention to the computer and took notes.

1. Denial and isolation
2. Anger
3. Bargaining
4. Depression
5. Acceptance

I scanned down the page to read about stress and grief, about what happens when people deny themselves the right to grieve. I took notes furiously, first on the five stages, then on the additional stress that can follow.

On a whim, I clicked out of the website and went to the one featuring the two extra steps of grieving. The pages were similar but different. I flipped a page in the notebook and wrote the seven stages on a clean sheet.

My eyes were starting to burn; I realized I didn't know the time. I looked at the little box at the bottom right-hand corner of the laptop screen. It read 2:47. I'd made it home by 1:00. Dad had opened the door for me and said "We'll talk about it later" as he locked up behind me. I'd rushed up the stairs without saying anything more than "I'm sorry." I'd gone to bed around 1:45. Which meant I'd only slept—and dreamed—for an hour. An hour?

It had felt like days.

I rubbed my eyes. I wanted to keep reading. I wanted to know more about where I stood in this grieving process, if that was what I was dealing with at all. Maybe I was just fine. Maybe I was just feeling sad.

And why shouldn't I? My mother had just died. My father had left me to go on vacation and come back with a wife. A nice wife, but nonetheless, she wasn't my mother. In a few months I would graduate from high school, and Mom wouldn't be there. I'd give my final performance for the studio, and she wouldn't be there. I'd go off to college, and she wouldn't ride alongside Dad in the car behind me, bags from Pier One and Crate and Barrel stacked in the backseat. I wouldn't see her dashing up the stairs of the dorm ahead of me, talking nonstop as she always did, saying things like, "Oh, Ami! Look at *this*! You're going to love *that*. Oh, how adorable *this* is."

She would not be there on my wedding day or when I gave birth to my children.

If I ever had them.

No, I probably wouldn't. I wasn't even sure I wanted to get married. I'd never even had a date, really. Just burgers and Cokes with my friends, all from the studio. It wasn't that I wasn't interested in boys; between school and the studio and Mom being sick, I hadn't had time for them. A thought came to me—in just a few months, I'd be expected to attend the senior prom. *The prom*. Another thing Mom would miss.

I looked at the computer screen one more time, willing myself to shut it after I read one tiny part, the part about anger.

Anger. Was I angry with Mom? Angry that she'd left me? Furious with her, perhaps, that she'd left me with these final words of accusation even in the middle of admonishment to forgive?

I pressed the point of my pen against the page and printed: *Why did you have to tell me these things?*

I went over the words—over and over—until they appeared as angry as I felt. I raked my teeth over my bottom lip before penning in script:

But how can I know for sure? Maybe it was all just a lie.

Only one way to know: ask Dad.

But I was smart enough to know I never would.

9

We've been going to Cedar Key as a family since before I was born. Dad and Mom went to the annual arts festival not too long after they married, fell in love with the place, bought a house—raised up and sitting right on the marshlands—where the family has since vacationed all summer and during special holidays. Mom took us girls there during those hot, sticky summer months when the days are long and the mosquitoes on the neighboring keys thick as the air. Dad came for the first two weeks and, after that, on most weekends.

By the time I was old enough to really enjoy the island, my sisters were grown. I'd beg Mom to let me take a friend along to keep from being bored. Not too many of the other moms and dads were willing to let their daughters go away for an entire summer, but Avery's parents at least okayed her coming for a couple of weeks at a stretch. Then, after Dad had spent a weekend with us, he'd take Avery home, bringing her back a week or two later for another couple of weeks.

During those times when I didn't have Avery, I had Mom—of course—but she often slept late and I'd never been one for that. Up early, raring to go. Our Cedar Key housekeeper,

Eliana, was always up with me, pulling sticky buns out of
the oven, pouring orange juice over ice, just the way I liked
it. Sometimes her daughter Rosa would drop by and hang
out, but she was nearly as old as Kimberly, so it was more
like having a sister there than a friend.

Even though we'd always spent the majority of the Christmas holidays at home, on the twenty-third of December,
we'd load the car up with our luggage and the gifts under
the tree, and drive the three hours toward our coastal home.
The "road to nowhere," Dad called it. "You can't get there
from here," he'd add with a grin.

The harbor town of Cedar Key rests at the end of Highway 24. If one was to drive to the end of the highway and
keep going, they'd end up in the gulf. There's no such thing
as "I took a wrong turn and ended up here." It's really the
end of the earth.

I guess that's why Dad and Mom loved it so much. For
them, it wasn't reality. It was paradise. They could let their
kids roam around and never worry about us, not once. "Keep
your eyes open for snakes" was the only admonishment I
ever heard.

That and "Be back by supper."

But that was from Eliana; as cook, she didn't want to see
a good meal wasted.

I wondered if that Christmas—the second Christmas without Mom and the first with Anise—would be spent in Cedar
Key or at home. After all, Dad hadn't taken his new wife to
our "island home" yet, and the holidays might not be the

best time for it. She'd not met Eliana or Rosa or any of the others we'd come to know over the years.

I half hoped he would and half hoped he wouldn't.

A few days after Heather's dramatics in our festive home and my staying-out-late escapade, Dad announced to Anise and me over supper in the dining room that we *were* spending the holiday in Cedar Key. Just like that and just like Dad. An "oh by the way" line that made everything in life just the way he wanted it.

Anise rested her fork ever so gently on her plate, tines turned downward. She drew the linen napkin from her lap, dabbed at the corners of her mouth, and said, "Ross, are you sure?" Her eyes shifted from him to me, back to him.

"Ami, what do you think?" Dad asked, not answering his wife.

I'm pretty sure my mouth fell open just then. I don't remember Dad asking my opinion about much of anything, ever. Other than those months when it was just him and me, and then it was "do you want to go out or eat in," "cheese or pepperoni" kinds of questions that weren't opinion based but more about level of hunger.

"Ah . . ." I said. Because, quite honestly, in this case I didn't have a solid enough opinion. I only knew that we'd *not* gone the year before and had only visited once or twice—Dad and me—since Mom died. Thoughts of how the place looked— every inch of it decorated by Mom—came to mind. At the house, Anise had only redone the master bedroom—and I don't blame her for that. But the cottage would be a totally different thing. The Windermere house "spoke" of Mom's taste, but the cottage "screamed" it.

"I'll take that as a yes," Dad said. He dug his fork into the mashed potatoes and slipped them easily between his lips.

"She said no such thing," Anise said. Her shoulders dropped, then squared again. "Honey," she said, her voice as calm as the water around Cedar Key after a summer storm, "maybe it's too soon. I haven't even *been* to the beach house yet. I'm sure the house needs a thorough cleaning."

"That's what I have Eliana for." Dad practically beamed with the words.

"Dad," I said, finding my voice. "Wouldn't that be a lot to ask of Eliana during the holidays? I mean, the place has got to be filled with cobwebs and dust. She's surely not up for that *now*."

I watched him cut into a piece of boneless chicken, bring it to his mouth, and chew. His eyes stayed focused on his plate as though he were thinking over what I'd just said. Maybe taking that whole "Ami's opinion" thing to a new level. I looked at Anise, who looked at me, and then we both looked at Dad.

When he looked up, he seemed surprised by our attention. "What?"

"Did you not hear what Ami said?"

"I heard her." He peered at me while cutting away at another section of his chicken. "Sweetheart, Eliana has been keeping the place clean on a weekly basis since the day your mother and I hired her. What would make you think she'd stopped? Because Mom died?"

Something inside me fell. My heart stopped and my stomach grew heavy. I put my fork on my plate, horizontally, the way Mom had shown me to do when I was done with my meal. I took a deep breath, dropped my napkin by my plate, then scooped up both as I stood. "I'm not hungry," I said.

"Ami, sit down," Dad said.

"Ross . . ."

I froze as Dad shot a warning look at Anise. "No." Then back to me. "Ami, sit down. We don't storm away from this table. Never have before and we're not going to start now." When I didn't move, he added, "Sit down and tell me what's wrong."

I pushed my chair with the back of my legs and stepped around it. "I'm just not hungry," I said, keeping my voice steadier than I felt.

Even though I was calling on more bravado with my father than I'd ever used before—or perhaps because of it—the room started to spin. I bent forward, dropping my handful of dishes and linen to the massive table where we always sat for supper. My hands pressed hard against the tablecloth and the wood beneath it. I squeezed my eyes shut, then opened them again.

Both Dad and Anise were beside me. "You're pushing too hard," she was saying while Dad eased stemware toward me. "Drink something, Ami," he said. "Here."

I took the glass and sat. Dad's arm eased me back into the chair; his hand stayed on my shoulder as I took a sip of cool water. I blew out a breath, then another until everything around me settled. Anise returned to her place, but Dad sat in the vacant chair next to me. "You all right, sweetheart?"

I nodded. Looked at him. "Dad . . ." I calculated my words. "Dad, can I ask you a question?"

"Haven't you always been able to do that?"

I smiled weakly. "Dad, what do you know about the seven stages of grief?"

"You mean the five stages?"

"There are some who say there are seven," Anise interjected. We both looked at her.

"When *my* mother died, Ami, I did a lot of research. I'm honestly not sure I went through all of the seven or even the five, but I understand the theory."

"Do you think you are going through stages of grief, Ami? Even now?" Dad asked.

I jerked my face toward his. "Even now? Dad, it's *only* been a year."

"I know how long it's been, Ami."

I felt my chest grow tight. "I'm sorry, Anise. No disrespect intended, but . . . Dad, you may have been able to get on with your life seven months after Mom died, but the rest of us haven't."

Anger became a color in my father's face. "Young lady, you listen to me." His eyes cut toward Anise. "Stay or go for this, Anise. Your choice."

Her brow rose. "I have no reason to leave unless you ask me to."

"If you're going to yell at me," I said, "then I want her to stay."

Dad's hands flew up in the air, then back down. "I have no reason to yell at you. When have I ever yelled at you?"

Had he meant other than right then?

I started to cry. It wasn't what I wanted to do. Not what I had planned to do. In my heart, I'd hoped to be able to broach the subject with Dad, to tell him about Mom and her words to me just before she'd died. He was my father, for crying out loud. Why should I be afraid to talk to him about something so important? One word from him either way—a yes or a no—and I would know if Mom had been out of her mind or sane as me.

Unless *I* was crazy.

"Ami, do you think you need to see a counselor?" Anise's sweet voice floated across the room. "I'm sure your father would see to it that you get the finest. Wouldn't you, Ross?"

"If that's what she needs."

I closed my eyes and sighed. "No. I don't need a counselor. I think I just need to get beyond this time in my life. Focus more on my dancing." I forced a smile and sent it toward my father. "So . . . a Cedar Key Christmas? Do you think Heather will go for it?"

"Why of course," Dad said. The smile on his face told me he was pleased we were past the subject of grief and counselors. "She'll see things my way; I'm sure of it."

Heather decided that weekend was the perfect time for us to do some Christmas shopping. She called me on Friday morning—I was on my way to school—to inform me she'd pick me up at five, we'd grab dinner somewhere, and then hit the mall. I reminded her I had practice at the studio.

"Ditch it this once," she said.

"Heather, I can't ditch it. The showcase is next Saturday."

"Then what are you doing tomorrow?"

I turned into the Dr. Phillips high school grounds, my car practically driving itself toward my assigned parking spot with the large panther paw print painted just above the number. "I have practice, Heather."

"All day and all night?"

Well . . . no.

"We're going from ten until three, I think. But I really should stick around and help close up."

"Someone else can do that this time. You and I need to get off by ourselves. This is actually perfect. Andre is off; he can be here with the kids."

Honestly, sometimes the way my sister ordered the lives of everyone around her was unnerving.

"All right then," I said. "Do you want to pick me up at the house or do you want me to come there?"

"No, I do not want to come to the house. Not after . . . ugh. Never mind. I won't get into that with you right now."

I pulled into my parking place and shut down the engine of my Mustang. "Did you and Dad have a fight the other night?"

"I'm surprised you didn't hear us."

"I left." I gathered my book bag and purse from the seat beside me, all the while keeping my phone wedged between my shoulder and ear.

"It was not a pretty picture to say the least, and I'm sure her royal majesty got quite the kick out of it."

I opened the car door. "Heather. If you're going to spend tomorrow night ripping Anise to shreds, I'd just as soon not go anywhere with you." Heather remained quiet. I shut my door with a pop of my hip against it. "Okay?" I continued.

"You know, Ami . . . I've always been there for you. You'd think you could be here for me now."

I wanted to laugh. I wanted to cry.

"There are things you don't understand because you're still young," she continued.

I stopped walking, stared up at the brick and stucco building, watched several of my fellow classmates filing into the school. Talking. Laughing. Making beelines to first period.

Maybe, I thought . . . maybe I *could* talk to Heather about what Mom had told me.

"Heather, I'm at school now."

First bell rang.

"So I hear."

"I'm going to be late if I don't hurry, so I'll see you tomorrow after practice."

I heard her sigh. "Hey, little sis . . . don't be mad at me, okay? I just can't wrap myself around Anise the way the rest of you have."

"It's okay," I said. "I love you, Heather."

"I love you too, Ami. See you tomorrow afternoon. It'll be fun. I promise."

Fun. Maybe. Sure. Why not.

But, more than that—hopefully—informative.

10

Heather has always been a sucker for Winter Park's Park Avenue, but no more so than during the Christmas season. Florida doesn't boast chilling weather in December but rather pleasant enough to sit outside the many coffee shops, restaurants, and cafés. Inside, stores brim with merchandise perfect for gift giving, and outside the brick-laid, live oak dotted streets are washed in colors from strings of seasonal lights and banners.

All that aside, enjoying Park Avenue has been the one thing Heather and I have had in common. It brings out the credit cards in her and the poet in me.

When Mom was alive, it brought out both for her. Dad's bighearted allowance meant her whipping a credit card out at every store, if we saw something we loved. We'd often sit outside the Briarpatch Restaurant, sipping on cappuccinos in the cooler months or enjoying decadent ice cream when it was hot (those days we sat inside). Being on Park Avenue now wasn't the same as being there with Mom, but—what with Heather looking so much like her and being so generous with Andre's credit card—it was close.

We started with Santa's White Christmas coffees and biscotti at Barnie's. Heather kept the conversation to my schoolwork, asking about the joys of being a senior and my dance troupe at school and the one at Straight to Broadway. She then asked the kinds of things people ask this time of year when they don't really want to talk about whatever it is that is on their minds: Christmas gifts.

"So what are you hoping for from Santa?" she asked, tipping her cup toward me as if it really held Santa's coffee.

I'd just bitten into my biscotti and was chomping away on it. To pass the time, I watched the white-blonde curls dance around my sister's temples in the afternoon breeze. She tilted her face up as she waited for my answer, closed her eyes, and allowed the moment to pass over her. She was so beautiful. Not just because she looked so much like Mom, but . . . I genuinely loved the color of her hair, the blueness of her eyes, the paleness of her skin. Mine was olive in tone whether I wanted it to be or not. As a ballet dancer, I'd prefer a fairer complexion, but we take whatever we are given in life and make the best of it. In my case, that meant staying out of the sunshine as much as possible during the summer months and out of tanning beds, which was the way so many of my classmates had taken to getting a tan.

Heather opened her eyes as I swallowed. I took a sip of my coffee and said, "I really haven't asked for anything. I mean, seriously, what do I need?"

"Oh, give me a break, Ami. You? Come on now. Surely you've mentioned *something* to Dad."

I shrugged. "Not really. Clothes, probably. But nothing he'd pick out. I'll take whatever he gives me in the form of a gift card." Best, I reasoned, not to mention that Anise would probably do an excellent job at picking out the right thing.

"That's a stocking stuffer for Dad, and you know it."

"I saw some boots on the Neiman Marcus website I wouldn't mind owning."

She smiled. "Send me the link. When I get around to speaking to Dad again, I'll mention it to him." She offered up a half smile.

"Thanks." I sipped on my coffee, struggling with whether or not—and even *how*—to tell her about Christmas Day. "What are your plans for Christmas?"

Heather placed her hands flat on the round table between us. "We'll let the kids wake up and have Christmas around the tree, of course. Kim and I were talking last night about her having Christmas dinner over at her house this year. You *do* know that Christmas Eve is on Sunday, don't you? I'm sure we'll go to service as a family that night."

"'We' as in you and Andre and the kids or 'we' as in our whole family?" I paused for a millisecond. "That would mean Anise too, Heather."

Heather frowned. "Well, I *did* mean 'we' as in our whole family. For one brief, glorious moment, I'd forgotten about Anise."

I sighed. This wasn't going to go well. Better to avoid it altogether, I decided. I glanced over my shoulder and down the sidewalk filled with shoppers and sample goodies outside the open doorways, meant to entice those who walked by. "So," I said, returning my attention to my sister. "Where shall we go first?"

She drained the last of her coffee. "You got out of that one, didn't you?"

I wiped my mouth with the small paper napkin imprinted with the Barnie's logo. "I don't want to fight, Heather . . . but I do want to talk to you about something. First, let's shop. Then we'll go to dinner. I vote for Pannullo's."

"You always do." She reached for her purse slung on the back of her chair. "And I always acquiesce."

I laughed at her. Maybe today wouldn't be so bad. At least I'd get good Italian food and some of my shopping done.

I decided to drop the bomb on Heather just before I left her house for home. She had walked me to my car. We'd practically filled the backseat with shopping bags stuffed with packages wrapped in Christmas-themed foil paper. I turned at my opened driver's door to hug her, to tell her I loved her, and then said, "Heather, like I said earlier, I have to tell you something."

Her blue eyes narrowed. "I'm listening. Suspicious that you've waited until now to 'tell me something.'" She hooked her index fingers in the air as she quoted my words. "But listening."

"Dad wants to spend Christmas in Cedar Key this year." I spoke quickly and winced, prepared for the worst.

Heather's porch light barely reached my car, but even still I could see her pale complexion blanch before her cheeks turned pink. "Oh, he does, does he?"

"Heather, Dad has a right to say where he wants to spend Christmas."

She gave me her best "are you serious?" look. "Have you been planning that line, Ami? Or did it just now come to you?"

I felt anger stirring inside me. "Why do you do that, Heather? Why do you treat me as if I'm stupid or something?"

"I suppose he's going to take *her* there," she said in an obvious avoidance of my questions.

"Anise, Heather. Her name is Anise."

"Keep your voice down. I don't want the kids running out here in their pajamas."

"No, Heather. That's not it and you know it. Truth is, you don't want your kids to hear you yelling at their favorite aunt about a woman they have seemingly no problem with."

Frustration at the truthfulness of my words washed over her. "I'll talk to Dad. Don't worry, Ami. You won't have to spend Christmas Day with Anise in Cedar Key. Not if I can help it."

I inched closer to the inside of my car. "That's just it, Heather. I don't mind going to Cedar Key this year. I really don't. It'd be kind of like having Mom there. What with all her things. The memories of past Christmases spent there."

"It took Anise all of—what?—ten seconds to totally redo Mom and Dad's bedroom. No doubt she'll have the beach house completely redone too."

"Can you blame her?" I asked. "On either account?"

Heather's face took on a firmness I'd never seen before. Anger flashed from her eyes. "Yes, I can. She has no right being here. She shouldn't have married Dad. Any woman worth her weight in salt would know better than to marry a widower not seven months after his wife of over thirty years dies. Not to mention before she's even had a chance to meet his children. His grandchildren." She looked around as if

99

to make sure no one was listening but me. "Let me tell you, Ami, I've got that woman all figured out, and I told Dad so."

"What does that mean?"

"It means I know the truth. She's nearly forty and never married. Never married? Women like that, Ami—just so you know—are the ones who have affairs with married men. Then, when all their options are used up and they are too, they latch on to a widower like Dad—handsome, well-to-do, established in his community, who knows nothing of her—and bam! They're married. I have no doubt whatsoever that she snared Dad while he was up there, knowing he was heartbroken and lonely. She seduced him into her bed and then convinced him they should get married so she could make all his middle-aged dreams come true." She slammed her fists into her sides. "Sorry to have to put it like that, but you're old enough to know the wherewithal of life, Ami."

I shook my head for what felt like ten minutes before I spoke. Before I could *even* speak. "First of all, Heather, yeah. I am old enough to know the 'wherewithal of life.' Believe me. Second, you don't know what you are talking about. You seriously don't. I live with them, remember? Anise didn't *seduce* Dad. She *loves* him. I've never seen such love as the way she looks at Dad."

Heather spewed in laughter, spraying my face in the process. I wiped my cheeks with my hands.

"You really are naïve, Ami. I love you, but Mom and Dad kept you too protected in the palace, princess."

I pushed my sister's shoulder with my fingertips. "You listen here, Heather Dutton. You don't know anything even close to what you think you know."

She pushed me back. "Don't you push me, Ami Sabrina Claybourne."

I pushed her again. "I will if you keep being stupid. And you are. You've got issues, Heather. You need to see a therapist or something."

She opened her mouth, and her jaw locked before she huffed and said, "What in this world are you talking about?" She waved her hands left to right, left to right. "No. I don't want to know. *I've* got issues? *You've* got issues, Ami. Especially if you think Anise Kelly is in *love* with our father."

Her teeth had now come together and she spoke through them. My sister, who I loved so much and thought to be so beautiful, looked more like a monster right then than a china doll.

"And *especially* if you think I'm going to Cedar Key for Christmas. Or that *any* of us are."

I dropped into the seat of my Mustang, reached for the door handle—which always seemed to be just out of the reach of my long arms and fingertips—grabbed hold of it, and slammed the door. I started the car, powered down the window, and said, "Oh, I'm going, Heather. I'm going even if Dad doesn't, so what do you think about *that*?" I watched her mouth drop open a final time before I turned to the backseat, rummaged through one of the packages, and pulled out a wrapped Ahava gift set. I threw it at her; she caught it. "Here! Merry Christmas!"

I jerked the car into drive and tore out of the semicircular driveway.

I needed to talk to someone. I wanted to talk to Dad, but that wasn't practical. Anise was out as well. Especially about this.

I called Jayme-Leigh, always my first choice after Mom. She didn't answer her cell phone, so I called the house. Isaac answered.

"Hey there, Ames."

I loved my brother-in-law enough to allow him to call me by the pet name. But only from time to time.

Jayme-Leigh had caused quite a stir in our typical Christian home when she married the Jewish Isaac Levy. Even more of a stir within our church. But, quite honestly, I'd never thought of Jayme-Leigh as being overly religious anyway. I had never thought of her as an *un*believer. I'd just never thought things of the church carried the same weight with her that they had always carried with Dad. With Mom. Or with Kimberly and Heather. Although, while Kimberly seemed to be more about relationship in her faith, Heather tended to be a little more traditional and set in her ways. Conservative to the highest degree. At least that's what I had always thought.

So when Jaymes brought Isaac home for the first time, there were a lot of "discussions" as to "just how far is this relationship going to go?" But whatever worries and concerns Dad and Mom had in the beginning, after really getting to know Dr. Isaac Levy, their opinions changed. Isaac was and is one of the finest sons-in-law (and, in my case, brothers-in-law) to ever be a part of a family. Mom used to say she could "wrap him up and take him home for dinner." Her way of saying she liked someone.

What Isaac had brought to our family was more than just

goodness; he'd taught us, as he observed the holidays and holy days of his faith, the connection of Judaism to Christianity. And, for that matter, how much we had to learn about Jesus.

I had a *lot* to learn about Jesus, I figured right then. What kind of Christian was I, pushing my sister in her own front yard? Throwing a Christmas gift at her, of all things.

"Hey, Isaac, where's Jayme-Leigh?"

"She got called to the hospital. One of her patients is not doing so well."

I nibbled on my bottom lip and inside my gum. "Oh. Sorry to hear that."

"Where you be?" he asked, switching the words to be cute.

"In my car. On my way home from Heather's."

"Uh-oh."

"What does that mean?"

"If you are just coming from Heather's and you're calling Jayme-Leigh, something must be up."

"It is. Heather and I had a fight."

"Wanna come over and talk? I'll make you some of my famous hot cocoa."

I smiled as I pressed the brakes of my car, inching my way into a lane full of other cars with drivers who had probably spent the better part of the day shopping. The streets were twinkling with Christmas lights and banners, just like on Park Avenue where, not a few hours ago, I'd had a marvelous shopping adventure with my sister. "I could live with that."

Twenty minutes later I'd made the ten-minute trip to Jayme-Leigh and Isaac's home. Heather called it "ostentatious for just two people," but I thought it was great. Okay, yes, it cost Jayme-Leigh and Isaac nearly a million dollars (or so I heard Mom and Dad say in a private conversation with each other), but the rooms weren't all that big and it *did* sit on Lake Down and they *did* have a pretty nice boat and two jet skis for the warm-slash-hot months, which were nearly all the months here in Florida. When Dad had gone to Maine, Jayme-Leigh and Isaac's was where I stayed because—in spite of its cost—it's warm and comfy and, best of all, no one there bugs me.

Like Heather.

Staying with Kimberly wouldn't have been so bad, but she had a baby, which is fine for her and I love my nephews to pieces but . . . the baby cries a lot at night and the oldest is bent on *not* going to bed.

Isaac met me at the front door, holding a large menorah. It practically towered over his head. "What are you doing?" I asked with a laugh. "Or is that the only flashlight in the house."

"You laugh," he said. "But your sister has me polishing it already. I was thinking that while I make that hot cocoa . . ."

"Oh no. I'm not polishing that monster."

I walked past the multi-stoned mezuzah shimmering in the porch light, touched it lightly with my fingertips the way my brother-in-law had shown me, and walked into the entryway. Isaac shut the door behind us. "It'll bring you closer to God," he said in a coaxing voice.

"I'm close enough," I answered, but I took the menorah anyway. "Point me to the polish." I added a dramatized sigh.

Isaac grinned in victory. "This way to the kitchen," he said, extending his arm and making a short bow.

"Ugh . . ." I moaned, but already I felt better. "So, what do you mean 'already.' When is Hanukkah this year?"

"The twenty-third it starts," he said.

We entered the kitchen, where an open tub of silver polish and a white cloth waited on the marble bar. I hitched myself up on a stool and started working. Isaac busied himself at the stove, where the ingredients for his famous cocoa were waiting on the nearby countertop. "Your sister brought home a pretty nice cake from the bakery this afternoon if you want a slice."

"Yum," I said.

"I'll take that as a yes."

"*Bevakasha*," I said, using the Hebrew word for "please." Isaac had taught me a few of the easier words and phrases he'd learned in Hebrew school, and I liked using them with him.

"Be sure to get in all the crevices with that cloth."

The menorah was ornate and heavy and, in my way of thinking, not in need of polishing. "I'll do my best." I looked across the kitchen and focused on his back. He wore a white dress shirt—the long sleeves rolled up to his elbows—and a pair of what I knew to be pretty expensive jeans. "Have you even bothered to change since work?"

He glanced over his shoulder at me and winked, making me smile. My brother-in-law was nothing short of gorgeous. His lashes would make a girl cry. He had a broad smile and white, perfectly even teeth. His eyes, though dark, twinkled in merriment. I'd only seen them looking anything other than gleeful once, and that was at Mom's funeral. Then they had turned from amber-brown to chocolate-brown, filled with sorrow.

"I haven't been home that long," he said. "Got caught up in something at the lab."

I set the menorah on its base and stretched my arms. "Hey, Isaac, can I ask you something?"

He poured milk from a gallon jug into the stainless steel pot before him. "Is it a question?" he asked, without looking up.

"Uh . . . yeah."

"Shoot."

I sat straight again, breathed in and out of my nose. "Do you think . . ." I wasn't so sure I could ask the question that had haunted me for so many months. Perhaps I could ask him something else. Something about spending the holiday in Cedar Key. Maybe ask if he thought he and my sister could spend Hanukkah there. With us, celebrating both holidays together.

"Do I think? Yes. Quite often." He spooned cocoa into the milk. "Helps when it comes to being a doctor. Next question?"

"Haha." Here goes nothing, I thought. If I couldn't ask Isaac, I couldn't ask anyone. "Do you think . . . Isaac, do you think Dad ever had an affair?"

11

Isaac laughed at my question before asking one of his own: "Where do you get such thoughts, Ami?" He turned from the stove, rested against the countertop's edge, and crossed his arms. "Heather?"

"No. Not really."

He returned to his stove-top preparations. The room had filled with the scent of vanilla and cocoa, which made my tummy rumble in anticipation. "Well, one thing I know about your father is that he's a virtuous man. He loved your mother very much, you know that, right?"

"I guess so."

"All right then. I don't know who would tell you such a thing, but whoever it was, she was obviously out of her mind." He mumbled the rest. "Which brings us back to Heather."

I grimaced. "I dunno."

He looked over his shoulder again. "So it *was* Heather."

I shook my head.

"Well, I doubt it was Kimberly, and I know Jayme-Leigh doesn't feel that way." He picked the pot up from the stove and, stirring with a wooden spoon, carefully poured the creamy dark liquid into two ceramic mugs.

"It was Mom."

He placed the pot on a hot pad before turning to face me. "Joan said that? Are you sure?"

"Mmmhmm."

"When?"

"Right before she died. That night Dad and Jayme-Leigh had to go to the hospital. Remember the three-year-old who died?"

Isaac brought the mugs of steaming cocoa to the dividing bar where I'd now slid the menorah away from me. "Yeah . . . I remember. Whipped cream?" he asked.

"Bevakasha."

He walked to the refrigerator, opened it without saying a word, brought back the Reddi-wip, and squirted thick peaks onto the top of our drinks. We picked up the mugs, toasted the holidays, and each took tentative sips.

Isaac blinked several times before saying, "Ami, you know, don't you, that when someone is as sick as your mother— what with all the meds she was being given and the overall state of her physical condition—she may have truly believed something like that. But it could have been as simple as a song she heard or a movie she and your father saw together and the plot got mixed up in her mind."

I rested my mug on the counter, cupped my hands around it. The warmth of it felt good, the scent of the cocoa filled me with comfort. "You think?"

"Don't you know your father better than that?"

I honestly wasn't sure if I did or I didn't. After all, he'd married Anise before a full year had passed. Maybe he had . . . *needs* . . . that Mom, in her condition, couldn't meet.

The thought gave me shivers and took my mind to places I didn't want to go.

"I guess so. I mean, if *you* think . . ."

"Hey, I'm a doctor, aren't I? I know about these things." He took a good swallow of his drink, leaving a whipped topping moustache along his upper lip. He swiped at it with his tongue. "The brain is so complex, Ami. We don't know nearly what we should know or possibly ever will know. Memories, every single one of them, are stored. What happens when we administer meds that tell the brain the body isn't hurting? Maybe it does its job but at the same time jumbles up those memories?" He shook his head, looked down. The dark, feathery lashes cast shadows along his cheekbones. "I'm sorry you had to witness something like that, and I wish you'd told us sooner."

"Sorry."

"Have you thought about discussing this with your father?" he asked just as I took a sip of my drink.

I nearly choked. "Did you put something funny in this hot chocolate or are *you* crazy? It was hard enough talking to you about it. I can't even talk to Jaymes about something like this."

Isaac smiled. "All right. All right. Calm down."

"I'm calm. But, no. No way."

He stared at me for several minutes before asking, "So where do you go from here then?"

I didn't answer for a long time. I just sipped my drink until it was nearly gone. "Isaac? What do you know about the stages of grief?"

He shrugged. "That's not my area of expertise, Ami, but . . . where do you think you are in the process?"

"Somewhere between shock and denial and pain and guilt. Which means I haven't really made a lot of progress. I should be way past that by now. It's been a year already."

Isaac laughed. "A whole year?"

I wrinkled my nose. I knew where he was going with this.

"Ami, don't expect yourself to follow some prescribed formula for grieving over your mom's death, okay? And don't let these nasty memories you have eat you up. Joan was one of the loveliest women I've ever known. So much grace and character."

"That's true."

"Focus on that. You're young, and that makes it easier to think about everything you have going on in your life. So think on that. Your mom's character, your own life, and her love for you, okay?"

I smiled. "Okay."

He slid the menorah back toward me with a grin of his own. "Now, get back to work, kiddo, and quit worrying about things that are more flight of the imagination than fact."

Kimberly refused to go to Cedar Key for Christmas, telling Dad and Anise (and me) that she just couldn't return there. Not yet.

Dad told me later that he was more worried about Kimberly now than he had been before. "Has she talked to you about any of this?" he asked.

I shook my head. "Not a word. Kimberly is so gaga over

her little family, I think that gives her some . . . you know . . . grounding."

Dad smiled at me as his arm came around me and squeezed. "Grounding? Where did you hear such a grown-up word?"

I melted into his hug. "Oh, you know, Dad. I read."

Heather, of course, pitched such a fit I'm surprised the police weren't called. Anise and I ended up sneaking out the back door, slipping into her car, and heading for the nearest Starbucks, where my stepmother treated me to peppermint tea and ginger molasses cookies. We were surrounded by coffee aromas, swing-era Christmas music, and joyful shoppers laden with packages and coats.

The weather had turned as cold outside as the inside of our house. Finally.

Two hours later, Dad called Anise's phone, reporting it safe to return, adding that Heather and family would *not* be joining us for Christmas in Cedar Key.

"Maybe we *should* wait a year, Ross," Anise spoke tenderly into the phone. Then: "All right. We'll come home in a little bit. How about treating Ami and me to dinner out tonight? It'll give you a chance to eat a steak." Whatever response my father gave her made her smile, and I smiled too.

Dad took us to Ocean Prime that evening, an uptown place with white tablecloths and blue leather chairs. It's also most definitely one of his favorite places to go for his coveted steak, especially since Anise had taken the cook's role in his kitchen.

At Dad's request we sat in one of the semicircular booths so we could make our holiday plans. I couldn't help but smile at my father. His eyes danced. In spite of our whole family not being together for Christmas, in spite of it being only a little more than a year since Mom died, he was going to his beloved Cedar Key. And he was taking his new wife.

I was beyond grateful Heather was nowhere in sight. Nowhere in earshot, for that matter. But I couldn't help but wonder if Dad would tell us anything about the conversation he'd had with my sister.

Correction. If he would tell me anything. Whether or not he told Anise was up for debate. Maybe he would. Maybe not. Knowing her, she wouldn't even ask.

But she did a fine job of asking a dozen questions about what to expect from Cedar Key—the weather, the people. The house.

"I called a friend of mine there," Dad told her, then looking at me, said, "Paul Poynton."

I nodded.

"Of course the tree has already been lit," he said. "So we missed that."

"But we'll get to see it, so . . ."

"Tell me about the tree," Anise said, placing her elbows on the table. She cradled a cup of coffee in her hands. I watched her inhale its aroma and take a sip.

"It's a cedar tree—naturally." I shrugged. "It's pretty simple, really. They decorate it with lights and ornaments. It's just fun being there, especially if the weather has cooled off. If we'd been there for the lighting, we would have sung carols and drunk hot cocoa."

Anise looked genuinely excited. "Anything else?"

"There is, of course, the boat parade." I turned my attention to my father. "Dad, will we be there for that?"

"Only if we're there on the sixteenth."

I frowned. "Dad. I have school until the twentieth."

My father's face registered disappointment. "Ah. Some-times, my little Ami, I forget you are still in high school."

"Dad!" I laughed in admonishment.

Anise touched Dad's arm. "Ross, what kind of thing is that to say?" But her face showed amusement.

"Sorry," Dad said. He craned his neck to try to spot our server. Catching his attention, he waved him over and asked for the check. Looking back at Anise, he said, "She doesn't *act* like a typical senior in high school."

"Well, let me get a pad and pen," I teased. "I'll take some notes on how I should act. Uh . . . maybe you'd like to tell me some of the things *you* got into?"

"No, I would not."

Anise straightened. "Oh, I don't know, my love. I think I might like to hear some of these things."

Dad pointed playfully at his wife. "You stay out of this, young lady. You already know enough about me to get me in real trouble." Dad's face pinked, as though he'd said some-thing he hadn't meant to.

Anise cleared her throat. Placed her palms against the table. "Personally, I'm glad we're going to Cedar Key this year." She looked at me, obviously dismissing what Dad had said. "Ami, after you get out of school on the twentieth, do you think you'd be up to heading over that evening?"

"Sure."

Anise smiled, but it looked forced. "Do we need to take anything?" she asked the two of us. "Any Christmas decora-tions or did Joan have everything there?"

113

When Dad didn't answer, I said, "She had quite a few things there for the holidays. All of them."

"Well, then. I'm sure whatever she had is perfect for what we need." She lightly touched my hand with her fingertips. "Your mother had lovely taste."

Because of the joint holidays—Christmas and Hanukkah—Jayme-Leigh and Isaac bowed out as well. Isaac explained the importance of them spending the time with his family, Jaymes reminded Dad that with him gone from the office, she really couldn't be too.

Dad said he completely understood. I honestly think he did. I think.

12

December 20 was the last day of school. Not even a day. A half day. Dad was so eager to get to Cedar Key—to get Anise to Cedar Key—we left our Orlando home around six o'clock.

In the dark.

Three hours later, driving down Highway 24 toward Cedar Key, I watched out the back window of Dad's Mercedes the silhouettes of palms, oaks, and pines as they whirred past us in the dark. In the front seat, Anise and Dad spoke to each other in muted tones. Dad, telling his new wife all about Cedar Key. Its history. How he and Mom had found the house before Kim was born.

It was a story I was certain Anise had heard before, but she hung on every word from my father's mouth as though it were the first time he'd told her. Or had ever even heard him speak.

I wondered if I would ever be in love with a man the way Anise was in love with my father. And, I couldn't help but wonder if Mom had treated Dad in such a way. I strained to remember, but nothing—not a single memory of this kind of devotion—came to mind.

Forgive him, Ami. You must forgive him as I have forgiven him.

Had she? Had Mom forgiven my father for what she'd told me that night, that awful night? Had he even done anything to be forgiven for?

"Ami?"

My head jerked toward the front seat. "What?"

I caught the reflection of Dad's eyes peering at me in the rearview mirror. They crinkled in delight. "You daydreaming back there?"

I smiled. "A little. Just thinking how good it will be to get there. My legs could use a stretch."

"Well, baby doll, I was just asking if you were getting cold back there."

"No, thank you. I'm fine." Actually the chill in the air felt good, a welcomed relief to the heat that never seemed to leave Florida. Perhaps the closer we got to the water, the chillier the air became. I didn't know. All I knew was that it felt like Christmas for the first time in a long time.

We crossed over Bridge Number Four—the first of the bridges one comes to before entering Cedar Key and the one right before Boggie Ridge, the area of Cedar Key where our house is. When Dad didn't slow down the car to turn onto our street, I said, "Dad? Where are we going?"

"I thought we'd take Anise to see what downtown looks like all lit up."

I nodded. "Oh. Anise, I hope you aren't expecting downtown Orlando or even Winter Park. This is a tiny seaside village, I guess you could say. Well . . . you'll see."

But if I'd thought Anise would be let down in any way,

I was wrong. She acted like she was seeing New York City during the month of December. "Look how adorable," she said upon spying privately owned decks jutting out into the marshlands, decorated by tiny, blinking white lights. One had lighted images of dolphin and manatees, starfish and oyster shells.

When we got to 2nd Street we looked up to see the street lamp wrapped in lights and boasting a lit "starfish." We inched our way up 2nd, observing the different seaside-influenced ornamentation, the occasional Christmas tree shadowed behind storefront windows. I unbuckled my seat belt and leaned over the front seat, pointing out things to my stepmother as proudly as Dad was.

Dad turned right onto A Street, which led to Dock Street. To our left and before us, the Gulf of Mexico shimmered in the moonlight. I pointed to the dark images of pelicans and seagulls sleeping on a dilapidated pier. Anise seemed completely delighted by the vision.

The birds aside, Dock Street was still awake. Christmas music wafted from both sides. The weather had dipped into the fifties, so the few people who were out and about had donned sweaters, scarves, and mittens to walk under the neon and holiday lights.

"This is fabulous," Anise said. "You're right, darling. This does remind me a little of home."

We turned right onto C Street, which took us to 1st, and then left onto 2nd.

"Dad, where are we going?"

"Just a minute, Ami," he said.

Dad pointed out the place the locals call "the spit," and

said, "We'll come here tomorrow night for the sunset. It's something else."

"Will we go to City Park for sunrise?" I asked, sliding to the back of the seat.

"Uh," Anise said. "I'm thinking more about sleeping in tomorrow morning." She twisted her neck to look back at me. "How about the next morning?" she asked with a wink.

I smiled. "Sure. Lazybones."

Dad laughed. He was happy. Even though three of his four daughters would not be celebrating with him, he had brought his bride and his baby, and that gave him joy. No matter what—no matter where the truth lay in my mother and father's marriage—I couldn't help but feel happiness too.

When we got to the house, I went online to see what time sunrise would occur the next day.

"Dad," I called from my bedroom, the one I'd shared with my sisters until—with them all grown up—there was just me.

"We're in the bedroom," Dad called back.

I walked from my room to the one Mom and Dad had shared since 1969 when they'd bought this place. Anise stood on one side of the king-size bed, Dad on the other. Both had their arms crossed, both were staring at the stark white linens and bedding Mom had decorated the bed with. Mounds of pillows rested at the headboard, making the bed look shorter than it actually was.

"What?" I asked, knowing instinctively that the two were in the midst of some deep discussion. "Is everything okay?"

Dad moved first. "Yes, of course it is," he said. "What did you need, Ames?"

"Um . . . just to tell you that sunrise is a little after seven in the morning. Seven-o-six, to be exact."

"All right."

"Do you mind if I take the car down to the docks to watch it? I'll leave here about six-thirty to six-forty-five."

Dad dug into his pants pocket, pulled out his keys, and tossed them toward me. "Here ya go. Just keep the noise level down when you leave if we're still in bed."

Anise looked at me, wide-eyed. As though she were in a panic. "Ami, would you mind horribly if we changed rooms tonight?"

"Change rooms?"

Her shoulders dropped and she smiled almost apologetically. "I know it's silly." She looked at Dad. "I know. But I just don't think I can sleep in this bed." Her hands clutched each other.

"I'm sorry, sweetheart. I hadn't even stopped to think . . ."

"I know that. You'd had the master bedroom at the house completely redone before I got there so it wasn't like . . . it was more like . . ." She looked at me again. "Ami, do you mind?"

"I think I get it. I mean, I've never been married and I've never even really had a boyfriend, but I can imagine." I glanced at Dad. "This," I said, pointing to the bed, "would be weird."

I looked around the room. Everything screamed my mother's name. Her taste and style. "So, why don't I take this room for while we're here, and then, Anise, when we get back to Orlando, you and I can start working on redecorating? I'd love to help with that."

Anise looked as though she could kiss me.

Dad pretended to look defeated, raised and dropped his hands, and said, "I'm suddenly feeling a pain in my credit card muscle."

Anise practically danced around the bed and into her husband's arms. "I love you, I love you, I love you," she said, planting kisses over his face.

Dad chuckled appropriately.

"One problem," I said, lifting my index finger.

They turned and looked at me. "What's that?" Dad asked.

"My room has two sets of bunk beds."

I slipped out of the comfort of my parents' bed, tiptoed across the wide pine boards to the master bathroom, dressed in a pair of jeans and a long-sleeved tee, brushed my teeth and my hair, and, sitting on the closed toilet lid, slipped into a pair of fur-lined boots.

Before leaving the quiet of the bedroom, I retrieved Dad's keys from the dresser where I had left them the night before, and then crept down the hall and into the kitchen. I rummaged through the bags of groceries we'd brought in but had not put away, found the box of instant hot cocoa with mini marshmallows, poured water into a mug from the drinking water jug, set it in the microwave, and waited for it to heat. With a travel mug of hot cocoa and a multicolored knit throw in hand, I slipped out the front door, clicking it shut and locking it behind me. Outside, I bounded down the steps, jumped into the car, and shivered. The weather was decidedly nippy. I loved it.

The car rolled into a parking space near City Park, just steps from the docks and the marina. I made my way to a park bench, huddled under the throw, and waited for the sun to make its debut.

An amber halo lay close to the water; Cedar Key was blanketed in shades of gray. Birds were already dancing in anticipation. I watched the thin clouds change from ashen to pink, to white, and then—as the sun crested—to magnificent gold. By now, my cocoa mug was empty. A boat carrying two fishermen had returned to the dock, and several walkers had stopped long enough to say "Merry Christmas," "Don't blink or you'll miss it," or "You're up awful early, young lady."

I liked the way the locals in Cedar Key spoke. More Southern than Floridian. Laid-back. These are easygoing people. Proud people. Hardworking people.

If I knew nothing else about Cedar Key, I knew that.

With nothing left to observe but the widening of the sun's reflection over the dark gulf water, I picked up, packed up, and drove home. When I pulled into the driveway, a car was parked to the left of where Dad usually parked. It was a car I knew well; the burgundy Buick Century owned by Eliana, the woman who'd cleaned up after us and who'd raised us kids as though we were her own, at least on weekends and during summer breaks.

My heart fluttered. I applied my foot to the brake pedal, rolling the Mercedes to a stop next to it. I pressed my lips together.

What was she doing here?

My breathing grew rapid. I glanced up to the front door, wondering if Anise had gotten up with Eliana's arrival.

Wondering how the two were finding each other. Wondering . . .

I opened the car door, closed it quietly behind me. The car keys jingled as they dropped into the pockets of my jeans. I pressed my hand against where they rested, as though to force them to stay put, and crept up the staircase like a cat burglar. Like a child sneaking in after curfew.

I tested the doorknob to see if the door was unlocked; it was. I opened it, slowly. Closed it even more slowly. From where I stood I could hear them speaking to each other as though they were in church. I strained to hear if there were only two voices. Or three.

Maybe Anise was with them. Maybe I wouldn't interrupt anything more than a getting-to-know-you session. Over coffee. And a plate of Eliana's homemade, steaming cinnamon rolls.

That thought alone made my stomach rumble.

I eased closer to the kitchen, rested my shoulder against the wall. Listened. Only two voices. Dad's and Eliana's. What were they saying? Nothing really.

"That Enrique," Eliana said, speaking of her grandson. Rosa's baby boy, born three years before. "He's the cutest thing."

"Tell me," Dad said, his voice encouraging.

"He can say all his ABCs, he can count to a hundred, and he knows his colors. The other day he says to me, 'Abby'— which you know he calls me—"

Dad chuckled. "Yeah, yeah."

"I want to die every time he says it, Ross. He says, 'Abby, when you were three years old like me, did you like to play on the computer?'"

122

I smiled. Cute.

Dad laughed too. "What did you tell him?"

"I said, 'Rique, when Abby was three years old, there was no such thing as a computer. At least, not like what you have at your house.'"

"And what did he say?"

"He said"—she giggled like a girl—"he said, 'Then, Abby, you must have been a kid a *long, long* time ago.'"

They laughed together. They sobered.

Get serious, Ami, I chided myself. This is just two adults talking about a precocious little boy. Two adults who have known each other for over thirty years. Why shouldn't they have a cup of coffee together? Why shouldn't they talk about their children? Their grandchildren?

But then Dad cleared his throat. Spoke. Said the words I'd hoped to never hear.

So it's true.

It was all horrifically true.

13

Jayme-Leigh
February 2005

The bleeding had started again. The third time in a month.

I walked out of the marble and walnut master bathroom of the home I shared with my husband, Isaac, and into our bedroom. The sleigh bed was thick with rumpled covers, topped by a cream-colored down duvet. I stepped onto the upholstered stepstool on my side of the bed, slid my body between the chocolate-brown sheets, pulled the duvet over my shoulders, and curled into a ball.

The pain grew deep in my abdomen, sent chills scurrying from my toes to my shoulders. I admonished myself; I should have taken something before returning to bed. I opened my eyes to peer across the empty side where my husband slept. When he was home. Lately, his work had kept him so busy, I'd hardly seen him.

The clock with the large digital numbers revealed the late hour. Nearly ten o'clock. Why, I wondered, did the house grow larger when the sun went down? And why did pain always increase?

I winced against the ache, wrapped my feet one on top of the other, grateful for the fuzzy socks . . . when was it . . . three hours ago I'd put them on?

The bleeding explained why I'd been so tired. Too exhausted to stay awake, even to read—my favorite thing to do at the end of the day. Stack of goose down pillows at my back. My husband at my side, doing the same.

I tried to snuggle further into the comfort of our bed only to have the pain shoot through me, pushing its way out from between my legs. "Ohhhhhh . . ." I groaned. I rolled over to the bed's matching end table. The moon cast enough light into the room for me to find my cell phone and press a two-digit speed dial code.

Isaac answered on the first ring. "Hey, honey . . . I was just about to lock up and come on home."

I sighed at the sound of his voice. Typically, it soothed me to the point of casting out any demon within my body, but not this time. "Isaac," I said, my voice strained.

"What's wrong?"

"I need you to come home now."

I heard a door close, a lock flip, keys rattle. "Are you bleeding again?"

"Mmm."

Footsteps quickened down the corridor leading to the laboratory where Isaac spent most of his days. And, lately, his nights. "That's it, J.L. I mean it this time. You're going to the doctor."

"Don't lecture me . . . just come home."

"I'm not kidding. If you don't make an appointment and keep it, I'm going to your father. I'm serious; do you hear me?"

Nature told me I had to get out of the bed. Return to the bathroom. "Isaac, it's pretty bad this time." I crawled from under the warm covers to the chill of the room. Even the heater wasn't making a dent in the recent, usual cold front that had washed over Central Florida. As soon as my feet touched the floor, I doubled over.

"It's been pretty bad every time, hon. Do you hear me?"

I made it to the bathroom. "I hear you." I gritted my teeth as I reached under the marble countertop for the box of sanitary napkins and retrieved what I needed. I hurried as best I could to the toilet. "Just come home," I managed to say. "I'm on my second pad in a half hour."

"You're going to the hospital. Tonight."

"I'll be all right if you'll just come home, Isaac."

The sound of his car starting caused my shoulders to sag in relief. "I'm calling your father."

I tensed again. "No."

"He can be there before I can, Jayme-Leigh. And he's a doctor."

"I know he's a doctor, Isaac. But he's also my father and he'll worry."

"That's his job, to worry."

From the looks of things in front of me, I knew he was right. Not about the worrying—though that was true too—but that I needed to get to the hospital. "All right, Isaac. Tell him. I mean, call him. And meet us at the hospital."

"That's my girl."

I finished with what I had to do, went to the medicine cabinet, and took out a bottle of oxycontin I'd been prescribed six months before after a severely sprained ankle. For several seconds I contemplated taking one before opting for simple over-the-counter naproxen. The last thing I needed was to tell a doctor I'd taken a narcotic prescribed for an ankle injury for menstrual cramping. No matter how relentless the pain had become.

I ran water into the glass-bowl sink, dropped two of the oval blue pills onto my tongue, allowed the water to pool in my cupped hand, and practically inhaled the water and swallowed. The pills crept down my esophagus. I cupped both hands under the running water and drank again. I pressed my face into a nearby hanging hand towel, all the while asking myself why I didn't just get a bottled water from the under-the-counter mini-fridge.

I must really be sick.

The wall clock—kept ten minutes fast—told me I'd been off the phone with Isaac for seven minutes already. Dad would arrive soon. I sat at the vanity, brushed my hair, and secured it with a scrunchie. I walked doubled over into my closet, found a pair of jeans, a tee, and a sweatshirt, and sat on the floor to dress. I pulled a small leather bag from the shelf, threw in a carry-on bag of toiletries I kept for when Isaac and I traveled, two pairs of underwear, and a clean nightgown. I knew better than to go with a pajama set.

I frowned as I looked at the ones I'd been wearing just moments before; they were soiled to the point of my having to throw them into a wastebasket.

"Rats," I said aloud. "I really loved those pjs."

Mom had given them to me. I'd wanted to wear them until they became threadbare, but nature had chosen differently.

I pushed my feet into a pair of fur-lined boots just as the doorbell rang.

Dad had made it in record time. Anise would be at his side, I was certain. Since they'd married five years ago, seeing Dad without his new wife meant that he and I were either at the office or the hospital.

I left my closet and walked through the house as the doorbell rang again. I could have called out, but it wouldn't have mattered. For one, I was too far from the front door and, for the other, I was too weak.

By the time I made it to the entryway, I had doubled over again. I opened the front door and slid to my knees, dropping the small bag next to me.

"Anise, start the car."

"Of course." I saw her gloved hand clasp the handle of the bag.

Dad's arm came around my hunched shoulders; the smell of his favorite cologne made me nauseous. I gagged, pressed my hand over my mouth, and gagged again.

"Sweetheart," Dad cooed. "I'm here now. Can you stand?"

I inhaled deeply through my mouth, an old remedy to quash nausea. I blinked several times. "I think so."

For his age, Dad's strength was remarkable. I believe—if necessary—he could have scooped me into his arms and carried me to the car. "Tell me what's going on," he said, closing the front door behind us. The night air was crisp, filled with the scent of dying fires from the neighbors' fireplaces.

"I'm hemorrhaging. Third time this month."

"When did it start?"

"Tonight."

"First time you've experienced this?"

I shivered. "No. Dad, I'm freezing."

"It's no wonder. You're running a low-grade temp."

I laid my head against his shoulder as we continued toward the car. Dad called, "Anise!"

She returned to us so fast I wondered if she'd been beside us all along.

"Baby, go back inside and get a coat for Jayme-Leigh."

Anise's hand came to rest on my arm, a momentary demonstration of comfort. "I'll be right back."

Dad helped me into the back of his Mercedes. The heater blew full blast and the leather seats felt warm. Still, I shivered. Dad closed my door, opened his. The car shifted under the weight of his getting behind the wheel. "Jayme-Leigh, when was the first time you had bleeding like this?"

"Six, seven months ago."

I heard the swish of his coat against the leather of the front seat. My eyes were closed, but I knew he had turned to gaze at me. "Have you seen anyone?"

I shook my head.

"Has Isaac known?"

I nodded.

"I'll talk with him later," he muttered.

"Dad . . . no . . ."

The front passenger door opened. I blinked to see Anise leaning toward me from her seat. She first laid my wool Burberry coat over me followed by a throw she'd found over the swan fainting couch in our bedroom. "I thought you'd like this too."

Dad backed out of the driveway before Anise could turn and buckle up.

"Sorry, sweetheart," he said.

"No, no. I understand."

I squeezed my eyes shut. The woman was nothing short of amazing. I'm not one to make a fuss over people, and I was as shocked as everyone else when, nearly five years ago, Dad brought her home (okay, maybe not as shocked as Heather). But I admit, she is a very special lady.

"Tell me if you need anything, Jayme-Leigh," she said.

I nodded. In spite of her special attentions, my teeth began to chatter. I balled my hands and shoved them under my jaw in an effort to keep them from rattling. The uterine pain lessened; the only good news on this night. Slowly, slowly, with the gentle rocking of the car . . . the stopping and starting . . . I felt myself ease into much-needed sleep.

"Sweetheart . . ."

My father's voice pulled me from someplace deep. I opened my eyes. A tan leather car seat faced me, a couple of feet from my nose. I felt both lost and snuggled into someplace comfortable. Drool had pooled under my chin; I wiped it away as I mumbled, "Hmm?"

"We're here."

"Where?"

"We're at the hospital."

I lifted my head. "Oh. Yeah." I cut my eyes upward to see Dad's face leaning into the car. "Where's Isaac?"

"I saw his car as we pulled in. Anise has already gone to find him. We're in the ER drive, sweetheart. Come on. I've got a wheelchair right here for you."

I moved to sit up, felt the reason for my being there rush to reality. "Dad," I whispered. "I'm hemorrhaging pretty badly."

"Right now?"

I nodded. "I'm scared to move."

"Well, you have to, Jayme-Leigh. Come on, now. You can do this."

I allowed him to help me out, horrified to realize my jeans were—like my favorite pajamas—ruined. Two hundred dollars. Trashed. And in front of Dad, no less.

True, he was a doctor. First and foremost, he was my father.

A broad-shouldered nursing assistant stood behind the wheelchair Dad helped me into. "Get her inside," Dad said. "Honey, I'm going to park the car and I'll be right there."

I nodded as I placed an elbow on the armrest, leaned my head into the palm of my hand, and felt the chair surge forward. Glass doors slid open followed by another set as we approached them. Hearing footsteps, I looked up. Isaac ran toward me. "I'm here," he said, taking my hand in his, walking beside us. "I've called Dr. Young. He'll be here in a few minutes." Isaac looked at his watch as though it would verify his declaration. He looked at the assistant. "You're to take Dr. Claybourne straight back," he said.

"Yes, sir," the young man said. "I know."

I squeezed my husband's hand. "I'm so glad you're here."

He smiled at me; my heart melted as it did each time he did so. Even in the midst of crisis, the man had such a way with me. But it had always been that way, from the moment we'd met as freshmen in medical school. My adorable histology lab partner, Isaac Levy.

I was all gone from the first flash of that smile, in spite of my resolve to *not* get involved with a man until after I'd gotten through my residency. I had worked too hard to let anyone—let alone a man—interfere with my life's goal. Or so I thought.

In high school I'd only dated one guy, and he felt the same as I: if we managed to get through school and we were still available, we'd revisit our relationship. And I pretty much thought that would be the direction of my life. I'd get my bachelor's in record time, spend four years in medical school, three years for my residency, and then see where life had taken Simon. If he were still available . . . well then.

But one smile—one line, really ("Hi, I'm Isaac Levy")—and all of life's plans shifted. And now, with each squeaky turn of a wheelchair's wheel, I knew life's plans were changing again.

I just knew it.

And Dad . . . Dad would have questions. Questions I would, finally, have to answer.

14

"Now I know why the patients I dealt with in residency hated these gowns so much." I plucked at the blue and white overly-worn-and-washed piece of cotton.

"It's not a name brand from Bloomie's, is it?" Isaac asked from beside me.

I turned my head to look at him. The plastic around the pillow squeaked. I sighed.

"I'm not going to make a very good patient, Isaac."

He kissed the tip of my nose. "Doctors never do."

I closed my eyes, faced forward again.

"How are you feeling now?"

I nodded. "Pain has lessened greatly."

"Dilaudid is good stuff."

I felt my lips spread in a slow grin. "Maybe we can take a case home."

My eyes opened when I heard the click of the door. John Young, my gynecologist, strolled in, chart tucked under his arm. He and Isaac shook hands, he made small talk with me, then got down to business. "I have some questions for you, Jayme-Leigh, and then I'll do a pelvic and we'll see what's what." He pulled a rolling chair to the bedside opposite Isaac. "We've gotten your blood work down to the lab already and should have something on that fairly soon."

"Okay."

John flipped open my chart. Beneath dark lashes, his eyes darted across the notes taken in triage while I studied his face. This late at night, he sported a five-o'clock shadow but remained expressionless. The trained look of a doctor, I thought. We must not give away our thoughts; no matter how positive, no matter how grim.

John inhaled deeply through his nose, blew it out.

"What?" I asked.

He pulled a pen from the breast pocket of his lab coat, clicked the top of it, and asked, "This started six or seven months ago?"

"Yes."

"This bad?"

"No. Not at all. Just mild bleeding between my periods."

"Until last month," Isaac interjected. "Last month she had some bleeding that was a little more profuse."

"I don't have your chart from the office with me, so forgive me for asking some questions that I'm sure you've answered before."

"No problem." I didn't expect John to remember the details of every patient any more than I was able to.

"You began your periods . . . when?"

"I was eleven."

John jotted a note in the chart. "A little earlier than most girls."

I smiled. "Mom had given me a book to read—you know

those books mothers give to their daughters—and not two weeks later, I started. She said, 'Jayme-Leigh, if I'd given you a book on skydiving, I believe you would have sprouted a parachute.'"

John smiled, but I could tell he wasn't amused. "And you've never been pregnant." His eyes locked with mine. "Ever?"

I shook my head. "No." Isaac squeezed my hand; until then I hadn't been fully aware he was holding it. I looked at him. "We've talked about it . . . in the future." I looked at John again. "Everyone thinks I don't want children. *We* don't want children. But that's not true. I just . . . we just . . . don't talk about these kinds of things with any and everybody. Not even family."

"She needs to get her practice up and going," Isaac said. "We thought maybe in five years." He shrugged.

"When you were away at school, were you ever diagnosed with cervical polyps?"

"No. Is that what you think this could be?"

John smiled at me. "Let me do my job before you start diagnosing, Dr. Claybourne."

I returned the smile. "Sorry."

"Okay. So, no cervical polyps."

"No."

"Periods been longer than usual?"

"Yes."

"What do they typically run?"

"Three to four days."

"And now?"

"Seven."

"With bleeding in between."

135

"Yes. The first few months, I thought I was just early. But last month and this month . . . it's been a week on, a week off, a week on, a week off."

"You've not had any abnormal Paps, have you?"

"No."

"Due for your next one . . . ?"

"In about a month. I have an appointment with you."

"Ah, well, that explains why you waited to call me." I processed the jab while John scribbled in my chart. "Painful intercourse?" he asked without looking up.

"Yes."

"What?" Isaac asked. "Are you serious?"

I looked at him. His face registered hurt and confusion. "I'm sorry. I didn't want to say anything. Plus, you've been gone so much lately, it really hasn't mattered much. I just thought maybe it was from in . . . frequency." I bit my lower lip as his cheeks pinked. "Sorry," I whispered.

"It's okay," he whispered back.

"Why are we whispering?" John asked.

We both looked at him. He grinned back. "Okay. I'm going to do a pelvic, get the lab work back, and then we'll talk some more. Sound like a plan?"

"Yes," I said.

He looked at Isaac. "Staying or leaving?"

Isaac brought my hand to his chest and pressed it against his heart. "I'm staying right here."

While we waited for the results of the tests, Dad came in, Isaac went to get a cup of coffee (the poor man hadn't

136

slept more than a few hours in the last forty-eight), and I catnapped. I woke no more than a half hour later. Dad sat in the same chair John had abandoned earlier. He was flipping through a magazine.

I craned my head to try to read the cover. "*O* magazine, Dad?"

Dad's head jerked. He tilted the cover so that a better view of Oprah Winfrey, dressed in holiday finery, could be seen. "It's even outdated."

"Only by a few months. We've got magazines in our office older than that, you know."

"Ami gave Anise a subscription for her birthday. Anise brought a couple along to give her something to do."

"I'll bet Anise likes reading the parts about gardening and flowers and cooking and such."

He tossed the magazine to the foot of the bed as he stood. "How are you feeling, kiddo?"

"Sort of weak."

"Don't worry about the office. I've got that arranged."

"I'm sure you do." I lifted my head and pulled the scrunchie from my hair, drawing my hair across one shoulder. "You haven't called my sisters, have you?"

"No. Not at this hour."

"Anise hasn't either, has she?"

"No. Told her not to. We know how private you are, Jayme-Leigh. We don't necessarily always agree with it, but we respect your wishes nonetheless."

I mouthed "thank you" then said, "Have you talked to Ami in a while?"

Dad's lips twitched. "She doesn't call much. When she

does, it seems like I'm always gone. Anise talks to her more than I do."

"She called me a month ago. Left a message. I've tried to call her back several times but . . . I guess we just keep missing each other."

Sadness registered in Dad's eyes; a father missing more than just his baby girl. After graduating from high school, she moved to Atlanta to continue in her studies. She snagged a position with a small ballet company there but continued in her goal toward the Atlanta Ballet. Thus, we'd hardly heard from or seen her.

"She's trying out for the Atlanta Ballet again soon," I said. "What is wrong with those people? Don't they know brilliance when they see it?"

"She'll make it this time," Dad said.

"What makes you so sure?" I asked, not really expecting an answer.

"Anise told me so." He winked.

"Well, then . . . by all means."

The door opened, and Isaac walked through carrying two cups of coffee, one he handed to my father. "Just like you like it."

"Thank you, son." Dad took a sip.

"I don't suppose you brought one for me?"

"Nope. Doctor's orders. You're officially NPO." He jerked his head toward the hallway. "Just saw John. He's admitting you for more tests so, nothing past those lips."

"Why am I NPO?"

"You'll have to ask him." He took a sip of his coffee, swallowed, then leaned over the bed railing. "But if you kiss me," he said, "you can at least have a taste."

I grinned. "I'd kiss you even if I couldn't have a taste." And I did.

John walked in. "Ah, look at these two, will you?" He shook my father's hand. "So, as you may have heard, I want to do some more tests in the morning. If I'm right in what I'm suspecting, we'll start talking surgery."

I felt my brow furrow. "What do you suspect?"

"John?" Dad said.

John cocked a brow in an expression that read: *I've done this a million times; like I said earlier, let me do my job.*

"Whatever it is," I said from my reclined position on the bed, "I trust you, John. I brought a small bag with a night-gown and some toiletries. I'm set."

Truth was, I'd already figured the few things it *could* be. Not knowing for another day—not knowing for certain—didn't bother me in the least. I've never been called stupid, but in this case, the less I knew—for now—the better. If I'd been my patient's parent, I'd feel differently about it. But I was the patient this time; seeing a hospital room from this position was uncharted territory for me. I'd have to take it one step at a time.

15

Within days, a number of procedures had been done, a diagnosis rendered, and surgery scheduled.

I was one of the rare cases of women below the age of forty diagnosed with endometrial cancer.

"Stage I," John told Isaac, Dad, Anise, and me. "So you're lucky."

I didn't feel lucky, but I nodded and said nothing.

"We'll perform a hysterectomy with a bilateral salpingo-oophorectomy," he continued, his voice professional and matter-of-fact. But his eyes were veiled in sorrow. And I knew why. I knew where his heart was.

But. It was what it was and it had to be done.

I swallowed hard. "What . . . what about . . ." I swallowed again, blinking back hot tears. "What about postsurgical treatment? Are we looking at radiation or chemo or . . ."

John patted my sheet-covered foot. "We caught this early, Jayme-Leigh. Although, with your symptoms starting back when they did, I'm surprised it's not worse."

"So," Dad interrupted, "what?"

"Pathology report looks good, Ross. CT scan doesn't

show any involvement in the lymph nodes." He turned to me. "Jayme-Leigh, I'll do an abdominal incision. That's going to allow me a better look than vaginally. But, for now, let's pray for the cancer to be contained."

Isaac ran his hand over the crown of my head. I read his thoughts. For now, surgery would suffice. No need for chemo. I would lose my uterus, my ovaries, my fallopian tubes, and any chance of ever having a baby. But I'd keep my hair.

After John left the room, I cleared my throat, pressed my shoulders against the hospital bed, and said, "This does *not* leave this room for *any* reason."

"But Jayme-Leigh," Anise said, her hands clasped in her lap. "You need your family around you now."

I reached for Isaac's hand. He wrapped both of his around mine. "I have my family," I said with a turn of my head toward him. We looked at each other in that way couples have of communicating without speaking.

I returned my attention to my father. "I'm firm about this, Dad. You know and Anise knows and Isaac knows. That is enough. I don't want this discussed with Kim or Heather or Ami. We'll tell the staff at work I'm having . . . a T&A. It takes adults longer to get over a tonsillectomy, so my absence will make sense."

Dad raised his brow and shook his head. "I don't agree with you, sweetheart, but it *is* your life and your decision. But . . ." He raised a finger. "You have to promise me you'll allow Anise and me to help you over these next few weeks."

I would need help. There was no question about it; Isaac would not be able to provide all that I would need. "I promise."

I kept that promise. For the first few weeks I'd managed to chat on the phone with my sisters, even Ami once, without any suspicions. When I was able to walk again without bending over, I attended family dinners. When Heather—naturally, Heather—commented on my slow gait, I told her I'd had some problems with my period, had a D&C, and everything was great now. Which was all true. I'd just left out the hysterectomy part.

Remarkably, she bought it.

One night, while at home, snuggled on our living room sofa under a light blanket and watching film noir on Turner Classic Movies, Isaac mumbled near my ear, "Tell me something, J.L."

"What?" I asked, popping a piece of popcorn into my mouth.

"Why *don't* you want your family to know about the surgery? I mean, I understand you are primarily a private person, but like Anise said, they are your sisters."

I sat up slowly. Not because I had to, but because I needed the extra time to ponder what my husband had just asked me. Lifting the remote and pointing it toward the large screen television, I paused the movie—*Daisy Kenyon*—using our newly purchased TiVo digital video recorder. I turned toward Isaac, set the bowl of popcorn and the remote on the floor, and laid my hand onto his arm, which now stretched across the back of the sofa.

"Isaac, you have to understand something." I pressed my lips together. "I grew up between Kimberly and Heather."

"I know that." He grinned. "I've been a part of this family long enough to have the birth order set to memory."

"Smart aleck." I patted his arm. "But you didn't grow up between the two of them." I picked up the blanket, now twisted around my body, and straightened it over the two of us. "Kimberly is more of a control freak than you realize. She's just subtle about it. She wants everything in life to be picture perfect. All the time. No mess ups."

"Really?" He shrugged. "I guess I've never noticed that about her."

"Because you didn't grow up with her. Believe me; we shared a bedroom for a few years. Now, you know me. I like things tidy. But Kimberly wanted everything to look like it belonged on a magazine cover."

Isaac chuckled. "I can believe that, based on what her home looks like now."

I shook my head. "I can only hope she'll let her boys be boys."

Isaac tweaked my nose between the knuckles of his first and middle fingers. "I bet she will."

"We'll see."

"And then there's you."

"Technically the middle child, you know, because Ami came along a little later in life."

"Mmm."

"And I liked to read. Kimberly wasn't that crazy about reading. She was a good student—a great student—but she was more interested in Barbies. And then in clothes and her friends. And then in boys. Heaven help us. There was this one boy over in Cedar Key when we were teenagers . . ."

Isaac scooted back to straighten himself, grinned, and said, "Oh yeah?"

I swatted him. "Stop thinking of my sister that way."

Isaac feigned shock and innocence, all with one look. "What did *I* say?"

I continued on without answering his question. "His name was Steven. Steven Granger. His dad owned the tour boat company there. Steven was a year older than Kim and, I admit, cute as a bug in those days."

"Not that you were interested."

"I wasn't. I just remember him being cute in a beachboy kind of way. Anyway, Kim was totally nuts over Steven. That whole summer, the summer of their romance," I said, adding finger quotes in the air. "It was just nearly pathetic."

"How old was she?"

"Sixteen."

"Uh-oh. That's dangerous territory."

"Dangerous enough."

"So what happened?" He glanced over to the television. "Because this story is becoming even better than the one on TV, and the one on TV is pretty good."

I reached for the bowl of popcorn, keeping an arm pressed against my abdomen. Even though nearly five weeks had passed and I had plans to return to work soon, I still felt as though I needed to support the surgical site. I placed the popcorn between us, shuffled a handful from one hand to the other. I chewed thoughtfully on a piece and said, "Steven went to college, got some girl pregnant, and Kimberly sulked until she met Charlie in college."

"Wow. Just like that."

"Just like that."

"Poor Charlie." Isaac grabbed a handful of popcorn, tossed one in his mouth, and chewed.

I finished off the little bit left in my hand, brushed the salt and crumbs back into the bowl. "What do you mean, 'poor Charlie'?"

"Well," he said, his mouth still working on the corn. He swallowed. "If Kim sulked *until* she met Charlie, that means she has pinned a lot of hopes and dreams *on* Charlie."

"Well, he's her husband. Shouldn't she pin hopes and dreams on him?"

Isaac tilted his head. "Maybe. But . . . there weren't any other boys between Steven and Charlie?"

"Not that I know of. And, if there were, I think I would have known. She was pretty vocal about the social aspects of her life."

Isaac nibbled on popcorn for a minute before adding, "And Heather we *all* know about."

"Little Miss Mother-to-All."

"Does she fit your birth-order theories?"

"Actually, she doesn't. I've done some research on this—"

"Of course you have."

"Haha. And, no. But the issue with Heather is that, while she was the youngest, she wasn't *really* the youngest. So, when Ami came along, she mothered her, I mothered her, and Kim was too much into friends to mother anybody. And, when Kim had her heartbreak over Steven, Heather mothered her too. With Mom, um, not being well, I guess Heather just grabbed her role by the horns and was happy doing it."

Isaac didn't say anything for a moment. Just chewed on

popcorn, took a long swallow of his Coke, and added, "So, why don't you want your family to know?"

"Kim has enough going on in her world and I'm not altogether sure she wouldn't—oh-so-casually—end up mentioning it to her friends or her Sunday school class or to some of the other teachers. And Heather would be over here clucking around me, and you know how much I despise clucking."

Isaac laughed, pressing a hand against the flat of his abdomen. "Gotcha."

"And Ami is away." I returned the popcorn bowl to the floor, picked up the remote, turned and positioned myself against my husband again. "Isaac?" I asked, pushing play.

"Hmm?"

"Do you think Ami is okay?"

"Sure. Why do you ask?"

I watched a few moments of exchange between Henry Fonda and Joan Crawford before answering. "I dunno. Just a hunch, I guess."

"Sister's intuition?"

"This is not kidding?" Joan Crawford asked of Henry Fonda.

"This is not kidding," Fonda returned.

I didn't answer. I let Crawford and Fonda do it for me. Later, as the movie credits rolled, I turned back to Isaac and said, "I'll never have my own baby." A tear slipped down my cheek. "Our baby."

He brushed it away with a fingertip. "I know. It's okay."

"I'll take care of the infants and toddlers and babies of everyone else, but never my own."

He withheld comment.

146

I pressed my face into his shirt and sobbed. "I'm so sorry. I'm so sorry."

Instinctively, his strong arms drew me closer. "It's okay, Jayme-Leigh. Seriously, babe. It's okay."

I shook my head. "No. No, it's not." Beneath my face, his shirt grew wet with tears.

"Remember we have Kim's kids and Heather's . . ."

"It's not the same. I don't want to just be somebody's doctor or somebody's aunt. I want to be a mother."

"Then we can adopt."

"I want one of my own, Isaac. Don't you understand that? I want to know what it feels like to be pregnant. To give birth. And now I never will. There's no going back."

Blessedly, he said nothing. And when I had cried until there was nothing left, I added, "Stupid hormones. I'm sure that's what's happening here."

"That, maybe. And, you're a woman who loves her husband, loves kids, and wants to have the one with the other." He tilted my chin so I was forced to look at him. "You do love your husband, don't you?"

I laughed and cried, drew my arms around his neck, and slid around until our faces were pressed cheek to cheek. "I love you so much, Dr. Levy."

"And I love you, Dr. Claybourne."

I leaned back. "That's Mrs. Levy to you, sir."

He leaned closer; I closed my eyes and felt his lips tenderly kiss each lid. "You bet you are."

One Friday afternoon, between seeing the Bateman baby and Zandra Brown's two-year-old, my energy level crashed.

Dizziness swept over me. I sagged against the rough wall, turned, and pressed the back of my head against it. From the other side, I could hear Mrs. Brown telling little Naomi to "stop moving around so much." Just then, Dad stepped out of room 7, which was directly across from me, and stopped short. "Jayme-Leigh?" he asked without moving.

"I'm just tired," I said.

He crossed the hallway in two steps, placed his hand under my elbow, and said, "Let's get to your office."

I nodded.

"I allowed you to come back to work too soon. John said six to eight weeks and here you are working within the fifth."

We entered my office without any of the staff noticing. Dad closed the door behind us, guided me to the maroon leather sofa on the opposite side of the room from my desk, and lowered me toward it.

"Let me get you a glass of water," he said.

I nodded again, pleased. My mouth was parched. Dad went to a mini-fridge where I kept small bottles of water. Seconds later, I guzzled the entire eight ounces without so much as taking a breath. I immediately felt better. "I needed that," I said.

"You need to be at home in bed." Dad sat beside me.

I cut my eyes at him. "Dad . . ."

"I'm not kidding, young lady."

Naomi Brown's chart rested on my knees; I placed my hands palm down on top of it. "If I'd been gone much longer, I'd have forgotten how to do my job."

"I doubt that."

I chuckled. "I felt fine, Dad," I said, turning serious. "Really

148

I did. And I've worked half days all this week, and each day I've felt better and better. I've been thinking that by next week I could come back full-time. And the dizziness I felt a few minutes ago just came on me without warning. This is a first. I promise."

Dad dipped his hand into one of the lower pockets of his lab coat and pulled out a cell phone. "I'm calling John."

I put my hand on his. "You'll do no such thing."

Dad cocked a brow at me. "Now you listen here, Jayme-Leigh Claybourne," he said. "I'm feeling guilty enough as it is."

My spine tingled. There hadn't been too many times in my life that my father had called me by my full name. And only once before had I heard him talk of feeling guilt, and that had been the night we'd gone to the hospital on a call, leaving Ami alone with Mom. "Why should you feel guilty?"

Dad's face grew somber. "Remember how I told everyone your mother had cancer?"

I nodded.

"You've kept that secret with me and . . . now, I have to wonder. Did God punish me by giving *you* cancer instead?"

I felt air rush out of me. "Dad . . . wouldn't that be God punishing *me*?"

Dad's eyes rested on mine. "I don't know. Anise says I'm wrong. That God doesn't work that way." He shook his head. "Maybe this is just my own guilt."

I patted his hand. "I love you, Dad." I shifted. "For that and so much more. Please don't feel that way. You're too smart for that. Cancer just . . . happens. You and I both know that. As doctors, we know it. It's a fallen world we live in, right?"

Dad seemed to ponder my words for a minute. "Do you ever get mad at God?"

"Do you?"

"Sometimes."

I gave him a half smile. "Me too. Sometimes."

Dad kissed my cheek. "Let me call John. I'm your father. Give me this much?"

I slid backward until I was resting completely into the sofa, all the while wondering why the men in my life felt they had to depend on each other to get their way. At the same time, grateful for them both. "Dial away," I said, closing my eyes. I listened as Dad gave the details to John, said "uh-huh . . . uh-huh" a few times, and then slapped the phone shut.

I opened my eyes. "Well?"

"He thinks you've overdone it. He wants you to go home, get some rest over the weekend, and if this continues, call him on Monday. Sooner if you need to. He said to tell you that you've risked hemorrhaging and that if you should start spotting, to not wait a second before calling him." Dad stood. "I'm getting one of the girls up front to drive you home."

"Dad . . ." But one look at his face and I threw my hands up. "Okay. Okay. I surrender."

"Good girl." He pointed at me. "Just sit. I'll send someone back here in a minute." He started toward the door. "Oh. And John said you may want to get a recipe book that has after-cancer recipes in it."

"Oh?"

"He said there are some fatigue-fighting snacks. Juices. Things like that."

"Oh."

"I'll tell Anise—she knows all about things like that—and have her pick one up for you from the bookstore." Dad left.

Minutes later, one of the receptionists entered. She was young—all of nineteen—and already married with a two-year-old. "Hey, BJ."

"Dr. Claybourne." She tilted her head. The thick brown hair she wore in a high ponytail dipped to one side, and her doe-shaped, rich brown eyes grew wide. "You need a ride home?"

I slid to the end of the sofa. "Looks like it." She put her hand on the doorknob. "I'll get my truck and drive it 'round to the back door," she said. "Just give me five minutes."

"I'll meet you at the back."

With the energy and precociousness of a five-year-old she placed her fists on her hips and said, "Do you want me to come back inside and help you outside? Dr. Ross said you had a weak spell."

I smiled at her with appreciation. "No, BJ. I'm fine now. I can make it." Realizing I still had the Brown file in my lap, I said, "Oh. BJ . . ." I extended the file to her. "Would you mind taking this to Dr. Ross and asking him to take care of little Naomi." I smiled. "I think her mother has her hands full in there."

BJ took the file and smiled back. "Don't I know it? If my Becca had as much energy as Naomi, I'd be too tired to come to work."

———

Until that ride home, I had little knowledge of BJ. I hadn't recorded to memory where she lived or the name of her husband, and I certainly had no idea what kind of car she drove. Dad and I had enough office workers—receptionists, nurses, insurance clerks, CNAs, and a PA who worked primarily with Dad—to keep up with the details of their lives would be a full-time job in and of itself. The only reason I knew BJ's age, that she was married and had a child, was because it had fallen on me to conduct her final interview. Those facts, which she had happily rattled off, had stuck with me.

I sat in the front seat of a brand-new silver Ford F150 4-door SuperCrew. I knew because BJ proudly said, "This is my new Ford F150, 4-door SuperCrew!" A child's car seat was strapped into the backseat, padded bar thrown back, a sippy cup and a crumpled blanket with duckies tossed onto the seat. For the most part, I sat without saying a word while BJ rambled on about her little girl. For every quality she possessed as a receptionist—and she was a good one—I found it obvious that she took her role as mother far more seriously.

About ten minutes from home, I broached a question I'd been asking myself since I'd pulled myself into the cab. "BJ," I said slowly. "How is it that a young girl like yourself—a vivacious girl like yourself—is driving a four-door truck?"

She laughed. "My husband—Randy—says it's a deer hauler if he ever saw one." She patted the black leather seat. "I picked it out myself. Bought it myself too. Randy said if I wanted it I could have it, but by golly I was going to pay for it." She winked at me. "So please don't fire me."

I blinked. She was too competent in her job; firing her was the last thing about to happen. "He said it's a . . . a what?"

"Deer hauler." She kept her eyes on the road while I kept my eyes on her. "You know, for deer huntin'."

"You . . . deer hunt?"

She grinned. "Sure. Randy's daddy owns some land over in Osceola County. We go there during deer season. Whitetails all over the place."

"And you shoot a gun? At a deer?"

"I got two of 'em last year." She grinned at me, albeit briefly. "You should try it, Dr. Claybourne. You'd enjoy it."

I laughed. "I think I'll pass."

She shrugged. "We don't do it for sport. We eat the meat. I'll bring you some venison steaks next week if you like. We've got plenty."

"I don't think I've ever had any venison."

"Some people think it's gamey. But I like it. I'll even tell you how to cook it so it's so tender you won't need to chew."

I smiled at the thought. "That's very nice of you. Can I ask you another question?"

"Sure." The ponytail swung behind her. "I'm pretty much an open book."

"Why did you decide not to go to school?"

BJ shot a glance toward me. "I went to school."

"I mean after high school. Surely you had a goal outside of working as a pediatrician's receptionist."

"Yeah. Well. I started dating Randy when I was a junior and he was a senior. After school, he went to trade school— he's the manager at Mobil Lube, you know. The one on Colonial near where we live," she said, as though I knew her address. "Anyway, I always figured he'd graduate from trade school and I'd graduate from high school about the same time. Then we'd get married. I couldn't imagine anything in this world I'd rather be than Mrs. Randy Stodden." She rolled her eyes. "I was and still am completely nuts about that guy."

I raised my brow but not enough that she'd notice. "He obviously felt the same way."

"Honestly? Not altogether."

"Meaning?" I asked, then added, "Turn left up here."

"Meaning he met some chickadee while he was at school and broke up with me so he could date her."

"It didn't last, apparently."

"Well . . . no. I mean, a month after he broke up with me, I found out Becca was on the way and . . ."

I swallowed. "I see."

BJ scooted back in her seat. "I hope that doesn't make you feel bad against me."

"No. Absolutely not."

"It wasn't like I was sleeping with every boy in school. In fact, Randy was my only, and he and I had only been together twice. For the longest time I thought that was why he'd broken up with me. You know. Because I had . . ."

"Yes. I understand." I took a deep breath around a knot growing in my chest. "Randy is obviously a responsible young man."

She smiled brightly. "He is. I mean, I was kinda worried he would say 'Good luck, girl' and leave me to it. But he did the right thing. We got married, we had Becca, and we couldn't be happier. At least I don't think we could."

I pointed. "Turn right up here. We'll need to stop at the guard gate, but they all know me."

"Got it." She drove on in silence, we made it past the guard, and she followed my instructions, all the while craning her neck to look out the windshield. "Sure are some nice houses around here."

"There are."

"I bet your house is something else, Dr. Claybourne."

"I like it. Sometimes I think it's too big for just my husband and me, but . . ."

BJ turned onto my street. "Don't worry about that. I'd be willing to bet that pretty soon you'll have your own little ones running around, filling up the empty spaces."

The knot moved to my throat. I could say nothing. I kept my focus on breathing around it. By the time she pulled the truck to my front door and I'd gotten the keys out of my purse, I'd managed to swallow it down. "Thank you, BJ. You're very kind to do this."

"Any time. And I hope you get to feeling better. Right now I'm glad I had a T&A when I was a kid and not an adult."

I opened the door and slid to the ground. "Yes," I said. I raised my eyes to the young woman who was the epitome of everything I'd never wanted to be. Uneducated in terms of a college education. Working *for* someone else and driving a truck she could hunt Bambi in. Pregnant way before she should have been.

But she was a mother. No matter what she may not have chosen as her way in life, she'd have Becca. "That was good for you," I finally said. "You have no idea how lucky you are."

16

Heather
March 2007

I was in deep, deep trouble. More than I could wrap my brain around. More than I could figure a way out of.

And, figuring my way out of things, well . . . that's a gift of mine.

But this was beyond me.

God! I looked up from the piles of papers—bills, invoices, threatening correspondences—and offered a pitiful prayer to the One who knows me best and loves me most. *How could I . . .*

But I knew the answer. I didn't need God to say one word. Not one. Other than, maybe, *Didn't I tell you so?*

I hate it when that happens. Not when God is right. He's always right. But when I am wrong. I hate being wrong.

Lord! Why didn't you stop me? Just once? Stop me before I made such a mess of things?

God remained silent. Again, not one word was necessary. I didn't need to "be still and know." I didn't need to open the

156

Bible, open it randomly as some people do, and then point and let God speak to me by chance. I didn't need to journal, not that I do anyway—who has time?—allowing my free mind to eventually come up with what God would say to my heart. No. I already knew the answer.

God didn't stop me *ever* because I *never* stopped long enough to let him.

I slapped both hands on the desk where I took care of our family's household expenses. The papers beneath shifted under the force. I slid them all together. Looked at each one, sheet by sheet. Credit card invoice by credit card invoice.

Robb & Stucky, where I'd bought our new bedroom furniture.

Thomasville, where I'd bought the living room and dining room furniture.

Macy's, where I'd bought the new china. And the new stemware. And the new flatware.

Dillard's, where I'd bought the new sheet sets and comforters.

Bed, Bath, & Beyond, where I'd bought the new towel sets.

Home Depot, where this whole thing started.

Oh, if Andre had only listened to me when I told him we should move to a new house. But no. He had to be practical. Logical. He just had to sit down and talk budget with me.

"If the budget is my job," I'd asked him from the middle of the kitchen—arms folded, feet braced apart as if I were about to lunge—"then why can't you just trust me?"

Andre sat in one of the kitchen chairs. He was as relaxed as a cat on a sunporch in the middle of the afternoon. Leaning back. One leg crossed over the other. Shirtsleeves cuffed and rolled twice toward his elbow. And looking as handsome as the day I'd married him, just less boyish, more man.

"Heather, honey," he said, almost as if the words were one. Heather-honey. I should have my name changed on my birth certificate. No longer Heather Elaine Claybourne. Instead, Heather Honey Dutton. "I do trust you. You've done a great job all these years, and goodness knows I didn't give you a whole lot to work with in the beginning. But I don't see what in the world we need to move for. This house is plenty big. It's in a good school zone. The kids have their friends right here in the neighborhood. We're near the church. We're near my work."

I threw up my hands. "I'm suffocating, this house is so small."

"It's nearly four thousand square feet."

"Thirty-five hundred and that includes the garage." I walked to the sink, turned on the water, and ran the dishcloth under it.

"Which is still plenty big enough for this family."

I added soap to the cloth, wrung it out, and started wiping the countertop, picking up whatnots, wiping under them, setting the whatnots back down. "Look at this, Andre. I cannot get some of the stains off this countertop. It's cheap and you know it. And even if I bleach it, what about . . ." I pointed to a place where the linoleum was seamed together. "That?"

"What about it?"

"It's buckling."

Andre chuckled. Stood. Walked over to me, slid his arms around my waist from behind, and gently stilled my hands.

"Stop, stop, stop," he whispered. "Goodness gracious, woman, but what you don't get all upset over the littlest things."

His breath blew warm on my neck, and I shivered. He could talk me into anything—and obviously he had, what with us getting married mere months after meeting. Ten months later we were holding twin babies.

"It's not little." I groaned, though I knew I wouldn't win this one.

"Tell you what let's do," he said, turning me to face him. He placed his hands on both sides of my face, splayed his fingers, and drew my lips to his for the tenderest of kisses. "How about if we remodel the kitchen. You go down to Home Depot tomorrow. Talk to someone who knows what they're talking about—goodness knows I don't—and see what it will take to redo the countertops, the cabinets." He glanced over his right shoulder. "The appliances are fairly new so I don't think—"

My shoulders sagged. "Oh, Andre, really. You can't expect me to upgrade this kitchen and not get new appliances."

"Okay, okay. We'll look at new appliances."

I grinned with such fervor my cheeks ached. I placed my hands on his waist, tickled my way around his trim torso until I had locked him in my arms. This time, it was me drawing him close and kissing him. When I leaned back to look into his eyes, I said, "What's my budget?"

A growl escaped from his throat. "Woman . . ."

"Well, I need to know," I said, pretending to be coy.

"Let's say twenty grand."

"That's it?"

His face—handsome and perpetually tanned—grew somber.

"I'm not kidding, Heather. That's as much as we can afford. You may keep the books, but I'm not so naïve that I don't look into them once a month."

I laid my forehead against his wide shoulder. "Okay, okay. Twenty and not a penny more."

"Now then," he said. "I believe the twins are at swim practice and Lenny is at Richie's. Right?"

"Mmmhmm."

He bit my earlobe. "Then my timing is perfect," he whispered.

It took three months to renovate the kitchen. Three months and nineteen thousand, eight hundred, and eighty-three dollars (and sixty-four cents) to be exact. The last bit of white dust and the last manufacturer's sticker had been removed in time for Thanksgiving 2006. I invited the whole family to come for dinner, including Ami, who declined.

Since she'd graduated from high school, we'd hardly seen her. She rarely called. And I frequently kicked myself in the rear for the fight we'd had seven years previously.

"But will you try to come home for Christmas?" I'd asked her.

"Yeah," she said, totally noncommittal. "I'll see what I can get off. But, just so you know, since being accepted by the Atlanta Ballet . . . I mean . . . this is a busy season."

"But surely you'll have Christmas Day off?"

I heard the deep sigh from the other end of the line. "I said I'll see what I can do and I will, okay?"

So, Thanksgiving Day, there we were, enjoying the fruits

of my new kitchen, all of us, save Ami. Of course, Anise brought several health-conscious dishes and then went on and on about the difference between a Southern Thanksgiving and a Northern one.

"If she doesn't like the way we eat," I mumbled to Kim, "then why doesn't she go *home* and enjoy the holidays with *her* family."

Kim popped my hand. "Shush, Heather, before Dad hears."

"I don't care," I said, but I whispered the words all the same. Not that he *could* hear, what with the kids yelling through their game of touch football in the backyard and the volume of the televised game in the family room. I felt my eyes fill with tears. "Kim . . ."

Kim turned to me. We stood together side by side in front of my new stainless steel stove, Kimberly adding seasonings to the white acre peas while I stirred the giblet gravy. "Hey, girl. What's wrong?"

I swiped at a tear. "I know I shouldn't act like I do." I sniffled. "I do, but I can't seem to help myself." Several tears made their way down my cheeks. "I just miss Mom so . . . so much, Boo. Some days I feel like I'm going to die right along with her. Like, I can't take another breath without her here."

Kim stopped long enough to rub my back. "I know, Heather. Me too. But Anise *is* nice and Dad seems really happy."

I didn't answer. I couldn't. My heart was raw when it came to losing Mom. I'd never felt as though I'd truly had either of them—Mom or Dad. Kim was the firstborn; she'd had them all to herself for a season of life. Even though I was the baby, Jayme-Leigh had been born smart. She and Dad had what seemed like an instant connection. And, it always felt like Mom and Kim had their love for photography and artsy things. Me? I had my baby dolls and then I had Ami, and then, later on, a few beauty pageants that drew Mom's attention.

With Mom gone, I'd had a chance to have just a little piece of Dad. Ami still needed him, of course. Jayme-Leigh and he spent hours together at work. But I could be a sort of surrogate mother for Ami and wife for Dad. Not in any weird way, just in the way that filled his need for a cook. A laundry washer. A floor sweeper. I was willing to do it all, just to have a little piece of him that was all mine. But, then, before I had a chance to settle in to my new role, here came Anise. I quickly found myself sharing Dad with a practical stranger. I wanted to be as accepting of her as my sisters had been, but I just couldn't seem to get past the hurt and anger growing inside me.

I took a deep breath, ready to change the subject. "By the way," I said, "I've noticed Charlie is getting gray fast."

She smiled at me. "Premature gray, I believe they call it."

I nudged her shoulder with mine. "He's still hot."

She giggled, cut her eyes at me. "I know, right?"

I slammed the spoon against the side of a new two-quart pot and said, "We are so lucky. You, me, Jayme-Leigh. All of us married such gorgeous men." Then I laughed, truly laughed, and it felt good.

Kimberly opened the drawer next to the stove and pulled out an oven mitt. "Let me check the bird," she said.

I stepped aside as she pulled the door toward her. I rested against the lip of the Silestone countertop just as the heat blew across me. I crossed one ankle over the other, figuring every wild curl on my head had just frizzed in delight. "Have you ever noticed how Jayme-Leigh manages to stick close to the men when the women are in the kitchen? She's in there, right now, watching a game, for crying out loud."

"It's who she is," Kimberly said, basting the turkey with its juices. "Besides, I'm thinking something else is going on with her."

"Like what?"

Kim shrugged as she reached for the oven mitt she'd removed just seconds before. "I can't put my finger on it, Heather. Just . . . something."

I hadn't noticed anything. Nothing more than her usual absence and indifference in my life. "I guess you also noticed Anise is right in there with her."

Kim looked up at me and rolled her eyes. She slid the rack holding the guest of honor back into the oven and shut the door. "Heather, you told her not to be in here, remember? She did ask."

I grabbed my sister's dark blonde hair, wrapped it into a makeshift ponytail at the nape of her neck, and tugged play-fully. "Whose side are you on, anyway?"

She pinched the tip of my nose; I let go of her hair. "Will you please stop being so rotten and give her a break? Just for today?"

I pretended to think about it. "No," I said. "Not today. Not any day." Then I tweaked her nose as she'd done mine. "Okay. Maybe *one* day. But in the meantime, big sister, keep your nose out of my rottenness."

If only I'd left everything alone. If only the remodeling of the kitchen had been enough. If only having the family over for Thanksgiving had satisfied me. But no . . .

In March—just when so many things were starting to happen with the kids and school and sports—Andre announced he had a weeklong seminar in Dallas he had to attend. *Had* to. And so, like the dutiful wife I've always been, I packed his clothes and drove him to the airport. I kissed him oh-so-sweetly at the curb.

"See you in a week," he said. "I'll miss you."

"Miss you too," I parroted.

A whole week. Kids' schedules busier than ever. Andre gone. Gone to Dallas. I could only hope he didn't meet a cheerleader.

As he walked past the sliding glass doors of Orlando International Airport, a single oversized carry-on wheeled behind him, I gripped the steering wheel of my car, sighed, and jumped when a traffic cop blew his whistle at me. "This isn't a parking garage," he barked.

I came close to sticking my tongue out at him, but refrained. I eased into the flow of traffic, drove along Concourse A's sidewalk until I reached the off-ramp leading to the 528. I was halfway home when I saw the advertisement for Robb & Stucky Interiors. The kids were in school, and since I had nothing really to do at home, I followed the directions to the nearest location.

The opulence and elegance of the store—not to mention the offer of warm oatmeal cookies and cappuccinos—pulled me in like the first cool days of autumn after a blistering Florida summer. I walked among and relished the homey

arrangements, the upscale designers of furniture, the taste-
ful "little things" that made each "room" invite me in, that
made me pretend it not only belonged in my home but that
it would *be* in my home.

Before I'd had time to reason my way out of the store,
I'd completed an in-store credit application, been approved,
picked out a bedroom set, drunk two cups of cappuccino,
and eaten three cookies.

I set a time for delivery, left the store—hands shaking,
whether from the coffee and cookies or the shock at what
I'd just done, I don't know—and drove down the street to a
Thomasville furniture store, where I repeated my actions—
minus the snacks. This time, I left with an in-store credit
receipt and the same delivery date, but now for the new living
room and dining room furniture.

I drove to the nearest mall, entered the food court, purchased a Chick-fil-A traditional sandwich, waffle potato fries,
and lemonade. After brushing the crumbs from my fingertips,
I walked to one end of the mall and entered Macy's. There,
with my zeroed-out Macy's card, I bought new china, stemware, and flatware. For kicks, I threw in new Waterford table
linens and Lenox napkin ring holders.

After walking my new purchases to the car, I returned
inside, this time walking in the opposite direction of Macy's,
straight to Dillard's, where I chose a Ralph Lauren bedding
collection, sheets included. The colors were perfect for the
wood tone of the new bedroom furniture. I had a fifty-dollar
balance on my card. I paid it off in customer service, then ran
the balance back up by several hundred dollars.

On the way home, with three hours left to shop before

the kids had to be picked up from their various after-school activities, I stopped at Bed Bath & Beyond for new towels, using my personal credit card and the 20 percent off coupon that had come in the mail the week before and had been stashed in my purse ever since.

That night I placed an ad on craigslist, offering the old furniture for a song. The phone started ringing immediately. I set appointments beginning at ten the next morning.

The following day, I took the kids to school, returned home, and got the house in order for potential buyers. By one o'clock that afternoon, everything was gone, including the everyday china, all the glassware and flatware from the kitchen, and the linens I kept in the dining room china cabinet. At two o'clock I walked through the front door of Dawson's, ready to purchase new draperies with my earnings.

Days later, by the time Andre threw his luggage into the backseat of my car and himself into the front, by the time he'd given me his "I'm back" kiss, I was nearly quivering with excitement and trepidation.

"I've got a surprise for you when we get home," I said, smiling. Hopeful.

I glanced his way. His eyes danced. "Oh?"

I gave him my best "come now" look. "Men," I said. "Not that."

"What then?" In the glow of street lamps I saw him kick off one of his loafers, lean down, and scratch the arch of his foot.

"You'll see."

"But *that* too, right? 'Cause I've missed you."

"That too. 'Cause I've missed you too."

He replaced his shoe, stretched his long legs. "I hate

airplanes. I managed to get the exit row, but it's still never enough room."

"Why don't you just get a first class ticket, Andre? We can afford it, and then you wouldn't be so miserable."

"Nah. I don't want to spend that much money."

I bit my lower lip. "Speaking of spending money," I said, "I guess there's something I should tell you before we get home."

17

Never in the history of our marriage—perhaps in the history of *any* marriage—has there ever been such an argument. At one point it became so verbally volatile, our children went into their bedrooms and shut and locked their doors.

I didn't blame them. I was nearly there myself.

We said all the usual things couples say in such situations.

"How could you do something like this without asking me?"

"I didn't know I was your child. I thought I was your wife." Which sounded so childish.

"I want you to take it all back. Every last bit of it."

"I will not."

"How do you expect to pay for all this?"

And then I said the most idiotic thing of all: "I'll get a job."

To which he laughed. Not happily.

A shame I'd bought those new linens; Andre slept in the guest room that night while I slept in our bed, alone.

We hardly spoke for days on end. Our children tiptoed around us. After a week I announced that I had secured a job at a local froufrou store, would work four hours a day, five days a week, and would pay the debt off myself.

"That's it?" he said. At the end of a long day, he stood in front of his chest of drawers, pulling a necktie from the collar of his shirt.

I leaned against the door frame of the nearby master bath. Threw up my hands. They landed against my sides. "What more do you want, Andre?"

"I want you to admit you were wrong in what you did. Heather, I would never dream of spending that kind of money without talking to you."

He was right, of course. Logical, normal wives just didn't do this kind of thing. I prickled, but so wanting the tension in our home to come to an end, I said, "I was wrong, Andre. I don't know what got into me."

He blinked slowly, smiled ever so slightly. "Come here," he said. I went into his arms; he breathed in deeply. "Thank you for that." He kissed my hair. "I've missed you."

"You too," I said.

"Promise me you won't do anything like that again."

I shook my head. Whether I meant I wouldn't promise or I wouldn't do anything like that again, I don't know. And I'm not sure how he interpreted it.

"And you won't allow this new job to interfere with your work as a wife and a mother. I haven't worked this hard this long so you would have to go out and get a job. We both agreed from the start you'd be at home with the kids."

"Yes, but I've caused this," I said, leaning back. "It'll work, you'll see. I'll keep up with what I do here, and I'll work for Margie McCombs four hours a day. I can do it, Andre. I can."

"Because," he said as though I'd said nothing, "what you always said was that you wanted to be the quintessential homemaker. A wife and a mother."

"I know. And I love my role in life, Andre. I do. I can't imagine it being any other way, but I know I can do this."

But apparently I couldn't. I lasted exactly five days at my new job. The first day one of the twins got sick at school, and after only an hour on the job, I had to leave to get her. The second day, the other twin got sick, and after two and a half hours on the job, I clocked out for the day and headed for the school. The third day, our twelve-year-old son Lenny called informing me I'd not returned his all-important paper for American History class.

"What do you mean, I haven't returned it?" I whispered into my cell phone, the very one I wasn't supposed to be using during work hours.

"Remember two nights ago? You asked me to bring it to you so you could read over it? You never gave it back."

I could see it. Oh yes I could. Sitting right there on my desk. Heavily researched. Neatly typed. Well-crafted sentences and an obvious A for my son. He was right; I had not returned it.

"Can't it wait until after I get off work?"

"Mom," he said. I could see his lips forming the words over clear braces railroaded across his teeth.

"Lenny, I can't leave my job."

"You left yesterday and the day before for Toni and Tyler. Besides, Mom, my class is next period, and the majority of my grade for the semester rides on that paper."

I swallowed. "I'll be there in less than an hour. But you should have remembered to get it back from me."

I could all but hear the eyes rolling.

"See you in a bit."

Two days earlier, when I'd told Margie about Toni being sick, she said, "Oh, dear. I hope she gets to feeling better."

Yesterday, when Tyler came down with the same twenty-four-hour bug, she said, "I understand." But she sighed deeply.

This time I got the exhale but not the words of sympathy or understanding.

"I'll be back, and I'll still work four hours today."

Without looking at me she said, "I already have someone else coming in at two, Heather." Then she locked her eyes with mine. "Just go."

I never really liked Margie anyway; this just added to the long list of reasons why. No consideration outside the needs of her store with cute but overpriced items.

Day four went off without a hitch. But day five dawned with my sudden realization that *this* was the day of my six-month dental cleaning. Canceling without a twenty-four-hour notice meant having to pay a rescheduling fee, which was more than I would actually make working.

Margie fired me over the phone, stating this clearly wasn't working out for either of us. She encouraged me to come by and get my paycheck the following Friday.

And so there I sat, at my desk, crying out to God with a pile of invoices and bills clasped in my hands, wondering how I would ever pay them. And then it hit me. I knew exactly what I needed to do, who I needed to call.

Dad.

———

I called Dad while he was at work, leaving a message on his cell phone. "No biggie," I lied. "I just needed to talk to you about something."

Dad called back about two hours later. "Hey, kiddo. What can I do for you?"

I cleared my throat. "Dad?" I said, forcing my voice to sound as much like a helpless little girl as I could. "Do you have some time when I can come by and talk with you about something?"

"What's wrong, little girl?"

I closed my eyes in blessed relief. "Can we just get together and talk?"

A stretch of silence filled the distance between us. "This doesn't have anything to do with Anise, does it?"

One thing about me: I'm loyal to my convictions. In the near seven years since their marriage, I had not relented in my negative feelings about their . . . marriage. "No, Dad. It's not about Anise. It's about me."

"You okay?"

No. "Well, yes and no. That's what I need to talk to you about."

Dad said I could meet him at his house that evening, but I begged away from it. I didn't say it out loud, but Anise would be there and I really didn't want to admit my financial failures in front of her. "Is it possible for us to grab lunch tomorrow? I can meet you anywhere you say. I'll even buy." I threw my head back at the last statement. *What in the world am I saying?*

"Don't be silly," Dad said. "Okay. Let's meet around noon at Anthony's Pizzeria for a slice of pizza."

"Sounds wonderful, Dad. I'll see you tomorrow at noon."

The following day, over a plastic red-and-white-checkered tablecloth and two slices of pizza, Dad listened while I regurgitated my "sin of spend" (as Tyler called it). I watched a look of disappointment cross his face. My heart sank. As angry as I could get with him about some of the choices he'd made since Mom died, I still hated the thought that I'd let him down, even a little, with my personal decisions. This was the man who'd wanted so much for me to go to college, finish college, have a career. When I'd chosen marriage over knowledge, it was Mom who soothed his ruffled feathers. And, while I know he's long been one of Andre's biggest fans, and he absolutely adores my children, and he sees me as a good mother, this was still way over the top.

"Dad?" I said when I'd finished my saga and he hadn't responded.

"Heather . . ." he began but didn't finish.

I leaned forward, clutched my hands together as though I were offering up a prayer to God. "I need your help, Dad."

Expressionless eyes met mine. "Go on."

"I need a job. Something I can do without getting fired because my children get sick." I gave him my best "please, please, please" look. "Is there *anything* in your office I can help with? Filing? Answering phones? Billing?" I squeezed my hands together. "I'm not too proud to come in at night and scrub toilets."

At that, Dad laughed.

"I'd have to talk to Jayme-Leigh."

"Ugh."

"Or, you could try your luck somewhere else."

"Okay. Fine."

"I'm sure we could use some help somewhere. I'll ask BJ. She's the office manager; she'll have a better idea than your sister or I will, but I'll still need to discuss it with her."

"BJ? That cute little thing is your office manager? What happened to Edwina?"

"Edwina retired."

"Retired?"

Dad stretched. "Yeah. I hear it's something you can do at sixty-two."

The next day, Dad called to tell me that he had discussed the matter with both Jayme-Leigh and Anise. I wanted to absolutely blow at the thought of his telling his wife, but thought better of such a notion. Then he told me Anise insisted they loan me the money I had indebted myself to everyone and his brother with and that I could work it off both at the medical office and at her floral shop. Anise, he said, thought I probably had great decorating talent.

I was just certain that wasn't a compliment but a slap in the face, seeing as my debt was décor-related.

I swallowed. Hard. "That's very kind of her," I said. "When do I start?"

When I had worked—and worked *hard*—for six months, when I had survived the summer with active kids, two part-time jobs, and a husband who continued to work long hours and was still holding a grudge, Dad called me into his office at the end of a Tuesday shift. I was tired and needed to get home to cook dinner but wasn't about to say no to my father.

I tapped on his closed office door, waited for the "come on in," and then entered. Dad was sitting in one of the two burgundy leather wingback chairs that faced his desk. The ankle of one leg rested on the knee of the other. He had a large book—one of those medical ones he and Jayme-Leigh are forever burrowing their noses into—opened wide in his lap.

He looked over his shoulder. "Hey, kiddo."

"Hey, Dad. You wanted to see me?"

He closed the book and shifted toward the other chair. "Come sit."

I did.

"I'll get right to the point. You've done a great job around here, and Anise says you've been exceptional at the shop."

I groaned inwardly.

"I know you are still not Anise's best friend and you may never be, but she's insisting that I offer you a weekend at the beach house."

Oh she did, did she? "In Cedar Key?"

The skin around Dad's eyes crinkled. "Do I own another one?"

I smiled. A weekend in Cedar Key . . . I could live with that. "Do I have to take anyone else?"

"Not if you don't want to. We weren't sure if you'd want to take the girls or if you wanted just you and Andre to steal away for a while."

I allowed my eyes to roam over the book titles on his bookshelf.

"You and Andre doing all right now?" he asked.

My eyes jerked back to his. "Yeah. I'd say so. After my 'sin of spend' he spent the first week sleeping in the guest bedroom but moved back into ours once I got a job. Things more or less got back to normal once I started working for you."

"And Anise."

"Yes." I crossed one leg over the other, pumped my foot up and down, back and forth. Cleared my throat to steer Dad back to the discussion about Cedar Key. "So, how's this weekend sound for my mini-vacation?"

"The house is all yours."

I threw my head against the leather and sighed. "Cedar Key! Here I come!"

18

"Guess where I'm heading?" I cheered into my cell phone.

"Where?"

I had left a voice message for Kimberly earlier, knowing she wouldn't get it until she had a break between classes. I also knew she'd not set foot in Cedar Key since Mom had died. From the sound of her voice, she could use a vacation as much as I.

"I'll give you a hint. My car is pointed toward the west and I'm on a long stretch of road between the Gulf of Mexico and Otter Creek."

"Oh. You're going to Cedar Key?"

I frowned. "Dad treated me to the weekend at the house. A whole weekend, Kimberly-Boo. No kids. No Andre. No working for Dad and Jayme-Leigh and, thank you, Lord, no working for Anise." I grinned. "Yippee!"

Momentary silence was followed by, "So what will you do with yourself, all by yourself?"

"Nothing. Or everything. You know how much I love the little artsy shops there. I'm going to buy myself a pair of earrings. And I'm going to sit on Dock Street in the evenings."

"Isn't it going to be awfully hot this weekend for sitting on Dock Street? Even at night?"

"I don't care, Kim. I'm going to be *freeeee*."

"Okay then."

"Join me!"

"What?"

I slowed my car for the truck pulling an airboat ahead of me. "Join me. Come on, Kim. I know you haven't wanted to come since Mom died, but you have to put that behind you. We can make new memories here. I bet Mr. Granger will take us out on a sunset tour in his boat."

"That's okay, Heather. I've got some things I need to do around the house this weekend."

"What? Name one thing. I dare you."

I heard my sister's long sigh. "Heather?"

"Are you crying?"

She breathed in. Out. "No. I'm fine."

"You don't sound fine."

"Look, Heather. I only have another two minutes before the children return from break. I can't get into this right now."

"Into what?"

"I can't—"

"Into what?"

"Ugh. All right. I think . . ."

I heard the deep intake of breath. Another exhale.

"What? What do you think?"

"I think Charlie is having an affair," she said so quickly I almost missed the meaning.

"What!"

178

"I have to go. Call you later. Have fun. If you do see Mr. Granger, give him my best."

With that, the call disconnected.

During the years of our youth, Kimberly and Mr. Granger's son, Steven, had something of a "thing" going. Summer romance, it's called. When she was sixteen and he was seventeen, it had heated up to the near-boiling point, though I know Kim managed to hold on to her virtue. When Steven had gone to college that fall, he'd met someone else, "got pregnant," got married, and—sometime later, from what we heard—got divorced. His wife had left him with their child—a daughter—and he'd spent the years since as a single father.

In all my years coming to Cedar Key—whether with Dad and Mom or with Andre and the kids—I'd only seen Steven once. He'd been standing at his dad's tour boat dock, talking to his father. A too-thin strawberry blonde child of about eight or nine skipped around him, waving her arms about like one of the pelicans and seagulls swarming nearby. I figured her to be his daughter, but I didn't approach to ask. The last thing I needed on my conscience was talking to Steven and meeting his child. The moment I saw my sister again, I knew, it would spill out of me and she'd be forlorn. Again. Even with Charlie and the boys, the memory of Steven had stayed bitterly close to the edge of her heart.

Charlie. Could he really be having an affair? No . . . Charlie adored Kim. Doted on his sons. He was a good husband. The best father. Kimberly was, no doubt, being overly sensitive about something. Hormonal. Yeah, that was it. She was hormonal.

Maybe even pregnant again. Okay, yeah, that was probably it. If Mom were still here, Mom would know . . .

I turned off Highway 24 and onto Boogie Ridge, down the road winding between thick live oaks and bushy oleander showcasing white and pink blossoms. Boogie Ridge is actually 154th Street, with a road that loops at the end, affording the houses along the way views into the bayou, spectacular both in the morning and the evening. I slowed my car over the bumps of what had gone from asphalt to sand, tires crunching over broken oyster shells.

Dad's next-door neighbor, an elderly woman named Patsy, stood to the left side of her house, hands splayed on her narrow hips, looking out over the marshland. She wore a pair of khaki slacks, a short-sleeved blouse, and a red oversized hat, the floppy brim of which ruffled in the slight breeze. Hearing my car, she turned, waved as though we were old friends, and started toward me.

The thought of entertaining the woman, kind as she was, didn't appeal to me. My brain scrambled for what I could say that would allow me to make a hasty retreat inside.

Opening the door, I had the perfect response. "Hello, Patsy. Awful hot, isn't it?"

"Honey," she said, moving toward me, "it's a scorcher, and it's not even lunchtime yet."

I decided my best plan of action was to walk to her, guide her homeward, and *then* I could follow through with my own mini-vacation plans. "How have you been, Miss Patsy?"

eck Out Receipt

inook - Hodgeville Branch Library
6) 677-2223
p://www.chinooklibrary.ca

day, November 15, 2019 4:53:35 PM
326

m: 33292900011010
e: Slow moon rising : a Cedar Key novel
terial: Book
e: 06/12/2019

al items: 1

u just saved $17.99 by using your library. You have
ved $115.38 so far this year by using your library!

ank you! If you would like to update your library
tification to telephone, email or text message, please
ntact your local library.

"I'm good for an old girl," she answered. "You're which one, now?"

"Heather," I said, placing my hand against my chest. "Ross's daughter."

"Not the doctor one."

"No, ma'am," I said, turning her back toward her own front door, which was really to the side of the house. "What were you looking at out here?"

"Just watching the world turn." She chuckled. "When you get to be my age, you can do that, you know."

"Now, Miss Patsy. I've only met you a couple of times, but I've never thought of you as old."

She cackled. "Well, I've still got enough get-up-and-go to get up and go and I'm old enough to enjoy the days and to go to bed when I'm good and ready." She chuckled again. "Which is usually pretty early, but you never know. Some nights I don't go to bed until ten o'clock."

I had to laugh. Patsy—whose last name I couldn't recall—was nothing if not cute. "How long have you been here now, Miss Patsy?" We'd reached the stairs leading to the door. She rested a hand upon the weathered wood railing.

"Just two years. Used to come here with Gilbert—my husband—for vacations. Brought the kids here in the summertime. Lost two of my babies here in a boating accident. Did you know that?"

I blinked. I'd had no idea. What sorrows must possess a person in the sunset years of life . . . Would mine be similar? "Two? At the same time?"

She nodded. "You'd think I'd never want to return, wouldn't you, with such a tragedy having occurred here." She patted the wood beneath her hand. "'When sorrow comes under the power of divine grace, it works out a manifold ministry.'" She blinked slowly. "That's from one of my devotional books. Sweet Heather, I'm here to tell you that, nearing the end of my life, the good memories far outweigh the bad. And there were plenty of bad." She smiled at me. "Come inside and have a bite of lunch with me. Keep a lonely widow company?" She winked.

This wasn't what I'd had in mind when I pictured my time in Cedar Key. "Uh, Miss Patsy, I really need to unpack and . . ."

"Well, you go do that. And then you march right back over here. Just come on up these steps and walk on in. I'll make us some sandwiches—I just made some of my homemade chicken salad—and we'll eat chips and drink iced tea. I won't take no for an answer." She walked up three of the steps. "Then you can go on and do whatever you came here to do." After several steps more she looked out over her lawn, called, "Come on, Oreo, let's go inside before you have a heatstroke."

A black-and-white cat came bounding toward me. I stepped back, and the cat shot past and up to its owner.

"I'll, uh—I'll be back in about a half an hour, I guess," I said, completely clueless as to how this woman had talked me into eating lunch with her.

"I'll be right here," she declared. She walked through her door and closed it gently behind her.

———

After lunch, I left Patsy's and returned to Dad's, somewhat shaken after hearing Patsy's story. I marveled at the faith she lived by and wondered if my own could stand up to the kinds of tests she'd endured. I wasn't sure if it had managed to survive the few bumps and bruises life had already left me with.

Once I got back to Dad's, I did what Patsy said she was about to do; I curled up on the sofa for a nap. But, sleep didn't come easy. I wrestled with myself. My heart. My life.

Everything had always come easily for me. I was the "pretty one," everyone said. Kimberly, the oldest. Jayme-Leigh, the smartest. And, when Ami came along, she was known as "the talented one."

But I was pretty and I knew how to use my looks to get my way in life. Mom once said if I went to a picnic without my basket, I'd manage somehow to get the best from everyone else's. High school was one fabulous party after the other. The homecoming queen's crown rested on my head, and I won a sweet number of local beauty pageants. Not that they meant anything, really, other than a way to connect with Mom.

I didn't want to go to college, but I enrolled anyway. It made Dad happy for a season, but I knew it couldn't last. As much fun as high school had been, I couldn't fake or pretty my way to a diploma. When I met Andre right away my freshman year, I knew I'd come face-to-face with my "way out." We fell in love and we fell hard, but more than anything, he was my ticket away from disappointing Dad. Dad didn't have to tell his colleagues I'd become a dropout; rather he could boast his role as the father of the bride.

Even with my misstep with the money spending, I'd managed to get myself out of hot water and into lukewarm without too much of a sweat. Not really.

Two hours later, I tumbled off the sofa, made myself a cup of coffee, thumbed through a *Coastal Living* magazine, then grabbed my car keys and my purse and went out to my car.

Minutes later, I was rolling into the Cedar Key city limits and to the 2nd Street stop sign. I turned left, keeping my eyes alert for an empty parking spot between the golf carts parallel parked with the occasional car or truck. I settled for turning in on C Street and parking next to the historic Lutterloh Store.

Lutterloh's, according to what I remembered, had been established in the late 1800s, back when sleepy Cedar Key had bustled. Getting out of my car, I stared at the old double doors and the time-stamped screens over them. The wide boards of the door frame had been painted rusty red, a perfect offsetting to the peeling white paint of the long-ago abandoned building and the square board columns straining to hold the second floor balcony aboveground.

I locked the car door, though I honestly don't know why. If ever anything or anyone was safe, it was here in Cedar Key. I scooted up to 2nd, onto the only sidewalk I'd ever stepped upon that I could say "had character," and into a local artist's shop where, if nothing else, I escaped the heat. I also bought a pair of handmade earrings but stopped short of a necklace outside my price range.

Later, I drove to Dock Street, parking across from the marina. Even though only two blocks from where I'd been earlier, it was much too far away to walk in the late summer heat. Knowing this place as well as I did, I knew warm weather would remain until sometime around Thanksgiving.

I walked the length of the street, darting in and out of shops, made several purchases (Cedar Key tees for Andre and Len, two adorable rope-chain bracelets with conch and starfish charms for Toni and Tyler, but nothing else whatsoever for myself). Upon exiting one of the shops near the fishing pier, I caught a whiff of shrimp frying somewhere close by. Coconuts Sports Bar was directly in front of me. Overhead, the Rusty Rim beckoned me forward; it had been a while, but memory told me the best coconut shrimp ever was a flight of stairs away.

I licked my lips and walked straight into Coconuts, turning left toward the stairs leading to the restaurant. I was nearly giddy with expectation as I stepped through the wooden door and into a room where small tables and chairs lined a wall of windows overlooking the Gulf of Mexico. And, beyond, Atsena Otie, one of the barrier islands. The original Cedar Key.

The room was empty save one person sitting alone—a woman with her back to me, dark hair flowing past her shoulders. From where I stood I could see she was wearing large sunglasses. Her slender fingers played with the base of a glass holding something appearing to be cold and tropical. Alcoholic.

A server standing behind the bar told me to "have a seat wherever."

I thought to sit as far away from the one and only other patron, but as I did, she turned toward me, hooked her index finger into the nose bridge of the sunglasses, and pulled them to the tip of her nose.

Her dark, red-rimmed eyes blinked in my direction. "Heather?"

I gasped. It had been a long time. Such a long time. "Rosa," I breathed out her name. "My goodness."

The server came around the bar, carrying utensils wrapped tightly in a paper napkin. "You want to sit with Rosa?" she asked.

I opened my mouth to speak but was unsure of my answer. I didn't really want to be alone, but perhaps Rosa did. She was obviously upset about something; this moment might not have been the best for a reunion.

But Rosa's hand swept toward the chair on the opposite side of the table. "Please. Join me."

"Okay," I said.

Rosa looked at the server. "Bring me another one of these," she said, tapping the rim of the glass. "And one for my old and dear friend Heather."

I'd never had a sip of alcohol in my life. Growing up, I had known Mom and Dad drank occasionally. Mom more than Dad. Much more. It was our family secret, Mom drinking as much as she did. Not that she was an alcoholic or anything close to it. She just liked her cocktails at night. And at parties. "I . . . uh . . . ."

"Do you want that on the rocks or frozen?" the server—DJ, her name tag read—asked me.

"Um . . ." Oh, why not, I reasoned. My whole life I'd managed to keep alcoholic beverages from my lips, but I was in Cedar Key, for heaven's sake. This was the one place Mom really let her hair down. Why shouldn't I? Why *couldn't* I? After all, I'd worked hard these past months, righting my awful wrong. What would this one hurt? "On the rocks," I answered.

"Salt?"

"Uh . . . sure."

DJ walked away. I looked at Rosa. "Hey," I drawled out. "Are you okay?"

She shook her head. "I got a call today. My father passed away."

"Your dad? I didn't even know you knew him."

She nodded. "I looked for him not too long ago. Found him in Colorado." She gave me a tear-filled smile. "I have half siblings too."

"You do?"

DJ returned with our drinks. "Let me know when you're ready to order," she said, pulling the menu from behind the napkin holder and placing it before me.

"Thank you," I said. "Just go ahead and put in an order for a coconut shrimp basket." I looked at Rosa, the glasses before her. The empty space on the table before that. "Do you want anything to eat?"

She shook her head no.

I didn't know much about drinking, but what I did know was that it wasn't best done on an empty stomach. I returned my attention to DJ. "Make that two baskets."

I studied the glass in front of me for a moment. The salt around the rim looked like glitter in the sunlight. I took a sip. Felt the tart play on my tongue and the cold slip down my throat. I looked at Rosa. "I'm so sorry," I said. "I know what it's like, losing a parent."

Rosa pushed her half-consumed drink away and toyed with the new one. "I don't know why I'm crying, chica. I didn't really know him."

"Because he was your father, Rosa. And fathers are special."

"Your father, yes. My father . . . not so much."

I took another swallow of the drink, appreciating the saltiness mixed with the sweet. "This is good," I said finally.

Rosa shrugged. "I'm not much of a drinker. Just . . . sometimes it takes away the sting of life, you know?"

"Yeah," I said. "I know."

But I didn't. With all the heartaches of my life, turning to alcohol to numb the pain had never been my way of doing things. I pouted. I cried. I stomped my feet like a three-year-old. Then, if all that failed, I turned on the charms Mother Nature and Mother Joan had given me. In the end, it was always being alluring that got me through.

But now, truth was, I'd just come face-to-face with the first thing I couldn't control with tears or feet-stomping or "being pretty."

I just didn't know it yet.

19

Kimberly
March 2008

Central Florida springs bring many things. The Easter season. The start of warmer weather. Budding flowers. Hordes of tourists to the theme parks. A renewed mass exodus of swimsuit-clad beachcombers heading east to such places as Ormond by the Sea, Cocoa Beach, and Daytona. But my family—my childhood family—used to take off for Cedar Key with renewed vigor during the springtime. Now, my husband, sons, and I spend our afternoons and Saturdays on soccer fields.

Charlie, my husband, doesn't put in the time I do. He used to. There wasn't a practice or a game he'd miss. Then, about a year ago, all we heard about was how busy he was at work. How much extra time he needed to spend at his family's landscape nursery.

Any comment from me was met with a defiant, "You want nice things, don't you? You want that our sons are able to stay in private school? That we can afford this oversized magazine cover house we live in?"

It always came back to me. To how I failed as a wife simply because I wanted my husband with us more than somewhere else.

But this evening, with its thick warm air and the occasional no-see-ums swarming up from the overgrown grass beneath the bleachers, Charlie had promised to be here.

I sat third row from the top, where I could watch for his car when it finally came in. I'd be able to see him slide out from behind the driver's seat, all six-foot-three of him. I'd see the familiar adjusting of his pants' waistband over narrow hips, the straightening of his broad shoulders. With the sun edging closer to the horizon, I'd witness its light skip across the premature silver of his hair and the casting of bronze over his skin.

Mad as I could get at the man, the very thought of his arrival motivated me to try to be a better wife. To give more of what he needed and, in turn, he'd then *want* to spend more time with me. With the boys.

I'd loved two men in my life, other than my father. What I mean to say is, I've been in love only twice in my life. I often wonder if the first time could even be considered love. I was sixteen at the time and . . . oh, who am I kidding? Puppy love, some would call it, but I was as crazy about Steven Granger as any sixteen-year-old had the ability to be. And, I'd thought, he was just as nuts about me.

We were a year apart in age; Steven was seventeen to my sixteen. His father owned a tour boat company in Cedar Key, and we—Steven and I—had practically grown up together. For years he was my "older brother" of sorts. Then, it happened. I cannot fully recall how or when, but one day I saw him . . . quite differently. With the tick of time, he went from *some*one to *the* one.

As that summer rolled in, I'd done everything I knew how to make myself irresistible to him. The right bathing suit. The right haircut. Poring over fashion magazines for just the right "look." And, my efforts had not been in vain. Steven had nearly stumbled over himself where I was concerned. We became "the item" that summer. I was hopelessly in love, and I thought he was too. But I was wrong.

The following year he went away to college, met a fellow student, got her pregnant, and got married. I'd never been so devastated about anything in my life. It was a heartbreak I thought I could never recover from.

And then in my junior year of college . . . I met Charlie.

We were a team, he and I. We talked and talked and talked . . . about everything. No emotion, no memory, nothing was hidden from the other. And, just when I thought any higher level of happiness could not be achieved, he proposed by putting a one-karat diamond ring in one of the hollow eggs of my Easter basket, the one Mom put at the foot of my bed until I was no longer a child in her home.

We married the following Christmas.

Our oldest son, Chase, was born in 1996, and three years later, Cody rounded out our little family.

After a couple of years of apartment living, Charlie and I purchased a Mediterranean-style home in Windermere, Florida, not far from my parents. I will be forever grateful for the close proximity of our homes during the time of my mother's illness and subsequent death.

Only months after Cody's birth.

And Charlie, God love him, was there for me the whole time. I didn't know fully whatever happened to Steven Granger, but I couldn't imagine anyone being as emotionally strong and supportive as Charlie had been. Now, he just seemed distant.

I rested my elbows on my knees and leaned forward, allowing my hands to cup each other. I tilted my engagement ring to the west and watched prisms of color escape it. Then, with Chase's team scoring another goal, I stood and cheered with the rest of the parents, siblings, and friends of the players. Watched my son, so handsome in his uniform, dance about the field and then chest-bump another player. I scanned the sidelines for Cody, who was standing with several other younger siblings, cheering as though he'd been the one to kick the ball.

As I returned to the hard metal bleacher, I turned again to see if Charlie might be pulling into the parking area of the rec department. Sure enough, his silver Acura 2008 MDX bounded in. I smiled. Breathed in, pleased. He was here. A glance at my watch told me he'd made it to see almost the entire last half of the game. Better than none at all.

I turned again to see him do exactly as I'd imagined he would. Slide out. Adjust. Walk proud.

I started to look back to the field when, out of the corner of my eye, I caught sight of Bunni Berno walking between the parked cars, making her way toward my husband. She waved, he waved back, detouring toward her.

Bunni Berno was younger than most of the soccer moms who attended practice and games. Or perhaps she just appeared younger. Everything on her had been sucked out or otherwise enhanced. I often wondered if anything about her was real. Her hair was bleached blonde, her teeth were capped, her skin was the finest golden brown a tanning bed could give, her nails were acrylic, and her body was either plumped up with silicone or as firm as a sixteen-year-old football player's.

I watched her from behind, tight jeans curving around her hips just so. The wide leather belt that made her waist seem only that much tinier. The clinging white cami.

I narrowed my eyes and pulled my sunglasses from my face just in time to watch them come together. To see her fingers splay along his abs to his sides. He seemed to glance up as though to ascertain his surroundings, then look back to her upturned face where he planted a kiss on her lips. It was brief, but it was unmistakable. And when it was over, her hands remained where they'd begun.

On my husband.

It was happening again. A year before I'd suspected his late hours at the office were nothing more than time spent hanging out where he didn't belong. He admitted he'd been with some of his employees from work, just having a beer with the boys. I wanted to believe him. I did. And I had nothing to weigh my suspicions on, but now . . . with this. And with Bunni, no less.

My only hope was none of the other moms were watching.

"I know what I saw."

"You don't know anything, Kim. You're imagining things

just like you did last year." Charlie pulled his belt from the loops of his pants and tossed it on our bed. Kicked off his leather boat shoes.

I pulled the belt from atop the comforter and walked it to Charlie's closet, where I hung it on a hook. I returned to our bedroom, jaw aching from being locked so long, in time to watch my husband pull his polo over his head and throw it to the same place the belt had been. I stooped to pick up the shoes, muttering.

"What?" he said.

I straightened. "Keep your voice down, Charlie Tucker. I do *not* want the boys to hear us arguing."

He jutted his face to inches from mine. "And just how do you think they could do that, Kim? They're downstairs and we're upstairs. There's approximately thirty-five-hundred square feet between us and them."

I snatched the shirt from the bed. "What does that have to do with anything?"

"What did you say? A minute ago? What did your smart mouth say?"

I walked away from him. Put the shoes on the shoe rack in his closet and the shirt into the dirty clothes basket before returning, again, to see him stepping out of his pants. He threw them toward me. I fumbled but recovered.

"Nice," I said.

"May as well. You're going to pick them up anyway, Miss Perfect."

I started to drop the pants to the floor, thought better of it, and instead put them in the same hamper as the shirt. I came back to the bedroom to see that Charlie had pulled his dorm pajama pants out of a dresser drawer and was slinging them over his forearm.

"You know what, Charlie? You are *not* going to make this about me. And, for once, you are not going to bully me into anything. I. Know. What. I. Saw. And with Bunni? *Bunni?* The tart of Windermere?"

Anger flashed across his face; for a moment I felt fearful. I'd not seen Charlie angry too many times in our years together but enough to know I didn't want to be on the wrong end of his fury. "That's real Christian of you, Kimberly. That kind of talk should get you nominated for sainthood."

I shoved my arms together. "Charlie, do not do this. I'm not kidding. I'm sorry, okay? I'm sorry I said that. But everyone knows about Bunni. Everyone knows what kind of person she is."

"Maybe you don't know *everything*. Ever stop to think of that?"

I sat on the corner of the bed, crossed my legs. "All right then, Mr. Know-it-all. I'm all ears. Tell me what I don't know."

Charlie walked away from me, toward our bathroom. "I'm going to take a shower. Get the boys to bed, will you? I'm in no mood for any of this right now."

An hour later I returned to the dark bedroom I shared with my husband. The light spilling in from the hall revealed a lump under the covers. Hopefully, Charlie was as much asleep as our boys; I wanted no more than to undress, get into my nightgown, and ease into my side of the king-size bed. Back turned to Charlie, I'd fight for every second of sleep I'd get.

I left the door open so I could see without switching on a lamp. I went into my closet, the twin walk-in of Charlie's, undressed, slipped my gown over my body, and then made a silent entry into the bathroom to wash my face, brush my teeth, and apply the natural night cream Anise insisted I try. So far, I was impressed.

I ran a large-toothed comb through the straight blonde hair that fell past my shoulders as it had since I was a teenager. In fact, I surmised while looking at my mirrored reflection, little about me had changed since college. In high school I'd worn my hair longer, but in college I'd had it cut by several inches. Even having had two children, my body had changed little. Maybe five extra pounds, but I needed every one of them. I'd always been slender. Tall and not overly curvaceous.

I turned to the side, keeping my eyes fixed on my body. I jutted my chest out, pulled the nightgown tight with my fists at my sides. My shoulders slumped. There were thirteen-year-old girls out there with more than I had to offer. No wonder Charlie had succumbed to Bunni Berno with her 38Ds.

I pushed my backside out. Nothing curvy there either. Not even close. I turned to face the mirror, extended my arms wide. I wore a baby pink cotton gown with little girl lace across the bodice. I wondered what Bunni wore to bed at night. Probably some little number, some little lacy teddy, if she wore anything at all. Something I could never bring myself to wear, not even in my younger days.

I frowned at my image. I'd had no trouble whatsoever wearing a skimpy bikini when I was sixteen and trying to impress Steven. Why, then, had I become such a . . . a prude in the privacy of my bedroom?

No. I wasn't a prude. I just liked what I liked. And I liked to sleep comfortable. Was there anything wrong with that? I didn't like enhanced body parts. God had made me just the way I was.

I flipped off the bathroom light, walked into the bedroom and over to my side of the bed. As quietly as possible, I pulled the cover back, sat, lay down, and pulled the sheet and comforter back over me in one movement. A full minute must have passed before I realized I was holding my breath.

I exhaled slowly. Closed my eyes. Forced my shoulders and back to relax into the soft tufts of the mattress.

"Hey," Charlie said from the other side of the bed.

I opened my eyes, stared at the ceiling. "Hey," I said back.

"You ready to listen now?"

20

"What is there to say, Charlie?"

Charlie rolled over to face me. With a single movement his arm reached across the distance between us, caught my waist, and pulled me to him as though I were a rag doll.

"Charlie . . ."

"Listen," he whispered in my ear.

His voice told me his teeth were gritted together. He was as determined to speak as he was that I would hear.

I pushed against him to put distance between us but didn't return to my side of the bed. "I'm listening."

"You're going to feel foolish."

I turned my eyes toward him. "Am I?"

"Do you know what Bunni does for a living?"

"Yes."

"Tell me."

He moved closer. Propped his elbow on the mattress, his head in his hand. I could smell soap and cologne. Toothpaste and mouthwash.

"She works in a bar. As a bartender." I heard the holier-than-thou tone in my voice and inwardly cringed.

"That's right. Two kids. An ex-husband who plays 'hit and miss' with his child support payments. She's busting her behind to keep her head above water six nights a week while her mother watches her sons. In fact, she was leaving the game, leaving the joy of watching her son play, so she could get to work on time."

I raised myself onto my elbows. "Charlie, I appreciate all that, but it doesn't account for her hands on your body and your lips on her mouth."

His right hand crept toward me; he laid it flat against my stomach. "You aren't listening, Boo. You're talking."

"I am too listening."

"She came to see me a couple of days ago."

"Where?"

"At work."

"What?"

"She came to ask me for a job."

"A job?" I sat up fully. Charlie's hand was left resting on my thighs.

"Mmmhmm." He looked up at me. "She needs the extra work. The economy being what it is, her tips are down. She's willing to work day and night. I told her I'd have to talk to Dad first, which I did, and then I called her earlier today and offered her a job. That's it. That's why she . . . she kissed me. It was just a show of appreciation."

I took a minute to think it through. The way she'd approached him. How she'd turned her face up to his. Put her hands on him as though she were comfortable with the intimacy of it. "Charlie," I said slowly, "she shouldn't be touching you the way she did. I'm *not* comfortable with that.

Surely you can understand . . . you wouldn't want another man touching *me* like that."

His finger drew lazy circles on my leg. Tickling. Enticing me to see this from his perspective. "I know. And you're right about not wanting another man to touch you. Just so you know, I'm not comfortable with what Bunni did either. I didn't really want to . . . to kiss her. She walked up, touched me the way she did, and said, 'I'm so thrilled I could kiss you.' I know I should have stepped back. I should have said something to discourage her. She just caught me off guard is all."

"Charlie . . ."

"I love you, Boo. You know that. And I'm sorry for blowing up at you earlier. I'd had a pretty bad day—one of my best guys quit on me, just up and quit. Dad was being difficult—and that just kind of topped it all off. All I wanted was to come to the game, sit next to my wife, watch my son play, and then take in dinner somewhere with my family. I'm sorry."

I slid downward until my body was snuggled up against his, drawing my nightgown into a bunch around my hips. As he wrapped his arms around me, I kissed his jaw. "I really, *really* don't like the idea of her working for you." I nibbled at his ear. "But I do feel silly, and I appreciate your being thoughtful enough to give her a job."

"You're killing me here."

"Good," I teased.

"If it's any consolation, she's working on one of the landscape teams. I'll hardly see her." His embrace grew more intense.

"You're a good man, Charlie Brown," I whispered. "Now

why don't you go over there and close our bedroom door like a good boy."

I was able to live in the fantasy of my hope for another month. Weeks of things being just fine. And when I didn't see Bunni at practice or at the games, I refused to allow myself to even think about the fact that she was working—somewhere— for my husband.

For him.

Not *with* him.

And then Heather called. Said she needed to see me. That we needed to talk.

"This isn't about Anise, is it? Because, Heather, I'm really tired of the way you treat her. Especially after she gave you a job last year so you could get yourself out of hot water."

"Ugh. No. This isn't about Anise."

I sat cross-legged on my bed. It was early on a Saturday morning. The boys were still asleep, a load of clothes was going in the washer, and Charlie had gone to work. An extra job he'd hoped to get one of his brothers—all the Tucker boys worked for their parents' landscape and design firm—to take but had been unsuccessful.

I smiled, remembering our earlier conversation. He'd said, "Then again, it's an extra paycheck in our account. What's say we take the extra money and take the boys on a Disney cruise?"

I'd inhaled so fast I'd nearly swallowed my tongue.

"Yes!"

Even now, listening to my sister, it was at the forefront of my mind. A four-night cruise with "my boys."

"So, what do you say? Meet me for brunch?"

"Ah . . . no. I can't. Charlie is at work and the boys are in bed."

"Then I'll come over."

I glanced around the bedroom. My eyes rested on one of the 16-by-20 black and whites of Chase and Cody my mother had taken not too long after Cody's birth and shortly before her death. "Well, sure. I guess. I can make coffee."

"That's fine."

I went downstairs, prepared the coffee, then went to the front of the house to wait for Heather's car to come into the driveway. When it did, I opened the door and watched her walk toward the house, sundress swishing around her. I ushered her into the kitchen and poured us two mugs of steaming coffee.

Heather looked resplendent sitting at the breakfast nook table with the sun spilling through the bay windows. Her hair has always been more white than blonde. Bombshells from the forties and fifties would have given their next MGM paycheck to have had hair like hers.

Not that she appreciated it. My hair is more dirty blonde than blonde. Somewhere between her twelfth and thirteenth year, Jayme-Leigh's turned to copper and Ami's had always been light brown. But Heather's . . . she was born a towhead and, from the looks of it, she'd die a towhead. A not-to-be-tamed, curly-headed towhead.

I joined her with the cream and sugar and two spoons.

She prepared her coffee. I did the same. She took a sip, swallowed hard, and then ran her right index finger around the rim of the mug.

"So what's going on, Heather?"

She wrapped her fingers around the mug, ran them over the top, and then back to the sides. "I'm just going to say this."

For a brief moment, I thought I could smell alcohol on her breath. It seemed to me I'd been able to do that more and more lately. Then again, it could have been some strong mouthwash. "Seems serious. Is it something with Andre?"

"No. Not Andre."

"The kids?"

"No."

I waited. When she said nothing, I added, "Dad?"

"No." She took a deep breath. "Charlie is having an affair with Bunni Berno." The eight words were spoken as one.

I started to laugh. "No, he's not."

She reached across the table, placed her hand on my arm. Locked her eyes with mine. "Yes. He is. And I'm furious with myself. I should have listened to you when you tried to tell me. I should have paid more attention to your needs rather than my own. I should have—"

"No, Heather! Listen. He wasn't having an affair then either. I was mistaken. He just went to hang out with some of the boys after work. He explained it to me."

"Kim, no. I swear to you, I'm telling you the truth."

I slammed my hands against the table. "It's not true!"

"I'm awful to come and tell you this, but I'd be even more awful if I didn't. You're my sister. I love you. But Charlie . . . Charlie is making a fool of you. Of this marriage."

I balled my hands into fists. Shook them at her. "*How* do you know this?"

She closed her eyes, opened them. Pushed her mug of nearly

untouched coffee away. "Bunni is a friend of a friend. Well, sort of a friend. Someone I know. And she's talking."

"Bunni or the . . . friend?"

"Bunni. To the woman I know. The woman I know doesn't know you and I are sisters and she . . . she thinks this is pretty . . . well, wonderful that *her* friend got such a catch."

My insides quaked. I felt cold on the inside, but my skin broke out in a sweat. Charlie. With Bunni. He'd lied . . . lied a month ago. Had he lied last year as well?

"What . . . what else do you know?" I ran my fingers through my hair, rested my forehead against the pad of the palm.

"Boo, I'm sorry."

I jerked my head up. Tears spilled down my cheeks. "What. Else. Do you know?"

"He's with her now. My friend—you don't know her—"

"You've said that."

"Oh. Well, she told me they've been hanging out after work. And they've been planning this . . . um . . . day. To-gether. For a while."

"Did she say where they were going to be?"

"The Peabody."

"On I Drive?"

She squirmed. "I'm not sure there's another one."

I left the table, rummaged around in the pantry for the Yellow Pages I never used anymore but could never bring myself to throw away, brought it back to the table, and dropped it on the glass top. I jerked it open, flipped the thin, mustard-colored pages until I found the number for the Peabody.

"What are you going to do?" Heather asked.

"I'm going to call."

She stood. Put her hand on mine. "Kim, wait. Think this through."

I brought my eyes to hers. "You're right. That's too easy, and it probably wouldn't work."

I left the room, ran up the stairs—careful to walk quietly past the boys' bedrooms—and into mine, where I'd left my cell phone lying on the bed. Heather was right behind me. "What are you going to do?" Heather asked again, keeping her voice quiet.

"Close the door."

She did. "What are you going to do?" She was beginning to sound like a parrot.

"I'm calling him from my cell phone."

"Where? At the hotel?"

"No, on *his* cell phone."

Heather sat on the bed while I stood next to my side. I dialed the familiar number, waited through four . . . five . . . six rings.

"You don't really think he's going to answer, do you?" she asked.

But he did. Before the seventh ring. "Hey, babe."

He sounded breathless. But that could have been my imagination. "Hey," I said back. I took in a deep breath. Forced myself to remain calm. Still, my insides shook. "I don't mean to bother you. I know you're busy." I wrapped my free arm around myself.

He laughed. A chuckle. I think it was a chuckle. "That's okay. You caught me at a good time."

I had? "I did?"

Heather drew herself up to her knees. Tucked the sundress under her legs. Sat back on her feet.

"Yeah," he said. "I just took a break. Sitting in the car, drinking some water."

I pictured him sitting behind the wheel of his SUV, sweaty water bottle in his hand, tipping it back to swallow one swig in succession of another. And another. Maybe Heather was wrong.

"Kim?"

"Oh. Yeah. I just wanted to say that I love you. I can't wait to take that cruise with the boys."

He paused. "You too. And me too."

"You too what?"

He chuckled again. Strained. Uncomfortable. "You know. Hey, I gotta go. Break's over and I'm the boss. So. You know."

"Well, if you can't say it, I'll just have to make you *prove* it later."

He chuckled a final time. "Bye-bye now."

He ended the call. I did too. Looked at my sister, who seemed paler than usual. "Come on," I said, heading for the door.

I left the room with my sister trailing behind me. We returned to the kitchen. I placed my finger under the main number for the Peabody, dialed, and waited.

"The Peabody Hotel on International Drive. This is Claire. How may I direct your call?"

I cleared my throat. "Yes. Um . . ." I blinked. "Can you put me through to a guest's room, please?"

"Name of the guest?"

I swallowed hard. Did I really want to know this? "Charlie. Tucker."

"Would that be Charles Tucker?"

"Yes."

"Hold for a moment, please."

The phone rang. And was answered on the third ring. By my husband. Who sounded more than a little frustrated. And winded. "Yeah," he said.

I squeezed my eyes shut, so much so they hurt. Colors burst from behind them.

"Hello?"

"Will you say it now, Charlie Tucker? Will you tell me you love me . . . now?"

21

Charlie returned home within the hour. By this point, Heather had gotten the boys up. She helped them pack and whisked them away for breakfast at McDonald's. From there she was taking them home. Or to Dad's.

She wasn't sure which.

I begged her *not* to take them to Dad's but knew she would anyway.

Charlie walked in the door leading from the garage to the kitchen, looking completely defensive. I had been waiting for him at the kitchen table, the same table where Heather had given me the news that changed my day.

My life.

He tossed his keys onto the countertop. Rested his hip against it. Crossed his arms. "Where are my sons?" he asked.

Your sons? "They're with Heather."

He nodded. "Is she the one who told you?"

"Yes."

"And she found out . . . ?"

"A friend of *your* friend. You know, Bunni? The girl who is just the hardworking mother who needed a job?"

"Stop it, Kim."

I stood. Took deliberate steps toward him. Stopped just inches from his imposing form. "Stop it? Stop it? That's all you have to say?"

"What do you want me to say?"

My fists hit him squarely in the chest. I pounded against him until he grabbed my wrists and held me at bay.

"Don't you *dare* touch me," I screamed.

"Kim!"

I felt my knees buckle, my weight give way. Charlie caught me, scooped me into his arms, and headed for the family room. I struggled against him. "Put me down," I said ridiculously.

He dropped me unceremoniously onto the sofa. Then he sat beside me, blocking me at the hip between his body and the back of the couch. "You need to listen."

"No. The last time you told me to listen, you lied to me." I started to cry. I'd been crying since Heather had left. I was sure I looked a fright. A far cry from the woman he'd just left behind at one of the swankiest hotels in Central Florida.

I tried to force myself up from where he had me pinned. He held on all the more.

"You need to calm down."

I placed my hands over my face. "Go away, Charlie. Go away and let me think."

Charlie stood. Adjusted his waistband. "Fine. You're not going to listen to a thing I have to say anyway. You never have." Then, "Look," he said. "It's not that I meant to hurt you. You or the boys. It's just that . . . you expect too much and I . . ."

I gave him my best "you've got to be kidding me" look.

"I can't breathe, Kim. I love my sons, but I can't breathe."

"*You* can't breathe," I repeated.

"No. I can't."

I waved him away. "Go away, Charlie. I can't even look at you right now."

He glanced over his shoulder. "All right then. If you need me, I'll be upstairs."

I didn't want him upstairs. I didn't want him in the house. But I didn't want him to leave either. If he left, he might never come back, and I couldn't honestly say I wanted that either.

There was more than just me to consider. More than our years together. More than the fact that he was the only man—excluding Steven, who had been nothing but a boy thinking he was a man—I had ever loved.

There were, of course, the children. Our sons. They loved their father. Adored him. Idolized him. They'd set him on a pedestal; if they saw him fall, what would it mean to their little psyches?

I had no clue what to do. I was stuck. Or was I?

The ringing of my cell phone from in the kitchen forced me off the sofa. I stumbled into the breakfast nook. Picked up the phone from the table.

Dad.

I wrestled with my choices. Not answer and hope this was just a random call. Not answer and find out later that he knew the truth and was calling out of concern. Answer and find out the call was just to check on me. Answer and find out that he knew. That he wanted to talk about it.

And I just couldn't . . .

"Hello?"

"Boo?"

"Hey, Dad." I didn't mean for it to happen, but the tears began. Gulping my words, I said, "I guess you've talked to Heather."

"Honey . . ." he said, the endearment trailing. "I'll be right there."

"No, Dad. Charlie is here and it might not . . . be . . . a good idea for . . ."

"What does he say, Boo? Have you asked him if it's true?"

"Dad. I caught him. I called the hotel and he answered. He told me he was . . . was working. He told me he was taking a break. And drinking water." The tears returned. Fresh and hot.

"Oh, Boo . . ."

"I don't know what to do, Dad. The boys . . ."

Momentary silence was followed by, "Meet me at my office, Kim."

"When?"

"How soon can you get there?"

"Fifteen minutes?"

"I'll see you then."

I didn't tell Charlie I was leaving. I figured it would do him good, so to speak, to hear the garage door open. To see me driving away. To wonder.

Sure enough, when I got to the edge of the driveway, he called. I didn't answer. It was a stupid mind game, I knew, but I felt vindicated by it. Almost.

211

The ringing stopped. Started again. After his third attempt, I turned my phone off. Let it go directly to voice mail, I thought. Let's see if you leave a message.

Dad's car was already in the parking lot; I wondered if he'd called me from the office. As soon as I pulled my Honda in beside his car, he appeared in the back doorway. His shoulders seemed to sag under the burden of my heartache. I understood this. All too well. When our children hurt, we hurt.

I once heard it said that parents can only be as happy as their saddest child. I had yet to learn just how true that statement was, but I felt I'd soon find out.

Dad had been through so much. Mom's illness. Her death. Heather's manic shopping holiday, which he practically bailed her out of. Jayme-Leigh's marriage to Isaac—whom we all love but were equally as concerned about the differences in beliefs. Then there was Ami's move to Atlanta. Not that it came as a surprise, but she'd hardly come home since she'd left. Barely called, Dad told me. I knew there had been a rift between her and Heather; this bothered Dad greatly. I had often thought how I would feel if Chase and Cody—as adults—were fighting. Not speaking. I would be heartbroken.

And now this thing with me. With Charlie.

Dad had always been crazy about Charlie. Thought of him—as he did Andre and Isaac—as the sons he never had. Knowing that Charlie had been unfaithful to the vows of our marriage would cut him at the deepest part of himself.

I got out of the car, ran to my father. His arms opened wide and I practically fell into his embrace. "Daddy," I cried, using a name by which I'd not called him since I was ten.

"It's okay, Boo. I've got you. We'll talk this out. We'll figure out what to do."

Dad's office smelled like rubbing alcohol and fresh-brewed coffee. We went directly to the break room, where he had already poured me a cup—had it sitting on the table with a neatly folded napkin beneath it. I wished he hadn't gone to the trouble. I didn't want it. Couldn't stomach it. I thanked him but didn't drink anything.

We sat across from each other at the little table where his and Jayme-Leigh's employees ate their lunches or nibbled snacks. Unlike the rest of the office—decorated in classic Pooh—this room had Mom's decorative touch. She'd made it warm. Inviting. A person with a workload like those who worked for Dad could come in for fifteen or thirty minutes or even an hour and find themselves completely relaxed. I only wished it could have that effect on me right then.

"Tell me," Dad said.

I spilled the story. I told him about my previous concerns and how Charlie had convinced me otherwise. I told him about Bunni. About the soccer game and the kiss. I told him about what had transpired in the last few hours.

"Why, Dad?" I asked with a blow of my nose into a paper towel, the only "tissue" I could find in the room. "Why do men do it?" I tossed the towel into the nearby trash can. Wiped at my eyes with my fingers before thinking better of it.

I heard my father inhale. Exhale. So slowly that had the room and everything around us not been so quiet, I would have missed it. "Boo, I can't speak for my sex in general. And I don't think that's what you need to concentrate on."

I looked up from mascara-smeared hands. "What then?"

Dad looked as though he were hurting as much as I. "What you need to concentrate on is not why *men* do things like this but why *Charlie* did it."

I felt myself go stiff. "Are you saying it's my fault?" *Maybe it is . . . Is it?*

Dad patted my hand. "No, Boo. Not in a million years. You are a good wife. A good mother. A good person. And with all that, Charlie still strayed. You have to ask yourself why *he* did it, not why *men*—or women for that matter—do it."

I nodded. "Yes. Yes. That's what I want to know."

Dad flexed his shoulders, rested his forearms against the edge of the table. His hands came together naturally, each finger folding between the corresponding finger of the other hand. "Boo, what do you want to do now? From here?"

I started to cry again. "I don't know, Dad." My words came between sobs. "I am so angry. And I'm *so* hurt."

Dad stood. "I'll be right back," he said.

I watched him leave, my tears stifled long enough for him to walk down the hall and then return with a clean hand-kerchief in his hand. "I just got this as a gift from one of my patients." He showed me the dark blue monogram stitched in one corner. "A set of them, actually." I took it from his hand. "Good thing I didn't take them home just yet."

He returned to his seat while I returned to my sobbing. I raised my head at one point, thanked him for allowing me to just cry, and he nodded. When I was thoroughly wrung out, when I couldn't bring any new pictures of Charlie and Bunni to my mind, when I could no longer envision myself beating them both like piñatas at a birthday party, I stopped crying.

I twisted Dad's handkerchief with my hands, staring at the rings on my left hand. Watching them taunt me. What difference had it made that we'd spoken vows? Made a covenant with each other? Why had we even bothered?

Dad cleared his throat. "Do you love him?"

My head jerked up. I shook my head back and forth. I had no energy for such a question as that, either. "I don't know anymore. I don't know."

"Well, now. That's not a no."

I shook my head some more. "It's not a yes, either."

"Boo, you have two boys to think about. Two sons. Now I'm not overly happy with Charlie right now, but he's the father of my grandsons and he always will be. That will never, ever change."

"I know, Dad," I said, sounding more like a thirteen-year-old than a grown woman.

"If you decide you cannot work this out with him, if you decide to get a divorce, you'll not be rid of him, you know. You'll have to deal with him in ways you never imagined. Visitation. Support. He will date other women."

I nearly gagged at the thought.

"Trust me. He will. Bunni Berno is fooling herself if she thinks Charlie is going to leave you and marry her. That much I'm sure of."

"Are you?"

He nodded. "But that doesn't mean he won't get married again, someday, and your sons will then have a stepmother. She may be as good as gold or she may become your worst enemy." I groaned; my head felt like it was going to explode. "The question you have to ask yourself at this point is whether

215

or not you think the marriage is worth fighting for. Or, if not, giving up and dealing with what comes next."

I pressed my forehead into the pad of my palms. Pressed against the agony. "Dad. Either way, I'm in the worst situation. I didn't do anything wrong and yet *I'm* the one who has to make this decision?"

Dad reached across the space between us, grabbed the back of my chair, and pulled it toward him. I felt his arms wrap around me. As easily as I'd done when a girl, I rested my head against his broad chest. Even with my stuffy nose, I was able to breathe in the scent of him. It comforted me like a memory of a summer's morning from my childhood. I hiccupped several times and Dad chuckled. "Oh, my baby Boo. You know I love you, right?"

I nodded.

"Then listen to the old dad. If you decide you want to try to work this out, I'm here for you. I can suggest a good therapist. A Christian therapist. She's the mother of one of my patients. This woman and her husband work together, and I think you'd both like them."

"Okay."

"But if you decide this is not going to work, I've also got the name of a good attorney. And I'm here for you, every step of the way. Anything you need."

I wiped my nose with the handkerchief. It wasn't as rough as the paper towel, but the newness of it scraped against my sensitive skin. "Dad?"

"Yeah?"

"What would you do?"

I felt his chest heave out. In. "I'd give him a chance, Boo.

I think you have a lot to salvage. And I know . . . I *know* . . . that the Lord can . . ." His voice trailed.

I raised my head. Looked up into his face. He appeared pained by something. Something deep. I knew my father loved me. Loved all of us beyond measure. The fact that my agony affected him in such a way nearly did me in. As if I weren't "done in" enough already. "Dad?"

He cleared his throat. "Kimberly, the Bible has a line in it. A most incredible line. I think a lot of Christians overlook it."

I sat up straight. Wiped my nose again, though it was now dry. "What is it?"

"It's from Paul's letter to the Colossians. Colossians 1:17 says, 'He is before all things, and in him all things hold together.' Do you know what I think that means?"

I shook my head.

"I believe that, before the world was formed by his Word, he knew that you would marry Charlie. And he knew that Charlie would do this awful thing. He knew how it would divide your home, crush your heart, and sever your vows. But he wants you to know that, in his hands, he can bring all this back together. And when it comes back together, it can be better than it ever was before."

"I believe that too, Dad."

"I know it. It wasn't always perfect with your mother and me, you know. We both made our mistakes within our marriage, and God still managed to hold us together." He smiled. "Either that or it was just your mother's stubbornness."

I tried to smile. "Yeah. Mom's. Sure."

"Well, that got me a half smile anyway. Okay, then. Take a step. One today. One tomorrow. Maybe two the next day."

"Can I take a step backward every so often?"

The skin around Dad's eyes crinkled. "Sure." He stood. "Let me get you the name of the counselors."

"Thanks, Dad."

While he was gone I took deep breaths. I was still angry. And hurt. And I wasn't sure how I was going to walk back into the house and face Charlie. I also was not sure how Charlie was going to react to counseling.

But, I decided, if he wanted to stay with me and the boys, he would go. We obviously needed help. Him more than me, I supposed.

I pulled into the garage. Turned off the car. Charlie's car was parked next to mine. He was home.

I slipped out of my Honda CR-V while the garage door jerked toward the cement floor. I closed the car's door. The garage was enveloped in shadows. I moved deliberately toward the door. Opened it. Stepped into my home.

Charlie sat at the kitchen table. His left arm rested on the tabletop, his hand around a coffee mug printed with WORLD'S BEST DAD in bold black lettering. The room smelled of coffee and cinnamon rolls. I glanced over to the coffeemaker to see half a carafe. To the stove to see a plate of half-eaten Pillsbury rolls dripping with creamy white frosting.

"I got hungry," he said.

"So I see."

"You look terrible."

I laughed. I didn't mean to, but I did. And it wasn't because I was amused.

"Been to see your father?"

"Yeah."

"Kim . . ."

I held up my hand. "Wait. I want to say something."

He took a sip of coffee. "Okay."

I stood glued to the spot where I'd stopped upon entering the room. I kept my eyes fixed beyond Charlie to a small table where a framed photo of our family stared back at me. It had been taken by Heather outside her home after a Sunday afternoon get-together. Four happy members of one contented family. At least three of us were.

"I don't want to talk about what happened. I only want to talk about what to do . . . where to go from here. And I think we need help. I think we need to see a counselor. Dad gave me the name—"

"No."

My eyes shot to his. "What?"

"I'm not seeing a counselor."

I should have known. I *did* know . . .

"The fact is, Kim . . . what I tried to say to you before is . . . I'm done here." He breathed deeply through his nostrils. "And I want a divorce."

22

June 2010

Dad was right. In the nearly two years since my divorce from Charlie had been final, we'd done nothing but test each other with our individual decisions. He found it impossible to settle down and act like an adult, and I found it even more difficult not to interfere in his life. Subsequently, I was forever questioning my sons after their weekends about what they did and who they did it with. Namely, I wanted to ascertain whether or not another woman was sitting in the place that had, at one time, been solely mine.

Dad was also right about another thing: Bunni Berno was a flash in the pan. She removed her kids from the team and, I heard later, moved to Tampa. She never even bothered to return to another game.

But Heather did. She came to every practice, no matter what was going on in her own life, and kept a watch so I wouldn't have to.

After Bunni there were others, but none I had to see. I only had to hear about them from Chase and Cody. Heather had stopped coming to the soccer field by then, which was just as well. It seemed to me that, over the past few years, she'd started drinking more often in the afternoons, turning herself into the socialite I knew she really wasn't. More than that, it was changing her personality. I didn't like the idea of her driving when sometimes she couldn't walk without bumping into something, usually me.

Eventually, Charlie had all but stopped coming to practices *or* the games, unless they fell on his weekends.

As the boys' new summer schedule loomed, I became more fretful of the time they'd spend with their father—their court-appointed four weeks of visitation in which I didn't see them at all. It wasn't healthy, I'd complained to my attorney, to Dad, to Anise, to anyone who would listen, for my sons not to see their mother at all for four straight weeks.

They all agreed, but Charlie's attorney—a snake in the courtroom if I'd ever seen one—was quick to tell the presiding judge that "four straight weeks" did not mean I could not contact them by phone or *ask* for, say, dinner with them. And, he countered, the four weeks after Charlie's were time they spent with me without seeing their father, so it was all fair. The point was to have, basically, four uninterrupted weeks with our sons and without each other.

I'd managed to survive two summers like this, but this year my concern grew based not on the length of time away from me but from the length of time with their Casanova father. I took the matter up with the court, to ask that if Charlie was going to have this time with his sons, it should be *with* his sons.

I lost miserably. So much so, the judge granted an extra

week to Charlie. After all, he'd missed spring break, Charlie told the judge. Never mind the boys had *asked* not to go and Charlie had said he was fine with that. Now—now that he needed something to use against me, he claimed he'd wanted to be with them but was *kept* from them.

Of all the . . .

Dad insisted I use this time for a trip to Cedar Key. His excuse was that, since our longtime housekeeper Eliana had recently died, he needed to find someone to take her place. I'd argued about it, telling him that (1) I didn't want to return to the place that always reminded me of Mom, more so than even the house I'd grown up in, and (2) he could always call someone in Cedar Key and find Eliana's replacement. But Dad was insistent, so much so I couldn't argue with him.

Whatever plans Dad had for me in Cedar Key—whether to find a replacement for Eliana or to just get away from it all—on the very first night there I ran into my old high school flame, Steven Granger. Seeing him was awkward at first, but then we began to see each other socially and, within too short a period of time, I found myself dealing with old feelings as well as new ones.

For one, Steven made me take a good, hard look at losing Mom. For another, he made me take an equally hard look at losing him, which felt like the most difficult of all. I found myself welcoming him into my life and shutting him out, often within the same hour.

Dad and Anise's elderly neighbor Patsy became my lifeline to understanding myself and to helping me return to a better relationship with God. She showed me a way of life in Christ that went beyond sitting in the pews on Sunday and saying grace before a meal or prayers at bedtime.

One Saturday morning, I'd had a particularly difficult phone conversation with Heather in which she told me she thought Andre was having an affair. I suppose she thought that, with my history with Charlie, I'd jump all over her accusations. Truth is, I was less concerned about that than I was about her drinking and some recent bizarre behaviors. Already, before lunch, I could hear ice clinking in a glass. Before we hung up, we had a rather brutal argument about it.

I went to see Patsy for advice. I found her not feeling well. In fact, in need of a doctor. I did what any good daughter of a pediatrician would do: I called Dad. He suggested I drive her to the nearest town with a doctor. Shortly after, Steven called. I told him what was happening, and in no time, he arrived at Patsy's with a medical doctor who happened to be vacationing in Cedar Key. Dr. Willingham wrote a prescription for Patsy, and then Steven walked him back to his car.

While they were out, I called Dad again. "Steven came with a doctor who is vacationing here and took care of Patsy. I'm sorry I haven't called you back already. The doctor is just leaving."

"Steven?"

My legs grew weak; I hadn't yet told Dad about Steven. About seeing him . . . dating him . . . feeling a little bit crazy when I was near him. I took a deep breath and tried to sound nonchalant. "Steven Granger. You remember him, don't you?"

"I remember him, yes. How is it that Steven Granger knew about Patsy?"

"I know what you're thinking, Dad. He just happened to call after I talked to you and—"

"Why was he calling you?"

I swallowed. "Because, Dad. We have a date tonight and—"

"You have a date tonight?"

"Dad, are you going to interrupt me every three words or are you going to let me finish?"

A moment of silence passed before he said, "I'm listening."

I turned toward the door to see Steven stick his head in and say, "I'll be right back."

I nodded. He closed the door behind him.

I walked briskly into Patsy's kitchen and sat in one of the chairs at the table. "Dad," I said, crossing my legs. "I don't understand the tone of your voice. Steven Granger is living here now. His father had a heart attack last year, and he moved back down to help with the business. We ran into each other, he asked me out, I said yes, and that's that."

"Not a good idea and you know it."

"Dad—"

"Hear me out on this one, Kim."

My jaw flinched. "Okay."

"I've never seen you so hurt in my life as you were at the end of your senior year."

"You mean other than when Charlie left me and the boys?"

"Well, of course. But you were older then. Steven was your first love, and he ripped your heart out."

"You sound more like a mother than a father."

"A father doesn't forget that kind of heartache when it's his little girl who's crying."

I rubbed my forehead with my fingertips. I leaned over as

though in pain. "That's sweet, Dad, but I'm not a little girl anymore."

"I know that. But you're still *my* little girl."

I smiled but remained silent.

I heard him sigh. "Well, then. Does it feel like it did twenty years ago?"

I straightened as I laughed. "Honestly? It's not as hormonally driven."

"I didn't need to hear that."

"I know you didn't. But . . . we had our second date last night. He got me to take pictures with his camera, Dad. And he made me laugh."

"I haven't seen Steven since you were kids."

"Well, he's not a kid anymore. Neither am I. And I don't know what all this means or where it will lead, but I have to tell you. I'm more than a little willing to find out."

"Just be careful, sweetheart."

"I will." I heard Patsy coughing from her bedroom. "Dad, I need to go check on Patsy. I'll call you later, okay?"

"Take it easy, Boo."

———

Later, after Steven had brought the prescription back and we'd agreed on pizza for dinner and that it should be eaten at Patsy's, where we could continue to keep an eye on her, I made a call I'd dreaded.

My brother-in-law answered with, "Hey, Kimberly."

"Oh, the joy of caller ID." I pulled up my feet to rest them on the aqua-painted railing.

"That and I've half-expected your call."

I wondered what he meant but decided against asking. Andre—a brilliant mind if there ever was one—was too astute for someone like me to challenge. "Are you able to talk right now?"

"It's as good a time as any."

"Are you at work?"

"No. I just pulled up to the library, to tell you the truth."

The library. It didn't seem like an Andre kind of thing to do on a Saturday. My stomach churned, half from hunger and the other half from concern. "Oh." I took a deep breath and plunged right in. "I talked with Heather this morning . . . more or less . . . and I'm very worried about her, Andre."

"Me too. I'm worried about her too." He paused. "I love her, Kimberly. I don't know what she's told you, but I want that much said before we go any further with this conversation."

I watched as a small flock of seagulls glided past me. They called to one another in screeches I was all too familiar with.

When I didn't say anything, he asked, "How's Cedar Key?"

"It's good. It's real good, actually."

"Heather told me she was surprised you'd gone. She told me about what happened when you were kids there. About Steven."

"Oh, did she now?"

He chuckled. "Anything to take the focus away from her and her problems."

I took another breath. "Well, since you've now brought it up, do you mind telling me what's going on with the two of you?"

"Did she tell you I'm having an affair?"

Right to the point. Wow. "She thinks you are."

"I'm not."

I closed my eyes at the revelation, praying he was telling me the truth. Charlie and I had been donned the perfect couple, but no more perfect than Andre and Heather.

"Can I be honest?" he asked.

"Of course."

"You and Charlie . . . do you know how often Heather held our marriage up to the mirror of yours?"

"What? No."

"Yes. If Charlie so much as winked at you during a family dinner, I caught it when we got home. 'Why don't you ever wink at me like that?' she'd ask. 'Why don't you love me like Charlie loves Kim?' It got to the point where, if I saw Charlie do anything for you, to you, whatever . . . I knew I had to one-up him. That whole 'new kitchen' thing. It was me, trying to give her the kind of home she wanted because I knew she was comparing our home to yours and to Jayme-Leigh's. Not that she'd ever admit it." He coughed sarcasm. "I told Charlie one time, I said, 'Charlie, I'll pay you half my annual income if you'll just *not* be so loving toward your wife in front of Heather.'"

I pressed my hand against my forehead. I was sweating profusely in the afternoon heat but couldn't bring myself to go inside and disturb Patsy. "What did he say to that?"

"He just laughed. He actually said—and I don't say this to hurt you or bring back negative emotions—that if I loved Heather a quarter as much as he loved you, I'd be just fine."

I scoffed at the news. "Do tell."

"He was joking, of course."

227

"No kidding, Andre." I dropped my feet from the railing and leaned over, fighting a wave of nausea that threatened to turn violent.

"I'm sorry. But if we are going to be honest here—"

"And you're *not* having an affair?"

"Kim. I told you. No."

23

I pictured Andre—if he was where he said he was—sitting in his black Navigator, the one with all the bells and whistles—outside the public library. Handsome hardly described him. The closer he got to forty, the more appealing he became. While my sister worried over every little laugh line and gray hair, Andre's only served to change him from boyishly cute to dashing. If he were my husband, I'd worry too.

"Then Heather is just imagining all this?"

"It's more than that, Kim. It's . . ."

I stood and started pacing the length of the balcony, hoping the action would bring enough of a breeze to cool me. "Andre, just say it, okay? If I'm going to help Heather, I need to know."

"You already know, Boo. You just don't want to say the words."

I stopped pacing. The sun beat against my back in perfect rhythm with my heart. I forced myself to focus on something—anything—in front of me. The water had turned to gray. The scattering of islands in the gulf were blurred by haze. Overhead, against the perfect blue of the sky, white wings fluttered as another flock of gulls headed toward the sunset. I blinked several times as I tried to force myself to find one thing . . . just one thing . . .

A *ping-ping* drew my attention to the oversized wind chimes hanging on the east side of Patsy's balcony. They echoed back the sun's light like a diamond under the display of Tiffany's lamps. I stared at the glint, widening my eyes, and told myself to not be weary. I knew this . . . I knew . . .

"I know."

"Then say it."

"I . . ." I couldn't.

"You want me to say it? Okay, I'll say it, Kim. Heather is an alcoholic. She's also addicted to prescription drugs. She's an alcoholic and an addict."

I sucked in my breath. "Andre . . ."

"And I'll tell you where I've been lately. I've been going to Al-Anon meetings after work. Not to a cheap motel with some floozy, like she's accused me of."

"Al-Anon?"

"Yeah. Al-Anon. Because I need help too, Kim. I've enabled her and I need help as much as she does."

"Enabled her? What do you mean? You've forced her to drink?"

"Don't be silly. You're too smart for that. Control, shopping, drinking, whatever. They're all coping skills she learned a long time ago. Long before we even met."

"I don't—"

"I'm the one, Kim, who has made sure she had whatever she needed from the pharmacy, which very well could cost me my job. But I'm not willing to sacrifice my *wife*. I won't lie and I won't enable her. Not anymore." His voice was strong, as if he'd rehearsed the words a thousand times so as not to get them wrong and in the repeating had come to believe what he said. Before I could reply, he added, "I won't treat this the way your dad did, Kim. I won't lose my wife to this disease."

The wind chimes moved, twirling round and round as though hurricane-force winds were upon the island. The screeching overhead reverberated in my inner ear. While the world turned upside down around me, I managed to find my chair. To sit. To remind myself to breathe. "What are you talking about?" I spoke through a clenched jaw.

"You know what I'm talking about. You've always known."

"No."

"Yes, Kimberly. Yes. Heather told me the way you used to play your mother. The way you used to get what you wanted by waiting until you knew she'd had enough to drink and you could mold the clay any way you wanted."

My breath came in ragged jerks. "No, no, no."

"Kim!"

I jumped, jolted back to the here and now and what my brother-in-law was saying to me. "Don't you talk to me like that, Charlie Tucker."

Andre groaned. "Oh, man. I'm not Charlie, Kim. I'm Andre. And I'm telling you the truth here."

I ended the call. One second later, I called him back. As soon as he said hello, I declared, "My mother died of liver cancer."

"Your mother died of cirrhosis of the liver. She was a functioning alcoholic, but an alcoholic nonetheless."

I raked my hand through my hair. My fingertips came back drenched in sweat. "No." I ended the call again.

And called him right back. "Andre, don't—"

"Don't what? Say it out loud? Determine that the cycle is going to stop here? I've got my own children to think about too."

I pressed my hand against my chest; my heart hammered beneath it. In spite of the news I'd just received, all I could think was that Steven was coming back with pizza and that Patsy lay in bed with a fever. "I can't talk about this right now," I said.

"If you want to help your sister—"

"Of course I want to help my sister!" I clamped my hand over my mouth and looked in the direction of Patsy's bedroom. "Andre," I continued, my voice softer, "I'm caring for an elderly woman right now. I'm at her home. I just can't . . ."

"The timing is off then." I heard him exhale. "But the subject has got to be faced. You can keep hanging up on me and calling me back and you can put it off indefinitely, but it's not going to change the facts. Your sister is an alcoholic and a drug addict. She knows it. And she knows you know it but won't address it."

"Just this morning . . . I tried . . ." My words tumbled out like soiled clothes from a laundry hamper. "She only ended up yelling at me."

"I know. Believe me, I know the sting of her alcohol-induced fury."

Anger rose from inside me. I blew air from my lungs like a bull ready to stampede. "So what are you going to do about it, Andre?"

"I'm meeting someone here at the library. There are some archived articles he wants me to read. He's going to help me get Heather into a crisis center."

"And she's okay with that?"

"No, she's not okay with that," he said as though I were an idiot. "She insists every night that she can beat this on her own. But every morning she's pouring vodka into orange juice just to get by to lunch. At lunch she has a little something to tide her over, and at five o'clock it's cocktail hour."

I hiccupped to force my tears back.

"The kids and I have talked," he continued. "They know they'll be without their mother for the summer, and they're okay with that."

"But how will you manage? Heather takes care of them."

"No, she doesn't, Kimberly. She pretends to take care of them. They've been taking care of themselves for some time now. And it stops. Monday she either goes in on her own, or I'll force the issue."

"Andre . . ." I swallowed. "I'll be back on Tuesday, I think. If you can wait till then, the kids can stay with me."

I heard him chuckle before he said, "You don't have to fix this too, Kim."

If he had thrown cold water on me, it wouldn't have had any less effect. "What?"

"I'm sorry. It's just . . . you know how you are. You want to fix everything."

"No, I—"

"Yes, you do. And I love you for offering, but we'll be fine. It's not like they're babies."

"I see."

"And I'm sorry if I sounded cruel about your mother. I've tried to talk to your father, but he's still not willing to openly discuss this. Even when it comes to making things better for his daughter."

I wiped my face with my fingertips, grateful I wore no makeup. "Have you spoken to anyone else?"

"Just Jayme-Leigh."

"And?"

"She agrees with me."

"Even about Mom?"

"Yes."

I couldn't say much. Andre was right; somewhere way back in my most honest place, I knew the truth about Mom. He was also right about how, when I'd been a teenager, I'd waited until the right time of day to ask Mom for favors. Questions that required only a "yes" and that would get me my way, especially when it came to doing what I wanted to do and with whom I wanted to do it.

And Heather had known too. And Jayme-Leigh. All our efforts to keep our best-guarded secret from each other had been for nothing, in the end.

That left only one sister. Ami. She'd been so young; surely she hadn't known anything.

Or, had she?

24

Ami
Summer 2011

In the spring of 2011, I made a decision to leave the Atlanta Ballet and open my own dance studio in the town of Conyers, a suburban town twenty-five miles east of Atlanta. Over the years I'd built my credit, made all the right connections, and then—when the time was right—I left the ballet company, rented a building perfect for a studio in a section of Conyers known as Olde Town, and set about getting ready.

I set a goal that Claybourne Center of Dance would open within three months from the keys being placed in my hand. In that time I worked myself silly—painting, installing barres and mirrors, proper flooring.

I advertised for instructors and they came. I hired for ballet, tap, jazz, and hip-hop. A friend I'd met while working with the ballet in Atlanta joined my endeavor as the contemporary instructor. As far as I could tell, I was ready.

Until . . .

One late July morning while I painted the front room, a

man walked in. I'd left the door unlocked—I was expecting some deliveries—so I wasn't alarmed at the sound of the wind chimes I'd hung from the ceiling to announce students and visitors.

"Be right with you," I said, not bothering to look, concentrating more on the task at hand. The fine detail of painting light blue "boxes" inside dark blue "boxes."

"Now that's fly." I'd come to recognize the voice of the UPS guy, and this wasn't his.

One look over my shoulder from where I stood on the stepladder had me thinking the same thing. *Fly.* Well-built, just a tad under six feet tall, tousled brown hair, shining dark blue eyes, boyish charm in a grown man's body. Totally cool. Totally fly.

When I found my voice, I said, "I'm sorry," although I have no idea what I was sorry for, other than the way I was dressed. My hair. My lack of makeup. Ponytail skewed, tendrils of hair slipping out. "Can I help you?"

He moved toward me, or perhaps it was the ladder, as I stepped toward the floor. "Yes, ma'am," he said, though I suspected him to be at least five years older than me. "You can if you tell me how to apply for a job here."

I landed, rested the paintbrush on one of the rungs, and extended my hand. He took it in his. "You have to apply with the owner," I said. "But the positions have all been filled for now."

"Ami Claybourne?" His voice held the Southern charm I'd come to appreciate since moving to Atlanta.

"Yes." I squeezed his hand and released it.

"Do you know where she is? I'd really like to talk with her . . ." He chuckled. "Beg a little."

I laughed along with him. "I am Ami Claybourne. And I'm not sure begging is necessary."

He pinked. Beautifully.

"And you are?"

"Gray. Gray Rollins." He extended his hand again as though we'd not shaken hands before.

"Nice to meet you, Gray." We smiled at each other. "So," I said, "what kind of job are you applying for?"

"I'm a certified Zumba instructor. I'm also a personal trainer." He looked around the half-painted, unfurnished room. "I don't know if you are planning anything like that."

I shoved my hands into the deep pockets of my paint-splattered, bib overall capris. "Oh. I hadn't thought of personal training. Or Zumba."

His face registered surprise. "Seriously? Seriously. You should think of Zumba. Zumba is . . . it's huge."

I blinked several times. "Yes, I know it is." I'd hardly been living under a rock, after all. "But, I was thinking to start simple. You know, because this is my first time going out on a limb like this."

He looked around. "What limb?"

I shrugged. "You know. A business of my own. A *studio* of my own."

He turned toward the window that pretty much took up the entire outer wall. He stared long enough that I was forced to look too. Beyond the glass. Past the awning-covered sidewalk. To the asphalt of the parking lot, sparkling in the afternoon sun. Nothing about the man was rushed, as though he had forever and a day to live his life and anyone else's that crossed paths with it. "So," he finally said. "You've been working for some other dance studio?"

"Ah . . . no. Well, yes and no. I've been with the Atlanta Ballet for the past few years."

"The Atlanta Ballet," he said, as though he were in awe. His lips turned up for a crooked grin. "That's quite an accomplishment."

I smiled. "Thanks."

He looked around the room—bare with the exception of a drop cloth and a ladder—and said, "So what *are* you planning to offer here?"

"Ballet. Tap. Jazz. Um, hip-hop—that's also pretty big right now—and contemporary. Maybe cheer. What do you think about cheer? Or ballroom. What do you think of ballroom?" I pulled my hands from the pockets and spread them wide.

"I think it's for old people."

I laughed. "Oh, come on. That's not true and you know it."

He laughed with me. I noticed that when he did—when he laughed or smiled—his brows shot up as though he were questioning something. I found it to be most adorable. "Okay, okay. Maybe not *old*, but come on! If you're going to have ballroom and cheer—which clearly is *not* for old people—you *have* to have Zumba."

I chewed on my bottom lip. "You're probably right."

"Probably? Have you taken a Zumba class?"

"No, I haven't. My roommate Shellie loves it though. She's always trying to get me to go. I just . . ."

"Just?"

"I just really, *really* haven't had time."

He smiled again, brows shooting upward. "See, there's your problem. You should take a class." He paused. "Or . . .

EVA MARIE EVERSON

at least let me give you a private lesson so you can see the benefits for young *and* old alike. Everyone gets something out of Zumba."

I agreed to the proposal. We decided he'd return a few hours later. I cleared as much debris as I could from Studio A before going into the back, where the finished bathrooms and changing areas would soon be. I washed my face, brushed my teeth, combed my hair, and wrapped it in a bun on top of my head. I finished by dressing in tights, a leotard, a pair of shorts, socks, and workout shoes.

Gray returned at two and gave me the workout of my life. Somewhere between walking out the basic steps and slinging sweat, I decided that having Gray Rollins's face on advertisements wasn't an altogether bad idea. So much so that, when we were done, I extended a glistening arm and said, "Mr. Gray Rollins, welcome to the staff of Claybourne's." I had no idea how I'd add Zumba to a nearly full schedule, but I'd figure out something, even if it meant running a class at midnight.

He slapped his hands together. "Yes!" He looked up. "Thank you," he said.

"You're welcome."

He laughed easily. "Oh, sorry." He pointed to the ceiling. "I was thanking God."

"Then you're a . . ."

"Christian. Yes, ma'am. All the way."

I wiped sweat from my face with my hands. "Me too. Though, I'll be honest. With the ballet taking over my life, I haven't found a church I've connected with."

"Then, you should come with my family and me to our church sometime."

239

I was pleasantly surprised. Since moving to Atlanta, my social life had been dismal. My world had been the Atlanta Ballet. No one I knew really went to church on a regular basis, and I had more or less moved finding a church so far down the to-do pile, it had grown dusty. "I'd like that. I really would."

We stood for a moment, both breathing heavily until Gray said, "Can I interest you in a little dinner?" He pointed, his finger running up and down the length of my torso. "I mean, after you clean up a little."

I looked at the mirrored wall across from us. I really was a sight. "I'm a mess, I don't deny that. But look at you," I said pointing to his reflection.

We both laughed.

"I don't deny it either." His eyes locked with mine in the mirror. "What do you say? Dinner?"

I nodded. "I'd like that."

We turned to each other. "Where should I pick you up?"

"Um . . . how about I meet you there?"

He jutted his head forward. "Because . . . you just hired me but you really don't know me and therefore you really shouldn't tell me where you live?"

"That's right."

"You *do* know we're here—just the two of us—alone. Right?"

"I know, but . . . there's a difference."

His face became solemn. "Believe me, Ami. There's not."

———

I learned over dinner at Las Flores Olde Town Mex that Gray's youngest sister had been the victim of a violent crime.

EVA MARIE EVERSON

She had elected to stay late at work to finish up a project that was past due.

"One of her co-workers—a man she'd never been overly comfortable around—had driven by, seen the lights on, and decided to come in and see if, according to him, someone had inadvertently left them on." Gray winced. "She was more or less trapped."

"Oh no . . ."

"Of course he said the attack was consensual. Men like that tend to see themselves as some kind of demigod women crave."

"I've met a few like that," I said. "I haven't dated a lot, but you can't be single in this town and not. So, I know what you mean." When Gray remained silent, I added, "Did he go to jail?"

He nodded. "After a very long trial. It was a he-said-she-said kind of trial. But God was good." Gray shook his head. Residual anger flashed across his face. "Promise me you'll be more careful, Ami Claybourne. When I walked in today, you were there alone . . . door unlocked . . ."

I wanted to mention that his sister had been at work with the doors *locked* and it hadn't mattered, but I refrained. "I know. You're right. I was waiting for a delivery. But, that's no excuse."

"And, I should have known better than to even suggest coming back without someone else there to take the lesson with you. My bad on that one. I just got excited about the possibility of working there. Most of my work has been in personal training, and with the economy down, I've been strapped." He smiled. Brows shot up. "Had to move back home with Mama and Daddy."

241

I placed my hands in my lap. Mama and Daddy. How charmingly Southern. "Question: if I hadn't been there alone, would you have asked me out for dinner?"

He narrowed his eyes in contemplation. "Maybe. You're kind of a cute one, you know."

Kind of cute . . . My time dedicated to the Atlanta Ballet had left me void of hearing such compliments. The men in my social circle were either gay or so used to seeing me looking as Gray had first seen me. I rarely dressed up. When I did, and when I needed a "date," it was usually someone from the ballet who accompanied me. Hearing this here, now, was nice. "Nice you can say that considering what I looked like when you walked in."

His brows lifted again, a characteristic I was beginning to appreciate. "I could see through the paint and the sweat to what you look like now, though."

"You could?"

He laughed. "No. But I'd seen a photo of you in the local newsletter where I read that you were hiring staff."

"Then why didn't you recognize me when you walked in?"

He laughed easily. "You look *nothing* like your picture. All that makeup. Why do girls do that to themselves, that's what I want to know. Just for one picture."

I buried my face in my hands and shook my head. "Oh no." Then I laughed. "I guess us theater kind of people think we have to go all out."

"I reckon." Using his fork, he cut into a piece of his chicken enchilada. "So, Ami Claybourne, tell me more about you. Did you grow up here in Georgia?"

"No," I said, taking a sip of water before concentrating on my shrimp burrito. "I'm from Florida. Orlando."

His eyes met mine. "Really?"

"Why so shocked?"

"I hear a Georgia accent."

I chewed and swallowed. "Whenever I call home, my family says the same thing."

"Tell me about home."

"I have three sisters."

He grinned. "And I thought I had it bad with two."

"You have no idea." I speared a shrimp and ate it. "I'm the baby. Kimberly is the oldest. She used to live not far from where we grew up, but she got a divorce and moved to Cedar Key."

"Is that part of the Florida Keys?"

I shook my head. "Everyone asks that. No. It's in the Gulf of Mexico. West side of the state. She went there for some R & R, ran into her old high school sweetheart, and the rest, as they say, is history. They got married about a year ago, and they're already expecting a baby."

"Ah. Sounds like the stuff chick flicks are made of."

I smiled. "Then there's Jayme-Leigh—she's a doctor, like our dad—and then, heaven help us, there's Heather." I speared another shrimp. "She is a pain in my rear." I felt instant regret, but I couldn't stop how I felt. A year earlier Andre had committed Heather to a Florida rehab center for alcohol and substance abuse. I'd never even known Heather to drink and had been more than a little shocked. Then again, not really. The apple hadn't fallen far from the tree with the exception that she'd been able to get through rehab and remain sober. At least, so far, so good.

"Step eight, Ami," Heather had said in one of the few

phone calls she and I had had since I'd moved away. "Make a list of all persons we've harmed, and be willing to make amends to them all. I know I've said some things over the years that have hurt you . . ."

Some things?

"And I want to say I'm sorry and I hope you'll forgive me. Especially for anything I may have done while drinking."

Since I hadn't even been aware there was a problem, I muttered, "Yeah, well. Sure. I love you."

She told me she loved me too. Life went back to normal, which, for me, was her in Orlando and me in Atlanta, our paths crossing as little as possible.

Gray laughed easily, bringing me back to our conversation. "In what way is she a pain in the rear?"

"In the trying-to-run-my-life way. She's such a . . . a . . . little mother. But I don't need a mother so I do whatever I can, whenever I can, to avoid her."

"Because you have a mother."

"I did."

He stared at me for a moment before saying, "Oh. I'm sorry, Ami." I could tell he meant it.

"Thanks." I tossed my hair. "Now I have a stepmother."

"Wicked?"

"No. Marvelous, actually."

"When did your mother pass away?"

"Nineteen-ninety-nine. I was sixteen."

"Ouch. When did your father remarry?"

"The following year. Not even a year after Mom passed away. It was hard news to hear but . . . Anise is really and truly wonderful, and I don't blame my father for loving her."

He took a long swallow of water. "But . . ."

"But what?"

"But, you do blame him for . . . ?"

I started to answer but stopped. I wanted to share—though I didn't know why—my heart with this man. On one hand, I told myself, Gray had shared with me the incredibly personal story of his sister's rape. In many ways, what my father had done was equal. In many ways, not. If I told him the truth, I would be swinging open a door I could never close again. If I kept it shut, then perhaps I could open a window. "Nothing," I finally said.

"Your mother's death?"

He was reading me—*how* was he reading me?—and he wasn't letting go. "In a way." I placed my hand over my mouth, then removed it. "I've never said that to anyone before. Not in so many words. Not in *any* words."

"Well, then I'm honored."

Our server came to the table, refilling water glasses and reminding us to leave room for dessert. When she'd walked away, Gray said, "Tell me about your dad."

"He's a pediatrician, like my sister."

"That just tells me what he does for a living. Tell me about *him*."

I looked across the dining room filled with guests and servers. The restaurant was not typical for Mexican fare. The décor was rich and dark. Tall vases with flowers stood at the end of the bar. A row of lanterns casting off warm light hung above it. Crisp white linen tablecloths draped square tables. The aroma of the best Mexican food I'd ever eaten blended with Latin music, adding to the ambiance. For a fleeting moment I thought that if Gray asked me for a second date, he'd have to work hard to outdo Las Flores.

When my attention returned to him, I said, "When I was a little girl, I thought my father was the man in the moon. He was handsome. Smart. Fun. Like a prince in a fairy tale."

"What happened?"

My breath caught in my throat. "I can't believe I'm telling you this," I whispered.

He crossed his heart. "Your secrets are safe with me."

"Are they?"

"Yes, ma'am. One thing I can say for myself, I'm a good secret keeper."

Twice in a matter of minutes, I found myself wanting to tell him what my heart had kept secret for so many years. Too many. I wanted to share with someone—some other human being—the hurt in my heart. My soul. I wanted not to have to carry this secret all by myself anymore. Not just about my father's alleged affair. I'd shared *that* with Isaac. Of course, he'd quickly shut it down.

But I hadn't known then what I know now. I hadn't calculated the rest of the story.

I now figured, if I shared with Gray, chances were he'd never meet my family, so the secret really was safe with him. I took a deep breath and plunged. Not too deep, just deep enough to get a reading. "When my mother was on her death bed . . . she told me something. Something about my father."

"What?"

"She told me . . . he'd had an affair." I shook my head. "Early on in their marriage. I don't know the other details, like how long it went on or if they were in love."

Gray laid his fork over his plate, placed his elbows on the table, and laced his fingers. "Why would she go and do a thing like that?"

I wiped my mouth with my napkin, took another drink of water, and dropped my hands into my lap. "I talked to my brother-in-law about this years ago. Not too long after it happened. He said Mom was probably just talking out of her mind because she was so sick. But I don't know."

"Your mother, was she on a lot of medication?"

I nodded. "I know. I know. That's what Isaac said too."

"So, she could have been delusional."

"She could have been."

"But?"

Here it was. Here was my chance to say out loud to another human being what I wouldn't even say out loud to myself. "There's more."

When my words trailed to silence, he said, "Do you want to share that part?"

Yes. No. Maybe. Once it was out, it was out forever. "Not really."

"That's fair. After all, this is only our first date. Maybe on the second? Third?"

I looked at him. He was smiling. "Yeah. Maybe."

Gray paused a moment. "Why don't you tell me, what did your mom say exactly?"

"That I needed to forgive my father, as she had forgiven him."

"Forgiveness is a gift, more to ourselves than to those who have hurt us." He blinked. "Have you? Forgiven?"

I swept my lips with my tongue. I felt tears pool in my eyes. One trailed down a cheek. When I was finally able to get my voice past the knot in my throat, I said, "I wish I knew."

25

Gray became a staple in my life. We went to dinner at least twice a week—often after work—and to church every Sunday. My studio launched successfully, and Gray's class—shock of shocks—was the most popular, especially with women in the thirty-plus category. More than anything, with the busyness of starting my business and keeping it afloat, I was able to avoid going back to Orlando for pretty much any reason. That didn't stop Dad and Anise from coming to Conyers, of course. But, they always stayed at a hotel near my apartment, which meant I could manage not to have to spend every waking minute with them.

It was during a visit in June 2012 that Anise talked my roommate Shellie and me into a day of pampering. On Dad. We went out for brunch, then to get manis and pedis. Afterward, we had a late lunch, went shopping for trinkets we didn't need, and finished the day with late-afternoon massages. It was great fun, but at the end of it I was more than ready to go home and crash.

Anise wouldn't hear of it. She insisted on picking Shellie and me up later for dinner, where she asked Shellie endless questions about her life, how work was going, who she was dating, and how often *she* got to visit her family.

I felt the sting in every question, especially the last one.

Shellie and I are roommates, but we've never been confidants. In the past months, Gray had filled that role. Shellie and I only shared a place to live and expenses along with the occasional conversation or movie when we were both bored and dateless. What *I* knew about *her* personal life was where she worked (a bank), who she dated (a guy named Bud), and where she was born and had grown up (Birmingham). Other than that—and the fact she went to visit her family at least twice a month—I knew nothing. It was that one final thing that made my heart sick.

"I go twice a month," Shellie said.

"Of course," I interjected across the restaurant's booth table, "she lives only two hours from her hometown."

Anise smiled in that gentle way she has and said, "That makes a difference, for sure." She turned back to Shellie, who seemed more interested in her high-fat dessert of red velvet cake with cream cheese and pecan icing than in catching a glimpse of the expression I was attempting to plaster across my face, the one that said, "Don't. Say. Anything. About. *Anything.*"

"So," Anise continued, "do you have someone special in your life, Shellie?"

Shellie nodded as she took a sip of her coffee. I did the same, glaring at her over the rim of the cup. Still, she didn't take notice of me. "I do. I see a guy named Bud." She pulled her long black hair into a makeshift ponytail, then released it before picking up her fork for another bite of cake. "Of course, his name isn't really Bud. It's Robert. But his family has always called him Bud."

Anise frowned. "I guess that must be a Southern thing."

Shellie's dark eyes sparkled. "I guess so." She took a bite of cake and said, "This cake is delicious. You two should have gotten a piece."

I looked at Anise. "The joy of being only 105 pounds soaking wet is that you can eat cake and it doesn't matter."

Shellie shook her head. "No, no. I'm able to eat this cake because I work out three nights a week with *your* boyfriend."

"Ugh," I said, replacing the cup on its saucer.

Anise's head whipped around. "Ami?"

I rolled my eyes, took a deep breath, and smiled at her. "Yes, Anise, I have a boyfriend."

"But why haven't you told us? In all these years, you've never really mentioned a boyfriend or even dating that much."

I could hear new hurt in her voice, which made me feel all the more guilty. "It's really not that serious."

"Not that serious?" Shellie said.

I did my best to tap her leg with my foot under the table.

"How can you say you're not serious? You go out to a movie at least once a week, to Bible study on Wednesday, to church on Sunday."

"Have you met his family, Ami?" Anise asked.

"Ugh," I said again. Every last one of them, including the one remaining grandparent, his maternal grandmother, whom he called "Ga-Ga."

"I'll take that as a yes."

I nodded. "Yes. Okay, yes."

The hurt look grew. "But, why not tell us? Is he a convicted felon or something?"

"No, of course not," I said. "He's a personal trainer and a Zumba instructor, which is what Shellie was talking about when she said she takes three of his classes a week." I frowned toward Shellie. "He's a good guy. A great guy, Anise, but . . . I've just not been ready to share him. Yet."

"I see."

Shellie's face held a look of recognition. She wiped her mouth with her napkin and laid it beside her plate. "I think I might need to go to the little girls' room so you two can talk more privately." She stood, grimaced at me, and walked from the table.

Anise took Shellie's place across from me and laced her fingers as she positioned her elbows on the table, a sure sign we were going to *talk*. "Ami," she said, so quietly that had I not seen her mouth, I wouldn't have caught my name. "I honestly don't understand. What has happened since you've moved to Atlanta? Have I done something to offend you in any way?"

"No, Anise. Of course not."

"Your sisters? Has one of them?"

It would be so easy to pin this on Heather. To talk about her obsession with mothering me. To say that since Andre had admitted her into a recovery center, I'd felt . . . what had I felt? Guilt? Sure, guilt. Guilt at not knowing she was drinking too much. Or too often. That she'd become . . . like Mom. But Andre's declaration that he would make sure his wife didn't turn out like his mother-in-law and Heather's stint in rehab were too fresh. I couldn't blame nearly a decade of avoidance on her. "No, not my sisters," I said. "I talk to Jayme-Leigh a lot and sometimes Kim. And I pray for Heather."

"You're talking quite rapidly, Ami. Are you so sure of yourself?"

"Yes."

"Then, if it's not me and it's not your sisters, it must have something to do with your father. And please," she said, raising a hand to stop me from interrupting, "don't say it's not. Don't think for a moment he hasn't felt it. That it hasn't hurt him." Her eyes shimmered with tears. "From the moment I met him, he spoke of you, Ami. Said there was something—he couldn't put his finger on it—something wrong between the two of you after Joan died."

She waited for me to say something, but I couldn't.

"When I came to live with you and your dad, you and I seemed to hit it off quite well."

"I liked you a lot, Anise. And, now, I love you. I do."

"And I love you. But your father . . . he *loves* you. So much more than I ever could. You and I don't have the same history. And, he's your father. He's always been your father. That's . . . you have no idea how special that is."

"Yes, I do. I know, but—"

"If you knew, if you really knew, you would call him more. See him more. He's made excuses for years now, but I just cannot sit back anymore and let this continue. Not now. Not knowing there is someone special in your life." She took a deep breath, but I could tell she wasn't done. "Ami, I've never really talked to you about my father."

I shook my head. From across the room, I noticed that Shellie had found a place at another table and that she was

252

sipping on a tall glass of ice water. She waggled her fingers at me, letting me know she saw me seeing her.

"My father left when my brother and I were little. He met a woman—my stepmother—and went on to have other children, my half siblings. Dad didn't live *that* far away from home, but he rarely saw us, and he rarely called. He made us the smallest part of his life possible without completely ignoring us. I never knew what it was like to have a real relationship with a father, and by the time I was mature enough to pick up the phone and try, it just felt silly. But you, Ami. You do. And when I think of how you have everything I ever wanted in a dad, but you seem to be so flippant about it—"

"That's not it, Anise. I know what a good dad he is. It's just—"

"What? Tell me, Ami. I'm begging you to tell me."

"There are things about Mom that I can't . . . things she told me before she died."

"Like what?"

I shook my head. It wasn't my place to tell Anise this story. It was Dad's, if he would even tell her at all. For ten years I'd been unsure of who my father really was. I knew he loved me. That he loved my sisters, my nieces and nephews. There was no doubt in my mind that he'd welcome Gray into the family—if we came to that—as he'd done my brothers-in-law. But the one thing I needed to know for sure, I couldn't ask. Couldn't say. Not to this woman and certainly not here in this restaurant. The best I could do was . . . "I promise to try, Anise. I'll call more often. Come home when I can. It's hard, really it is, with the studio."

"We know that, sweetheart. Why do you think we're so

willing to drive up so often? But, your father isn't forty any-more. With age comes the difficulty of not being able to go like he used to." Her eyes widened. "I'm not saying he's old, but I think you know what I mean."

I laughed lightly. "Anise, you really love my father, don't you?"

"More than my own life." Her eyes swept over my face. "What about you and . . . what's this young man's name?"

"Gray." Heat rushed to my cheeks.

"Ah," she said. "I see."

I pressed my fingertips against both sides of my face. "See what?"

"You've fallen for him, eh?"

I shrugged, but my grin felt as though it would split my face. "He's a very special man. And, Anise? He's never *tried* anything. I mean, I know he . . . he *loves* me and he . . . oh, how do I say this?"

"He wants you?"

"Yes." I looked away. "I can't believe I'm telling you this. But I . . . I know this would be important. To you. To Dad. Gray . . . he's been very much the gentleman. He's . . . he's passionate, but appropriately so. And keeping our relation-ship right before God seems to mean as much to him as it does to me."

Anise reached across the table and took my hands in hers. "Oh, Ami. I'm so happy for you."

"Like Shellie said, we go to church. To Bible study. To dinner and occasionally to the movies. Mostly we stay with the Singles Over Thirty group in the church because Gray is over thirty even if I'm not quite there yet."

"Wisdom. Absolute wisdom. I'm proud to hear it. Ami, can we meet him? Dad and me?"

"Ohhhh . . . Anise. Am I ready for this?"

"Are you ready for this? What I want to know is whether or not *Dad* is ready for this. His baby. In love." She squeezed my hands before releasing them. "Have you said the *L* word yet?"

I nodded. "Yeah."

"The *M* word?"

I had to ponder what she meant. "Oh, you mean marriage?"

"Mmmhmm."

Excitement was written all over her. "Only in passing. We're not picking out china patterns or anything like that. Not yet."

"Hmm," she said. "I wonder what he's waiting on."

"Yeah," I said, as though the thought was conspiratorial. But, truth be known, I knew the answer. Gray was waiting for me to introduce him to my father. An old-fashioned guy who would only propose the old-fashioned way.

Well, as it seemed, he'd be meeting my father soon enough.

26

Gray met Dad and Anise the following day when they went to church with us. Afterward, Dad took us out for lunch, where he kindly peppered Gray with all the questions I imagined he would. Gray answered each one, impressing both Dad and Anise, if the looks on their faces were any indication.

That night, after the evening service, Gray and I went to a local diner for a cup of coffee and to talk.

"I like them a lot," he told me. "I don't know why you've waited so long to introduce me."

"You know," I said. "And you know you know."

Gray took a swallow of coffee. He never picks up a cup or a mug by the handle; instead his fingers loosely hold the rim, allowing it to dangle beneath the umbrella of his palm. After he returns the mug to the table, he turns it so the handle faces him, then to the left, toward me, to the right. It's his way, I suppose.

"I know what you think you know," he said. "But after meeting your father . . . he's such a great guy. What I mean to say is . . ."

I blinked rapidly. Waited for his words to come. When they

didn't, I pushed my cup of coffee a few inches toward Gray. I didn't want it anyway. "Are you calling me a liar?"

His eyes pierced mine. "No. No, of course not."

"Then what are you saying?"

"I'm just saying . . ." He shifted the coffee cup a quarter turn. "Maybe what your brother-in-law—what did you say his name is?"

"Isaac."

"Yeah. Isaac. I think maybe he was right. Maybe your mother was just, you know, not in her right mind at the end there."

I felt myself flush. Anger rose to the surface. I clenched my fists. What did he know about my mother? What did he know about the dynamics of our family? I shook my head. "I don't think so," I said, a little more cynically than I intended, especially considering that Gray didn't know the *whole* story of the conversation I'd overheard between Dad and Eliana. "I've tried to reason it that way, but I don't think so, Gray."

Gray lifted his cup, took another sip of coffee. "You know your dad better than I do, but that doesn't matter. All I'm saying is, I like him. I like him a lot."

My anger subsided. It made little sense to take my father's past sins out on Gray. "I'm glad you do."

"And Anise too. Great woman."

"I told you you'd like her."

His tongue darted out to wet his bottom lip. "You know, Ami, I'm glad to have met your father because . . . you know I want to, I *hope* to marry you, right?"

The flame of anger completely dissipated. "I know."

257

"We don't talk about it a lot. I've tried to stay away from the subject, to be honest with you."

"Why?"

He shrugged. "Well, the thing with your father, for one." His index finger darted back and forth between us. "This thing with us, for another."

"What thing?"

He chuckled, fixed his eyes on his coffee mug, started turning it again. "Ami, come on, now. You know and I know that once we say we're getting married, it's going to be no-holds-barred." His Adam's apple slid up and down in his throat. The muscles in his arms flexed. "Not that we don't have feelings for each other as it is, but I think we've done pretty good about keeping everything pure before God."

I ran my fingers across my cheeks. "I can't believe we're having this conversation in the middle of a restaurant," I said, leaning over so only he could hear me. I hoped.

He grabbed my hand and pulled it toward him. "I can't afford to say this anywhere else, Ami. If we talk at your apartment—if we start talking about how we feel and about being intimate once we're married—I'm afraid we'll become intimate before we're married." He cast a glance over his shoulder. Back at me. "I don't want to talk outside in the car. Same thing. Same obstacles and temptations. I can't even afford to talk to you outside the church in the parking lot. *That's* how I feel about you."

I blew a pent-up breath from between my lips. "Wow. Me too, Gray. I'm grateful to have met someone like you who . . . who does what it takes to wait. I know we're an anomaly. Maybe even within the church."

"You're right there; we are. For a long time I struggled with that, I'll be honest. I'd look around at the young men and women in my church—in any young adult program—and I'd hear them proclaim their love for God, for Jesus, for his teaching. All the time, everyone knew this couple or that couple were already being intimate with each other. That used to practically torture me until I finally realized that, unmarried and completely untried at that point, it wasn't my battle. This wasn't between me, them, and God. This was between them and God." He swallowed. Blinked. "Thing is, Ami, I want God to honor *this* marriage. That's the one God has asked me to deal with. And, difficult as it is, I'm willing to do whatever it takes now for his blessings later."

I smiled all over myself. "So," I said, drawing out the word. "What do we do from here?"

He sat up straight. "I'd say, Miss Ami, you and I just carry on like we have for a while. A little while." He smiled. The brows shot up again. "A very little while. Godly as I'm trying to be, I'm still a human and you are still smokin' hot, okay?"

I laughed. "You're not so bad yourself."

"Thank you," he said, strutting in his seat like a bantam rooster in a hen pen. "Okay, then. When the time is right, I'll do the proper thing. I'll talk to your daddy, I'll buy you a ring, we'll pick out china and silver and crystal and linens." He winked. "My mama is going to be tickled pink that she gets to help with this."

My mother would have been too, I thought. But I said nothing. I just smiled and nodded.

Two months later, Gray and I went to Orlando so he could talk to Dad. The entire family—with the exception of Kimberly, who now lived in Cedar Key and was "too pregnant for the three-hour trip"—came to the house for a cookout, which Heather organized and ran while Dad stayed inside, away from the heat of the Florida summer. When dinner was over, the family had left, and the house had settled down, Gray came into the kitchen where Anise and I were sneaking another piece of strawberry shortcake.

"Caught you," he said, laughing.

We turned from the counter, both of us gasping and giggling like schoolgirls.

"Oh, Gray," Anise said before turning back to the bowl of sweet berries, which she then spooned onto slices of pound cake.

I stood ready with a tub of Cool Whip and a large spoon. "Want some?"

"Nah," he said, patting his abdomen. "Like my daddy says, I gotta keep up my schoolboy figure."

I knew the six-pack that lay under his black Hurley tee. I'd seen it a number of times when Gray stripped out of a sweaty shirt before hitting the showers at the studio. It never ceased to amaze me; as much as I worked out, there was a part of me that was still soft. There seemed to be little on Gray that wasn't solid muscle.

I winked at him before plopping the whipped topping on the berry-covered cake Anise had slid my way on a plate.

"Where's your dad?" he asked.

Anise continued with her task. "He's in his office." She looked at me. "Today's festivities wore him out, I'm afraid."

I turned to Gray. "You know where his office is?"

"I think I can find it." This time, he winked at me. Mouthed, "Wish me luck."

I nodded, all the while feeling my knees go weak.

"Here," Anise said, extending her plate of dessert. "Whipped cream, please." Then, "Oh my goodness gracious."

I looked from the door Gray had just walked through to Anise. "Like I said, very Southern turn of phrase there."

"Oh no you don't, trying to make this about me," she said as I plopped Cool Whip onto the top of the berries. "He's going to talk to your father, isn't he?"

I smiled and wrapped my lips around the cream-layered spoon.

"Ami?"

"Yes, but don't tell Heather. Please don't tell Heather."

Anise placed her plate onto the counter and wrapped me in her arms. "Oh, Ami!" She jumped up and down, forcing me to do the same.

We both laughed.

"And," I added, "don't say anything once they come out of the office. He wants this to be totally old-fashioned. He's going to ask Dad. We'll go back to Atlanta, and I'll have to wait for him to propose."

Anise looked to the ceiling. "We get to plan a wedding," she said. Looking back at me she added, "Oh, please tell me you want a wedding."

"Of course."

"With all the trimmings?"

I could hardly believe I did, but I did. "Every single one. Something old, something new . . ."

"When do you think he'll ask?"

I shrugged, picked up my plate, and headed to the table with it. "Grab us a couple of forks," I said, "and I'll get the milk. You want some milk?"

"Perfect."

I glanced to the door again. "How long do you think they'll take?"

"Knowing your father," she answered from the flatware drawer, "they'll be in there a while."

"You think?" I pulled a nearly full gallon jug of milk from the top shelf of the fridge.

"Oh yeah. He's going to want to talk about virtues and what he wants for your future."

"Virtues," I said, walking the milk to the counter beneath the cabinet where Anise and Dad kept their glasses. All things considered, it would be an odd thing for Dad to talk to Gray about, but . . . whatever. "No worries there. Believe me."

September slid into Atlanta with a week of thunderstorms and weather dipping to unseasonable lows. This was our kickoff month at the studio. A new school year had begun, and our official first day of the new year was the Tuesday after Labor Day. The rain started on Sunday, lingered all day Monday and Tuesday, and somehow managed to get worse on Wednesday. Dark clouds hung over the entire greater Atlanta area. Car accident reports went up and every class at the studio began fifteen minutes later than scheduled due to traffic holdups.

Gray decided that going to the Wednesday night Bible

study we'd joined was out. Instead of our leaving the studio together, he headed out first for the apartment he'd recently rented for himself—the one I assumed I'd eventually move into—and, an hour later, I left for mine. We talked on the phone for a while around nine, our usual banter.

I opened the studio doors on Thursday at one in the afternoon. For nearly an hour, I worked on the books before a few of my staff came in. An early afternoon Over 40s ballet class started at two along with Gray's Over 40s Zumba. We liked to get the older students out before school let out and the place swarmed with tots, tweens, and teenagers.

About two-fifteen the door to my office opened. Genice, the ballet instructor, stuck her head in. "Hey, Ami?"

I looked up from the August financials spreadsheet. "Yeah."

"Do you know where Gray is?"

"Gray?"

"His class has pretty much all gathered in the front room, but he's not here yet."

I looked at my cell phone resting on my desk. "He hasn't called." A tingle went over my body. Ominous, as if my heart knew something was amiss.

"Laura said he hasn't called the front desk either."

"Is the weather still pretty bad out there?"

"It's a gully washer all right, but it's not like him to be late and not call."

I reached for my phone. "I'll call."

The call went to voice mail, and I left a message. "Gray? Hey, it's Ami. Um . . . you're late." I tried to draw from the storehouse of humor I kept deep inside. "I'm going to have to dock your pay if you don't have a good excuse, you know."

I looked at Genice. She smiled, though the smile didn't seem heartfelt. "Okay, um, call when you get this."

I returned the phone to where it had been just moments before and stood. "I'll go talk to the class," I said, smoothing the front of my jeans as though they were wrinkled.

Just as I reached for my phone, it rang. I looked from Genice to it and said, "Bet that's him. Probably couldn't answer in traffic." I picked up the phone. Caller ID indicated that, sure enough, it was Gray. "Gray?" I answered.

"Ami . . ." The voice on the other end of the line was hardly recognizable. It was raspy. Torn into a million pieces.

I looked at Genice. Fear must have registered in my eyes. "Gray?"

"Ami, I . . . I need you. I'm sorry I haven't called you yet, but . . . I need . . ."

"Gray, what's happened? Where are you?"

"I'm at home. I'm at . . . I need you." His words broke off and into sobs. "I couldn't call before. I . . . just got back and . . ."

"Back? Back from where?"

"I need you."

"I'll be right there," I said.

I'd only gone to his apartment once, and that was six months ago when a group of us from the church had helped him move in. I hoped I could remember how to get there, or that the address was still stored in my car's GPS. About that time Laura skidded into the door, running smack into Genice.

"Sorry," she said. "Ami," she whispered. "I have to tell you something *now*."

264

"I'm coming," I said to Gray. "I love you." I ended the call. "Laura, for heaven's sake, what is it?"

"I just got a call from my mom," she said, breathless. "She said it was on the news."

I shook my head lightly. "What was on the news?"

"Gray's sister . . . the one who was raped . . ."

"What about her?"

"She was killed last night."

My backside made hard contact with the top of my desk. "What?"

"The man who raped her, they let him out of prison on an early release program. Mom said that the news said he broke into her house and . . . it's pretty gruesome, Ami. He raped and tortured her before he killed her."

Bile rose in my throat. I swallowed it back. "Oh, Father . . ." I felt myself go dizzy.

Genice went to the side of my desk, where I always kept my purse. She grabbed it up and tossed it at me. "Go, Ami. But drive careful." She handed me my umbrella. "We don't need anything happening to you too."

I walked out of the office, through the hallways and the crowd of waiting women in the front room. I didn't bother to open the umbrella; I drew it close to my chest along with my purse and walked straight out into the pelting drops of water. When I arrived at my car, I fumbled for my keys, which had fallen into recesses of satin and leather. By the time I'd gotten inside, I was soaked and shivering. I flipped on the seat warmers, started the car, turned off my preset radio station, and activated my GPS. After pushing a few keys, I found Gray's previously entered address, pressed go, and waited.

"Drive fifteen feet and turn right," the automated voice said.

I flipped the windshield wipers to the highest speed, pressed against the accelerator, and started out of the parking lot. But before I could reach the traffic light leading me onto the highway, sobs racked my body with such force, I had to pull into another parking place.

I opened my car door, leaned my head into the pouring rain, and vomited onto the asphalt below.

27

Anise
First Week of December 2012

The melodious voice of Dick Haymes singing "O Come All Ye Faithful" filled the living room of our Cedar Key home. While Ross busied himself getting the Christmas tree into the stand, I sat in the middle of the sofa and opened boxes of ornaments, each wrapped in white tissue paper. I placed the ornaments on the coffee table; the tissue I folded and placed back in the boxes. I had managed to unwrap three boxes when the coffeemaker beeped in the kitchen, letting me know the coffee had brewed and was ready to pour.

"I'll do it," Ross said, as though reading my mind.

He groaned as he rose from the floor, balancing himself with a hand pressed against a knee. When he stumbled, I shifted on the sofa and pushed the box on my lap to the cushion.

"I'm okay, I'm okay," he said.

I was already half up. "Are you sure?"

He smiled at me. "Sit back down, Anise. I'm just an old man trying to stand too quickly."

"Ross."

He flexed his shoulders. "Seriously, hon. I just stumbled. It's not a big deal to stagger a little when a man is seventy-two. You'll see one day."

I pulled the box of ornaments back onto my lap. He was halfway to the kitchen when I said, "Fifty is hard enough, thank you."

To which he laughed. "Oh, to be fifty again."

When he returned with his fingers wrapped around the handles of two Christmas mugs of steaming coffee, he said, "Why don't you put that aside for a minute and let's go sit outside on the balcony. It's a shame to waste a day like today putting up a tree."

I took the offered coffee, looked down, and said, "I really want to have this done before Kim and Steven and the kids get here for the official lighting of the Claybourne Christmas tree."

"Yes, yes." He held out his hand. "I know. We'll get it done, I promise."

There was nothing I liked better than sitting on that balcony with my husband, looking out over the water, wondering if a pod of dolphins might show themselves playing in the sunlight. I also loved waiting for the sunset. Watching the colors of the marsh and water change. And if a slow moon rose over those same marshes—especially in the light of day—it just made my life better than it already was.

I set the box aside, took my husband's hand, and allowed him to guide me to the balcony, where a patio set—one I'd purchased recently from Home Depot—awaited. Amazon teak. Two chairs, one end table. Ross moved easily to his preferred seat and I sat in mine.

"You were right," I said. "The weather is too gorgeous to miss."

"Nice part of living in Florida in the wintertime."

I took a sip of my coffee. "But I miss Maine's snow blanket on Christmas Day," I said. "And having *cold* weather to make the season feel right." I sighed. "But I'm happy there is, at least, a chill in the air." Then I smiled at a new thought, which I chose to keep to myself. People in Cedar Key—when the weather hit sixty-nine—dragged out their winter coats. Where I'd grown up, that was considered a heat wave for this time of year.

Ross glanced across his shoulder to look at me. "Why don't we plan to go back up there next year? Spend the holidays with Jon and his family?"

I smiled. "I'd like that. It's been a few years now."

His hand glided through the air toward mine. Mine did likewise. Our fingers entwined. "I should have thought of that this year."

"You mean now that we're a couple of semi-retired old folks."

"One of us, at least."

In the early fall, Ross—fatigued beyond what he was normally able to handle—decided, finally, to take partial retirement. He'd argued that, as a doctor, he should be able to work until he walked out of his office door and into his grave. I agreed with the theory, but—as he'd said—his "get-up-and-go had got up and went."

We—Ross, Jayme-Leigh, and I—decided Ross would work two days a week, Tuesdays and Wednesdays. This would give us more time in Cedar Key but raised the question of what to do about my business.

On a whim, I offered it to Heather, who—miracle of miracles—decided to take it. I always knew she had great talent and more organizational skills than most people gave her credit for, and she's proven me right.

Ross kissed my hand. "What time will Kim be here?"

"About seven-thirty. I told her we'd have dinner, then dessert in the living room with the lighting of the tree."

"She's doing real well, don't you think?"

"I do."

Adjustments in the Granger household had not come easily, but anytime families start over or blend, there is a season of fine-tuning. Truth be told, the adjustments with the boys had been so slight, no one really noticed. Cody had been more upset than Chase—leaving his friends and his father to move three hours away—but had eventually come to love working with his stepfather in his tour boat business. Boys and boats were a good combination.

It was the business that had brought Steven back to Cedar Key. He had lived as a single father in Atlanta for most of his adult life. When his father had a heart attack, he returned. His daughter, Eliza, had been in college at the time; a young woman abandoned by her mother when she'd been no more than six. As soon as Steven introduced his daughter to his fiancée, she and Kimberly became fast friends. Something inside each drew them together. Their relationship was a beautiful thing to watch and one I could reflect easily on.

Both Kim and Ami had accepted me without question into their family. Jayme-Leigh's acceptance had come slowly but without a fight. Heather's, of course, had been another story entirely.

Right around the time Ross decided to go into semi-retirement, Kimberly and Steven presented us with the most amazing gift, a granddaughter. They named her Patricia Joan. Patricia, for the woman who lived next door to us in Cedar Key until this past summer when God called her home. Joan, of course, for Kimberly's mother.

Losing Patsy was difficult for all of us. For one, no one expected her death to come when it had. She'd not been ill and, at seventy-eight, had been planning to celebrate her birthday the following week with family and friends. She had been quite busy with and excited about the preparations.

It was Kim who found her body. Kim, who'd developed such a kinship with her, called Patsy at least twice each day. She always said "to check on her," but I think it was more that Patsy gave Kim such wisdom. Patsy was the epitome of what all women hope to "grow up" to be. Fine. Gentle. Astute. When Patsy hadn't answered her phone all day, Kim decided to drive over. She used the spare key Patsy had given her and found her sitting on the balcony, head resting on the back of the chair, hand around a glass of weakened tea. Her face bore a faint smile, as though she'd looked up to see a loved one, and then, in the next breath, slipped into the arms of Jesus.

Three months later, the baby arrived. But, that blessed event came on the heels of news even worse than losing Patsy. Ami had called in early September, shortly after Labor Day. Gray's sister had been the victim of a vicious attack, killed in a murder-suicide by a man who'd served time for raping her years before. For a while, my concern lay solely with Gray, then it shifted to Ami as well.

Ross and I had gone up for the funeral and found Ami to be unusually jumpy. Nervous. I asked her about it several times, but she blew it off, saying, "Wouldn't you be?"

Later, lying next to Ross in our hotel room bed, I said, "It's more than just her future sister-in-law's murder. I know it."

Ross shook his head. "Nah, Anise. From what I read on the internet, this was pretty gruesome."

"I understand," I said. "But it's not like she walked in on the crime scene. I'm telling you, something is not quite right here."

Two weeks after the funeral, Ami called to inform us she and Gray had married in a simple ceremony in their pastor's study. "We couldn't imagine having a wedding now," she said. "And we can't imagine waiting a year, so Gray and I decided this was the best way."

I heard her sadness. Her disappointment. But there was something more. Something I knew she wouldn't share until she was ready. If ever.

I took another sip of coffee, leaned my head back, closed my eyes and swallowed, and tried to imagine what death had felt like for Patsy. Looking out on these same waters, taking a sip of iced tea, and then . . . *home*.

The December air—warm and breezy—blew over my face, lifting my hair and tickling my skin. I opened my eyes again to watch a pelican soaring across the marshes, here and there striped with brown. I watched him dip lower and lower, gliding across the water with grace. He dropped suddenly to just below the surface, came up with a large fish dangling from both sides of his beak.

"Got him one," Ross said. "Lunch is served."

I squeezed my husband's hand, looking his way. "Oh my, Ross!" I stood quickly.

Ross's face registered alarm; he must have felt what I saw at that very instant. A red trickle of blood seeping from his nose. He touched it lightly with his fingers, drew back his hand, and studied the tips.

"I'll get you a tissue," I said, already stepping into the house.

I put my coffee cup on an occasional table in the living room, dashed into the powder room, and pulled out three tissues. I returned to find Ross tilting his head forward and pinching the nostrils. "Here, honey. Here," I said, waving the tissues in front of him.

Ross applied them immediately under his nose and held them there. He removed them two or three times before saying, "It stopped."

I squatted before him, resting my hands on his knees. "What happened?"

"Just a nosebleed, Anise. They happen from time to time."

A nosebleed and a stumble . . . "Do they happen to *you* from time to time?" I took the bloodied tissues and stood again. "I'll go get you a wet washcloth."

When I returned I found Ross staring at the marshes. I handed him the cloth and sat next to him, where I'd been just moments earlier.

"Well?" I asked.

"Well what?"

"Does it happen to you a lot?"

He shook his head. "No. I think I may have a sinus infection."

I realized I'd left my coffee in the living room but didn't feel inclined to get it. "Wouldn't you know if it were a sinus infection?"

He shrugged. "Maybe. I've been a little tired. Felt a little headachy. So . . ."

I sat back in my chair and crossed my legs. "I want you to get a checkup. Talk to Jayme-Leigh next week when we're in Orlando."

"I'm due for my annual in a few months."

"Ross. I don't want you to wait a few months. Please."

He patted my hand as though I were a child. "All right, sweet pea. All right."

Ross and I decided to have lunch at Kona Joe's the following afternoon, choosing to sit on the back deck overlooking the bayou. I stared at a dilapidated pier. Years ago, it had been a place for lulling the days away, fishing pole cast over the blue-gray water, the line disappearing into its depths, waiting for a nibble. Men and women wearing straw hats. Children with hair bleached and cheeks kissed by the sun. Now, no one would dare take a step out onto the sun-stripped wood. After twenty yards or so, it dipped into the water, then rose again, like a roller coaster rail. At the end, where only supporting posts struggled to stand, seagulls perched, looking out toward the small shrub-filled islands dotting the waterway. I inhaled; the world smelled green.

"Gorgeous, isn't it?" Ross asked me.

I nodded. We sat at a small table; my elbows rested upon it. I'd clasped my hands together and brought them up under my chin. "Takes my breath away, Ross. I wonder, sometimes, what it would have been like to have been a part of the Timucuans. To have lived off this land. This water. Everything here is . . . it's a glance to another time. Another way of life." I rested my cheek against my hands and smiled at my husband. "No wonder you wanted to bring me here. And no wonder you and Joan wanted to buy the house when you first found Cedar Key."

Before sitting outside, we'd ordered quiche and coffee. When the red door from the middle of the wraparound porch opened, Edie—one of the café's owners—stepped out, carrying two plates. "Here you go," she said.

I rubbed my palms together. "Yum, yum."

The door opened again; Edie's husband Joe stepped onto the porch, bringing the coffee. "Edie made that herself this morning," he said, obviously proud of his wife's abilities. "And you really ought to try the cobbler she made for dessert."

"Peach?" Ross asked.

"With ice cream," Edie answered.

"We'll take two," Ross said.

"Make it one," I answered. "One of us has been trimming down." I jerked my head in Ross's direction. "And one of us has not."

"Don't think you're taking a bite of my cobbler," Ross said.

I picked up my fork and speared the quiche. "Oh, I'll take a bite, all right."

Edie and Joe left us to our lunch. When we'd eaten the quiche and Ross had managed to save one bite of the cobbler for me, we returned to the inside of the café to thank them and to wish them a happy Saturday.

A few new customers had walked in and were milling around the dining area. We said good-bye and turned to leave just as the door opened.

Rosa and her son Mateo entered.

"Well, hello there," Ross said, reaching to kiss Rosa's cheek.

"Dr. Ross." She returned the gesture. She looked back to her son, who towered behind her.

He extended his hand, shook Ross's. "Dr. Claybourne," he said.

"How are you doing, son?"

"Good, sir."

"I can't get over how tall you've gotten," I said.

Another patron of the café opened the door; we all shifted toward a small table to the right of the door where coffee condiments were placed.

Rosa looked up at her son and smiled. "After twelve or thirteen, boys just seem to shoot up."

I folded my arms. "How old are you now, Mateo?"

"Fifteen," he said. Perfect white teeth beamed behind his honey complexion and beneath coal-black eyes. "Hey, Dr. Claybourne, Chase and I decided we're going to fix up his stepdad's pontoon for the Christmas boat parade."

It was Ross's turn to fold his arms and beam. "Is that right?"

"Yes, sir. We're building what looks like a Christmas train, painting it. It'll go on the front of the boat. We'll line the boat with those little traveling lights, you know what I mean? Put a caboose on the back."

"Where are you working on it?"

"Mr. Steven's shop behind the house."

"Oh, I see. Well, you boys let me know if you need any help. I wouldn't mind spending time doing something like that."

"Who do you have set to ride with you?" I asked. I looked at Rosa to share a smile but held back. She watched her son with such intensity—pride mixed with anxiety.

"Chase and me, of course. Cody, maybe."

"So, just the two, maybe three, of you?" I asked.

"No girls?" Ross added with a laugh.

Mateo blushed. "Well, you know . . . maybe. That's why it's a maybe for Cody."

The four of us laughed together. Ross patted Mateo's upper arm.

Rosa spoke up. "If there are girls, Dr. Ross, then *I'll* be on that boat."

"Mom," Mateo said, "you are not going on the boat with us. No way, no how."

We laughed again.

Ross shook Mateo's hand again. "Son, you let me know. I'll check with Chase or Steven to see when you boys might be working on the train again."

"Thank you, Dr. Claybourne."

Ross and I said good-bye to Rosa, said good-bye again to Joe and Edie, and stepped outside onto the porch. We slipped our arms around each other's waists and walked toward our car.

I looked at my husband's face. He was positively beaming.

28

Saturday evening I hung up the phone and went to the living room where Ross was watching television. "Guess what," I said.

He smiled at me. "Gray and Ami are coming for Christmas."

I frowned. "How'd you guess?"

He laughed lightly. "I could hear you talking on the phone." He jerked his head toward the kitchen where I'd been. "You're only a room away, you know."

I returned to where I'd been sitting before the phone rang, before I'd left for that one room away, so as not to bother Ross. "I know, I know. You're brilliant." I clasped my hands together. "Oh, Ross, won't it be wonderful? Kim is already here. I bet we could get Heather and her family to come here as well." I jumped from my seat, dashed down the hall and into our bedroom, returning moments later with a pad and pen, jotting names and ideas within the lines.

"Now what have you got going there?" Ross asked. He held the remote up and paused his show. "Woman . . ."

I sat again. "Just making a list. Do you think Toni and

Tyler are going to be home from college this year? They were hardly around last year."

"Somehow," Ross said, leaning his head back, "a ski trip in Colorado took precedence over being with family. Call them crazy."

I made a note to find out what Heather's family plans were. "You're in fine form tonight, Dr. Claybourne." I tapped the paper with my pen. "I'm going to call Jayme-Leigh and beg her and Isaac to come. Hanukkah started last night . . ."

"Mmmhmm."

"The boat parade is next Saturday."

"Steven says the boys have the boat ready."

I looked up from my doodling. "Did you ever go by and help them with it?"

He shook his head. "No. I guess they got it done by themselves." He exhaled heavily. "But I look forward to seeing it."

My heart felt heavy. "Are you okay, Ross?"

He closed his eyes. "Just tired."

"It's these trips to Orlando," I said. "Right smack dab in the middle of the week. Why don't you think about fully retiring? Or maybe work just one day a week. Like on Thursdays? We can go over on Wednesday night, return on Friday. Wouldn't that be better?"

He answered with a faint smile.

"Ross?"

"I'm just thinking about how Southern you've become."

I felt my shoulders drop. "Now where did that come from?"

His eyes opened and he looked at me. "Right smack dab?"

I purposefully drew myself upright. "I will choose to ignore that." My eyes fell to the paper in my lap. "If Heather and her family can come and Jayme-Leigh and Isaac can come . . . I'll ask Kimberly if Heather's family can bunk over there. We'll be full up here, but . . . oh, Ross. Won't it be marvelous?" I repeated. "The whole family here?"

He didn't answer. I watched him carefully. The slow rise and fall of his chest. The relaxed state of his lips. He'd fallen asleep, leaving me to frown instead of wonder at how handsome he remained. Oh, how much I loved him! So much more than I ever thought possible.

I stood quietly, pulled a throw from a basket where I kept a stack of them, and laid it gently over my husband before stepping down the hallway into our bedroom, where I called Heather to discuss the possibilities of their coming.

My suggestion was met with a few uhs and ohs before she added, "You say Ami and Gray are coming?"

"They said they'd be here the twenty-first. The winter showcase is next Saturday, the studio is closed all next week, but they have office work to attend to and then they have loads of shopping, she said."

"How did she sound?"

"Happy. In spite of the strains during these first months of marriage."

"I'm so glad. I've been worried." She chuckled. "But you know me. I'm always worried when it comes to Ami."

"You've been a good sister."

"No, I haven't. But I'm working at getting better. At letting her be an adult. Now, a wife and, one day, a mother."

"Oh, gracious. I can hear what your father would say if he heard you say that."

Heather put on her best "Dad" voice. "Now, let's not go racing ahead of time, Heather."

I smiled. It felt good to banter with Heather. It had been too long in coming. "So, what do you think? Christmas? What are the kids doing this year?"

"They'll be home. I absolutely demanded it. Last year was one thing, this year is another. I refused to have Christmas two years in a row without my babies."

"So, when do you think you could come in?"

"I'll need to talk to Andre, of course, but if Ami and Gray are coming in on Friday, I suspect we'll come in on Saturday. Give them some time with you guys before we arrive. Have you talked to Jayme-Leigh?"

"No. And, to be honest, I need to call Kimberly and see if you guys can stay there."

"Or we can rent one of the condos near the park. I'll call Boo. You call Jayme-Leigh."

After we hung up, I did just that. She said she was open to coming but had to check their schedules. Who was on call and whatnot. When we'd exhausted all talk of the holidays, I told her I wanted to talk about something else. "Let me go check on your father first," I said. I tiptoed down the hall to make certain Ross was still asleep. He was. I returned to the bedroom, sat in one of the two cream-colored upholstered chairs I'd just brought in from Orlando, crossed my legs, and looked around in an effort to gather my thoughts.

Since marrying Ross, I'd redecorated this room twice. The first time because Ami had reminded me that the original master bedroom had been where her mother and father had resided during their trips to Cedar Key. Ross gave me

281

carte blanche when it came to making the beach house my own, and I had done just that. For years we slept in what had originally been the girls' room, but when he and I decided to live in Cedar Key on a more permanent basis, I thought it time to turn the larger room back into the master suite. Ross gave me a wink and said, "Knock yourself out." And I had.

I'd had the walls painted the creamiest of white. Brought in Country French furniture, added occasional pieces in dark wood, created a sitting area that faced away from the bed and toward the water. I bought a thick cream-colored area rug that allowed the dark hardwood to peek out from under the walls and windows. The only artwork I hung were portraits of our grandchildren on one side of the room and portraits of the girls and their spouses on the other.

The pictures had been taken on the beach of Atsena Otie, among the driftwood and the ancient oyster shells.

Just being in this room gave me a sense of belonging. Of peace and contentment. I could not help but be happy here. No one could.

"Jayme-Leigh," I now said into the quiet of the room. "Are you still there?"

"I'm here."

"I want to talk to you about your father."

"What about him?" Her voice held the same no-nonsense tone it always did. If there was an iota of concern, she never allowed herself to drop to the dramatic.

"I'm concerned. He's been so tired lately. More tired than I think he should be at his age."

"He's nearly seventy-three, Anise."

"I know that. I know. But I also know his virility, if I may be so bold to discuss that. Not just intimately, mind you. In every way."

"I see," she said, sounding almost professional in the remark. "I'd hoped his working two days a week would help."

"What do you mean?"

"Back in September—when he first approached me about this—he said he was getting too old for five days a week and wanted to spend more time puttering about. More time in Cedar Key. Of course, I'd noticed his aging. And I'd thought dropping back to two days a week would help."

"It did. Then it didn't," I said. "At first, he seemed better for having made that decision. But in the last couple of weeks he's just not been himself. He's napping more than usual. We were talking just a few minutes ago and he dropped off to sleep without so much as a yawn."

My stepdaughter said nothing at first, then, "Anything else?"

I thought of the nosebleed. Of how Ross had said it had happened a few times before. I decided to mention it along with, "I've also noticed he's lost a few pounds. He's been pretty smug about it, but I can't say his appetite has changed all that much. Not enough to account for it."

"Hmm. He hasn't said anything to me when we've been at the office about the nosebleeds or the weight loss."

"See if you can't coax something out of him, Jayme-Leigh. His annual is a few months off, but I don't feel good about waiting."

"Ah, doctors. We do make the worst patients."

"So I've heard."

"All right, Anise. I'll talk with him on Tuesday when I see him, encourage him to make an appointment."

"Thank you."

"No problem."

"I'll let you go. Please call me when you know more about Christmas."

"I'll find out something tomorrow. I promise."

We hung up. I absentmindedly pulled the December/January issue of *Coastal Living* magazine from the table between the chairs, dropped it into my lap, and opened the cover, which boasted a beachfront living room with a white Christmas tree, decorated with ornaments of seaside colors. As I thumbed through the pages, my eyes fell to a photo of a festive wreath, sprayed with baby's breath, starfish, pinecones, and tied up with a big red ribbon. *I could do that*, I thought, momentarily missing my work at the floral shop.

I walked over to the bed, retrieved the pad and pen I'd left there, and added a few notes for our next trip to Orlando. *Go to Michaels. Get wreaths. Baby's breath. Starfish.*

Our home, I decided, would be more festive than ever this year. Our children would be here. All of them. I knew it. It would be the most marvelous Christmas since Ross and I'd married. Absolutely.

Ross and I returned to Orlando late Monday evening. I drove; Ross had insisted he was fine, just too tired to drive in the dark.

In December, dark came too soon.

With the exception of the gentle piano of Philip Wesley

playing on the CD player, we traveled in silence. I kept my eyes on the narrow two-lane roads between Cedar Key and Ocala. I glanced toward the shadows of trees and bushes, and the outline of fences, which set the boundaries of horse farms. I looked for the familiar stretch of rolling land where nothing stood but an ancient oak, naked arms stretching upward while Spanish moss dripped toward the ground like an old man's beard.

Once we reached the highway, I sped past the billboards announcing the fun life Central Florida had to offer. The attractions. The shopping centers. Ron Jon. Neon signs over convenience stores and drive-thru restaurants were no more than a blur. I no longer had to think about the path I was taking. Where I was going. When to go straight and when to turn. This had all become familiar.

But my life had taken a new road and I knew it. Loving and marrying a man over twenty years my senior came with a price, and this was it. Ross had been so energetic when we'd met. I'd seen men twenty and thirty years younger unable to keep up with him. There were times I wondered if I could. His work had always been demanding, but he rose to meet it with vigor. On our weekends in Cedar Key, he enjoyed taking the boat out, walking down trails, and exploring. Both there and in Orlando, he enjoyed participating in the social activities. He read voraciously, staying up late when he couldn't put a book down, rising early the next day without complaint. And in our intimate moments, he was nothing short of amazing.

But, even that seemed to be dwindling away. Becoming fewer and farther between. I missed it, but more than that, I missed *Ross*. I missed our rousing conversations. Our never-ending efforts at one-upping each other. I missed his energy around me, drawing me, spurring me onward. Still, I knew—I *knew*—that if we'd reached that time when he slowed down while I remained "youthful for fifty," I would grab hold of this new era of our lives with the same love and devotion I'd had from day one.

That night, after we arrived home, I parked the car in the garage, turned to him, and shook his shoulder until his eyes fluttered open. I told him we were home now. Told him, sleepyhead, it was time to wake up and go to bed. He wiped drool from the side of his mouth, chuckled, and said, "You drive this car so well, Anise, I slept the whole way home."

I smiled, but I didn't feel the humor.

Inside the house we stopped in the kitchen for drinks of water and to take a moment to flip through the mail Heather had brought in every day and dropped on the countertop before watering our plants. Having created two stacks—one to shred and one to go through later—we went upstairs and prepared for bed. Stepped out of our clothes. Tossed them into an empty hamper. Took showers. Dressed for bed.

I stood at my bathroom vanity, staring into the mirror at his reflection from the opposite side of the room, all the while pretending to rub night cream along my cheekbones. He wore pajama bottoms and a tee. They hung on him, but only so much that I could tell. His wife, who knew him best.

He didn't notice me, noticing him. Picking up his toothbrush. Applying a glob of toothpaste. Bringing both to his mouth to begin the task of doing what I knew he'd done three times a day for as long as he could remember. I watched as he braced his left hand on the side of the sink, elbow locked, head down, moving it from side to side.

I placed the top of my night cream onto the jar. Turned it without looking, keeping my eyes on this man, this splendid man I'd been blessed enough to marry. I felt my heart flutter as he spit into the sink, drew back, spit again. His head came up, eyes locking with mine, mirrored image to mirrored image.

I turned. "What is it?" I walked across the marble tile—emblazoned in colors of the sunset—looked into the sink, and saw blood swirling in the foam of toothpaste and spittle. Ross leaned over, spit again. Bright red blood splattered against cream-colored porcelain.

"Ross!" I placed my hands on both sides of his face, forcing his mouth open. Tiny blisters dotted across the gums, each one open and bleeding. "Ross, what in the world?"

He stepped away from me, ran his hand along the right side of the touchless faucet. Cold water spewed into the sink, rinsing away the evidence as he bent over it, scooping water into his mouth, swishing, spitting until finally the blood stopped coming.

I handed him a towel I didn't remember getting. He swept it across his lips. Turned his head toward the mirror. Opened his mouth to investigate. Looked at me. Painfully so.

"What's wrong?" I whispered. I felt myself trembling in my core, past the knot of what was to come. What had already begun that I could not stop.

"I don't know," he said. "It just started."

"Get dressed," I said. "We're going to the hospital."

But my husband shook his head. "I'm fine, Anise. I'm not bleeding out. I'll see Kyle as soon as he can fit me in."

I knew that look; I wasn't going to get past it. "All right. But compromise. Tomorrow. I'll call Kyle's office first thing. He'll see you right away, I know he will."

Ross kissed my cheek. "Yes, ma'am."

"Then I can call?"

"You can call. First thing in the morning." He slipped his hand into mine, brought it to his lips, and kissed it. "Let's just go to bed for now, Anise," he said. "I'm bone weary."

29

Dr. Kyle Ryan's office was ultramodern and part of a quadruplex. Ross and I walked into the building's atrium filled with plants and fountains spewing water that emitted splashes meant to calm patients and their family members. If they were anything like me, they were anything but relaxed.

The reception areas of the individual offices were visible through walls of glass. Automatic doors slid open upon sensing an approaching visitor.

Standing in the center of the atrium, I could see that each office looked the same. A curved receptionist's desk cut from wood and marble in front of peach-painted walls and under low recessed lighting, a waiting area of modern office chairs, a flat-screened television for entertainment, a door leading to where tests were taken and truths were told.

Whether or not one wanted to hear them.

Ross and I stepped through the sliding doors at one that Tuesday afternoon. He'd woken earlier, feeling tired but okay to work, he'd told me. "Half a day," I said to him. "I've got you an appointment at one. I'll pick you up."

I spoke with Jayme-Leigh privately before her father had

come out of one of the patient rooms in their office. She agreed something didn't seem right with her father, told me she had talked with Ross for a few minutes and that he, remarkably, had admitted he needed to see a doctor. He felt it, she said, in his bones.

"Don't worry, Anise," she said, patting my shoulder. "He's healthy. Always has been. This is probably just something little that he'll take a few pills for or some vitamins and be all the better for it."

I shook my head. I wanted to feel assured. "Maybe so," I said. "But did you see the blisters in his mouth?"

"Probably just a virus. Or, maybe he's low on B12. Is he taking vitamins?"

"Of course. He's married to me, remember?"

"How does he take them?"

"The B12? We both take a B complex sublingually."

"Hmm. Okay. Let's just wait and see, Anise. Don't go borrowing trouble, I believe is the old saying."

"All right, Dr. Claybourne," I answered with a weak smile.

That weak smile continued, from Ross's office to Kyle's office, where we were taken right back—a privilege of being part of the medical community. We were escorted to a set of scales, which Ross stepped on without hesitation. So different, I thought, than when I am forced upon them. I'd drop my purse, slip out of my shoes. If I wore contact lenses, I'd pop them out. Ross not only stayed in his shoes, he didn't remove his wallet.

And still, his weight was considerably less than normal for him.

Inside the exam room, Ross had his vital signs taken. Blood

pressure was a little low, but heart rate seemed fine. Temp was normal. The nurse asked about his symptoms; he gave them. She looked into his mouth. Without flinching, said, "Okay, Dr. Claybourne. Dr. Ryan will be in with you shortly."

As soon as the door closed behind her, I said, "You've lost twelve pounds."

From the exam table he cut his eyes over at where I sat in the one chair the room afforded. "So I have. It's just like you, sweetheart, to notice the exact number."

I didn't answer. We sat silent, spending long moments looking at medical posters in expensive frames and at the one painting in the room, a Thomas Kinkade that I decided to stand and study while we waited. "Footprints in the Sand," I said, reading the brass plaque bearing its title. "This is one I've not seen before."

"Reminds me of Cedar Key," he noted.

I turned to look at it again. "The colors. The pinks and blues and lavenders he's painted into the sky."

He blew air from his nose. "I'm already ready to go home, Anise."

I looked at him again. "What do you mean?"

"Back to Cedar Key. I think I'd rather be there than here. We should think about selling the house here."

"Now? In this market?"

He shrugged. "It's paid for. Whatever we get is gravy."

"What about when we come here on the days you work?"

He stared past me. "I'm talking about fully retiring, hon. I realized this morning, as much as I love my work, I just can't do it anymore."

I walked over to him, placed my hand over his, where it

291

rested on his thigh. "Ross," I said easily, "Kyle will figure out what this is and you'll feel better. Let's not make any decisions until after you're feeling better. Deal?"

He brought his eyes to mine. "Deal." His eyes studied me for a moment before he said, "You're pretty, you know that?"

I laughed, leaned over, and nuzzled him, not caring where we were or who might walk in. "I love you, Dr. Claybourne. You'd better not be too sick, you hear me?"

"I love you too. And, yes ma'am." He winked. "It's a virus, Anise. Jayme-Leigh and I are both sure of that. So, you stop worrying, okay?"

I nodded. "Yes, sir."

But I knew I wouldn't stop worrying, not until we knew for sure. We were sitting in the family room, reading, when Ross's cell phone rang. He pulled it from his pocket, looked at the face, and said, "It's Kyle." Then into the phone, "Hey, Kyle. What's the word?"

I watched him from my chair. He said a few "uh-huhs" and "all rights" until a final, "Okay, Kyle. I'll see you in the morning . . . sounds good. Thank you, my friend."

He ended the call, sighed, and looked at me. "We're going to run another blood test in the morning."

My heart quickened. "What kind of blood test?"

"He wants to repeat the CBC."

"Why?"

Ross stared forward, rubbing his forehead with the fingertips of his right hand. "It's nothing, really. My hemoglobin is a little low."

"What does that mean?"

He raised his brow as he looked at me. "Probably nothing,

hon. Anemia, I'm guessing. As I've been saying for years now, I need more steak in my diet."

I breathed a sigh of relief. "Oh, well you must be thrilled. You have an excuse now when it comes to my no-red-meat menus."

Ross clasped his hands together and shook them heavenward. "Thank you, Lord! You *are* on my side."

"Posh," I said as he settled back into his book. "Ross? Do you think that's it? Really? You just need a few more steaks in your diet?"

His eyes remained riveted to the page. "I'm sure it is, Anise. I'll go back in the morning, have the test run again, and be sitting in front of a fat juicy steak tomorrow night at dinner."

Kyle suggested we not return to Cedar Key as we would normally have done, but Ross insisted that we return before Saturday's boat parade.

"I'll not miss seeing the boys," he said to me after ending the call that had come late Wednesday afternoon. "So, like it or not, we're heading back on Friday."

We were in our bedroom, getting ready to go out to dinner. I sat on the edge of the bed, picked up a brown suede boot, and pulled it onto my foot. "Ross, why don't we wait and see what Kyle says about that?"

Ross left the room for his closet, returning with a tie dangling from each hand. "Which one?"

"The left one." I pulled on the second boot and fluffed my calf-length skirt over my legs.

Ross tossed the right-hand tie onto the bed and started

the process of putting on the left. When I noticed how hard his hands were shaking, I stood and said, "Here. Let me." I adjusted the tie to the right length of both sides and teased, "You were never very good at this."

His shoulders squared. "I beg your pardon, madam. I've always been a good tie tie-er."

"Whatever you say, Dr. Claybourne."

"You just like to have your hands on me, that's all."

With the tying done, I ran my hands down the muscles of his chest as though to smooth nonexistent wrinkles from his shirt. "You know me well."

When I turned to get my purse from the dresser, he swatted my backside. "You bet I do."

I sent a smile his way. "Are you ordering a steak tonight?"

"You better believe I am. With mushrooms and mushroom gravy and a big baked potato with all the fixin's."

"Did Kyle mention if that was okay?"

Ross pulled his sports jacket over one arm. "Yes, as a matter of fact, he did."

"Then you eat it to your heart's content." I crossed my arms. "But tell me this: why are you listening to Kyle when it comes to eating steak but not when it comes to staying put in Orlando until all the tests come back?"

Ross's hand cupped my elbow as he guided me toward the door. "Don't argue with me, woman. I'm *going* to be at the boat parade. I don't care what the test results are."

He may not have cared, but I did. "Ross . . ."

"Nope! No arguments tonight. I'm hungry, I want a steak and a baked potato and I may even order something healthy like steamed asparagus or some such nonsense."

"Yum. White asparagus with olive oil sabayon. My taste buds are doing a happy dance even as we walk down these stairs."

"So happy for them."

I wrapped my arms around his arm as together we descended the back staircase leading to the kitchen. "If you're good, I'll let you have a taste."

"Then I'll be bad." His eyes slanted toward me.

I squeezed his arm. "I just may like that even better."

The call came the following morning while I worked on my Christmas wreaths at the kitchen table. Earlier in the day, Heather had brought a breakfast basket of muffins, a decadent coffee, and seasonal fruit bowls along with a copy of the *Orlando Sentinel*. While I worked on my project, Ross sat in the family room, reading the newspaper.

As soon as I heard him say, "Good morning, Kyle . . . pretty good. Enjoyed that steak last night as though I'd never had one before," I stood. Walked over to the doorway separating the kitchen from the family room, where Ross sat in a favorite chair. I leaned against the door frame and watched as he continued with, "Mmmhmm . . . all right . . . I see." He took a breath and his eyes closed before he added, "Kyle, I want to go back to Cedar Key this weekend to see my grandson in the Christmas boat parade. If I promise to be back on Monday . . ." His eyes had opened and he smiled. "Thank you." A stretch of silence was followed by, "Thank you again . . . I'll see you then."

As he closed his phone, I crossed the room and knelt in front of him. "Well?"

Ross cupped my chin in his hand. "We need more tests."

My heart hammered and I felt dizzy. Looking at him, I could see how pale he'd become, even more so over the last couple of days. "What kind of tests?"

He sighed deeply, and his hand fell from my face, almost as if he didn't have the energy to hold it there. "I don't want you to get upset unnecessarily . . ."

"What kind of tests?"

"A bone marrow biopsy."

The room stood still. Life, as I knew it, stopped. A new one entered our home, uninvited. Unwanted. Tears swam in my eyes; they were as unwelcome as the news.

When I said nothing, Ross continued. "Do you know what that is?"

"Of course I know. What I want to know is, why?" I sat on my feet, which were wrapped in thick socks.

Ross folded the paper and dropped it to the floor beside him. "Kyle thinks we may be looking at a form of leukemia."

I dropped my face into my hands and sobbed. "I knew it . . . I knew it was something bad."

Ross leaned forward, pulled me into his arms. He shushed me, lovingly, as though I was the patient and he was perfectly fine.

"Will it hurt?" I whispered into the wet spot I'd made on his shirt.

"The procedure?"

I nodded.

"Not a bit. Maybe a little the next day, but I can handle it."

I wrapped my arms around his neck and buried my face into the hollow where it met his shoulder. "I love you so much," I said, hiccupping. "I couldn't bear—"

He shushed me again. "Don't jump ahead of this story, Anise."

I pulled away. "Why are you waiting until next week? You should be doing this tomorrow, no?"

"You heard what I said to Kyle. I want to go to the boat parade. A couple of days either way isn't going to change anything."

"And Kyle is okay with that?"

"If he weren't, I wouldn't be going." He wiped the tears from my cheeks with the pads of his thumbs.

I sniffled several times. "Should we . . . should we call Jayme-Leigh?"

"I will."

"What about Heather?"

"No. She'll make more out of it than necessary. And not Ami, either. She's got enough going on."

I shook my head. "Sometimes, Ross, I can't handle all this grief life brings our way. I really can't. I think I'm strong. I act like I'm strong. But, the truth is, I'm not."

He took my face in his hands and brought my lips to his for a light kiss. "You are stronger than you know. But this time, sweetheart, you don't have to be."

My arms went around his shoulders and I snuggled into him again. Inhaled deeply and took in the scent of Irish Spring and his favorite cologne. "Ross," I whispered.

"What, my love?"

"What do you think? Do you think you have leukemia?"

Because I trust your opinion on everything.

"As a doctor, I'm thinking yes."

"And as my husband?"

"I'm praying no."

30

Kimberly

Saturday morning came too soon, as did most of my days. Sometimes I wondered what I'd been thinking, getting pregnant at this stage of life. A woman's forties were for trying to keep up with teenagers, not 2:00 a.m. feedings and stinky diapers.

In spite of the challenge—and the occasional thought of what my daughter's teen years will be like—I wouldn't trade little Patsy for anything. To be honest, I didn't think I could love someone so little with this much passion ever again. Nor did I think I could be this happy. But Steven, my boys, Patsy, and my life in Cedar Key are my world.

I didn't think I could love again—not after Charlie had taken my heart, chewed it up, and spit it out. I was wrong. Moving to Cedar Key changed my heart. Steven changed my way of thinking. He broke down the walls I'd been living behind most of my life. He showed me how, as the oldest of four extraordinarily different daughters, I strove for excellence. Precision in every detail of life. Always doing my best.

Being better than I had to be. Steven taught me how to rely on God, trusting in his ways. Even when his ways meant a baby in my early forties. Not necessarily planned, but we'd not done anything to keep it from happening, either.

Cedar Key had taught me something else: how to relax. How to *live* my life. How to sit down, sit back, and watch it roll in and out like the tide. I now know how to enjoy sunrise and experience sunset in ways I'd forgotten.

Not that life is always easy here; it's not. We find pleasure, yes, but we work hard too. During the summer months, when the sun beats down, Steven is out in one of our tour boats, guiding vacationers and nature lovers. This past summer, with an increase in tourism, we added another boat and put my stepdaughter, Eliza, to work. When they weren't spending their half summer with their dad, Chase and Cody worked alongside Steven.

Chase took to the business quickly. I often found myself daydreaming about the day he would take over, or—at the very least—become a partner. His love for boating and the water was evident in nearly everything he did, including the Christmas boat parade preparations.

He and Rosa's son worked for weeks on decorating one of Steven's two pontoons. This morning, Rosa and I were meeting for a midmorning cup of coffee at Kona Joe's to discuss some particulars. Namely the two teenage girls who were planning to ride the boat with our sons. How could it be that I had a son old enough to date and a daughter still nursing?

I placed my feet on the cool wood of the bedroom floor. Steven was still sleeping, his lips parted, and a gentle snoring emitted from them. His light brown hair was tousled on the pillowcase; he looked as much like a little boy as he did a man.

My heart performed a somersault.

I tiptoed into the bathroom, showered, and changed into my clothes. If Patsy stuck to her typical schedule, she'd be awake shortly. I went into the kitchen, turned on the coffeepot, and then walked into the nursery just as she stirred under a light blanket. "Hey, punkin," I cooed as I walked to the crib.

Patsy made baby grunting noises, quivered as I picked her up, and snuggled into me after I laid her over my shoulder.

"Morning." I heard Steven's voice behind me.

I turned. He stood in the doorway, wearing a pair of blue and white striped pajama bottoms and no shirt. His hair was still a mess and his eyes remained sleepy. "Good morning. You're just in time for her first feeding of the day."

He grinned at me. "Then I'm right on time. Watching this is amazing."

"Would you bring me a glass of ice water?" I asked my husband without looking at him. "I forgot again."

Steven returned minutes later, a cup of coffee in one hand, a glass of ice water in the other. I reached for the glass, took a long swallow, and went back to giving our daughter the attention she deserved. Steven hovered over us for a moment before sitting on the carpeted floor, stretching his legs out front and leaning against the painted-white closet door. He slurped and swallowed a sip of coffee. "Whew . . . hot."

"Isn't that the point?" I placed the glass on the floor before pulling Patsy from her happy place and shifting her to another.

"I guess so. What's on the agenda for you today?" He rubbed a hand over his early morning beard.

"I told you yesterday. I've got a coffee date with Rosa."

"But you don't drink coffee while you're nursing."

"I'll have some decaf tea." I made a playful face at him.

"Where are you meeting?" He drew his legs up to sit criss-crossed.

"Kona Joe's."

Steven nodded. Scratched what I figured to be an imaginary itch on his chest. "I have a ten o'clock tour. Are you taking the baby with you?"

"Absolutely."

He took another sip of coffee. "What's this meeting about, anyway?"

When Steven and I reunited after more than twenty years apart, my childhood friend—the girl I'd loved like a sister—had been anything but pleased. I didn't get it then. I still don't. She and I managed to talk through some old issues, but our relationship, even after I married Steven and moved to Cedar Key, has remained strained. Friendly, but cautious. "She wants to talk about the boys taking the boat out tonight with Claire and Crystal."

Steven chuckled.

"What's so funny?"

"I'm thinking about you and me at that age." He tilted his head. "Remember?"

I felt flush. The memory of the way we'd felt for each other as teenagers was enough to make me run into my oldest son's bedroom, scream, "No way, no how!" and then bar the door. "Oh, Steven . . ."

He chuckled again. Took another sip of coffee.

"It's not funny." I raised Patsy to my shoulder and patted her back.

"Don't worry, Mom," he teased. "I'll talk to him." He stood, stretched. "He's a good kid."

"*You* were a good kid." I didn't dare mention Brigitte and their untimely pregnancy, which resulted in Eliza.

"He's a better kid. How about that?"

I didn't feel the least little bit comforted. "You'll talk to him? What will you say?"

"Kim, it's not like he and I have never had this conversation before, but I'll remind him about treating a lady with respect, about God's ultimate will for us when it comes to our bodies."

Patsy burped. Steven beamed with pride.

Men . . .

"Let me ask you a question," I said, standing. "Did your father have similar conversations with you?"

Steven's brow rose. "No."

"Really?"

"Trust me. He's a good father and he was wonderful when I was growing up, but that is one conversation he and I *never* had. Not even when Brigitte and I got ourselves pregnant with Eliza."

"That brings me not even a sliver of relief," I said, now from the changing table.

"Your dad and Anise going to meet us here or at the dock?"

"Here."

"All right." He stepped toward the door. "Have fun with Rosa."

"Uh-huh."

"You girls play nice now, you hear?" With a final chuckle, he padded down the hall.

I was eager to see and speak with Rosa. I arrived ten minutes early, spoke to Edie and Joe, who oohed and aahhed over Patsy and talked about how much she'd grown. I ordered a cup of hot tea and some of Edie's quiche, then went into the dining room overlooking the bayou to wait for Rosa, who was ten minutes late. Sometimes, I do believe, she does this kind of thing on purpose. By now I had eaten the quiche and was on my second cup of tea.

"I'm sorry, I'm sorry," she said, leaning down to kiss my cheek. "I had a client call me at the last minute."

Rosa owns Cedar Key's most successful real estate agency.

"Well, you certainly smell pretty," I said.

She dropped dramatically into the chair opposite mine. Edie appeared in the doorway between the front room where patrons order and the dining area. "Rosa, the usual?"

"Yes. Thank you." She looked at Patsy, who slept at my feet in her carrier. "Adorable. I cannot believe you have a baby."

"Sometimes I can't either."

"If I got pregnant right now, I'd . . . well, I don't know what I'd do."

"You'd survive, just like I'm doing."

Rosa waved her hand as though she were pushing the conversation to some other place. "It's Natori."

"What is?"

"My perfume," she said, looking at me as if I couldn't have possibly forgotten my statement.

"Oh," I laughed. "Yes. I thought it smelled familiar."

In my years as a wife, mother, and schoolteacher, I rarely wore anything beyond body spray. I *knew* Natori, of course. Heather often wore it. I, quite frankly, couldn't imagine spending that much money for something I'd wash off later.

But, for Rosa, it made sense. She was nothing short of exotic and elegant. Even now, on a Saturday in December, sitting in an island café overlooking the marshy bayou, she was dressed to the nines. Off-white straight-leg gabardine pants, a cashmere top the color of warm toast, and a lacy shawl she wore slung over her shoulders had my jeans and button-down Ralph Lauren shirt looking like they'd come from a secondhand store. As for scent, I wore Eau de Mother's Milk.

"I'm glad you asked that we get together, Rosa," I said. "I think we—as the mothers—need to talk about, well, the rules for tonight."

Joe sauntered in just then with Rosa's specialty coffee. "Just the way you like it, madam," he teased.

She thanked him, and he talked for a moment about tonight's festivities and then rejoined Edie in the front. Other patrons had entered the café; two entered the dining room and sat at the first table they came to. The others had gone to the tables along the balcony overlooking the bayou.

"That's why I wanted to talk to you." She swiveled the coffee stirrer in the cup a few times. "After all, remember when we were young? This is Mateo's first . . . date, if you want to call it that."

"Chase's too."

"My son is insisting that we—his father and I—not tag along. He says there will be enough adults in other boats, that the journey from one side of Dock Street to the other is not that far, and that we need to trust them."

Camaraderie comes in strange packages. "I think I've heard those exact words from my son."

"Remember us at that age?" she asked.

I didn't answer; I chose to take a sip of tea and glance down at Patsy again.

"Manny says he's going to have 'the talk' with him."

"Steven says the same thing. About Chase, I mean."

"And Manny says they're good kids."

"Ditto."

"Then why am I so worried?" She chewed on her red-stained lip.

"I totally trust Steven's ability to communicate with Chase—Chase follows him like a shadow—but I think I'll have my father talk to him as well."

Rosa's face went dark. At first I thought a cloud had covered the sun and had dimmed the natural light in the room. But when she took a shaky breath and sighed, the color on her face returned to normal. "I'm sure that will be good too."

"Why the . . . is something wrong?"

"No, why?"

Patsy stirred in her carrier. Fussy cries and a few chubby leg kicks indicated she was awake and ready to be picked up. Half of me wondered if Rosa had kicked the carrier to keep from answering my question.

I scooped my daughter up and to my shoulder. I dug into

the diaper bag hanging from the arm of my chair until I found a bottle of water. I popped the cover off with my thumb and wiggled the nipple into Patsy's mouth. She took to it with the same vigor as she took to me.

"There we go," I said. I looked up at Rosa, knowing I could argue with her about the expression I'd seen but deciding instead to get to the point of our sons. "So, what time did you tell Mateo to be home? Or, did you?"

"Manny said we'd meet them where the parade ends and then, as a family, continue on with the evening. Chase and the girls are welcome to hang with us. We'll keep a close watch, I promise. Are you planning to go to the chili cook-off?"

"Yes. And I've entered Max in the doggie parade. I'll go home after that. Dad and Anise are coming to the house, and then we'll all go to the cook-off together."

She didn't say anything at first. Her eyes shimmered with tears. Then, "You are lucky, chica, having . . . them. I know you lost your mother way too soon. So did I, truth be told. We are never ready to lose them, are we?"

"No."

"Hector was . . . no real father to me. When he died, I was more upset about the fact that I'd never had any real relationship with him at all. I cried not for what I lost but for what I never had."

I cradled Patsy closer to me. By now her eyes had fluttered shut again. "I'm sorry, Rosa. I really am. And, you know, if you ever need a father figure, Dad has always had a special place in his heart for you."

Rosa's eyes traveled to the window and beyond. Mine did the same, to see if I could ascertain what she had seen that caught her attention. Other than the usual scene, nothing out of the ordinary stirred. "He has, hasn't he?" she said.

"He's a good man."

She looked at me again. "Yes. I suppose he is."

"It was weird," I told Steven. We were in our bedroom getting dressed for the night's festivities—the community chili dinner to be held in the park, the boat parade, and the grand finale, which was when Santa Clam arrived at the park in an airboat. We'd already had the doggie parade in the park, where my golden retriever Max and I had dressed alike. Max brought home 2nd place. I brought home Max, who went in search of his new housemate, Patsy's cat, Oreo. I can only assume to show off his ribbon.

The little bit of light leftover from the day managed to sneak in through the open windows. Our room was bathed in gray. I switched on the bedside table light. Amber shot across our bed and pooled on the floor.

Steven stepped into a pair of jeans and looped the buttonhole around the button. He wore a tee but had yet to don the long-sleeved shirt I'd set out for him. "What do you mean by 'weird'?"

I sat on the side of the bed to pull Uggs over thick white socks. "I don't know how to explain it." I adjusted the top of the boots over black leggings. I also wore a mid-thigh-length red cowl-neck sweater, which was cinched at the waist by a wide black belt.

"Explain Rosa," Steven said. "I've never completely understood her."

I turned to look at my husband. "I admit . . ."

Steven shoved both shirts into the waist of his jeans, tucking . . . tucking. My gracious, how this man had me wrapped around his little finger, and he didn't even have to try. "What?" he asked.

"I'm just thinking how absolutely adorable you are," I said, walking to him and slipping my arms around his waist. "You. Me. Back here, say in . . ." I glanced at the digital clock on Steven's side of the bed. "Five hours?"

He kissed the tip of my nose. "You betcha."

I stepped back and extended my arms. "Are you sure I don't look like Santa's elf?"

He pressed his lips together. Smirked. Mirth filled his eyes. "Maybe a little."

I walked toward my closet. "I'm changing."

Steven grabbed my hand and pulled me back, drawing me into his embrace. He pressed his lips against mine. "I have a thing," he said, "for elves. Did I ever tell you that?"

I shook my head.

"I do."

"Mmm?"

"Mmm."

"So don't change?"

"Well . . . in five hours."

I laughed against his mouth just as the doorbell rang. "Dad and Anise are here."

"You, sweetheart, were just saved by the bell."

I kissed him quickly. "And you definitely had the talk with Chase?" I asked at the closed door.

"He's good to go. Are you going to finish telling me what was so weird about Rosa this morning?"

I twisted the doorknob and shook my head. "Maybe later. It was just . . ." I shrugged. "Something in the way she reacted about . . . I dunno." I looked at the door. "What do you think? Should I have Dad talk to Chase?"

"Leave it be. I don't see any reason to make more of this than it is."

I opened the door in time to hear Cody shouting, "Pop! Nana!"

I sighed. "Okay. All right. I can do this. I can watch my son on a boat with some . . . girl."

Steven headed to where he'd left his shoes. "You'll be fine."

"Maybe I'm as slightly off-kilter as Rosa." I heard commotion from the front of the house. "What in the world?"

Cody ran down the hall toward me. Wispy blond hair billowed around his head. "Mom! Hurry! Pop's got blood pouring all out his nose!"

31

Jayme-Leigh

Isaac found me at the dining room table surrounded by volumes of books and with my laptop open in front of me. Next to it, a legal pad, on which I furiously made notes.

He stepped up behind me and kissed the top of my head. "What are you doing?" he mumbled.

"What do you think?"

He sighed deeply. "Hon, it's nearly one in the morning."

"I know what time it is, Isaac."

He backed away, walked around the antique mahogany table, and sat in one of the six shield-back needlepoint chairs. He laid his forearms along the highly polished tabletop and leaned over. "So what have you got?"

I laid the pen down, ran my nails through my hair, catching the scrunchie and pulling it through. Throwing it between two large volumes I said, "Nothing I like reading."

"If you want to share, I'll listen."

I shook my head. "I don't even know how to say these words. It's one thing talking about it to a patient—not that

I've ever had a patient with AML—but this is my father, Isaac. My father . . ." As soon as the tears started to burn my eyes, I looked from my husband to a large, framed replica of Sir Edward Burne-Jones's *An Angel*.

Focus, Jayme-Leigh. Focus. Wings made of feathers. Blue feathers. Halo of flowers. An angel gently blowing into the slender horn. Lovely, lovely . . .

I returned controlled attention to my husband. "I'm going tomorrow to be tested. To see if I'm a match."

Isaac rubbed his eyes before answering. "Do you really think, Jaymes, that with your chemo treatments a few years back, you are going to be a candidate?"

"Stupid cancer." I slammed my fists onto the table. "What is wrong with this world that we have to deal with all this?" In one sweep, I managed to knock several of the books to the floor.

My husband stood slowly. He walked to my side of the table. Squatting, he picked up each book, closing them quietly and placing them back on the table in a neat stack. "I want you to listen to me," he said, placing his hands on my knees and drawing them around until they faced him.

I looked into his incredible eyes. There couldn't have been more compassion or love there if he'd had three.

"Are you listening?"

"Yes." I wasn't happy, but I was listening.

"You can't beat yourself up over this. Your dad getting sick is no more your fault than when your mom got sick or when—what was that child's name? The one you grieved over so?"

My heart cinched. "Eryaka Johnson." Eryaka had been

my first death after medical school. Lovely African-American child, only ten years old with an infectious smile and overly large ebony eyes, who suffered and withered away from sickle-cell anemia under my care. I'd nearly quit medicine after she died. If it hadn't been for Dad, I probably would have.

"You don't have the kind of control you'd like to have when it comes to sickness and death." He stood, pulled me to my feet, and walked me into the living room. He dropped onto the sofa, bringing me with him. We shifted until we found comfort, Isaac's arms draped around me protectively. Lovingly. "Listen," he whispered into my ear.

I was starting to hate that word.

"Take a deep breath and tell me what you've found out. Let's talk logically about what you can and what you cannot do."

I gritted my teeth long enough to think through what I wanted to say. "Isaac," I finally began, "when my father told me he had AML, my first thought was, 'What is AML?' I mean, I *know* what it is, but I couldn't imagine leukemia being in any way connected to my father."

"I know."

I turned enough to see his face. "No, you don't know, Isaac. Both of your parents are alive and well. My mother is *dead*. My father is *dying*. You and I both know his chances of surviving this disease are slim to none. Less than slim to none." I started to get up. There was still much to research, and knowledge was power. Knowledge would at least give me a head start on what was about to happen to my father. To my family, none of whom knew what lay ahead.

Isaac's arms tightened. "Stay. I know you. You'll sit up all night reading and you'll gain just enough insight to be argumentative with the experts."

I struggled against him, but he was clearly not going to let me up. When I relaxed against him, his arms remained flexed for a moment before easing.

"Let me," he said.

I faced forward. "Let you what?"

"Let me do the research. That's what I do, after all. I'm in research, am I not?"

"I guess."

"Jayme-Leigh . . ."

"All right." From a logical, intelligent standpoint, he was right, of course. I was so emotionally involved, I wasn't reading or discovering anything that was making me less anxious at what lay ahead. "All right."

We remained quiet until he asked, "What is your dad planning to do about the others?"

I sighed. "He said he'd tell them at Christmas when everyone is there." I took another deep breath. "He said he'd give them all the options he's looking at. The meds, the chemo, the possible transplant, if we can find a match."

"His siblings would have been the best chance."

"I know that. But with Uncle Morris and Aunt Kathleen both gone already . . ."

"Okay. So the chances are slim. But there's always Kim and Heather and Ami."

Tears fought their way to the surface again. In the recesses of my mind, I screamed. Loudly. A wail tearing at my soul in its release. I bit down, hard, on my bottom lip. "I'm going to get tested, Isaac. I know the results will probably be negative, but I have to at least try."

His lips pressed against the side of my head. "Then try. I'm not going to stop you. But I think you and I both know—"

"Stop. Just stop. I don't want to talk about what I know. I want to know what I don't know."

Isaac wisely said not another word. Within minutes I heard rhythmic breathing, telling me he had fallen asleep. I made a final attempt to slip out of his arms, but by reflex they tightened again.

Too exhausted to fight further, I closed my eyes and allowed myself to drift away. Tomorrow—a final thought came to me—I'd see what needed to be done for testing. If I was even a four-point match to Dad, maybe they'd let me donate my bone marrow.

But, if not me . . . okay. Maybe Kim. Or Heather. Or Ami.

32

Ami

Gray and I had been on I-75 south for over an hour and hadn't said more than a few words to each other. My husband had made it clear he wasn't happy about spending the Christmas holidays with my family in Cedar Key from the moment I told him "we have to," and he'd kept the sour mood pretty much ever since.

"We must," I'd said to him earlier that month. "We spent Thanksgiving here with your family. We have to spend Christmas with my family."

Gray lay sprawled across the sofa with one foot on the floor. He wore sweatpants and a tee, which was wrinkled because he'd had to fish it out of the dirty laundry or go bare chested. His left arm covered his forehead. The wedding band I'd placed on his finger just months before caught the sunlight streaming from a nearby window. "Since when do you care, Ami? When was the last time you spent any significant holiday with your family?"

I crossed my arms. "I don't deny I haven't been home in a while, Gray. But I think now . . . more than ever . . ."

Gray sat up, bringing his knees to his chest and wrapping his arms around them. "Now more than ever I need to be with *my* family. Don't you think? It's Christmas. The first without Carole."

I did think he needed to be with them. Of course I did. More than that, his family needed to be with him. But I also had needs, namely to be with my family. Dad and Anise. Jaymes. Kimberly-Boo. And, yes, even Heather. Especially now.

"I'm going to Cedar Key for Christmas," I told him. "I know I'm supposed to 'submit to your authority,'" I said, hooking my fingers in the air. "Whatever *you* decide is best for us. But I need to be with my family right now. Stay if you want to, but *I'm* going."

He threw his head back in exasperation. "This has nothing to do with 'authority.'" Gray mocked my hand motion. "Not to mention that you're twisting Scripture, Ami." For a while I watched his lips move with his eyes closed until, finally, he looked at me and said, "All right. All right. It's only fair, I guess. After all, you haven't seen your family since the funeral." He blanched. "And we did spend Thanksgiving with mine so . . . yeah. It's only fair."

In spite of his acquiescing, the near-constant tension we'd experienced since Carole's murder remained between us. Written in the air. Laying in the wake of the way his muscles flexed when I touched him as though my hand was made of hot coals. Or, when he touched me, whether as a husband reaching for his wife or what just came naturally when two people lived together.

We'd been married three months. Everything I had hoped and believed for the two of us hadn't come to be. The wedding with all the trimmings would never be. The weeklong honeymoon we'd talked about would have to wait. Possibly for years. The first year of what should have been wedded bliss—of getting to know how he squeezed his toothpaste tube and his learning to accept my tossing dirty clothes on the floor—was instead a year of strain. The man who'd murdered Carole had seen to that. That, and so much more . . .

"Do you want to listen to something else or should I just turn it off?"

I looked from the passenger's side of my car to where Gray sat in the driver's seat. One hand rested lazily over the top of the wheel, the other on his thigh. "What?"

His eyes darted from the traffic on the highway to the radio dial and back again. "The radio is becoming nothing but static. Do you want to listen to something else?"

I hadn't been listening to begin with. Mercy Me's "Joseph's Lullaby" faded in and out. "No. Not really."

Gray pushed the on/off button. Silence seeped into the car.

"It's getting lighter outside." I wrapped my jacket tighter around my body. Even with the heater on, the car was nearly as cold inside as the weather outside. Or maybe it was just me.

"Sun will be coming up soon." Gray's eyes scanned to the east and back again. "I can't believe the traffic is already this bad. I guess a lot of folks have the same Christmas plans as we do."

"When do you think we'll stop for breakfast?"

"You hungry?"

"A little."

He shot a glance toward me, his brows up in the charming way that still made my heart beat a little faster. "You feel up to eating?"

I shook my head. "Not quite yet. But I shouldn't wait too long."

"What are you hungry for?"

I didn't bother to look at him when I answered. "Anything but fast food."

"Got it. So, do you want to go to a sit-down restaurant?"

Yes and no. Just the thought of breakfast foods cooking, the myriad aromas—eggs, greasy home-styled hash browns, pancakes and syrup—blending together stirred the acid in my stomach. I took in a long breath through my nose and blew it out between my lips. Slowly. Slowly. Repeat.

"Do I need to pull over?"

I shook my head. "I'll be okay in a minute."

Gray remained quiet. Blessedly. Then: "Hey, Ami?"

"Mmm."

"How much longer did the doctor say before the nausea stops?"

"He said most women find relief by the beginning of the second trimester."

"Then shouldn't you be over this already?"

I closed my eyes, easing my head back against the headrest. "He also said some are sick their entire pregnancy." *Dear Jesus, is this my punishment? Or just Eve's in general?*

I felt his hand touch my belly. I jerked, whipping my head toward him.

"Sorry." His hand returned to his thigh.

"It's okay. You just scared me."

After several moments of additional silence—painful silence—he said, "Have you decided whether or not you're going to tell your parents? About the baby?"

"Not yet. I'm not showing so . . . if I can keep this awful nausea at bay, they won't have any reason to know." After all, we'd only been married three months. At six months . . . maybe it would be easier to admit. Easier to own up to what had happened. What we'd sworn wouldn't happen until after we married.

And I could just hear Anise now, asking me if I'd asked Jesus for forgiveness and, when I said of course I had, telling me to stop carrying the guilt.

So sensible. So much truth. But the other side of that truthful coin was that, while I had accepted Jesus's forgiveness, I had not accepted my own. How could I with Gray carrying enough guilt for the two of us?

He forced a smile and sent it my way. "What do you want to bet Heather will see it all over your face?"

"Ugh." That thought alone made me want to ask Gray to pull over.

"Well, maybe not. After all, my family hasn't guessed yet, even with you spending most of Thanksgiving either in the guest bedroom or over the toilet bowl."

I guess she has a touch of the flu . . . it's been going around the studio, he'd told them. A lamer excuse couldn't have been made up. I figured their minds were elsewhere.

I spied a billboard boasting home-cooked meals at down-home prices. "Let's stop there," I suggested.

"Sure."

"And please don't order anything fried."

"I wouldn't do that to you."

The simple line meant more than he could imagine. I pretended to smile, just as he had earlier. "Do you think you could talk everyone else in the restaurant into the same?"

Gray eased the car up the off-ramp. "I'm thinking no."

I slipped my hand over his, and for once, he didn't seem to mind. "Gray?"

"Mmm?"

"You know what I'm more worried about than my family realizing I'm pregnant?"

"What's that?"

"That they'll see the tension between us and wonder why."

"And if they do? What will you tell them?" He flipped the turn signal to indicate that we, as well as about six other cars, were heading right from the off-ramp.

I sighed. "That's a good question."

We eased up in the line of traffic. "Why don't you tell them the truth?"

I cut my eyes to him. "I don't think so."

"And if you decide to?" Gray cut his eyes to meet mine. "Who will you blame? Me or you?"

33

"Me," I answered.

Gray turned right. "You shouldn't. I've told you that. I hold myself fully responsible."

He eased into the left lane, following the signs for the restaurant.

"What's the old saying?" I asked. "'It takes two to tango'?"

"Still," he said. Gray pulled into the parking lot of the restaurant and brought the car to a stop. He turned the key, removed it, and clutched it in his hand. He turned to me, and that same hand pushed my hair over my shoulder. "Look at me," he said.

I did.

"We've been over this and over this."

I felt tears burn my eyes. "And still, we're not moving forward. Even our pastor told you that *you* were not to blame, Gray. Didn't he say that when two people are in love and about to get married, a trauma such as Carole's murder can cause emotions already too close to the surface to spill over? Isn't that what he said?" Tears slipped down my cheeks. I was so tired—so tired—of the strain between us.

"Verbatim. And in my head I know he's right. But in my heart"—he pointed to his chest—"I blame myself. I shouldn't have let you into my apartment that day. Not that day. I needed too much and—"

"And I was all too willing to give you everything you needed. Don't forget that."

That dreadful, rainy day in September, when the deed was done and we could do nothing but hold each other, we both cried. Gray begged me for forgiveness, which on one hand I somewhat appreciated, but on the other only brought additional shame to the humiliation I carried. I told him then—as I'd told him many times since—that of course I forgave him.

But our problems grew when he could not forgive himself. The very afternoon we buried Carole, he pulled me aside in his family home and told me we either had to get married right away or break up. "The way I see it," he said, "this is the only right thing to do. I was going to propose at Christmas but . . . now that we've been together . . . physically . . . we'd be foolish to think we wouldn't do it again." He pinked as his eyes squeezed shut. "Wanting you was already bad enough. Now it's worse. So . . . pray about it, okay?"

"Okay."

"Tomorrow morning. I'll call you then and you can tell me what you've decided."

Gray's eyes were filled with so much sadness and angst, I didn't have the heart to ask him what I should do if God didn't have an answer for me by then. Besides, I knew my answer.

The last thing I wanted was to get married on the sly. And the other last thing I wanted was to live my life without Gray. The latter being more critical to me than the first. I naïvely assumed that with both of us having asked God for forgiveness, we could move on as if nothing had happened. I told Gray the next day that, yes, I would marry him. "Just arrange everything," I said. "We'll keep it quiet like you've asked until after we're married."

Our pastor insisted on conducting what little bit of pre-marital counseling he could work in beforehand, and that we continue with counseling at least two times a week after the wedding. We'd been faithful to that, although—where Gray was concerned—it didn't seem to be helping. He continued to carry blame, which to me was tantamount to throwing God's forgiveness back in his face. That burdensome guilt had seeped into every fiber of these precious early days of our lives together. Even our most intimate moments were plagued by the shame Gray could not let go of.

We both cried when we discovered I was pregnant. And we asked ourselves if we should pretend it was one of those quirky things that sometimes happens to a couple on their honeymoon. Or would we own up to our sin?

"That's for you to decide," our pastor had said. "But in all honesty, I don't see where it is anyone's business but yours, Ami, and yours, Gray. No one—and I mean no one—should be so rude as to ask."

"But if they do?" Gray asked. "Then to lie is to sin again, is it not?"

"It is," the pastor said. "Which is why I suggest you two decide soon how you intend to answer should someone ask."

So far, we were answerless. Forgiven but broken. Tired but forced to keep going.

"Ami. Gray." Anise greeted us in a whisper as she opened the door to the house in Cedar Key. Scents of fresh-ground coffee and sugar cookies met me with full force. I held my breath until my stomach adjusted. "You're finally here."

"What's wrong?" I asked, exhaling. The silence within the house held more power over me than the coffee and cookies. So did the grim look on her face.

"Nothing. Dad's just fallen asleep in his chair and I didn't want to wake him." She pulled me into the entryway with Gray close behind. "How was your trip? Are you tired?"

I removed my jacket as my eyes studied her. "Long. And yes."

She looked at Gray as though nothing was wrong as she took our jackets and hung them on a coatrack that hadn't been there the last time I'd come. "Y'all were on the road how long?"

"Nearly eight hours, what with meals and rest stops," Gray answered.

I gave him my best "no you did not" look, hoping the mere mention of my frequent trips to the bathroom would not give away our secret. When Anise looked at me, I calmly said, "I had too much to drink at breakfast and lunch." I pointed to the coatrack. "New?"

She nodded. "Pier One. Isn't it perfect for the entryway?"

"I like it. Yes. Why is Dad asleep at one-thirty in the afternoon?"

Anise clasped her hands together. "He's just overly excited about your being here. Woke up too early this morning." She glanced at the still-opened door. "Do you want to bring your things in now or wait?"

"I'll go get everything," Gray said. "It's just one suitcase and a big bag full of Christmas gifts." He kissed my cheek before adding, "I'll be right back."

Anise wrapped her arm around my shoulder. "How are you, Ami? How's married life treating you?"

Not that great, thank you. "It's . . . different. I was single too long, I guess."

"You?" she said with a smile. "I was single nearly forty years. And I've only been married twelve." She blinked. "Twelve. But I have loved . . . *loved* being married to your father." Her gray eyes shimmered beneath new tears.

"Anise? What's going on? I can tell something's not right."

She shook her head. "Nothing we need to discuss right now. Just some changes in our lives that we'll talk about tonight as a family." She patted my arm and drew me into the family room, where my father slept in his recliner. Faint snoring filled the room, nearly inaudible under the tune from a Christmas movie playing on the television. "We were watching the holiday lineup on Hallmark when Dad dropped off." Anise picked up the remote from the table next to Dad's cushy leather recliner. With a casual push of a button, the television went mute.

Even with her nonchalant attitude, I couldn't believe what I saw. "How much weight has Dad lost?" *And why does he look so pale?*

Anise sat on the sofa, and I right beside her. "Anise?"

"Dad's not been feeling well, Ami." Her eyes avoided mine. "We've asked Heather and Jayme-Leigh to come in today rather than wait. Heather and her family have nearly taken over Harbour Master Suites. She called just before lunch to say they were here."

"Are Jayme-Leigh and Isaac staying at Kim's?"

Anise nodded. "They'll be in town in a couple of hours. Jayme-Leigh closed the office early." She patted my arm. "Would you like a cup of coffee?"

"Do you have any decaf tea?"

My stepmother's brow furrowed.

"Just a mood I'm in," I said, hoping to sidestep what, to me, was obvious.

Anise seemed to brighten. "I have ginger tea."

My rolling tummy leapt in anticipated relief. "I can't tell you how perfect that would be," I said.

34

Kimberly

Dad's news hit harder than when we were told of Mom's prognosis. Surreal. That's what it was. Surreal. I kept thinking, *Where is the script for this?* as though I should have been handed one upon entering my father's home. Something to skim before greeting my sisters. To memorize, if there was time, so I could know what I'd been slated to say at my father's matter-of-fact medical report. How I should react. Even the questions I should ask.

"I don't know," Heather said after moments of stunned silence. She cleared her throat, as though the words she wanted to say had gotten stuck there. "I don't know a lot about leukemia, but I do know there are various types."

"That's right," Jayme-Leigh supplied. The adults sat together in the family room. Some on the sofa and love seat. Others in chairs brought in from the dining room. Dad sat upright in his recliner with Anise on the armrest. Her arm draped protectively over his shoulder. Dad's hand rested on her knee, caressing it. "Dad has AML," Jayme-Leigh continued. "Acute myeloid leukemia."

Heather stood and faced Jayme-Leigh. "You knew already? You knew and you kept this from the rest of us? How long have you known?"

Andre pulled her back to her place on the love seat. "Sit down, Heather. This is not the time."

Heather's pale complexion turned crimson. An angry face jerked in the direction of her husband. After their eyes met, and communicated, the natural peach returned to her cheeks. "Sorry, Jayme-Leigh."

Jayme-Leigh nodded in acceptance.

"Dad?" I said. "Will you answer Heather's question?"

Dad was visibly exhausted. Earlier, he'd blamed it on a sleepless night in anticipation of his family being together. Of seeing Ami for the first time since she and Gray married. I hadn't fully bought it; something about the night of the boat parade, the nosebleed, and seeing the gaunt look of my father since wasn't jibing. Now I understood. I understood all too well.

"Do you mind if I explain it?" Jayme-Leigh asked.

"Somebody explain it," Ami said before burying her face in her hands. "Oh, *Daddy*!"

Gray slipped his arm around her waist and drew her closer. "Shh-shh-shh. Listen to your sister for a minute."

Jayme-Leigh looked to Dad. "Dad?"

Dad nodded as though he only had the energy for that much.

Our sister leaned forward, clasped her hands together, and looked at each of us, eye to eye, trained physician to the "family of the patient."

"AML—in Dad's case, adult acute myeloid leukemia—is a type of cancer. The bone marrow—that's the flexible tissue in the interior of your bones—makes abnormal white blood cells, or red blood cells, or platelets."

"Platelets," Ami repeated. "What's that?"

Jayme-Leigh touched a deep scratch at the center of her hand as she looked at Ami. "It's the cells in the blood that, when you cut yourself like I did the other day, gather at the wound and keep you from bleeding too much. They're produced in the marrow."

"Oh."

Gray squeezed Ami closer to himself again, her arm draped between his knees.

"Keep going," Heather said.

"So, AML is a cancer of the blood and bone marrow."

I pressed my palms together, looked first to Steven, then to Dad and Anise, and finally to Jayme-Leigh. "I take it you and Dad have already talked about his prognosis?"

"We have."

"Naturally," Heather muttered.

"Heather," I said. Then to Jayme-Leigh, "What about treatment?"

Anise shifted uncomfortably on the armrest but remained planted firmly next to Dad, who swallowed hard enough that his Adam's apple bobbed. "Girls," he began, "I've had a number of tests, including a bone marrow aspiration, and . . ." He closed his eyes. "Jayme-Leigh . . ."

Jayme-Leigh's jaw appeared locked in place until, finally, her lips parted. "First you have to understand that there are subtypes of AML and that becomes part of this equation.

Dad's age is another part. Our best hope would be to get this thing into remission—"

"Our best hope?" Heather said.

"Wait, wait," Andre interjected. "I know something about this kind of thing." He looked around the room. "You've taken time to look into all this, right, Dad? There are a lot of options out there."

"We're looking at two phases of treatment right now."

"Explain," Heather all but demanded.

"It's a lot to understand, Heather," Jayme-Leigh said.

Heather's eyes flashed. "Don't talk to me like I'm stupid, *Jaymes*."

"I'm not. Look, Heather, I'm a doctor and I've had to spend hours studying this. It's not my specialty."

"Ladies," Steven said. I looked at him. He glanced Dad's way. "Is this helping your father?"

Dad blinked slowly, a silent thank-you.

Ami spoke next. "Can we just get to the bottom line? I'm really, really not in the mood for a science lesson or health class or . . . whatever." All color had drained from her face.

Heather's frustration exploded in hers. "That's rich, Ami. You don't come home in—what?—forever? Dad is sick, he could be dying, and *you* don't want a science lesson? How much more spoiled can you be?"

"Whoa." Gray raised a hand toward Heather.

"Stop it!" Anise slapped her hands together as she stood. "Right now, all of you! I won't have this, do you understand me? I won't!" With that, she collapsed on the chair's armrest again and buried her face in her hands. Her sobs were heartbreaking.

Dad gathered her in his arms.

"I'm sorry," Ami said.

"You should be," Heather seethed through clenched teeth.

"Don't talk to her like that," Gray demanded. "And she's not spoiled. She's pregnant and she's not feeling well."

"Gray." Ami turned, warning him with her eyes.

"I'm sorry. But I'm not going to let her talk to you like that."

"Ami?" I asked. "You're pregnant?"

Now she, too, burst into tears, as though expecting a baby was the worst possible thing that could happen. Which I found somewhat strange, considering Dad's diagnosis. I glanced at Steven. "My gosh, what a mess."

Isaac stood. "Can I have everyone's attention here?" he shouted over the din.

Remarkably, the room's ruckus died down to a few shocked gasps and overwrought sniffles. "I've watched your father and stepmother agonize over this news, I've witnessed your sister work herself silly every night, researching, trying to find an answer to this . . ." He looked at Dad, then to Ami. "Ames, yours is both fascinating and exciting news. And I can imagine the last thing you want is to listen to gory details. If you need to lie down, please don't hesitate to go to your room and rest. I'm sure Gray can fill you in later, no?"

Gray nodded. "Sweetie? Do you need to lie down?"

Ami shook her head. "I'll be fine. I want to know about Dad."

"Isaac?" Dad said. "Will you and Jayme-Leigh explain everything while *I* go to my room and lie down?" He looked at Anise. "Hon? Come with me, will you?"

No one spoke as they wrapped their arms around each

other and, with a good night, left the room. When we heard their bedroom door open and then close, Isaac said, "Okay. Like JL was about to say, the first thing we want to do is to try to get this thing into remission. So, we have what is called 'remission induction therapy.'"

"What will that do?" I asked.

"Kill the cancer cells."

"Then?"

"Next is postremission therapy. We want to destroy any remaining cancer cells that would cause a relapse. Now we can look at chemo . . . radiation . . . stem cell transplant . . . clinical trials . . ." Isaac returned to his seat next to Jayme-Leigh. "Do you want to explain about donors?" he asked her.

"Basically, it's this," she said, again giving each of us her individual attention. "We need to see if one of us is a candidate as a donor for Dad. Typically, his siblings would be first in line, but—"

"They're both dead," Ami whispered to Gray.

"Ami, you're out. And, well, so am I."

"Why?" Heather asked. "Are you . . . ?"

Sadness fell over Jayme-Leigh. "No. No, no. Truth is, I had cancer myself a few years back. So . . . I most probably wouldn't be—"

"Cancer?" I asked. "When? What kind?"

Jayme-Leigh raised her hands to stop me. "It doesn't matter right now. I'll tell you later. I will. I promise."

Heather shook her head. "Let me see if I have this straight, Jayme-Leigh. You knew about Dad. We all know you knew the truth about Mom. And now you're telling us you had cancer and never told any of us about that either? Is there anything else we need to know?"

Jayme-Leigh stared at Heather without blinking or answering until Steven said, "So that leaves Boo and Heather."

"That's not very good odds," I said.

"Just so you know and, hopefully, won't put too much pressure on yourselves, most donors come from donor banks," Andre said.

"That's true," Isaac said. "But we'd like to start with family first. So, as soon as we can, we'll test and see."

"What about the grandkids?" I asked.

Isaac shook his head. "Only the ones over eighteen. *If* it comes to that. But, with each generation, the likelihood of being a match lessens."

"Got it," I said.

For several minutes no one said anything. Finally, Jayme-Leigh offered an apology. "I'm sorry. For not being able to say anything about Dad to the rest of you until tonight. For not telling you about my cancer. For . . . well, for a lot of things."

"I'm sorry too," Heather said. "For . . . a lot of things."

"Me too," Ami said.

"What are you sorry for, sweet Ami?" I asked.

She smiled weakly at me. "For not coming home more often."

I went to her, dropping to my knees and wrapping her in my arms. "You're here now. That's what matters."

I hardly slept, and when I did, my dreams were fitful. Mom—beautiful one moment and skeletal the next—flitted in and out. My father—young and tanned—stood on the beach of Cedar Key. He threw a Frisbee to my sisters and me, all of us in our teens and standing bikini-clad and waist-high in the gulf. Each of us screaming, "Dad! Throw it to me! Dad!" Laughter filled the seconds between our cries. Without warning, his youth disappeared and he stood before us, the older version of himself, blood pouring from his nose and mouth. Jayme-Leigh, Heather, Ami, and I struggled to get out of the water, to make it to where he fell to his knees.

Ami said, "I have to take care of the baby."

I looked at her. She had stopped in her push to get to Dad. She now wore a white peignoir that billowed in the water. She cradled a newborn in her arms, and I felt torn between running to my sister and her baby and running to my father.

"Kimberly," Jayme-Leigh called to me. I turned toward her voice. She now wore a hospital gown. "I have to take my chemo now. Go get Dad. You're the oldest. Go get Dad."

By now Heather had made it to shore. She yelled at me, "Boo, I've got it. I'm the closest now. I'll get Dad, take him to the hospital, and help him with his chemo. Don't worry, I can handle it."

Then, in that way dreams have, I was sitting in my father's office break room, crying into a paper towel, Dad sitting beside me. "I think you have a lot to salvage. And I know . . . I *know* . . . that the Lord can . . ." His voice trailed.

"What, Dad? What can the Lord do? Dad? Dad?"

Steven gently rocked my shoulder. "Boo. Kimberly. Wake up."

I opened my eyes to early dawn in our bedroom. My tongue felt swollen, my mouth dry. Moist tears clung to my eyelashes. "What?"

"You were dreaming."

"I was?" My eyes scanned the ceiling. "Oh. I guess I was."

"Dreaming about your dad?"

I nodded as I shifted my weight to my elbows. "Yeah. I gotta get up. Patsy will be awake soon."

"Do you want to talk about it?"

"No," I said, swinging my legs over the edge of the bed and touching my feet to the chilled, hardwood floor. "I'm good."

Steven pushed himself until he sat fully up, his back against the headboard. "Do you know what today is?"

I tied the sash of my robe tight along my waist. "No, what?"

"The twenty-second of December."

I had to think a moment. "Oh. Yeah." I pulled my hair into a makeshift ponytail and secured it with a scrunchie I'd tossed to the bedside table the night before. "Looks like we're going to live, huh. So much for the Mayans." My voice caught in my throat. "We're going to live," I said, now crying. "But Dad. What about Dad?"

Steven gathered me into his arms, shushing me. "It's okay, Boo. Everything is going to be okay."

"It's not, Steven. Let's face it. We're talking leukemia here. Dad isn't twenty-one. And I've already lost Mom. If I lose Dad, what will I have?"

My husband didn't answer right away. Then: "Me. The boys. Patsy. Your sisters. Anise."

"But my parents, Steven." I pulled away from him and wiped my cheeks with my fingertips. "The two people who brought me into the world. The two people who, without them, I wouldn't exist. I guess I . . . I'm just seeing how fleeting life really is. How final death . . ."

"You know better than that." He stroked my arm. "Our lives don't stop here, Kim. Our lives go on and on. Everlasting life, remember. From the moment we asked Christ to be our Savior, we *chose* eternal life."

"I know all that, Steven, and it brings a certain amount of comfort. But Dad won't be *here*. With me. With us."

Quiet moments followed while the stroking continued. Finally, Steven said, "Do you believe your mother is with God?"

I nodded.

"Do you ever talk to her? From your heart?"

"Yes. All the time. Things I would say if she were right here. She may not actually hear me, but it makes me feel better to say them."

"Because," he added quickly, "in your heart, she goes on and on."

I sent a soggy smile his way. "You're starting to sound like that song from *Titanic*."

"Uh . . . yeah. What I'm saying—badly, I admit—is that your mother and all your memories of her remain in your heart. So when you speak *to* her, you are speaking to your heart. When your father dies—whether sooner or later—he'll be there too. Just like our sweet friend Patsy is there. We carry our loved ones with us, long after they're gone."

I let the words seep into my spirit. "You're right," I said. "You're so right." I kissed him sweetly. "What would I do without you?"

His eyes studied my face; they grew moist. "May you never find out," he whispered.

I nodded, unable to discuss death and dying another minute. "I have to get up. Wash my face. Feed the baby. Go to the market. We're nearly out of milk, and you know how much those boys of ours consume every morning."

Steven stood. "I'm outta here myself. Tour boats don't drive themselves, and the island is crawling with visitors."

"Just the way you like it."

"What's not to like?"

I managed to get to the market before the boys woke. I parked on the side of the painted blue building, in front of the mural of Cedar Key's earliest Native American residents. I stepped out of my car and closed the door, not bothering to lock it or to roll up the windows. In spite of my heavy mood, the weather was glorious.

How could that be? Hadn't the weather been told of my father's diagnosis? His prognosis? Hadn't a notice gone out informing the blue sky and the breeze ushering salt air across our little town that my sister and I would soon go through the agonizing process of being tested and waiting for word as to whether or not we were a match?

I shook my head as I entered the store, freeing my thoughts. The familiar blended smells of fresh seafood and an old building met me. I spoke briefly to Maddie, the clerk, before heading straight to the dairy.

I jerked a gallon of milk off the shelf, resting it between the crook of my arm and on my hip bone.

"What brings you out to the market so early on a Saturday, chica?"

I turned toward the familiar voice. "Hey, Rosa."

The faint smile on her face turned serious. "What's wrong?"

338

I blinked back tears. "It's my dad. He's . . . he told us last night. He's . . ."

Rosa took a step toward me. As always, she was fashionably dressed, and the smell of her perfume wafted around her. "He's what, Boo? What's wrong with Dr. Ross?"

"He's sick, Rosa. He has AML."

"I don't know what that is."

"It's a kind of leukemia. A cancer."

Her dark, almond-shaped eyes filled with tears. "Noooo," she whispered. "What . . . what will he do? He'll be okay, won't he?"

I shook my head. "I don't know, Rosa. Jayme-Leigh and Isaac tried to explain everything to us last night. There're steps to be taken. Chemo maybe. Radiation maybe. Stem cell transplant if we can find a donor. Heather and I . . . we're going to be tested."

She came closer. "When?"

"I—I don't know. We didn't get that far."

"You said you and Heather. What about Ami and Jayme-Leigh? Why aren't they going to be tested?"

"Jayme-Leigh isn't a candidate because . . . well, she's just not. And Ami is pregnant."

"Little Ami is having a baby?"

The milk grew heavy and cold. "Yeah." I tried to smile. "Can you believe that?"

Rosa didn't answer the question. "So, what if neither you nor Heather is a match?"

"The next step, I guess, is a donor bank." I shrugged. "The best bet is siblings, but Dad's are gone. Next would be children and after that, I . . . I honestly don't know all the answers, Rosa. It's all so new."

Rosa looked away from me. Her eyes grew darker. Intense. Tears spilled from them and her head quivered. "Mama, tell me what to do," she whispered.

"Rosa? What is it?"

Her focus returned to me. "Chica," she said, her whispered words continued. "Can you . . . can we talk? There's something I need to tell you. Something it's time you knew."

35

Anise

Ross slept fitfully for most of the night. His waking, turning, sighing kept me awake along with him. Not that I minded so terribly. Every conscious moment with my husband was another to treasure. To count as special, even in the midst of sickness.

Instinctively, I knew our nights were numbered.

Then again, they had always been.

From that first evening back in Seaside Pointe when we'd collided on the steps of the inn, the ticking of the clock had begun. The countdown had started. The pendulum swung. Like most couples, we simply were not aware.

With the exception of Steven and the grandchildren, by lunchtime the following day the entire clan had returned. Heather's older kids had volunteered to watch Patsy and "hang out" with Cody. Chase had gone to work with his stepfather. I'd put together a lunch of homemade chicken salad sandwiches, which I served with homemade potato chips, grapes, and carrot sticks. We ate scattered between the kitchen, dining room, family room, and balcony. Conversation rattled on, but no one really said what was on their mind.

Considering the general loss of appetite Ross had experienced lately, he ate fairly well. When we'd finished eating and the dishes had been rinsed and were stacked in the dishwasher, I returned to the family room to find him sleeping soundly, once again, in his chair. Around the room his daughters sat quietly, watching him. Doing the same thing I'd been doing since learning of this terrible disease and its effect on our family. Just watching. Taking it all in. Counting the minutes.

An hour or so later, Ross woke in a sweat; he'd started running a fever. I went with him into our bedroom. While he stripped out of his damp clothes, I found him something comfortable to change into, then I stepped back into the family room to ask Jayme-Leigh what would be best to give him.

"I'm on it," she said.

Later, when the fever had subsided and Ross felt well enough, he asked that we go out to the balcony outside our bedroom so he could watch the day come to its end.

"Of course," I told him.

After we settled in our patio chairs, he asked, "Where are the girls?"

"In the kitchen. They're all busy making dinner together. It's a sight to behold."

Ross smiled weakly. "I'd have to see that to believe it." Then: "And my sons-in-law?"

"Watching an old *Law and Order*. I'm not sure which version of it. *Special Victims Unit*? *Criminal Intent*? Anyway, one of those."

December's chill fell around us as the sky turned a darker gray. "Ross, are you cold?"

"A little."

"Just like you not to complain," I said, rising from my chair. I went into the bedroom, retrieved a throw, and was tucking it around him when Ami suddenly appeared at the open French doors.

"Hey, sweetheart," I said.

Ross turned his head and smiled. "My baby," he said. "I want to talk more about this upcoming addition to my family."

Ami pinked. "Yeah, well . . . I still haven't wrapped my mind around all this."

An uncomfortable expression crossed my stepdaughter's face, as though something were terribly wrong. "Is everything okay in the kitchen?" I asked.

"Yeah." She rolled her eyes. "Believe me, Heather has everything under control."

Ross snorted. "I'm sure she does."

Ami's smile rose and fell in one movement. "Um . . . can I talk with you a minute, Dad?" She looked at me apologetically. "Alone?"

Ross cocked a brow. "Anything you want to say in front of me, Ames, you can say in front of Anise."

I continued to stand near my husband as Ami wrung her hands, then ran the palms along her slender hips. "I . . . um . . ." She looked so sad; I couldn't help but feel sorry for her. "This isn't about me. Or the baby."

Ross sighed. "Whatever it is, I have no secrets from my wife."

She raised her chin by a fraction of an inch. "All right then." She sat in my chair, pressed her knees together. I watched her eyes dart back and forth to some unseen pattern on the floorboards. She licked her lips, took a deep breath, and said, "There's one more."

"One more what, sweetheart?"

"Daughter."

I looked at my husband, who immediately looked at me. "What did you say?" we said together, now giving Ami our full attention.

"I can't be a donor because of the baby, and Jayme-Leigh can't because of her past cancer. Heather and Kim may or may not be candidates. But . . ." She breathed in and out several times. Rapid, shallow breaths. "There's one more daughter, and I think we should at least be honest about it. See if she is. A match, I mean. I mean, maybe I'm jumping the gun, Dad, but . . ." Tears spilled from her eyes. "I just can't hold this in any longer." She hiccupped. "Maybe I'm just being hormonal, I don't know, but I can't . . . and I can't lose you, Dad. Not now."

Ross's own breath left his lungs as though they were a tire with a nail pierced through the rubber. His brow furrowed. He leaned forward, rested his elbows on his knees and his face in the palms of his hands. "How do you know that?" he asked, looking to his daughter.

"Mom told me."

"Mom?"

"Joan knew?" I asked.

Ami looked at me sharply. "You've known, haven't you? You're not shocked by what I'm saying as much as the fact that I'm the one saying it."

344

I nodded. "I've known."

"I told her before we married," Ross said. "Ami, how did your mother know?"

Ami shrugged. "I don't know, Dad. She just knew."

"When did she tell you? *Why* would she tell you?"

"That night . . . when you and Jayme-Leigh had the emergency and Mom was so close to death. You left me alone with her. Remember?"

Ross nodded.

"She was out of her head that night. At first I thought it was just nonsense. But then when we went to Cedar Key that Christmas after you married . . ." She looked to both of us. "I overheard you and Eliana talking, and I knew, then, that it was true."

"Oh, Ami." Ross groaned. "I'm so sorry, honey." He leaned back in his chair. He was tired already; this, I knew, would remove any level of energy he had left.

"Dad? Does Rosa know?" Ami asked.

He shook his head, unable to verbalize the answer.

Ami returned her gaze to the floor. "I never told the others. No one knows except Gray and me."

"I appreciate that, honey. But what I want to know is, is this why you left? Stayed away so long? Because you couldn't . . . couldn't live with this? Couldn't . . ." He didn't finish his thought, though I felt I could have, had I been asked to. Ross's fear, all along, had been that Ami was somehow angry with him for something he wasn't aware of.

With the question hanging between us, Ami remained quiet. She blinked a few times, then brought her long hair over one shoulder. "Yeah. I just—I just couldn't wrap my head around it. That you, of all people, would . . ."

Ross shifted a little in his chair. "Do you want to ask me any questions?"

"Is it okay? Okay to ask?"

"If it weren't, would I tell you that you could?"

"All right, then. Well . . . I mean . . . what happened, for starters?"

Ross rubbed his forehead with the fingers of one hand. "Fair question. All right. After Boo was born, right after, your mother started to . . ." He trailed off as he looked at his child, all grown up with one of her own on the way.

"Drink again?"

He chuckled, but it wasn't a happy laugh. "You know about that too?"

"That same night. Mom told me. She said she wanted me to know the truth so I'd never make the same mistakes she had. She said she didn't have liver cancer like everyone thought. But, to be honest, I'd already known, or at the very least, suspected before that." She smiled. "Remember how much I loved to play dress-up when I was little?"

"Of course."

"I went into Mom's closet for my dress-up clothes. There was always a bottle of wine or cans of beer stashed somewhere. Hidden in shoe boxes and hat boxes. Or just plain ol' boxes." Pain etched across my stepdaughter's thin face.

"Oh, Ami," I whispered. My heart ached at the thought of this child searching for a floppy hat to go with oversized wedges only to find cans of beer and bottles of wine.

She cast a weak smile toward me. "It's okay. Part of growing up, I guess."

"No, sweetie. No, it's not. Or, at least, it shouldn't be."

346

There was a moment of silence before Ross cleared his throat and said, "Back then, back when Kim was born, Eliana talked her into going into rehab. She loved your mother like a sister; you have to believe that."

Ami grimaced.

"It was all me, Ami. I took advantage of the situation." He swallowed hard. "I don't make any excuse for it. It's just how it was. I was hurting. I couldn't believe that after Kim was born Joan would go back to drinking like she did. Back then, I didn't understand the disease. How it works. How it destroys. I stayed in denial for an awful lot of years, so how would I know?"

"I thought you weren't going to make any excuses."

"It's not an excuse. It's just the way it was. I was lonely. I was hurt. Scared out of my mind. Eliana was in such a bad marriage. Hector treated her like a punching bag." He shook his head. "Yet, she was always so strong. So tender and giving in spite of what life took from her. Well," he said, looking directly at his daughter, "you remember."

"I do. And she was." Ami swiped her tongue over her bottom lip. "How long did the . . . did the affair last?"

Ross chuckled again. "There was no affair. It was one night. One time. One." He held up an index finger. "We both cried afterward. Promised it would never happen again. And it didn't." He swallowed. "She told me two months later she was pregnant and she was quite certain the baby was mine."

Ami looked out over the marshes. She folded her arms across her chest, crossed her legs, and slumped her shoulders. "I know all about 'one nights.' This baby," she said, looking down, "was probably conceived one night when our defenses—Gray's and mine—were down. Right after Carole got killed. That's why we got married so quickly." Her eyes widened. "Not because of the baby. We didn't even know about the baby until after we'd gotten married. But, because, Gray felt—we *both* felt—that once that door had been opened, it couldn't be closed so easily and then reopened again later. So I guess . . ." Her eyes turned sad. "I guess I know what it's like to . . . mess up. Who am I to cast a stone?"

"No stones necessary. But," Ross said, reaching for his daughter's hand, "you do whatever you can to make it right. Sounds like that's what you did too."

Ami sighed so deeply I was surprised she had air left in her lungs. "So, then what did you do? Once you found out? I mean, you were already married to Mom, and obviously you didn't leave her to marry Eliana."

"No. Hector was a drunken fool who could be easily . . . deceived. Eliana and I both agreed that to say anything truthful at that point would only disrupt everyone's life. Joan was doing better. In fact, she was doing so well, I thought she'd licked her problem." He made a tsking sound with his tongue. "I told Eliana I would provide for the baby. Everything she needed and then some."

"And you did?"

"Right down to college. And there are CDs in the bank for Rosa's children, as Eliana's grandchildren, when I . . . when I'm gone."

The three of us sat silent for several minutes. The early evening air turned thick with palm fronds rustling and marsh critters chatting. The smell of the marsh rose to where I leaned against the railing of the balcony. "Ross," I finally said, "if there is a chance, even a small chance, that Rosa is a match . . . well, that's one more chance."

"No. I won't hear of it."

I clasped my hands together. "But why not? To be honest with you, if the girls all tested negative, I was going to suggest it. But now Ami has . . . why not?"

His head jerked toward me. "And have her think that her mother . . . ? No. I'll die first."

"No, you won't." The voice came from beyond the opened doors. Kimberly stepped around the corner, and she leaned against the frame. "I'm sorry. I was eavesdropping."

Ross dropped his head along the back of the chair. His eyes rolled as the lids fluttered shut.

"Dad," Kim said, her voice firm.

He opened his eyes again, looked at her. "What, Boo?"

"She knows."

"What?" the three of us spoke in unison.

Kim folded her arms, crossed one ankle over the other. "Rosa knows. She knows she's your daughter. She's known for a few years now."

I exhaled a breath that had caught in my chest a minute earlier. "I've wondered . . ." I said, but no one responded.

Ross's gaze fixed on his oldest child for endless seconds. "How? How did she find out?"

"Her mom . . . on her deathbed." Kim looked at Ami. I watched her swallow. "Sound familiar?"

"How weird is that?" Ami whispered.

Kim looked at her father. "She thought Eliana was talking out of her head at first, but then . . . apparently there were some correspondences. Legal papers."

Eventually he looked at me and said, "Be sure your sins will find you out, Anise. Isn't that what they say?"

I grimaced. "Not 'they.' Moses said it to the Israelites about their behavior as they entered into the Promised Land. I'm afraid *they* have taken it out of context."

Ross sighed again. "It's still the truth." He chuckled. "All these secrets I've kept and look where it got me." He looked at his daughters. "Your mother's drinking. Her disease. Jayme-Leigh's cancer. My one night with Eliana, which led to a lifetime of secret-keeping. And where did all this get me? Sitting on a balcony, dying, with not a secret left inside."

"Dad," Kimberly said. She dropped to her knees by his chair. "We all have our secrets. There's not a person alive who won't take something to their grave they keep hidden in their hearts." She kissed his temple. "And you're not dying, Dad. Don't say that you are." Tears filled her voice. "Please don't say that."

Ross kissed her cheek in return. "We're all dying, sweet pea. Question is, how do we want to spend the days we've got left? I've spent too many of them holding on to things that, in the end, didn't matter anyway." He looked at me and back at Kim. "Does Rosa . . . does she hate me very much?"

Tenderness rose in Kimberly's eyes. "No, Dad. At first, yes. At first she was angry with you, with her mother, and—she told me earlier today—with me for having had the treasure of calling you my father."

"What changed her feelings?" I asked.

"Manny told her to go back and reread the letters between Dad and her mother. He said that when she did, she'd see that Hector—her legal father—had done as little as possible for

350

her. Dad, on the other hand, had done everything he could, going above and beyond, expecting nothing in return. As a father himself, Manny told her Dad's actions were impressive. There are so many fathers out there who would have denied the whole thing and let the responsibility fall solely on the mother's shoulders."

"No," Ross said. "I couldn't have done that. I may not have been perfect, but I couldn't have done that."

Kim leaned closer to her father. "Dad, this is why you understood about Charlie, isn't it? This is why you said you understood all too well the power of Christ's forgiveness. Of how he 'holds all things together'?"

Ross patted her cheek. "No one knows how the blood of Christ works better than this sinful man."

"Or this sinful woman," Ami whispered.

I smiled at her. "Or *this* sinful woman."

"You?" Ami said. "You're practically my hero when it comes to walking out your faith."

"What are we talking about?" Heather's voice came from inside the master bedroom.

We all turned. Heather wore a Christmas bib apron over jeans and a light cream-colored sweater. She had a red dishcloth in one hand and a wooden spoon in the other.

"Come join us," I said. "You may as well hear this too."

36

The family gathered in the family room. By now, Steven had arrived. At what point, I'm not sure. "What's going on?" Isaac asked.

Andre reached for the remote control and turned off the television.

"Anise is going to share a story," Heather said.

I hadn't expected this. Hadn't thought I'd ever share such intimate details with my husband's children and their spouses. Yet, here I was, about to tell what I'd only shared with Lisa and Ross, the story of how Jesus had come into my life and had taken what was broken and spoiled and made it into something whole and pure.

As usual, Ross sat in his recliner and, as usual, I chose to remain near him by perching on the thickly padded arm. He wrapped his arm around my hips and patted my leg, letting me know that what I had to say was safe with those I'd loved like blood. That I was safe with him.

Oh, how I knew that. How I'd always known that.

I cleared my throat. "When I was a little girl," I began, "my father and mother divorced. My father remarried very shortly thereafter." I took a moment to glance at Heather, who raised her eyes as though surprised to hear we had a commonality. "My mother, brother, and I learned to live without a man in our lives. My brother and I were both studious, both active with friends and ballet and tennis. My mother worked hard to provide for us, and—on the outside—we appeared to be doing all right.

"Inside, I grieved the loss of my father. But he'd built a new family, one he seemed totally enamored with, while pushing ours aside like yesterday's newspaper. As I grew older, I became somewhat infatuated with older men. Even in high school." I glanced down at my husband, who smiled.

"Old men," he said.

"Older," I corrected. I breathed in the scent of a vanilla-scented candle and Italian food simmering in the kitchen. "My best friend Lisa used to call it my 'father complex.'

"Well, one day, when I'd become a woman and was working with my mom, I met a man—older by ten years—who traveled a lot in his job. He told me he was single. That he had an apartment in a nearby town. He came through often enough that we established a relationship. An adult relationship. The first of its kind for me." I took another breath. Exhaled. "He was everything I thought I could ever want or need. Strong. Secure. And he adored me." I looked at my hands and made an effort at rubbing my fingernails with the pad of my thumb. "But as it turned out, he wasn't single at all. He had a wife. Kids. A *real* life.

"I was devastated, of course. And totally ashamed that I'd

given myself to this man who had so obviously little regard for me." I closed my eyes against the shame of my story.

Ami sighed loudly and I opened my eyes, questioning the look of confusion on her face. "I'm sorry," she said. "It's just that I . . . I guess I always thought . . . in my mind . . . that you were some virginal bride."

I bit my bottom lip and smiled. "I was. Spiritually speaking. I, uh . . . I realized—once my heart had begun to mend—that the one factor that had been missing from my relationship with Garrett was any kind of spiritual aspect. I'd been raised a Christian. I knew God's Word. I'd accepted Jesus as my Savior when I was about twelve . . ." I looked at Isaac, whose eyes were sympathetic and filled with compassion. He nodded, indicating I should continue. "But I'd left all that within the confines of the church building when it came to my relationship with Garrett. As though there were two sets of rules between God and me. Two covenants. One was for when Garrett was in town and one when he was not.

"So, I returned to my knees, asked Jesus to forgive me, to cleanse me, and to purify me."

"Purify me with hyssop, and I shall be clean; wash me, and I shall be whiter than snow," Isaac supplied. "Psalm 51:7."

The room stood still. Then, Ross said, "How beautiful, son. And appropriate."

"There are more things our faiths share," Isaac added, "than we don't. Don't think for a moment I don't take in everything you have said to me." He took his wife by the hand. "All of you."

"Then," Kimberly interjected, keeping her eyes locked

with mine, "you became a new creation, like it says in First Corinthians."

I nodded. "That's right." I smiled at an old memory. "Lisa used to say I was a new critter, borrowing on the translation that says we are new creatures." Light laughter floated through the room, then subsided as they waited for me to continue. "When I met your father," I said, smiling again at my husband, "I was spiritually pure. When Jesus forgave me, it was as if my relationship with Garrett never happened."

"Wow," Ami said.

"And," Gray added, "to make it any other way is to throw the blood of Jesus back in his face. To say, 'Your blood is good enough for others, but not good enough to cleanse the sins *I* have committed.'" His cheeks flushed. "I guess I needed to hear that as much as anyone." His eyes found his wife's. "I'm sorry, Ami," he said quietly. "I'm so sorry." Then, looking up, he added, "I'm sorry, Lord. I've been very wrong. Very, very wrong."

Gray and his wife wrapped themselves in a hug.

"Sorry for what?" Heather asked.

"None of your concern, Miss Priss," Ross said, his voice strong and sure.

Andre leaned forward, cracked his knuckles, and then said, "As a father, I have to ask: whatever happened between you and your dad, Anise?"

"Nothing," I said. "Nothing has changed with my father."

"Why not?" Ami asked. "I mean, if Christ holds all things together like Dad has always said, and he makes all things new, why haven't you reconnected with your father?"

I didn't have an answer for that. "I honestly don't know,"

I finally said. I smiled at my family, who seemed to be waiting for more of an explanation. "I guess I got comfortable with the way things were and just never thought to rock the boat." I shrugged. "If you are rejected time and again, you tend to be gun-shy."

Steven nodded. "I can somewhat sympathize. My daughter rarely hears from her mother. As much as she tries to act like it's okay, I know deep down it hurts. Even after all these years. Still."

I swallowed hard. I hadn't seen my father since the night I graduated high school. Even then our conversation was strained. In the years since, he'd made little effort to contact me, and I'd made less effort to contact him. He was alive; I knew that much. I received occasional Christmas cards from one of my half siblings, and my stepmother sent a birthday card every year. Both she and Dad signed it, and I often imagined her standing over him, forcing a pen into his hand. "I suppose," I finally said, "I thought it was up to him to reach out to me. He hasn't, so . . ."

"Hmm." Heather cocked her head at me. "I was just thinking how hard you worked to reach out to me. Difficult as I was."

Andre chuckled. "There's an understatement."

"Can I get a witness?" Kimberly said.

"All right. All right," Heather said, throwing up her hands. "I wasn't looking for an all-out attack over here. I'm just saying . . ." She looked at me again. "Maybe it's something you should think about. Pray about. One thing we should all admit to right now is that every story has more than one perspective."

True. I nodded but said nothing.

"Well now," Ross said from beside me, "I do believe I smell something delicious coming from the kitchen. Lasagna, perhaps?"

Kimberly stood and smiled. "Two of them actually. One spinach lasagna for Anise and Ami and Gray and one made with everything for the rest of us carnivores."

Gray raised a fist as we all stood. "To the kitchen, I say!"

"Last one in has to wash the dishes," Jayme-Leigh cheered us onward. "Unless it's Dad."

"Why start now, huh, Dad?" Andre teased.

"Why indeed?" I added.

Ross slipped his arm around my waist and I his as we followed our children into the next room. "Looks good from back here, doesn't it, Anise?" he asked.

I kissed his cheek. It was clammy, and I feared his fever had returned. "It does indeed, my love. It does indeed."

We both squeezed. "Ross, listen to me for a second. I think you should tell Rosa about your cancer," I said before we reached the kitchen. "Ask her to be tested."

"I know you do. And I love you for feeling that way."

I stopped and turned my husband into my arms. "I love you more than I have words to say, Ross Claybourne. Don't ask me to live without you."

He smiled at me; his eyes turned misty. "You will one day, you know."

I kissed his lips gently. "But no time soon. Okay?"

"Yes, ma'am. I'll see what I can do."

"Merry Almost-Christmas, Dr. Claybourne."

"Merry Almost-Christmas to you too, Mrs. Claybourne."

Heather stuck her head back into the family room. "Come on, you two. My gosh, can't you stop with your lovemaking long enough to eat dinner?"

I smiled at her. "Never," I said. "I'll love this man until I die."

"Or I," Ross whispered.

I looked at him fully. "No, sir. I had it right the first time."

37

Present Day

None of the girls—and that included Rosa—were a match for Ross. And, though we kept our hopes up about finding a match from a donor bank, that didn't seem to be happening either.

In 1908 a group of Seventh Day Adventists got together with a pocketful of change—$4.93 to be exact—and a bank full of commitment and prayer. With that they bought a farmhouse, which was converted to a treatment facility for patients with tuberculosis. Today, on that same piece of property, Florida Hospital Orlando—one of the seven Florida Hospital locations—stands. But even a century later, their mission has remained the same: to extend the healing ministry of Christ.

I know this bit of trivia because, in time, my life became endless days of sitting next to my husband's hospital bed on the third floor of that same hospital. I read books, flipped through magazines, and when those no longer kept me from feeling as though I was going stark raving mad, I read hospital brochures. I now know about everything from what to expect during an endoscopy to all the fine points of the hospital's Well Baby Program.

Time became more about dying and less about living. But I felt the love of God because of the hospital's mission more than I could have anticipated. The staff treated us—and every patient we met—with the tender loving care one often hears about but rarely sees. In the process of such grief, they brought much-needed comfort to Ross's body and to my soul.

Losing a loved one without warning is like waking up and discovering the sun has stopped shining. But losing a loved one over a long period of time—no matter how short that time is—is like waiting for the sun to set and knowing that once it does, it will never rise again.

I've watched the sun set time and again in Cedar Key, so I know how slowly it sinks toward the horizon. Yet, once it reaches a certain point, a particular place in the orb, it drops quickly. Too quickly. Blink, and you've missed it.

Many evenings, Ross and I drove out to Shell Mound. We stood at the end of the pier, our hands clasped, our shoulders rubbing against each other, waiting for this magnificent moment of nature. Then, after the sun puddled into the green grasses, the black rush, and the blue-green water of the marsh, we'd wait for the afterglow, that moment in time when the clouds become brilliant colors of gold, orange, and red. And, as it always has and most likely always will, the sky enflamed, as if God decided to lead his children, once again, to the Promised Land, and we had become them.

Later, as we drove along County Road 326, the slow moon rose—full and brilliant—as a night-light illuminating our path home.

He and I would never again experience those moments this side of Glory, but we talked of them often in that hospital room. "Remember when," he began, his lips barely moving.

I'd run my fingertips through his hair, marveling at the silver against the crisp, white pillowcase of the hospital linen set. "When what, my love?" I'd ask, and then he'd whisper Cedar Key memories.

"I remember," I'd say.

To which he'd reply, "But will you remember always?"

"Always and forever," I'd whisper back. "Always and forever."

In spite of the market, or perhaps because of it, we'd sold our Orlando home and nearly every piece of furniture in it. So, when I was not at the hospital, when I was not thinking about keeping infection away from my husband or about whether or not it was safe for him to be wheeled outside to the atrium so as to feel the warmth of the sun upon his skin, when I was not reading to him, or watching him sleep, or chatting as much as his energy level would allow, or dealing with an endless parade of medical professionals . . . I stayed at Jayme-Leigh and Isaac's home. They made me feel welcome there, providing a comfortable guest room with a private bath and the openness to talk or ask questions, and the respect to remain quiet when silence was what I craved.

As a family, we agreed that when the time drew near—as near as it could get without actually happening—Ross and I would return to Cedar Key. We'd bring hospice in. We'd do everything we could to make Ross feel comfortable as he left his earthly home for the one his Savior had prepared for him. "I'd like a house with a view of the marshes," he'd tease, and we'd all laugh. Or pretend to.

Eventually that day came. When I arrived at the Cedar Key house with Ross, Kim was already there, as was Heather, who had prepared the staff in the floral shop to take over for as long as need be. When we pulled into the driveway, they—along with Kim's boys and Steven—stood on the landing of the staircase, ready to help our beloved upstairs.

Ami and Gray had flown down every other weekend, until her doctor said she was getting too close to delivery and could no longer travel. Ross missed seeing his baby grow with child but managed a few minutes on the phone with her each evening.

I prayed that Ross could hold on until the baby came.

And, at the same time, I prayed God would go ahead and take him. It's strange, really. I couldn't bear to watch him suffer and yet I couldn't tolerate the thought of life without him.

Early on we'd agreed that once Ross ran to the arms of Jesus, I'd stay in Cedar Key. Jon begged time and again that I consider returning to Maine, but the truth be told, once life in Cedar Key gets into your veins, all other locations fall short. It had become, for me, both home and the closest thing to heaven I could reach this side of heaven.

Our return to Cedar Key brought another guest and brought her often. Rosa had her cleaning crew disinfect every square foot of the house before we arrived, and she came by about three times a week with cooked or frozen meals for us. Always plenty to eat, plenty to store.

"I can't thank you enough," I said to her one afternoon

while Ross napped. I sat at the kitchen table while Rosa poured two cups of coffee.

"There's no need to thank me." She blinked several times; I knew to force back the tears. "I finally get to do something for him." Rosa walked the mugs of coffee to the table and sat next to me. "You look . . . very tired."

I stammered in my laughter. "I never knew it was possible to be this exhausted and still breathing, believe me."

Our coffee remained untouched, in spite of the creamer and sugar between us, waiting to serve their purpose.

"I wish," she whispered, "I wish I had told him sooner. That I knew. I only found out a few summers ago, but . . . we would have at least had that." Her eyes shot up to mine. "He would have accepted me, don't you think?"

I wrapped my hands around the mug, thinking about my own father. For a fleeting moment I wondered what might have happened had I gone to him with the way I'd felt about things. Adult to adult. No secrets. No presumptions. Just a fresh slate and a chance to begin again. "Rosa," I said, returning to the woman before me, "when he first told me about you, he spoke with such pride. Did you know that?"

Her tears refused to stay put. "He did?"

"Oh yes. He told me how difficult it had been to watch you grow up from afar. No matter, he said, he'd always been pleased with you. Your choices in life. And that he'd liked Manny from the start."

Rosa pulled a napkin from the napkin holder. She dabbed under her eyes before blowing her nose. "What else did he say?"

I prepared my coffee, stirring the spoon slowly. "When

your sons were born, your mother called him. And she sent photographs. And every time he came here, she updated him on what was going on in their lives."

"Really?"

I took a sip of coffee. "Really. I want you to look at me and listen carefully, okay?"

She did.

"You are welcome here. You spend as much or as little time with your father as you need, okay?"

"Okay," she whispered. She then placed her face in her hands and wept openly, mascara and eyeliner smearing to her chin. Not that she cared. Not that either of us did.

We had cleared out the guest bedroom to make room for Ross's hospital bed and all the other medical paraphernalia involved in keeping a dying person alive just a little while longer. I had wanted Ross to return to our bed for our final weeks or months or however long God allowed. But he wouldn't hear of it.

"When I'm gone," he said, "I don't want you feeling strange about being in your own bed."

"What I feel," I told him, "is strange *now*. Me sleeping in that big bed without feeling your body next to mine is more than I can bear."

This was a fight I would not win. Another fight I would not win. No matter how many times I waged war with God over my husband's illness, I was clearly being defeated. And, where my husband spent our final nights together was also not open for debate. So, to help with the compromise, Jayme-Leigh and Isaac brought the chaise lounge from their bedroom to Cedar Key. We placed it against the wall of the guest room, parallel to Ross's bed; it became my bed for the duration.

My brother Jon and sister-in-law Cheryl called every day, and my dear friend Lisa called at least three times a week. Over the years our phone conversations had dwindled to once a week . . . then once a month . . . sometimes every other month. But after hearing of Ross's illness, she called regularly, always offering hope. Always offering to pray before we said good-bye.

During one such conversation she mentioned how tired I sounded.

"I am," I admitted, "but I have to keep going. There will be time to sleep when . . ."

After a moment or two of awkward silence, she said, "Remember when we'd sit out on the back porch of the inn and sip hot herbal tea?"

I breathed in deeply, imagining the scent of raspberry tea and the sea-salt air. "I miss those days. And your heirloom tea set. It added to the atmosphere, I always thought."

"Do you take time to sit out by the marshes you are always telling me about for a cup of hot tea?"

I chuckled. It was a weary one, but at least my lips curled in a smile. "I'm afraid I've taken to coffee."

"What have those Southerners done to you?" she teased. "I suppose you only drink tea when it's iced and syrupy sweet."

I didn't answer, except for a noise that sounded something like "Hmm . . ."

"Will you do me a favor?" Her voice was now whisper-soft.

"What's that?"

"Will you promise me that, when this is over, you'll at least come back to Seaside Pointe for a visit? Jon said you refused to discuss moving back, but . . . please come for a visit? Stay with Derrick and me at the inn?"

How strange life is, I thought. How it turns on itself. Not so long ago, my husband had gone to the inn in search of respite after losing his beloved Joan. Soon, it would be my turn to seek solace among the peaceful places God had so lovingly designed for his children. "Yes," I told her. "I will come."

Several days later, a large box marked "fragile" arrived in the mail. It was from Lisa. I took it into our bedroom so Ross could watch me open it. His eyes danced with delight as, one at a time, I removed bubble wrap from Lisa's heirloom tea set, the one Derrick's mother had given to her on her wedding day, lovely with its yellow daffodils and green ivy.

"There's a card," Ross noted.

I popped the envelope's back flap with a fingernail in need of attention and pulled the note card from within.

"What does it say?" he asked. "Read it to me."

"Friends are flowers in the garden of life," I read from the front of the card, then turned it toward him.

"Is that all?"

I opened the card and shook my head. "No. She signed it: *Don't forget to take care of Anise.*"

"Hear, hear."

I held the teapot and pressed it between my breasts. "Dr. Claybourne, could I interest you in a cup of hot tea?" I asked.

"I would love that," he answered. "Especially if I get to drink it with you."

———

There came the day when Ross was in an unusually talkative mood, as though he'd rallied back to the living. He'd asked me to read to him from the Cedar Key *Beacon*, and I did. We discussed all the fine points of the articles and talked about the Community Calendar of events we'd have to miss this year, as though next year we'd be sure to attend each and every one. Both of us, together.

"I wish," Ross said, "that I could go to at least one more chili cook-off at the Eagle Lodge." A brow cocked teasingly.

"That's just what you need, Ross Claybourne," I said from the chair placed flush against his bed and facing the headboard. "Chili."

He chuckled. "You've been a good wife, Anise, but I sure do wish you'd not been so bent on your 'no red meat' way of life. Think of all the steaks I've missed."

I wanted to give a snappy comeback to remind him that he may have missed a certain number of steaks, but look at all the days I'd added to his life with the diet I brought to it. I didn't, of course. In the end—whether we are vegetarian or meat lover—our days are numbered by God. With all the healthy eating at our dining room table, death still hovered outside the door. The proverbial truck that *could* hit you, no matter a healthy lifestyle.

"You've been a good husband," I finally said. "The best. Without fault. And I want you to know that I don't regret a single minute of knowing you, loving you, and being your wife."

"You sure can get sappy when a man's about to breathe his last," he teased me.

"Ross . . ."

His hand, so pale against the bedsheets, rose and found its way to my cheek. I slipped mine into it and rested my head against all the strength he had to offer. "I don't know what I did to deserve you, Anise, but it must have been something pretty fine."

"Everything you have done, Ross, has been good."

"Well, no. That's not true. Let's at least be honest."

"But look at what God has done, my love." I straightened, gathering his hand in both of mine. "Remember when we all sat around the family room, just days before Christmas, talking about the redeeming grace and mercy of Christ?"

"Wasn't that something," he said, his voice growing weak.

"It was. It surely was."

He closed his eyes. I could tell by his breathing that he was becoming less energetic; his burst of vitality gone too soon. I thought he'd fallen asleep, and I was willing—perfectly willing—to sit and watch him for the duration. But then he said, "I am remembering something else." His eyes fluttered open.

"What's that?"

"That we also talked that day about you and your relationship with your father."

I glanced away from his watered-down eyes to the bedside table, where a collection of framed photographs of Ross and his children and his grandchildren caught the light from the opened window. They were there, every single one of them, Rosa and her sons included. "I wish," he said softly, "that I'd reached out to Rosa sooner. But I thought . . . I thought I'd be rejected. And I thought I'd have to admit my wrongdoings and *that* would be more painful than not being in her life." He shook his head ever so slightly. "I was wrong, Anise."

I leaned in close. "What are you telling me, Ross?"

"That just as you got a second chance at redemption after your relationship with Garrett and I got a second chance after my one night with Eliana . . . maybe what your father needs is just that. A second chance."

"I gave him so many more chances than that, Ross," I said. "After I reached adulthood, he never really bothered to contact me except for those birthday cards I'm sure my stepmother made him sign."

"You don't know that for sure, do you? Did you ever call to thank him?"

"No."

"Well then."

I shook my head. "Ross. He sent flowers to Mom's funeral but didn't bother to call or even to send a handwritten card."

"How would you have felt if he had?"

I had no answer for that. I had never bothered to think in that direction. "I gave him a second chance," I said, as though that settled the issue.

"Did you really, Anise? Did you really give him a chance?"

I thought I had. I truly thought I had.

"Maybe there is more to your father's story than you know. Just like there was more to mine. To my daughter's." He winked at me. "Just promise me you'll think about it, okay?"

I squared my shoulders. "Okay."

"Promise."

"I promise. I'll think about it."

"That's my good girl," he whispered. "Now then. I think I'll nap if that's all right with you."

· I laid my head next to his bony hip. "That's perfectly fine with me. And when you wake, we'll have our tea."

When it was over, when we had whispered our last good-byes and cried through our "I love yous," when I had held my breath as Ross took his final one . . . and when we had taken his body back to Orlando for the funeral and then brought it again to Cedar Key for the burial, I thought about that conversation a lot.

Just as you got a second chance at redemption after your relationship with Garrett, he'd said, *and I got a second chance after my one night with Eliana . . . maybe what your father needs is just that. A second chance.*

Days later, when I'd convinced my family and friends I would be okay my first night in the house alone, I sat out on the deck of our home, pondering it all. The sun had risen earlier on the day of Ross's funeral, and before it set we had buried the love of my life. People had come by in droves. I thought I'd never seen so many gathered in one place to honor the life of one man. But why wouldn't they? He was everything and more than what the pastor relayed in his sermon. Husband. Father. Grandfather. Pediatrician loved by thousands over the course of his career. Friend who would be missed by many. Son of the late Dr. Paul and Mrs. Frances Claybourne. Child of God. At seventy-four years of age, gone too soon.

I would never see his face or hear his voice again. Not in this lifetime. Already I missed them both. I missed them so terribly and felt lonelier than I'd ever felt, even as a child wanting nothing more than her father's attention.

Before long, a full moon hung over the marshes and the black rush. In its light I could make out the silhouettes of large birds flying home for the evening and, through the palm fronds, hear the sweet breeze of nightfall.

A strange sense of knowing came over me, as if something in my life had been left undone and now—now of all the moments of my life—it was time to bring it to completion. To honor my husband's wish for me. I didn't necessarily *want* to finish it, but knew—instinctively—that in order to continue on, to be able to breathe even, I had to.

I stood. Walked into the living room. Past Ross's reclining chair. I allowed my fingertips to trail along the headrest as I moved slowly by. I made a steady path down the hallway and into the master bedroom where, that night, I would sleep alone.

I found my purse where I always kept it, in one of the shoe compartments of my closet. Now, I opened it, dug around until I found my cell phone, and sank slowly to the floor.

I leaned my back against the mattresses. Pushed the power button until the face lit. Dialed a three-digit number.

"Verizon 411," the automated voice said. "What city and state?"

"Albany." I swallowed. "New York."

A pause was followed by a man's voice, which said, "Albany, New York information. What listing, please?"

I closed my eyes and drew my knees to my chest. "I'm looking for a residential number. First name is Chris. Or maybe Christopher."

"Last name?"

"Kelly," I said, my voice choking on the knot formed in my throat.

"I have a Christopher Kelly on Whitehall Lane."

Whitehall Lane . . . yes. Across the pages of time I heard my father say to my brother and me, "Welcome to Whitehall Lane. This is now your *other* home. Isn't it something?"

I opened my eyes. "Yes, that's it. Whitehall Lane."

"Thank you for using Verizon. Hold, please."

The phone rang only once before I heard the oddly familiar—though aging—voice. "Chris Kelly," he answered, just the way he always had.

I opened my mouth to say something, but the breath caught and held in my chest.

"Hello?" he said, the *o* sung in a melody.

A voice in the background asked, "Who is it, Dad?"

I sucked in a breath. "Hello," I said quickly, though hardly audible. I squeezed my eyes shut again and felt the stinging there.

"Who is this, please?"

I could hang up, I thought. Hang up and pretend this never happened. That it didn't matter and that, really, it never would. That he could go on with his life and I could go on with mine here in Cedar Key as though our earlier lives hadn't happened. One painful door kept closed.

But it *did* matter; it mattered because of everything I'd lost in one man and gained in another. It mattered because of what Christ had asked of me.

Maybe what your father needs is just that. A second chance. Forgive . . . seventy times seven.

Truth was, just as Rosa and Ami hadn't known their father's side of the story, I didn't know my father's. Maybe there was more . . . and maybe it was worth the try to find out. Another second chance.

"Hi, Daddy," I said, eyes wide open. "It's me. Anise."

Acknowledgments

I am sad the Cedar Key novels have come to an end. I feel as though, for the past three years, I have lived with these people. I know them as well as I know my own family. As with others of my characters and stories, it will be a while before they leave my heart and mind.

There are so many folks to thank, and I just know I'm going to forget a few of them. First, thank you to all my friends in Cedar Key, Florida! (Kona Joe, I gave you a speaking role this time!) I want to bask in your sunrises, sunsets, and slow moons . . . always! Why can't every day be a day in Cedar Key?

Thank you to my friend Dawn from Maine, who I asked about all sorts of details when it comes to living in such a beautiful state. I miss you guys!

Larry Leech, thank you for the things you shared with me about Bar Harbor, Maine (my Seaside Pointe). The fact that you and Wendy have visited there and I have not . . . well, I'm not bitter. Not really.

Beverly Goode (Edna from Cedar Key), who provided the name "Seaside Pointe."

To Laura Menfree, who shared a piece of her story with me.

Mark Hancock, without your knowledge of how life's bumps change our behaviors, shape and mold us, I would not have understood Ami's story at all. I'd have written it completely wrong.

Dr. J. Shan Young, thank you, thank you! I know oncology is not your specialty, but being a doctor and a friend is. Your help was remarkable.

Robi Lipscomb, sweet friend, thank you for the place to crash by the beach so I could write without interruption. Unless, of course, you count my walks on the shores of Ormond Beach as interruption.

Deb Haggerty, for reading behind me as I wrote and for giving me the pointers to fix problem areas. Also, thank you for your final read-through. I trust and value your opinion more than you can know.

Donna Postell (my old backyard friend), who provided Rosa's son's name.

Shellie Arnold, I bow at your feet. Having you as my crit partner makes me a better writer than I could have ever thought to be on my own.

Mr. Jonathan Clements, agent to end all agents . . . *todah raba*!

As always, to my Baker/Revell team. Every one of you . . . Vicki, Kristin, Michele, Deonne . . . the list goes on and on.

To my huggy hubby, who puts up with my moods while I write. "Don't talk to me, I just wrote an emotional scene." Or, "Let's go do something fun; I just wrote a happy scene!"

And to my Y'shua, for all the second chances . . . *ani ohevet otkha* (I love you).

Eva Marie Everson

For more information about

The seven stages of grief:
www.recover-from-grief.com/7-stages-of-grief.html

Becoming a bone marrow donor:
www.marrow.org/Home.aspx

Cedar Key, Florida:
www.CedarKey.org

Eva Marie Everson is the author of over twenty-five titles and is the Southern fiction author for Revell. These titles include multiple-award-winning *Chasing Sunsets*, *Waiting for Sunrise*, *Things Left Unspoken* and *This Fine Life*. She is the coauthor of the multiple-award-winning *Reflections of God's Holy Land: A Personal Journey Through Israel* (with Miriam Feinberg Vamosh) and, of course, the Potluck Club and the Potluck Catering Club series with Linda Evans Shepherd. She is also the author of *Unconditional*, based on the award-winning movie. Eva Marie taught Old Testament theology for six years at Life Training Center and continues to teach in a home group setting. She speaks to women's groups and at churches across the nation and internationally. In 2009 she joined forces with Israel Ministry of Tourism to help organize and lead a group of journalists on a unique travel experience through the Holy Land. She is a mentor with Christian Writers Guild and the first president of Word Weavers, a successful writers critique group that began in Orlando and has since become the Jerry B. Jenkins Christian Writers Guild Word Weavers. She serves on its national leadership team. Eva Marie speaks at writers conferences across the country. In 2011 she served as an adjunct professor at Taylor University in Upton, IN. Eva Marie and her husband Dennis enjoy living "life on the lake" in Central Florida, are owned by two dogs, and are blessed to be the grandparents of the best grandkids in the world. Eva Marie considers a trip to Cedar Key the perfect respite.

Meet
Eva Marie Everson
at
www.EvaMarieEversonAuthor.com

❋

Connect with her on her blog
My Southern Voice
www.evamarieeversonsouthernvoice.blogspot.com

❋

Find her on
 Eva Marie Everson
 EvaMarieEverson

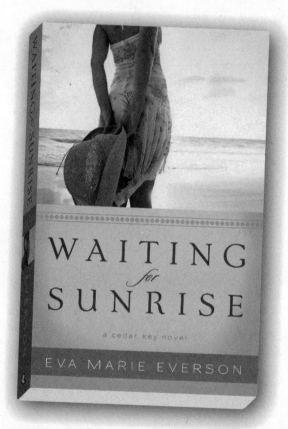

"A LOVELY AND DEEPLY MOVING
STORY. I DIDN'T JUST READ THIS
STORY, I LIVED IT!"

—ANN TATLOCK, award-winning author
of *The Returning*

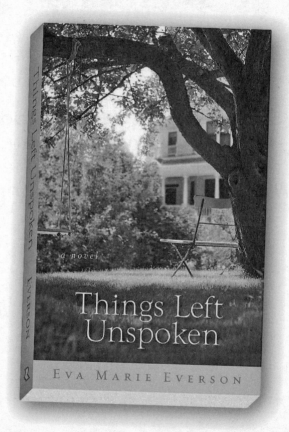

Jo-Lynn isn't sure she wants to know the truth—
but sometimes the truth has a way of making itself known.

Be the First
to Hear about
Other New Books
from Revell!

Sign up for announcements about
new and upcoming titles at

www.revellbooks.com/signup

Follow us on **twitter**
RevellBooks

Join us on **facebook**
Revell

Don't miss out on our great reads!

Revell
a division of Baker Publishing Group
www.RevellBooks.com